THE KIRKWOOD SCOTT CHRONICLES

CHRONICLES

Skelly's Square

By

Stephen Black

DEDICATION

Dedicated to Fionnuala, Adam, Hannah and Rebecca.

CONTENTS

CHAPTER 1 THE RIDGE 1

CHAPTER 2 POLYHEDRAL PALS 5

CHAPTER 3 ROUTINE 34 8

CHAPTER 4 ABOVE 12

CHAPTER 5 THE STUDY 14

CHAPTER 6 PRETEND POLICEMEN 16

CHAPTER 7 DOUBLE TROUBLE 19

CHAPTER 8 EVERY SHERIFF NEEDS A DEPUTY.....................23

CHAPTER 9 NIRVANA GIRL 27

CHAPTER 10 THE DIRTIEST WEE SHOP IN BELFAST 32

CHAPTER 11 ROUTINE 17 35

CHAPTER 12 OFFICE SMEAGOL..37

CHAPTER 13 EMILY'S WALL 39

CHAPTER 14 MILKY COFFEE, TWO SUGARS 43

CHAPTER 15 MY DEAREST EMILY 46

CHAPTER 16 BUCKIE FOR BREAKFAST 50

CHAPTER 17 MR BRADLEY'S TOY SHOP..................................54

CHAPTER 18 CARNAGE IN CUBICLE ONE 60

CHAPTER 19 KINGS FOR A DAY 64

CHAPTER 20 BANTER 69

CHAPTER 21 GUNTHER..74

CHAPTER 22 MY DEAREST EMILY II 77

CHAPTER 23 THE BROTHERS FITZGERALD 80

CHAPTER 24 THE DAY IT HAPPENED 84

CHAPTER 25 HELLO HANGOVER 88

CHAPTER 26 NATASHA..92

CHAPTER 27 THE LION TAMER WHO COULDN'T TAME LIONS 99

CHAPTER 28 MULBERRY SQUARE...107

CHAPTER 29 THREE'S A CROWD 111

CHAPTER 30 TRICKY TRICKSTER SAVES THE DAY 114

CHAPTER 31 CASTLE STREET CAPERS.....................................117

CHAPTER 32 MOVE...120

CHAPTER 33 SIX FEET OVER..124

CHAPTER 34 LOST JOURNAL 127

CHAPTER 35 REGROUP 129

CHAPTER 36 SCOFFEE 132

CHAPTER 37 FOR ONE NIGHT ONLY 134

CHAPTER 38 LET THEM COME..142

CHAPTER 39 HERE WE ARE 144
CHAPTER 40 POSH GIRL 150
CHAPTER 41 MY DEAREST ENEMY 154
CHAPTER 42 BIGGER FISH TO FRY 157
CHAPTER 43 MEET CORNELIUS DOBSON 160
CHAPTER 44 WAKE UP, IT'S A BEAUTIFUL MORNING 163
CHAPTER 45 A LITERARY TARDIS 167
CHAPTER 46 URBAN MURMURS 170
CHAPTER 47 PAPER SIFT 173
CHAPTER 48 ADEUS MEU AMIGO 175
CHAPTER 49 TRUST HIM 178
CHAPTER 50 CARROT CAKE CONFESSIONAL 181
CHAPTER 51 CHASE SCENE 184
CHAPTER 52 RODRIGUEZ 188
CHAPTER 53 BATTLE LINES 193
CHAPTER 54 THE LEAFY SUBURBS 196
CHAPTER 55 HAVEN'T YOU FORGOTTEN SOMETHING? 202
CHAPTER 56 LAY OF THE LAND 204
CHAPTER 57 ROUTINE 64 208
CHAPTER 58 ABDUCTION 210
CHAPTER 59 PARK LIFE 215
CHAPTER 60 ABYSS 219
CHAPTER 61 JIMMY JAMES 222
CHAPTER 62 REVELATION 225
CHAPTER 63 REHANNA 227
CHAPTER 64 WET RAIN 230
CHAPTER 65 THE FITZGERALD BROTHERS 233
CHAPTER 66 FOR THE KINGDOM 235
CHAPTER 67 MAKE IT END 240
CHAPTER 68 SAMUEL 241
CHAPTER 69 THE GATEHOUSE 244
CHAPTER 70 THE SCOURGE 249
CHAPTER 71 COUNCIL OF WAR 257
CHAPTER 72 A LITTLE ROAD TRIP 261
CHAPTER 73 STRANGERS IN A STRANGE LAND 265
CHAPTER 74 SKELLY'S SQUARE 269
CHAPTER 75 THE DRUMMER BOY 274
CHAPTER 76 THE FOURTH CHILD 277
CHAPTER 77 RAINBOW GIRL 280
CHAPTER 78 ARDGALLON 283
CHAPTER 79 SHE KNEW SOMETHING THEY DID NOT 286

CHAPTER 80 PILLOW TALK 290

CHAPTER 81 RESTORATION 294

CHAPTER 82 FLAG OF TRUCE 298

CHAPTER 83 SAY HELLO TO MY LITTLE FRIEND 302

CHAPTER 84 BREAKFAST OF CHAMPIONS.......................................306

CHAPTER 85 THE BRIDGE 311

CHAPTER 86 THE DUMMIES GUIDE TO SAVING THE PLANET 314

CHAPTER 87 IT IS OUR CALLING..317

CHAPTER 88 THESE BOOTS WERE MADE FOR WALKING..........................324

CHAPTER 89 GANDALF ON SPEED 331

CHAPTER 90 A TIME TO END ALL TIMES..337

CHAPTER 91 WHAT GOES AROUND 341

ABOUT THE AUTHOR 345

ACKNOWLEDGMENTS

Thank you to my family, friends and fellow bloggers for supporting me through this process. To my BETA readers - Meredith Jackson, Shae Jackson, Katie Nurton, T R Noble, Joanne Fisher and Helen Orr. To Laura Dobra for her incredible first edit. To Yanina and everyone at Kindle Book Publishing for making this a reality. Special thanks to Graham and Anne McCartney and the Johnston's my spiritual family. Finally, to God for putting up with me.

CHAPTER 1

THE RIDGE

Sunday, 18 June 1815

Waterloo – nine miles south of Brussels

8:30 p.m.

It became a rout in the end.

The Prussian columns swept over the battlefield from the west like a swarm of locusts devouring the Imperial Guard, Napoleon's pride and joy. One minute his elite force was bearing down on the wavering Allied lines with victory in their sights; the next they were retreating chaotically back across the valley, hysteria spreading through their ranks. Hardened veterans threw down their muskets and ran for their lives.

Smelling their fear, the Prussian cavalry crashed mercilessly into the fleeing French. Cries for parley were ignored, and men were butchered where they stood. Bogged down in the cloying mud, all semblance of order evaporated from the French ranks; the smoke cleared from the battlefield to unveil the true extent of the carnage. Beleaguered British and German units advanced to the crest of the ridge they had defended all day and peered down at the blackened shell that was once the elegant farm complex at La Haye Saint.

Faint and faltering at first, cheers rose from the Allied line into the slate-grey sky, growing in volume and belief with each passing second. Men hugged one another and fell to their knees, laughing and crying in equal measure. Officers shook hands and slapped each other's backs while the first plunderers got to work rooting through the tunics and trousers of the dead; irrespective of whether they were friend or foe. Hip flasks were passed around and a barrel of wine somehow conjured up from the middle of one of the British squares. Pipe music began to drift across the battlefield and regimental colours were raised in relief as much as victory.

The battle, which would become known as Waterloo, had ended. It was the evening of 18 June 1815.

To the sound of his adoring men, the tall, gaunt Duke spurred his chestnut charger, Copenhagen, along the ridge, followed by what remained of his staff. He pulled to a halt and swung around in his saddle to survey the battlefield with dark, piercing eyes. The memoirs written of the day would have him everywhere, at the forefront of the fighting. His very presence inspired all. The men would later regale each other with the time 'Old Hooky' sought refuge within their square, urging them to hold firm against the murderous French artillery which scoured the Allied lines, indiscriminately tossing heads and limbs into the smoke-clogged air.

Beneath the calm veneer he was as exhausted as the next man, both physically and mentally. It had been the closest-run thing and he acknowledged it could just as easily have been his own army retreating in disarray towards Brussels, had Blücher not arrived at the eleventh hour to turn imminent defeat into the defining moment of the Duke's career. Aged forty-six, he was now a legend, his name indelibly transcribed in the history books. But at what cost? The blood of thousands of brave men? The Duke sighed. If this was victory, then he did not care much for it.

Arthur Wellesley, Duke of Wellington, sighed and ran the sleeve of his greatcoat across his forehead. The mud and soot of the battle clung to his sweaty brow and he suddenly wanted nothing more than a cool drink, a hot bath and then deep, impenetrable sleep. Below him the French were in full retreat. Bonaparte would no doubt be halfway to Paris by now, but that was the least of Wellington's worries. The broken remnants of both armies lay before him; a blanket of human misery. The dead were everywhere and the groans and screams of the wounded were already challenging the songs and cheers for domination of the skies. Bodies twitched and shuddered. Some cried for water, some for their mothers, and others for a bayonet to put an end to their agony. Riderless horses careered across the plain, driven mad by their injuries, hurdling the piles of bodies which stretched for miles in every direction.

The Duke had taken in such sights before, but never on such a scale. The Peninsula had been a brutal slog; however, it was nothing compared to this. He knew in his heart that he would never fight a battle like this again. This had been a day like no other. He felt giddy, a mixture of fatigue, elation, and horror at what his shattered senses were taking in. It had a mesmeric beauty to it, and he was utterly under its spell, so much so, that he was initially unaware of

Ponsonby drawing alongside him. The two old campaigners sat side by side in their saddles, their mounts snorting and pawing at the ground; they too were eager to leave the stench of death behind.

'Damned close-run thing my Lord, but the day is ours. Marshal Blücher has sent a messenger. He requests the honour of leading the pursuit.'

'Of course. Tell the marshal I shall meet with him at La Belle Alliance. Our lads are out on their feet and the horses blown.'

'As you wish my Lord,' Ponsonby nodded curtly, wheeled his horse around and urged it back along the ridge. Behind Wellington a knot of aide-de-camps had nervously formed, awaiting their orders. He forced himself to focus on the many matters that required prompt, decisive leadership. He rattled off instructions with a calm efficiency honed by years of hard-earned experience, forged across the battlefields of Europe.

Before tapping Copenhagen's flanks to begin the journey to La Belle Alliance, he took one last look at the scene before him. From where he sat atop the ridge, his attention was drawn to the right. Several hundred yards below in the valley, a large body of troops lay motionless on the ground, in textbook square formation. Their colours were speared into the ground at the centre. The flag hung limply, and despite straining to make out the regiment in question, the Duke could not. It had been a common tactic throughout the day; infantry lying flat on their bellies to lessen the chances of being targeted by the devastating French artillery batteries.

'Morris,' he motioned for one of his aides to come alongside him. 'Who are those men? Tell them to stand up. The battle is over. No need to lie in the mud when the day is won.'

'Yes, my Lord,' replied the young officer. Morris spurred his horse forward and guided it down the slope, gingerly picking a path through the dead and dying from both sides. The Duke resumed issuing brief but detailed orders to other aides. Yes, the battle had somehow been won, but there was still so much to be done. His attention was elsewhere as Morris pulled his mount to a halt and dismounted at the edge of the square. He did not witness the young man picking his way through the bodies and searching for some sign of life.

He would find none.

The Duke looked up from a letter he had been handed of news from the right flank, as the young aide drew before him again. He noted that Morris could not have been more than twenty years old. His father was a wealthy man, if Wellington was thinking of the right family, and purchased the boy's commission at considerable expense. It had all seemed so terribly exciting at first. Travelling to the Continent to put the old enemy to the sword. Well, now Morris had tasted the reality of war, and the excitement had well and truly worn off, to be replaced by fear and exhaustion. The boy was as pale as a ghost.

'Well Morris. What news? Spit it out,' he demanded impatiently.

Morris swallowed hard before answering. This was the Duke of Wellington he was speaking to, so he was anxious to conduct himself in a manner befitting to his family. 'My Lord, it saddens me to report they are dead. Every last man,' He paused, as if to compose himself. 'And boy,' he added quietly.

'Boy? What are you talking about, Morris?'

The young officer reached inside his tunic and produced a square of cloth which he handed to his childhood hero. Unfolding the cloth, the Duke studied it closely, realising he was holding the colours of the 49th Somerset Regiment. They were one of the oldest regiments in the British Army, with a roll of honour as long as his arm.

'Skelly's Somerset's,' he remarked quietly to nobody in particular, before looking up and enquiring urgently, 'What of their Commanding Officer? Colonel Skelly?'

What little colour was left in the young officer's cheeks drained away. 'Dead sir. I found him at the foot of the colours with sabre drawn. The honour of the regiment is intact.'

An older officer spoke up from behind. 'Most remarkable sight I've ever seen. Fought as a square and died as a square. Bloody heroes every last one of them.'

The Duke returned the colours to Morris and wheeled away. 'Indeed, but we have business to attend to, gentlemen, before we start handing out the medals.' He shook his reins and Copenhagen responded instantly, man and horse in perfect harmony. As the entourage made their way down into the valley and across the battlefield, the cheering spread like wildfire. Hats were thrown in the air and at last the moans of the dying were drowned out by the roars of the living.

The Duke heard neither, for he was consumed by his own thoughts. Yes, Skelly was a hero. A hero whose actions most likely won Wellington the battle. But Skelly was dead, and Arthur Wellesley was alive and victorious. And it was the living who wrote the accounts of days like this where reputations were forged, and legends made. The truth was important to him, but only where he could mould it to his own advantage. His enemies were many that day, and not all of them had been wearing French uniforms. Yes, he would tell the story; but he would also make certain that the exploits of Colonel Augustus Skelly and the 49th Somerset's would never see the light of day.

Wellington gritted his teeth and shook Copenhagen's reins to pick up the pace. 'Damn you Skelly. I pray you rot in hell.'

CHAPTER 2

POLYHEDRAL PALS

Friday, 29 August 2012

Belfast, Northern Ireland

5:45 a.m.

Kirkwood always set his alarm earlier than was necessary as you never knew what the new day might bring. Not that he needed an alarm clock. He was always awake before the allotted hour.

The dice made sure of it.

There were two of them, a throwback to his *Dungeons & Dragons* playing days as a school boy. A four-year love affair with elves and orcs which effectively dashed whatever slim hopes he ever harboured of having a girlfriend during his teenage years. That, and the small matter of being unable to string two sentences together in the presence of the opposite sex.

He stared at the dice which sat daring to be rolled on the desk opposite his bed, in the box room of the cramped terraced house in South Belfast he called home — or as homely as shared rented accommodation with an extortionate monthly rent could be. His real home was almost seventy miles away in the market town of Omagh, but he had little reason to visit it now. His older sister, Katie, emigrated to New Zealand several years ago after her husband secured a position teaching something to do with computers at the University of Auckland.

Kirkwood and Katie were never particularly close, but he still felt miffed at the time. It was as if she was moving on, rebuilding her life whereas he … well, he wasn't. At least his mother remained, or so he thought, until the patter of tiny feet from Down Under proved too tempting, and she moved out last summer to be close to her new grandson. It was sold to him as an open-ended visit which, almost a year later, showed no sign of ending. They kept in touch via awkward Skype conversations and perfunctory emails, and he was always being invited out to visit, but the reality was his dead end, administrative job with Optima Financial Solutions provided nowhere near the finances for such an extravagant trip.

So here he was, treading water in Belfast with a 2:2 degree in Modern History from Queen's University which wasn't worth the paper it was printed on. He could have pursued a master's degree upon graduating but chose instead to drift from one crappy job to the next before securing a six-month temporary contract at Optima; which, despite his best efforts, they kept renewing. That was over two years ago. Kirkwood drifted from one pay day to the next, frittering away what little money was left after rent and other bills, on the occasional Ben Sherman shirt and drinking sessions with his equally delinquent mates, Gerry and Grogan. Yes, life was a laugh a minute.

At least it was Friday, and what's more; pay day Friday. The Scott coffers were replenished, and he had booked half the day off work to meet the Terrible Twins at their favourite city centre inn for an afternoon of self-imposed liver abuse. It was tragic that this was the highlight of an otherwise drab existence, but there you had it. Kirkwood Scott was in a rut — no, make it a chasm, from which he saw no escape. His life would have been utterly nondescript were it not for the dice.

He sighed before throwing back the duvet and swinging his legs out of bed. It was ridiculously early considering he didn't have to be in work for over four hours yet. Best to get up now though and deal with whatever his little polyhedral pals had in store for him. It could be five minutes, or it could be five hours. He cupped them in his hands, a blue four-sided die which resembled a mini pyramid, and its gaudier, twenty-sided yellow cousin. Rolling them was the first thing Kirkwood did every morning, before the first Diet Coke of the day, even before his morning ablutions.

He didn't want to roll them. He had to roll them.

He launched the dice across the desk and watched as they rattled and bounced before coming to rest. He had performed this task almost every day for the last nine years. It never got any easier, each time his heart flipping into the back of his throat as he awaited the axe to fall upon his exposed neck. Those hated dice, the physical manifestation of a mental disorder which had plagued him since the day it happened. A day he would never forget.

Kirkwood watched the dice as they settled. Two numbers stared resolutely up at him. 2 and 17. He groaned and looked at his alarm clock again, which now read 5:48 a.m. The dice had spoken, the routine was decided, and all Kirkwood could do was comply. Making work at a reasonable hour seemed a much less likely proposition, now that he was about to embark on Routine 34.

CHAPTER 3

ROUTINE 34

7:49 a.m.

Kirkwood had been running for what seemed an eternity before his watch triumphantly announced he was at the ten-mile mark of the required fifteen which the routine insisted upon. He was averaging a steady nine-minute mile pace which was just as well if he was to have any hope of making work, without awkward questions being asked by management.

The run incorporated loops of Albert Park, an oasis of verdant tranquillity set amidst the bedsits and boutiques of this most desirable part of South Belfast. It provided a sanctuary of calm for early morning dog walkers and coffee sipping office workers, craving ten minutes of solitude before another day jolted into action. Kirkwood stuck to the main path which hugged the shore of an ornamental oval lake at the heart of the park. He knew from bitter experience one circuit of the lake was exactly a mile, having completed Routine 34 some fourteen times over the past three years. It was as flat as a pancake, which suited just fine, and bar the occasional surly swan, he largely had it to himself, any morning the dice brought him to its ornate metal gates.

The lack of any breakfast ensured the first half mile up the Lisburn Road to the park entrance was a chore, but once he found his rhythm he plodded comfortably enough around the lake, regulating his breathing and heartbeat as best he could considering it was almost a month since he last ran in anger. That was when he had rolled a 12, which only necessitated a three-mile saunter, and it was a relatively pain free experience which he completed inside half an hour. Routine 34 was a whole different ball game; the worst possible scenario when it came to running-related routines, of which there were six in total, ranging from three to fifteen miles in length.

Kirkwood Scott, to the casual observer, did not merit a second glance. He was spectacularly ordinary, from his mop of dark brown hair three weeks overdue for a trim, down to his suggestion of a belly, which gave away his love of beer and Chinese takeaways. He was your archetypal scruffy, underachieving 25-year-old male, running around a park because he had decided to have the first of his many mid-life crises a decade before everybody else. Yes, spectacularly ordinary on the surface. But still waters run deep, and Kirkwood Scott's were bottomless.

He silently chastised himself for not investing in proper running gear after the last fifteen-miler the previous October. The cotton T-shirt he was wearing was already drenched in sweat and starting to chafe against his nipples. Kirkwood ruefully accepted they would be bleeding freely by the time he finished, ensuring his post-race shower, if indeed there was time for one, would be a painful, scream-saturated process. His left knee was also beginning to throb alarmingly, and he knew he would be hobbling like an octogenarian the following day. The alternative, however, was not worth thinking about. Any amount of discomfort was preferable to the wave of anxiety which engulfed him as he thought about the consequences of failing to complete a routine. Shaking his head to dispel the thought, he gritted his teeth and lurched on into the eleventh mile.

The routines had been part of Kirkwood's life since the day it happened almost fourteen years ago. Every morning, without fail, he rolled the dice and took whatever fate befell him on the chin. The numbers rolled with the twenty and four-sided dice would be multiplied to provide the number of the routine he was required to perform. There were forty-nine in total, varying in their complexity, but each designed to control Kirkwood's every waking moment and ensure he remained a slave to the chaos that had plagued him since his school days. They were all written down, but he rarely referred to the list as each one was engraved on his memory, like a drunken tattoo you bitterly regretted getting once you sobered up the morning after.

He was branded; a prisoner to a mental disorder, which over a decade of medication, counselling and other therapies had failed to tame. The many physicians and psychiatrists he squirmed in front of unanimously agreed on a name for it. Obsessive Compulsive Disorder. They called it OCD — he called it a living hell. Potato, Potatoe, Tomato, Tomatoe, Let's call the whole thing off.

He had read countless books about it and attended several support groups; you name it, he gave it a go. In fact, he was somewhat of an expert on the subject. Type OCD into a search engine and you could disappear down any number of online rabbit holes. How it was perfectly normal to entertain intrusive, unwanted thoughts. We all had them. *Did I turn the oven off? What would happen if I let go of the steering wheel? If I step on that crack in the pavement will I have bad luck for the rest of the day?* The difference was, such thoughts took up permanent residence in the minds of those with OCD, whereas, for the remainder of the population, they vanished as quickly as they appeared. Normal people just shook their heads, dismissed the thought as ridiculous and got on with the rest of their day.

Kirkwood knew he wasn't normal; far from it. He also knew OCD varied from person to person. It was a shifting, restless monster, as difficult to corner as an oiled piglet. For one person it might emerge as ritualistic hand washing and cleaning routines. This was the commonly held perception of the disorder that led to the often used 'Oh I'm a little bit OCD,' from the uneducated, who insisted upon spotless kitchens or bathroom floors you could eat your dinner off. Kirkwood shuddered whenever he heard the phrase; it was the equivalent of someone running a rusty nail along a blackboard. One was not *a little bit OCD*. Part time membership of Club OCD was not an option. It was a ravenous mental monster, that, if unchecked, laid siege to your beleaguered mind until your defences crumbled. You were either OCD or you were not. There was no middle ground.

It could take a million forms. There were as many strands of the disorder as there were grains of sand on your average beach. There were no boundaries or limits, no recognised dress code or etiquette. Anything went, and all were welcome on the terrifying OCD rollercoaster ride. Every victim — for that was what they were — was unique. The only common denominators were the unwanted thoughts (the obsession), and the corresponding routine or compulsive act that had to be performed to alleviate the anxiety associated with those thoughts. Yet the compulsion only eased the obsessive thinking for a limited period and, if anything, strengthened the urge to succumb again to ritualistic behaviour the next time the thoughts took hold.

Kirkwood was no different from any other poor sod in its grip. Except he was. With him it was 'The 49'. Routines that evolved and grew in scope and scale ever since the day it had happened. Before then, there had only been the one routine. The simplest, most basic of acts he performed every day without fail to prevent something bad from happening. Something very bad. Day after day, without exception, he had complied. Until the day he didn't. That was the day it happened. It was the day everything changed forever.

One routine became two, two became three, three became four. As he entered his teenage years there were twenty, by his twenties, it had doubled to forty routines. Until now, just shy of his twenty-fifth birthday the list stretched to forty-nine. It had stayed that way for eighteen months, as if the disorder had reached its allocated quota and had decided enough was enough. Yes, forty-nine was a grand number. That would do.

If you asked him to, Kirkwood could have rattled off all the routines without drawing breath. It was his party piece, not that he was invited to many and, even if he were, this was the last topic he would have wished to discuss. It was his shameful secret, a rotting albatross tied to his neck, which he was unwilling and unable to reveal to anyone but a few trusted confidantes; even then, they didn't know the full extent of his suffering. He had tried everything within his power to shake 'The 49', but all his efforts failed miserably. He had come to accept they were part of him, just as he was part of them. It was how his particular cookie had crumbled.

He groaned and glanced at his watch again, willing the miles to pass quicker as his body threatened to rebel with every passing step. Looking down at his aching legs, he suddenly had an out of body experience, and felt totally detached from them. It was as if he was a kite buffeted on all sides by violent storms, with only a thin thread of pain tethering him to the ground below. All the routines had their hellish aspects, but when it came to sheer physical displeasure, 34 was in a league of its own. He struggled to focus his thinking on anything but the many steps which still lay ahead of him. The relief of those final few strides would be all the sweeter today as it was pay day Friday. He planned to spend as much of the coming weekend as humanly possible at the bottom of a pint glass. Kirkwood didn't drink because he particularly enjoyed the taste of it. He drank to forget the crushing reality of the routines.

They were real, as real as life and death, and failure was not an option when it came to them. To fail was a sure-fire recipe for disaster. Not for Kirkwood, but for the countless strangers whose fates hinged upon him religiously adhering to them. It could be a chartered flight between Paris and Tokyo that exploded in mid-air, a sleepy, rural Illinois high school visited by an ex-pupil wielding an assault rifle; or a motorway pile-up at rush hour that left eight dead. It mattered not; the carnage was as indiscriminate as it was brutal. Trying to understand was futile. All Kirkwood needed to understand was if he failed his daily routine, then that day's bad news was his fault. It had been that way since the day it happened, and it always would be.

The logical, rational part of his mind screamed that it was insane to believe his actions were responsible for the carnage played out on the television news. But it was always swept away by the chilling certainty he was to blame, and it was his fault; he was always culpable. Kirkwood kept running. Two and three-quarter miles to go. No, he wasn't normal. His OCD was unique to him and nobody else. There were 'The 49', but there was something else; an even darker secret that would never see the light of day.

For the OCD had a voice. It had a face. It had a name.

And that name was Skelly.

CHAPTER 4

ABOVE

They watched from above as he laboured around the lake. It was a tiresome, tedious task but all routines had to be verified and this day was no different from any other. Their eyes were everywhere as far as the routines were concerned. The Colonel insisted upon it. He claimed it was the bread and butter of the job — the meat and potatoes as those bloody Americans referred to it. The young man below cut a sorry figure as he ground out the miles. Had he looked up, of course, he would have seen nothing but a clear blue sky framing an orange and white jet, as it climbed away from the city's airport. They were no more than fifty feet above, but he could see them no more than a blind man could see the end of his nose. They existed on the electromagnetic spectrum far beyond the range of the human eye, beyond the range of any eye on this stinking planet.

Had they revealed themselves, the primitive life forms below would most likely have fallen to their knees proclaiming they had seen angels or demons. Such was the limited range of their puny minds. They were both, but they were neither — magnificent new creations who once walked the Earth like the one known to his kind as 'Kirkwood' did now. That had been centuries ago, however, when they were spewed, gasping and flailing into the world from between their mothers' legs. They had died as one, yet some of them died as heroes, while others died as villains and cowards. Their deaths were futile and soon forgotten; others had gained the plaudits on that muddy, bloody day. History was such a fickle mistress.

Yet where were these charlatans now? Long dead and buried, remembered only by the lifeless granite statues pigeons now defecated upon at will. They deserved nothing less for standing on that accursed ridge and watching impassively as the square collapsed inwards upon itself, slowly, irrevocably subsiding beneath the relentless wave of musket and cannon ball fire, which battered their ranks into submission.

Dismembering. Decapitating. Decimating.

They had rallied by the colours, a last desperate show of defiance, screaming in the face of certain death. Fallen, stabbed and bludgeoned until the last glint of life had been extinguished from their desperate eyes, their blood soaking into the cloying Belgian mud.

Fallen.

Forgotten.

Forsaken.

The Forsaken. Now risen to pursue a glorious resurrection where blood and bone would no longer restrain them from wreaking a terrible revenge on this bloated, rancid lump of rock. They had honed their skills on other worlds, preparing for this day. For Earth was their world, a world that had abandoned them. An abrogation that would make its imminent destruction all the more delicious to them.

All that stood in their path was the thirteen-stone sack of putrid pus trudging around the lake beneath them. It was as baffling as it was laughable. Yet somehow the only force that could stop them was being housed within this pitiful figure. Crush him, and the gateway was open for them to flood unopposed onto this plane of existence. They despised it as it had despised and discarded them. But it was only a matter of time. They were told by the Colonel to remain patient and resist baser instincts to plunder and pillage. This was a war of attrition he had warned, so for now, they waited.

For now.

CHAPTER 5

THE STUDY

9:15 a.m.

The shower was as horrific as anticipated. Kirkwood leaned against the tiled wall and bit into his forearm as the scalding hot water connected with his chest. It was as if red-hot invisible pokers were being applied to both nipples. He endured two minutes before he was forced to hop out and tentatively towel himself dry before dressing for work. Thankfully there was no dress code in force at Optima for paper-pushers like him, who were never allowed within a mile of the general public. It took less than a minute to change into his regulation attire of a checked Ben Sherman shirt and distressed blue jeans. He sniffed dubiously at a pair of black socks on the bedroom floor before deciding he could get another day out of them. Lastly, he hauled on his beloved steel-capped Timberland desert boots.

Standing in front of the wardrobe mirror, he matted down his damp hair into some sort of order, knowing he only had forty-five minutes to make work. Turning up outside recognised core hours was frowned upon, and he had already received a verbal warning earlier in the year for tardy timekeeping. Never a wise move when one was on a temporary contract. Picking up his wallet and keys from the desk, he studiously ignored the dice. He turned to leave the room but as he did, a searing pain erupted behind his left eyeball, stopping him dead. Kirkwood hunched over and wobbled before falling back onto the bed. Clenching both eyes shut he was rewarded with a kaleidoscope of shifting coloured orbs, dancing on the back of his eyelids. It was an intense, relentless pain and the accompanying nausea meant there was little hope of returning to an upright position anytime soon.

Anyone else would have been scrambling for the migraine tablets but Kirkwood realised it would be a pointless exercise on his part, knowing he was headed one place and one place only. He had been through this particular pain barrier a thousand times before and knew exactly what lay on the other side. Gritting his teeth, he attempted to channel the pain to a part of his brain where he could control and contain it. Unfortunately, this was merely the unpleasant aperitif; an equally disagreeable main course was waiting in the wings, the moment the pain subsided.

Kirkwood did not know if this process took seconds, minutes, or hours. It didn't really matter as time was immaterial where he was going.

He opened one eye and then the other. It was as if he had never been away.

He was standing in the Study.

CHAPTER 6

PRETEND POLICEMEN

March 1995

Omagh, Northern Ireland

Kirkwood Scott would have been just like any other ordinary eight-year-old boy
if it were not for the extraordinary responsibility he bore. While Katie, his older
sister, played her music and swooned over whatever pop star was flavour of that
month, Kirkwood was preoccupied with saving his father's life. This meant he
didn't have time for hobbies and interests which filled the days of other
ordinary boys. No, for he had much more important business to attend to.

Kirkwood realised this made him special. Not special as in top of the class
special or captain of the football team. No, this was a different kind of special
which Kirkwood could share with nobody else; not his parents, not his sister,
not even his best friend Brian. This special was not for public consumption. As
to do that would jeopardise the operation which consumed his every waking
thought.

He was young, but he wasn't an idiot. He knew only too well that bad things
happened. Growing up in Northern Ireland you couldn't avoid it. Every time
his parents watched the news, the stony-faced presenter would solemnly
announce another shooting or bomb attack. Grainy photographs of grinning
victims from happier times would flash across the television screen, followed by
images of broken relatives shuffling behind wreath-laden coffins.

Sometimes the wreaths would form sets of letters which didn't make a lot of
sense to Kirkwood; 'UDA' or 'IRA'. There would be flags draped over the

16

coffins which were carried by men in uniforms. He recognised some of these as the pristine uniforms of the policemen and soldiers who patrolled his home town of Omagh. But he was less familiar with others. Men wearing white shirts, black berets, and sunglasses. Were they French? What were they doing in Northern Ireland? And why were they wearing sunglasses in a country where it was permanently cloudy and, more often than not, raining? Everyone knew the sun always shines in glamorous places like Paris. Did it explain why they always looked so grumpy as they stood by the gravesides? Wouldn't you, if you had to move to a dump like Northern Ireland?

He recognised other words as well, crafted from the lilies and carnations which adorned the coffins; words like 'Father', 'Son', and 'Brother'. Kirkwood wished they had done something like that at his cousin William's funeral, the only one he had ever been to in real life. But his aunt and uncle had a lot on their minds at the time, as did his own parents, so he never mentioned it to anyone. It would have been inappropriate for a start and, besides, Mum and Dad didn't like talking about it. On the few occasions they spoke about William afterwards, they went through the motions and spouted a few generic comments such as, 'He was a good man,' or 'He would have liked that,' before quickly changing the subject. Nobody mentioned how he died. It was a secret the grown-ups never discussed. They all seemed a bit embarrassed by it, which made little sense to him. A lot of grown-up stuff made little sense to him.

His father was a driver for a local furniture store and spent his working week delivering armchairs and dressing tables all over the town and surrounding area. On one occasion, he even made a delivery to Belfast on a Saturday and allowed Kirkwood to accompany him. Perched high in the cabin of the lorry, Kirkwood had felt like the most important boy in the country. It was his first time on a motorway, and once he had overcome the fear that there was no oncoming traffic in the overtaking lane, he had marvelled at the experience. He had laughed aloud as his father pushed the van to its limit, the speedometer touching a breath-taking sixty-five miles an hour. Kirkwood clung on tight and had imagined he was on a rocket ship hurtling into space with his father, not knowing what adventures in far-flung galaxies lay ahead for them.

His father loved adventures. He used to let Kirkwood sit on his knee to watch reruns of old John Wayne movies. He idolised the film star and would make Kirkwood and Katie giggle, swaggering lopsidedly to the kitchen table at dinner time before telling them to 'Get off your horse and drink your milk,' in a cringeworthy, cowboy drawl. His mother tutted disapprovingly and told him to stop being so silly, but when she turned away Kirkwood always caught her smiling indulgently. Dad loved the cowboys so much he had a second job at the weekends, when the furniture store was closed. This involved going out every Friday and Saturday night after dinner to help the policemen catch the bad French men, who kept shooting and blowing up people on the news. Thankfully nothing like that happened in Kirkwood's town, but only places like Belfast where all the French men seemed to live. This made sense because that was where the airport was; so, it seemed reasonable anyone visiting from Paris would reside close to the airport.

Kirkwood was a bit worried when his father first told Katie and him about the new job, but carefully explained he was only a pretend policeman, and not a real one. He helped the real police as they were so busy catching bad guys, they didn't have time to do all the other jobs requiring attention; like guarding the station in the centre of town. His job was to stay there when all the real policemen were out catching those 'pesky Parisians.' Kirkwood snorted with delight whenever his father said that in his best *Scooby Doo* villain's voice.

When he was at the station, or 'on duty' as the grown-ups called it, he opened the barrier to let cars in and out and answered the telephone. Stuff like that. The bad French men never came near the police station in the centre of town as (*a*) it was too far to travel from Belfast, and (*b*) they knew if they did, they would be captured and thrown into the underground dungeon, where they would have to stay for a very long time. Dad said the dungeon was a horrible, dark, wet place, and the food prisoners got to eat was leftover school dinners served up in a bucket. Double yuck!

This eased Kirkwood's mind somewhat, but he still worried. He was a natural worrier and fretted over most things, even though his Sunday school teacher, Mr Campbell, told him it was a waste of time because Jesus said not to worry, and Jesus was never wrong about anything. Kirkwood had nodded thoughtfully at the time but still had his doubts, no matter what Jesus commanded. And besides, try telling that to the families of all the policemen who were now sitting up in Heaven, thanks to the French men. So, Kirkwood reserved the right to worry and hoped Jesus would understand. At least there was comfort in knowing there were no French men in Heaven because they were too nasty, and there was no way they were getting past Saint Peter at the pearly gates.

It was a pity there were no pearly gates to protect his father. That's where Skelly came in.

CHAPTER 7

DOUBLE TROUBLE

Skelly sat like a malevolent alley cat in his favourite padded armchair, nose buried in a copy of *The London Times*. Sly, rheumy eyes peeked briefly above the broadsheet to acknowledge Kirkwood's presence before returning to its contents. He would speak when he was ready and not a second sooner. Kirkwood knew it was risky and pointless to initiate a conversation that would rile the old man in front of him. Despite the expensive trappings of his surroundings, this was a place you didn't want to spend a single second more than you had to.

Kirkwood blinked, his headache was gone as suddenly as it had descended upon him, and looked around. He had been visiting the study for almost fourteen years and nothing ever changed. To his left an imposing black marble fireplace was home to a blazing, crackling furnace. In front of it sat a basket of kindling, which Kirkwood never saw Skelly avail of, to fuel the flames. Despite the intense heat he would have expected standing so close to such a blaze, he felt nothing. He might as well have been standing in front of an open fridge. The fire emitted no heat whatsoever. He shivered involuntarily as if someone or something had walked over his grave; perhaps this study was his grave for all he knew.

Skelly sat between the fire and a sturdy rustic oak desk piled high with various files and papers. Kirkwood had never known Skelly to be behind the desk despite the latter's complaints about the amount of his time taken up attending to tiresome administrative tasks. 'I'm a soldier, not a damned clerk,' he once huffed in his clipped Home Counties accent. 'I'm paid to run a regiment, not a bloody corner shop.' He never expanded upon who his employer was, or the nature of the desk work, and Kirkwood thought it better not to probe any further on the matter.

A polished circular stone acting as a makeshift paperweight sat atop the heap of papers which defied gravity as they permanently teetered on the verge of collapse. Skelly once told him it was a souvenir from some siege in a long forgotten colonial outpost, as unpronounceable as it was obscure. Skelly liked to boast about his military exploits but, despite hours of research both online and in the military history section of the city library, Kirkwood had been unable to find any reference to a Colonel Augustus Wilberforce Skelly.

Behind the desk was a huge bay window flanked by deep green drapes which were always drawn. No matter how many times he visited, or rather was summoned to the study, Kirkwood was never able to determine what lay outside. He was unable to make out any landmarks, not even the faintest silhouette, which might have provided a clue as to his whereabouts. For the sake of what remained of his sanity, he always imagined it was a stately pile somewhere in leafy Cambridgeshire but suspected this assumption could not be further from the truth.

Despite the absence of any visible lighting, the study was always bathed in a sleepy half glow which Skelly declared added to the ambience of the environment. To Kirkwood's right were a series of floor-to-ceiling bookshelves, which ran the entire length of that side of the room. He estimated they must have housed thousands of books, yet each tome was identical in appearance to the next. Bound in deep burgundy leather, their spines contained embossed gold lettering which always loitered beyond his vision. Even if he squinted, he could never quite make out the words or numbers, therefore, he had no idea what their content was. The harder he tried, the more frustrating this task became until he convinced himself the lettering must be shifting before him; a shimmering mirage masking their true meaning from his straining eyes. It was just another mystery in a room full of mysteries.

Skelly shattered Kirkwood's thoughts with a loud 'Harummppphhh', as he theatrically folded the newspaper and set it down on a small circular wooden desk beside the armchair. On it were an expensive looking cut-glass decanter and tumbler. The decanter was three-quarters full of a dark red liquid, from which Skelly poured a generous measure before reverting his attention back to his guest.

'Sorry to interrupt your busy morning, but just wanted to touch base with you before things get too messy later on with your delightful friends.' He raised the tumbler to his lips and drank deeply, revealing a set of stained, yellow teeth. Broken blood vessels crevassed ruddy cheeks, combined with jowls that flowed over a shirt collar giving him the appearance of an aristocratic Jabba the Hutt. Mutton-chop sideburns swept down either side of Skelly's face, bushy and untamed. They were greying, and complemented an unkempt mop of thick, wiry curls, which receded from the temples, leaving a single bushy tuft that was separated from the main body of hair by a widening expanse of mottled forehead.

'I shan't be bothering you for the remainder of the weekend, but it will be business as usual come Monday. No rest for the wicked and all that.' He crossed perfectly-creased brown corduroy trousers to reveal a startling pair of yellow socks bedecked with tiny, red prancing ponies. A pair of expensive-looking brown brogues completed the bottom half of the attire. *Probably hand-stitched,* thought Kirkwood as he studied his own scuffed boots.

'X marks the spot,' mused Kirkwood as he contemplated his feet which were resolutely planted on the plush, green carpet, which matched the drapes. He would have shuffled them nervously had he been able to, as a visit to the study was never a pleasant experience. That would have been a futile exercise, though, for in all the years he had been visiting Skelly's lair, he had been incapable of moving a muscle from the waist down. He simply stood there and listened to Skelly. Stock-still, unable to move and unable to run. Just like all those years ago when they lowered the coffin into the gaping grave.

'It goes without saying we shall expect your behaviour to be of the highest standard during this period of leave,' Skelly continued, clearly warming to the task. He took another sip and smacked thin, cracked lips. The beige shirt he wore was immaculately pressed, a darker brown check running through it, which matched the corduroy trousers. The pièce de résistance, however, was a gold-coloured waistcoat and matching cravat. Kirkwood never saw Skelly without a waistcoat and cravat, just like he never saw him in the same outfit more than once. The man had more clothes than Victoria Beckham, but there the similarities ended. The media portrayed her as a heartless bitch, but everyone possessed a heart, somewhere, even if entombed deep within a block of ice. It just required the right person to melt it. Everyone except Skelly. Kirkwood doubted such an organ existed within his obese body and if one did, it was a cold lump of rancid flesh incapable of any semblance of compassion or empathy.

'I know the score,' Kirkwood replied miserably. 'I've been doing it long enough'. He mentally kicked himself, hating that his contempt for Skelly was revealed in the manner he spat out the words. The old bugger would no doubt get a kick out of that. He fed off the misery he imparted into every aspect of Kirkwood's life.

Skelly smirked. 'Now don't be like that young man. We've known each other for far too long to allow ill-feeling to enter into our little arrangement.' He paused before his next words, the half-light glistening off eyes which, while rheumy, still sparkled with a malignant intelligence that simultaneously intrigued and terrified Kirkwood. They were a deep, chocolate brown which would have been warm, and reassuring had they not been at the centre of such a monstrous visage.

'I have always viewed us as friends. Family even. I've known you for so long I often regard you as the son I never had. No time for a wife, you see. I was betrothed to Kind and Country. Children would only have been an inconvenience.'

Skelly shifted in the chair, folds of flesh rippling within tight clothing like an oozing oil slick, carried on a rolling swell. 'Yes, a son,' he continued. 'And I know deep down you have always viewed me as a father figure. Given what happened to your own.' He paused, enjoying the mental anguish he was inflicting on his immobile victim who stood helpless before him. Kirkwood knew if he displayed the slightest flicker of emotion, Skelly would know his work was done and the poisonous quiver he had unleashed had struck home. They both knew that. It was all part of the sick game the old man played with such artful malice. A game that showed no sign of ever ending.

'Can I go now?' Kirkwood breathed deeply, refusing to succumb to the acidic bile, which rose from the pit of his stomach to gather at the back of his throat. Skelly knew him inside out and back to front, but he wasn't going to rise to the bait this time. He had been relishing this weekend since last pay day and he wasn't going to let the old goat ruin what little of a life he had.

'Very well. Off you go. But I will be monitoring your progress over the next day or so.' Kirkwood realised he must have allowed his apprehension at those words to creep across his features because Skelly chuckled before continuing, 'Oh, don't worry. I won't cramp your style. No doubt you will be looking to find yourself a new young lady friend. Such a shame about Natasha. What a delightful creature she was.' The tip of Skelly's tongue flicked across his bottom lip as he raised the tumbler and drained the remainder of its contents, watching his blade finally slip between Kirkwood's defences.

'Oh, but one last thing. Seeing as I'm being so magnanimous and issuing you with a weekend pass, I think it's only fair you return the favour. I think an extra routine is in order before the festivities begin in earnest, don't you? Off you trot now and roll those dice again. Toodle pip!' The mocking smile said it all. Game, set and match to the Colonel.

Kirkwood blinked several times, adjusting to the sudden change in lighting and room temperature. He was back in his room, lying on the bed as he was before Skelly's unwanted invitation to wherever the hell he resided. He looked at the alarm clock which informed him that he still had forty-five minutes to get to the office. Time stood still where visits to the study were concerned. Kirkwood sighed and forced himself to his feet. He picked up the dice, rolled and groaned. Pay day Friday was off to a stinking start. Inebriated oblivion could not come quickly enough.

A 1 and a 17.

Routine 17.

CHAPTER 8

EVERY SHERIFF NEEDS A DEPUTY

Kirkwood's father got to carry a badge like a sheriff, just like the good guys in the movies, although he was slightly disappointed to discover it was only a bit of laminated plastic with his father's name and photograph on it. He kept this in his wallet as opposed to a shiny, metal star, which John Wayne always wore pinned to his chest on the big screen.

They also gave him a green uniform, a baton and a set of handcuffs. Dad solemnly informed them that he only used the baton at Halloween to crack open walnuts, and the handcuffs were reserved for naughty boys and girls who refused to keep their rooms tidy, bring down their dirty clothes for washing, or help their mother with the dishes. When he said this, his eyes twinkled, convincing Kirkwood he had no intention of ever carrying out such a threat. Even if he had, it was a good deal better than facing Mummy when she was on the warpath, wielding her dreaded wooden spoon like a tomahawk.

Then there was the gun. Kirkwood had never seen it, but knew Dad kept it on a shelf in his bedroom wardrobe, out of reach of the prying hands of curious children. He knew this because one night some men came to their front door in the dead of night, shouting his father's name and telling him to let them in, as they needed help. The commotion had roused Kirkwood, but he was so afraid he hid his head under the covers and pretended to be asleep. He heard Mum and Dad whispering loudly from their bedroom. Whenever they were having a 'serious' conversation they didn't want Katie and him to hear, they whispered louder than they normally talked. Kirkwood never quite worked out why grown-ups did this, but it was funny, nonetheless. On this occasion, however, it was anything but funny. He was terrified and began praying to Jesus to make the men at the front door go away.

The next sound that had filtered through the paper-thin wall separating them was Dad rummaging in the wardrobe, followed by his mother's frantic voice — 'Don't be going down to them, John, with that gun! For God's sake, phone the station. You're going to get yourself killed!' Dad must have gone out onto the landing, because Kirkwood heard the creaky floorboard; he always knew to avoid it when sneaking downstairs to the biscuit tin whenever he woke up feeling hungry during the night. Dad had shouted down the stairs asking the men who they were and what they wanted. They had said something he couldn't make out, before Dad had told them to, 'Get the *beep* away from my house or I'll shoot, and I don't care who you are or where you're from.'

Kirkwood remembered covering his ears and huddling deeper under the covers. Everything always seemed better under the bed covers. He had never heard his father swear before, apart from the time he dropped a tin of paint on his foot while redecorating the bathroom — and it was only the word beginning with the letter *s* and ending in a *t*, which meant poo, that was nowhere near as bad as the F-word. Kirkwood hoped Jesus hadn't been listening but was sure that, even if he were, he would have turned a blind eye to his father's indiscretion, given the circumstances.

Kirkwood wasn't sure if he had dozed off, for the next he knew, a dazzling, white light was flooding his bedroom, casting crazy patterns on the ceiling before vanishing as quickly as it had appeared. Poking his head above the covers he was greeted by, not alien life forms seeking to abduct him and experiment on his body, but instead, the reassuring sight of his mother who had told him everything was alright, and to go back to sleep. When he asked what was going on, she had told him some silly, drunk men had come to the front door, but Dad chased them off. The police and army were outside and would patrol the area for the rest of the night in case they came back. She had kissed him on the forehead and told him he could have the next day off school, given his sleep had been disturbed.

Falling back onto his pillows, Kirkwood's mind had been a flurry of mixed emotions. On the one hand, he was delighted he was missing school as it was lumpy mashed potatoes, rubbery cabbage, and fatty beef Monday, which he hated; but on the other, why did Dad need to keep a gun if he wasn't a real policeman and the French men had no interest in him? It was all a bit confusing and his head had started to ache. As he had drifted off to sleep, he had vowed to do everything in his power from that night onwards to help Dad when he went out on duty with the real policemen. He understood he couldn't physically go with him but there had to be something he could do to protect him. Dad was sheriff of the town after all and, if he had learnt nothing else from the cowboy films, he knew one thing; every sheriff needed a good deputy to back them up. He would become his father's deputy.

Life settled back into its normal routine, but Kirkwood continued to wrack his brain for days as to what he could do to help his father. Initially, he was at a loss, but was gripped by a growing uneasiness that he had to conjure up something — and quick. The weekend was coming around fast again, and Dad would be heading off into the night to guard the police station in the centre of town, which reminded Kirkwood more and more of a castle every time he saw it.

The police station stood alone, with its imposing concrete walls and iron gates. It housed a radio mast which towered over the surrounding area and could be seen from any vantage point in the town. If a visitor ever asked you for directions to the police station, not that anyone ever did, all you needed to do was point them towards the mast. Kirkwood reckoned the real policemen must love their music to have such a good mast, which no doubt could pick up radio channels from all over the world; even as far away as Paris. He told his father this once and he had laughed, replying that they listened to special radio shows which were only for policemen, soldiers, and secret agents, like James Bond.

Kirkwood had wanted nothing more than to venture inside the police station and explore its interior, but when he asked, he was told it was cold, dirty, and no place for a young boy. There were rats in the dungeons and sometimes they ventured to the surface in search of food. This had made Kirkwood's mind up for him, because if there was one thing he hated more than French men, it was rats. He saw one once, fat and sleek, scurrying across the school playground from the back of the kitchens, where it was no doubt feasting on the day's disgusting culinary offering of soggy chips, coagulated baked beans, and rock-hard sausage rolls. That night he had dreamed he was safe in bed, only to discover there was a rat at the bottom of the bed gnawing on his toes. He had jumped up and hopped about the bedroom, desperately trying to shake off the rodent that locked its jaws onto his big toe; except the toe was a sausage roll, and he could only look on in helpless horror as it chewed relentlessly through the pastry exterior towards…

Thankfully he had woken up then, in a tangle of bedclothes, gasping for air and coated in a sweaty sheen.

That had been the end of his aspirations to visit the police station. Instead, he decided to build his own castle-like construction within the safer, vermin-free confines of his bedroom. This way, he could protect his father without ever having to confront a rodent, or murderous Parisian.

Instead of policemen, it would house his growing collection of toy soldiers. He christened them the Company, and their job was to assist in protecting his father whenever he was on duty. Kirkwood accepted the responsibility, but with it came routines. Lots of routines. Yet they were a small price to pay, if it meant keeping his father safe. For a long time, the arrangement worked perfectly well.

Until the day it happened.

CHAPTER 9

NIRVANA GIRL

Friday

9:18 a.m.

Kirkwood slammed the front door and the Study behind him, scurrying up Glasgow Street towards the Lisburn Road as fast as his reluctant legs would carry him. Rush hour was at its peak and the road was a blur of passing traffic and pedestrians. As he neared the top of the street a gaudy pink double-decker bus, advertising the latest blockbuster cinematic release, trundled past his stop. He waved frantically in the hope that he could catch the driver's eye and convince him to pull over but to no avail. The bus carried on and, realising the next one would not be along for another twenty minutes, Kirkwood faced the grim realisation he would have to walk to work. Two miles in forty-two minutes with flayed thighs. Pay day Friday was getting better all the time.

17…

The physical pain was nothing compared to the mental discomfort he was experiencing at the thought of a second routine. And not just that, but a 17. Skelly was making certain Kirkwood would have to work for his weekend pass out of Camp OCD. As he turned left onto the Lisburn Road and began the gentle descent into the city centre it was as if an anvil had been dropped on his chest, such was the heaviness he felt, underpinned by a faint but persistent nausea and deep unease which occupied every cell of his body.

A steady stream of students and young professionals were making their way on foot to Queens University and the city centre beyond. Kirkwood gingerly joined them and focused on ignoring what lay ahead, reluctantly embracing his chafed nipples and thighs like uninvited guests. He was in agony as he hobbled along, but at least it took his mind off the almost inevitable humiliation which awaited him upon his arrival at Optima.

Thanks to 17…

His passable impersonation of an arthritic crab earned Kirkwood more than one bemused look from fellow early morning commuters. Two student nurses exchanged giggles as they passed at the entrance to the eyesore that was City Hospital, which dominated the skyline like a discarded yellow and grey Transformer robot. Architecture and acid, *never a clever combination*, he thought, shuffling past the young women.

By the time he reached the bustle of Great Victoria Street, in the heart of Belfast, the inside of his thighs were screaming foul murder. He suspected one of his nipples had started to bleed afresh but was afraid to check for fear of uncovering a bloodbath. He zipped up his leather jacket, and tentatively threaded a path through the steady flow of humanity pouring from the nearby bus and rail terminus. The image of Skelly's smug, sadistic face loomed large in his mind, leaning forward in his armchair at the prospect of the horror show that was Routine 17. Kirkwood's heart began to pound like an insane cymbal-clashing monkey.

He negotiated an uneasy turf war taking place between a pamphlet-waving older man in a fluorescent bib and an 'I Love Jesus' baseball cap, who was going toe to toe against two well-dressed Jehovah's Witnesses who had set up shop on the opposite side of the pavement. The majority of passers-by studiously avoided eye contact with both factions and their conflicting interpretations of the afterlife.

'God Bless you, son. I'll be praying for that limp.'

In his efforts to veer clear of the Jehovah's, Kirkwood had unwittingly fallen within the territorial waters of the street evangelist. The wily, old fisher of men needed no further invitation and thrust a religious tract into his hand. Kirkwood offered a weak smile of gratitude before giving the pamphlet a cursory glance. 'Do You Know Where Your Life Is Going?' queried its headline, against the backdrop of a cross atop a storm-ravaged hill. 'Nowhere fast,' he sighed, raising his eyes skywards as a middle-aged woman began to edge tentatively off the roof of the Europa Hotel several hundred feet above. Suspended by all manner of hooks and harnesses, she looked over her shoulder and fearlessly waved down towards her not so confident husband and kids who stood below rattling charity buckets. Kirkwood crossed the street at the beeping traffic lights and trotted painfully into Ahmed's Mini Market for his daily fix of Diet Coke. He had been hopelessly hooked to the beverage since his university days when existing on a diet of aspartame and 'Pro Plus' caffeine tablets allowed him to survive sleep-deprived, all-night cramming sessions in advance of final exams.

Despite a grizzled, tabard-wearing cleaner permanently mopping the floors and wiping the shelves, the premises always emitted an unsettling aroma Kirkwood could never quite put his finger on. His best friend, Gerry, was convinced it was rat urine, but Ahmed's permanent offer of four tins of Diet Coke for a pound made this stop off a no-brainer for an addict of Kirkwood's limited means. He nodded at Ahmed who glumly reciprocated the gesture as he laboriously pushed a trolley loaded with goods down the aisle. Despite almost two years of loyal custom, Kirkwood doubted if he had exchanged more than ten words with the shopkeeper. A tacit, unspoken understanding existed between them whereby, as long as Ahmed continued to undercut the Tesco Express next door, Kirkwood would continue his daily pilgrimage to the store. And no multinational conglomerate or rodent in need of a pee would ever sever that bond.

Kirkwood exchanged two of his precious pound coins for eight tins of the good stuff from a hatchet-faced Mrs Ahmed at the counter. He had never seen the woman smile and she wasn't about to end that sour streak today. As it was pay day, he treated himself to a five-pence plastic bag as opposed to cramming the tins down the inside of his jacket. Kings for a day, right?

As he exited the mini-market he checked the time again. His Garmin dispassionately informed him he had eight minutes to reach the office. He quickened his step as best he could and grimaced as his chafed nether regions howled in protest. He was a fighting a war on two fronts and losing them both. Arriving at work a millisecond past ten o'clock would evoke the wrath of the ever-vigilant office snitch, Brian Jenkins, who happily touted tardy colleagues to impress senior management. And even if he did arrive on time, there was still the Grand Canyon of Routine 17 to negotiate before the weekend's festivities could begin. This one was going down to the wire but that's what life with OCD often boiled down to; keeping all the balls in the air while ensuring all daily routines were crossed off the list.

'Any spare change, mister?'

Kirkwood looked down to his right to locate the source of the thick Belfast accent. A stick-thin man in his early twenties was wrapped in a sleeping bag outside Tesco Express. Beneath dark eyes set deep within cavernous sockets, was a small green India ink tattoo on his left cheekbone; a cross no less. Beside him another street dweller sat as if bowed in prayer, their features obscured by a hooded top, which was clearly several sizes too large. They were scribbling furiously into a notebook.

'Sorry mate. I'm late for work,' Kirkwood blushed with embarrassment. He would normally throw a few coins in the polystyrene cup at the man's side that was being used as an impromptu collection receptacle. The fear of Skelly and a failed routine unfortunately overrode all other considerations. Lives were at stake. Images of collapsing tower blocks and chemical-warfare strikes in the Middle East flooded his mind as he stared into the unblinking eyes of the young man.

17. And seven minutes to make it to Optima. Screw it up and it's…

All. Your. Fault.

'No problem, mister. Have a good day.' The skinny male was already looking towards his next potential benefactor. Kirkwood smiled apologetically and walked on. The other rough sleeper did not look up, immersed in whatever they were writing. He made a mental note that if he saw the two of them again next week, he would give something.

It was as if what happened next occurred in slow motion. The scribbling of the street dweller, rough sleeper, homeless person, or whatever the government chose to call them in order to massage the statistics and mask what was really happening on the streets — continued unabated. As Kirkwood neared them, he realised they weren't writing, but drawing; sketching a profile with a pencil stub, blunt and no more than three inches in length. Yet the detail was exquisite, the contour and shading bringing to life the face emerging at the hands of the talented artist huddled before him.

The face being sketched was unmistakable. The ruddy cheeks. The outrageous mutton-chop sideburns. The upper lip curled in a snarl beneath those mocking, malevolent eyes.

Staring at him from the page was a figment of his frazzled imagination. An apparition who resided within his savaged psyche, one he had never spoken of to another living soul.

Skelly.

Kirkwood stopped dead and stared as the hooded figure applied the finishing touches to the sketch. They abruptly looked up, as if aware they were being watched, and Kirkwood found himself staring into the pale blue eyes of a young woman, no more than eighteen or nineteen. Strands of jet-black hair poked out from under the hood which made her deathly-pale skin even more startling. Kirkwood realised his mouth was hanging open and as hard as he willed it, the words he needed to say would not come.

The young woman's surprised expression rapidly dissolved into a scowl. 'Do you want to take a picture? It'll last longer!' She began to stuff the notebook and pencil into a battered Adidas satchel by her side.

'I'm sorry,' stammered Kirkwood. 'It's just…'

'Is he hassling you?' the stick man intervened, jumping to his feet and squaring up to Kirkwood. 'What's your problem, mate? You get a thrill out of perving at wee girls in the street?'

'No…I…It's…' Kirkwood started to sweat profusely, acutely aware he was attracting puzzled looks from passers-by. He needed to be at his desk in five minutes which was never going to happen if he became embroiled in a public brawl. Besides, he had never thrown a punch in anger in his life, so he didn't fancy his chances against the stick man who towered a good four inches above him.

'Come on, Danny. Let's go. Don't be causing a scene.' The girl, now on her feet, pulled at her friend's tracksuit top and began to drag him away. She glowered at Kirkwood one last time before melting into the crowd.

'Consider that a warning, mate!' bellowed Danny, jabbing a finger in Kirkwood's direction before turning and following her.

Kirkwood froze, torn between pursuing the girl and the nagging need to get to the office on time to start Routine 17. He took a step towards the young couple before doubling over, the same intense pain as before, harpooning his left eye socket. He grimaced and the decision was made. Skelly always got his way.

He took one last, despairing look at the girl before she disappeared. The back of her black hoodie carried the name of his favourite band, Nirvana, in bold yellow, along with their trademark cross-eyed smiley face. It was insane. Was this a sign? Kirkwood turned and began to jog the final few hundred yards towards the Optima building, oblivious now to the chafing. He reckoned he would just make it before ten. He also reckoned he would muddle through Routine 17 before finally muddling through twelve pints of strong lager.

But above all else he vowed to find Nirvana Girl. For the first time that morning, indeed the first time in many mornings, he sensed the weight lifting slightly from his heart. Kirkwood began to quietly sing to himself.

'With the lights out, it's less dangerous….'

CHAPTER 10

THE DIRTIEST WEE SHOP IN BELFAST

9:54 a.m.

Danny peered into the cup to gauge how much they had gathered since setting up outside the Tesco Express. Rush hour was starting to die off and the steady flow of office workers making their way into the city had subsided to an irregular trickle. A quick mental calculation and a rattle of the cup brought a smile to his face. They must have cleared over twenty pounds, despite the best efforts of that creepy guy to freak out the girl. Ever since he had hooked up with her, business had boomed for Danny Keenan, street entrepreneur. Most people wouldn't give him a second look, correctly predicting that any contributions to the Keenan business empire would be frittered away on vodka and pills.

'Come on Meredith. We're sorted. Breakfast is on Uncle Danny.'

She was as weird as sin, always with her nose stuck in that bloody notebook. He asked her once what she was writing, and she mumbled something about writing letters to a friend back home, wherever that was. Danny hadn't pushed the subject as he didn't particularly care. Theirs was a relationship of convenience. He provided her protection at night and, in return, she pulled at the heartstrings and purse strings when they went begging during the day. She told him she was eighteen, but she could easily pass for younger. The punters loved the little-girl-lost look, and Danny loved the sound of their coins rattling in his cup.

'Yeah coming,' she sighed, struggling to keep pace with his long strides. Danny slowed slightly to let her catch up and winced in the process. Despite the warmer weather, his joints still ached from a night spent in a doorway at the side of the Europa.

'Usual spot I take it?' she asked.

'Aye,' replied Danny, emptying the contents of the cup into his hand and secreting them about his person. 'Oblivion here we come.'

They glided like ghosts through the city centre, invisible to the early morning shoppers and gangs of camera toting tourists who avoided them like they were lepers. Homelessness was not contagious but try telling that to Joe Public. They were incapable of seeing beyond the generic stereotype that if you lived rough, you were undoubtedly a drug-crazed psychopath intent on robbing them blind — with a stab wound to the guts for good measure.

'Slow down, Danny!' Meredith was now half jogging alongside her lofty companion in order to keep up. He stood a good head above her and his long legs covered the ground in a deceptively economic manner. Apparently, he had been a half decent footballer at school, a centre back who played for the Cliftonville youth team. There was talk of some of the English and Scottish teams wanting to look at him but then the wheels had come off in spectacular fashion.

'You keep up then.'

Meredith swore quietly and quickened her step again. She caught a reflection of herself in a store window as they turned left onto Royal Avenue, which was Belfast's primary shopping thoroughfare. Even in the baggy hooded top and tracksuit bottoms, it was clear to all she was painfully thin, having lost ten pounds since she fled home ten months ago. The Bitches at Ashcroft would have killed for the cheekbones and deathly pale complexion she now possessed. Her thin, dry lips were cracked, and a beauty of a cold sore was breaking out on the upper one to compliment the shadows beneath once striking blue eyes.

'I look like crap,' she sourly remarked to nobody in particular. No wonder that guy gawked at her like she had two heads.

'What's that?''

'Nothing,' she replied, pulling her hood back to allow what little breeze there was to cool her face. *God you're so unfit Meredith*, she thought. *Whatever happened to the girl who used to be able to run a seven-minute mile?* Shoulder-length black hair stuck to her face; a mixture of sweat and grease. She was long overdue a shower but that wasn't a priority at the moment. Her head was pounding as if a rave party was kicking off inside her skull and her brain felt like it had shrunk to the size of a pea, such was the raging hangover gathering momentum by the minute. She had already thrown up twice since waking, and Danny's breakneck pace was doing no favours with regards to keeping down whatever little was left in her stomach. She was relieved when they finally veered left onto Castle Street and their destination came into view.

Danny pushed the door open and walked into Healy's Newsagents; possibly the dirtiest shop in Belfast. Even by Castle Street's grimy standards it was dire, the layers of dust on the shelves, warding customers off from the mostly out of date stock. The proprietor, Dominic Healy, was slumped over a stained wooden counter, buried in that morning's edition of the *Irish News*. He looked up as the rusted bell above the door announced their arrival and his ancient, grizzled face broke into a greedy grin, as bleary eyes identified the first significant sale of the morning.

'Ah, my favourite two shoppers,' he boomed, spreading both arms wide in exaggerated greeting. 'What can I tempt you with this morning? A Chateau Latour 2009 perhaps? Or how about a cheeky Remy Martin Louise the Thirteenth? Interested?'

'We'll have the usual — and hurry up Healy, this place stinks,' said Danny, looking over his shoulder to make sure that their transaction was being conducted in privacy. Behind him, Meredith was already unzipping her bag in anticipation.

'Right you are, young Daniel,' Healy replied, before disappearing through a door behind the counter. Danny and Meredith stood in agitated silence, eager to be on their way as quickly as possible once the transaction was complete. Shards of daylight struggled to penetrate the grimy shop front, doing nothing to improve the drab interior. Healy eventually emerged from the bowels of the store clutching two bottles of Buckfast tonic wine and a ten-glass bottle of Smirnoff Vodka. He set them on the counter and Danny reciprocated by spilling the contents of his pockets beside them.

'Is that enough?' he asked edgily, eyeing the bottles in front of him. Meredith peeked out from behind and fixed the old man with her most doe-eyed expression, perfected from almost a year of surviving on the generosity of others.

Healy looked at her, before considering Danny's financial offering. 'No, it's not, but I'll turn a blind eye this time, considering you are two of my most loyal and valued patrons.' He began to scoop up the coins and deposit them in an archaic till which looked as if it belonged in a museum. Danny handed Meredith the bottles which she carefully placed in the Adidas bag as if they were precious gems. They had already turned and were halfway out of the store when the elderly shopkeeper shouted after them.

'Do come again. Open every morning from 7:30 a.m. Cheapest drink in town. No identification required.' He chuckled to himself. The youth of today. No manners. But they would be back again tomorrow, and the day after that.

They always were.

CHAPTER 11

ROUTINE 17

9:59 a.m.

As the lift lurched and began its ascent towards his office on the third floor of the Optima building, Kirkwood leaned back against its back wall, closed his eyes and attempted to regulate his breathing. His heart was thumping against his ribcage like a crazed woodpecker pecking its way to freedom. He would be at his desk within the allotted time. Part One of Mission Improbable was complete. It didn't get any easier from here on in, though. Routine 17 wasn't the most physically taxing or mentally challenging, but it was certainly one of the most embarrassing. Running fifteen miles was a total pain fest but was still chicken feed compared to the ordeal lying ahead.

Kirkwood Scott, amiable Administration Officer and eternal slacker, was about to make a Grade A fool of himself.

Routine 17 – 'Upon arriving at your designated place of work you must approach the first person you see on five separate occasions within the working day, and ask them a question about the first topic of conversation they engage you in. Failure to complete this routine to the satisfaction of all relevant parties within the allotted timeframe will result in it being ruled null and void. The normal terms and conditions will then apply.'

Kirkwood had every one of 'The 49' memorised to the last word. He exhaled deeply as he exited the lift and walked down the corridor towards Business Support Two, knowing that upon swinging left onto the expansive open planned office, the first co-worker he set his eyes on would be an unwitting participant in the farce which was to follow.

To the satisfaction of all relevant parties. Kirkwood struggled to suppress the ball of rage threatening to erupt from within and send him screaming from the building. There was only one relevant party who pulled the strings when it came to the routines, lurking within his deepest cerebral grooves, scrutinising his every move.

Skelly.

Even the name caused an icy shiver to rake a jagged path down Kirkwood's spine. It was always Skelly and if the routine was failed there were always consequences. Kirkwood winced. In the last year alone, he had failed six routines. Six. Meaning he had successfully completed the other 359. But that counted for nothing as those six resulted in the deaths of forty-seven people.

It was crazy. It was illogical. It was stark, utter madness.

Yet the grief and guilt which consumed with each passing catastrophe was as real as if he had pulled the trigger, detonated the explosive device or lost control of the juggernaut himself. Today could not be the seventh time. It could not.

Steeling himself, Kirkwood strode purposefully into Business Support Two and stopped. He took in the frenetic surroundings where dozens of colleagues busied themselves answering phones, tapping keyboards and filing documents. From the far end of the office, a slicked-back mop of silver hair popped up from behind a computer terminal like a demented meerkat and glared at him with barely contained contempt.

'Morning, loser. In by the skin of your teeth again?'

Of all the people he didn't want Routine 17 to involve, Brian Jenkins, office dork and brown-noser extraordinaire, was the name at the top of his list.

The same Brian Jenkins who Kirkwood now found himself staring helplessly at.

Somewhere deep, deep within himself he heard a throaty Home Counties chuckle.

CHAPTER 12

OFFICE SMEAGOL

10:01 a.m.

'Morning, Brian.'

Kirkwood felt like a gladiator entering the arena as he traversed the various aisles and pods of desks which separated him from one of the most unpleasant creatures he ever had the misfortune of meeting. Brian Jenkins, aka Smeagol to most of his colleagues, was in his early twenties but could have passed for many, many years older. It wasn't just his gelled back, prematurely grey hair. He dressed like an old man, talked like an old man and oozed his way through every miserable second of his existence like an old man. Having joined Optima straight from school, he had already risen to the dizzy heights of Pod Leader; placing him above Kirkwood in the organisational food chain. And oh, how the odious little weasel loved it.

Jenkins shifted uneasily in his chair, wary of the jovial nature of Kirkwood's greeting. He tugged nervously at the starched collar of his regulation white shirt with its accompanying ghastly grey clip-on tie.

'Can I help you?' he snapped. 'For if this isn't work related, then I have a mountain of invoices to get through. I haven't time to chew the cud with deadbeats like you. Some of us take pride in our work.'

'As do I. As do I, Brian,' replied Kirkwood, hovering over the divider which separated Brian's lair from the adjacent desk. While outwardly he appeared relaxed and genial, inside ripples of anxiety were beginning to lap at his thin veneer of calm. Routine 17 had begun.

Work. He could have foretold the little toad would bring it up first. He was as predictable as he was loathsome. Kirkwood leaned over the divider, causing Jenkins to protectively place a hand over the neatly stacked pile of invoices on his desk.

'I've often wondered how you manage to process them so quickly. I'm sure you must have to work to a very tight deadline.' Kirkwood put forward what he hoped was his most winning smile.

Jenkins relaxed a fraction but nothing more. 'Well yes I do actually. An exceedingly tight deadline. Which is why management entrust it to me as opposed to a slacker like you who would undoubtedly screw things up.' *If he was made of chocolate Jenkins would eat himself*, thought Kirkwood, as he fought to conceal his disdain for the self-important peacock pouting and preening before him.

'So, what time do they have to be on the system by?' asked Kirkwood in as casual a tone as he could muster. With that question he had nailed his colours firmly to the mast and buckled in, as the OCD rollercoaster jerked into action.

That was the question. The question he would have to ask Jenkins five times before the end of the working day. The question that Jenkins would have to *answer* five times before the end of the working day. A working day scheduled to end at lunchtime when he was due to meet Gerry and Grogan for an afternoon of alcoholic abuse.

Jenkins eyed Kirkwood cautiously, not sure if the question was genuine or some subtle attempt to mock and belittle him. The morons he worked with often resorted to such childish antics, such was their jealousy of his strong work ethic and popularity with management.

'Well...it's the same every month. They must be input by noon on the last Friday of every month. Which is...' He checked the clock on the wall above. 'In precisely one hour and fifty-seven minutes. So, if you'll excuse me please.' He pushed his jam-jar spectacles up the bridge of an angular nose and resumed pecking at the keyboard, glancing to and from the stack of invoices and the screen, where a spreadsheet crammed with columns and rows of digits grew ever longer.

'No worries. Catch you later.' Kirkwood turned smartly on his heels and made his way back across the office to his own desk. A smattering of colleagues looked up from their various tasks and smiled or grunted greetings. He collapsed into a swivel chair and began logging onto his computer, before peering up at the wall clock.

10:04 a.m.

Jenkins wasn't the only one working to a tight deadline.

One down, four to go. The first question was easy. It was when he started asking it again and again that the real fun and games started.

CHAPTER 13

EMILY'S WALL

10:08 a.m.

Leaving Healy's, Danny and Meredith crossed Castle Street and headed down a side street, away from the steady dribble of workers still heading into the city centre from the taxi ranks and multi-storey car parks that hugged its edges. To their left, Westland's Bookmakers was already plying a steady trade as regulars flitted to and from it, clutching their betting dockets with dreams of emerging victorious later in the day, grasping wads of bank notes. The reality was the majority of their slips would be lying crumpled on the betting shop floor by the end of the day; discarded in disgust as hopes of new-found wealth evaporated in front of them on the shop's giant plasma television screens. Meredith's father did not teach her much but always maintained he had never known a poor bookmaker.

'It's a mug's game, dear,' he warned her once, after she begged him to place a bet on that year's Grand National. 'It might seem like a harmless bit of fun now but let me tell you, it's the first step on the road to ruin. One bet leads to another and before you know it, you're lying in a doorway begging for loose change.'

Meredith smiled sadly at the prophetic irony of his words, given her current plight. This was her tenth month on the streets, yet her parents hadn't come looking for her once, even though they lived less than twenty miles away and she had been sighted on numerous occasions by friends and acquaintances of theirs. They were as embarrassed of her as she was appalled by them. She often daydreamed about what she would say if they sought her out. It would be a colourful conversation; she was certain of that much.

*

One of the many rules and regulations she was forced to adhere to within the repressive confines of the Starc household was that one must never resort to foul language. Swearing was viewed as evidence of a limited vocabulary, and even more limited career prospects. A boy she briefly dated from the church youth group had once dared to say 'shit' in the presence of Mrs Starc, which was the end of that fleeting romance.

It was one of the few domestic edicts which stuck with her, given the abrasive nature of her current lifestyle. Meredith was not one for swearing and resisted the urge to lapse into the language of her street peers where every sentence was riddled with expletives. If her parents were to appear before her now, though, she was prepared to make an exception and drop the F-bomb from a great height upon them. It would have been the death of her mother, but oh so worth it.

'I need to see a man about a dog,' Danny interrupted her thoughts. 'You okay if we meet up in the square in about an hour?'

By 'meet a man about a dog' he actually meant a drug deal. Danny's career as a small time criminal and car thief in the west of the city came to an abrupt halt when the local 'community representatives' paid him an unscheduled visit with a crowbar and several baseball bats. It was delivered as a gentle reminder that, unless he desisted from his anti-social activities, the next time it would be a bullet in the head as opposed to a severe beating. This rudimentary example of social justice left him in a bad way. Three operations later, he still suffered constant pain in both legs which often left him squirming in agony in the various doorways they co-habited. The prescription painkillers he now gulped down in decidedly unprescribed numbers were the only relief he found. Washed down with copious amounts of cheap alcohol of course.

'Sure. You trust me with the drink? I promise not to leave the country, but you can have my passport if it helps set your mind at ease.'

'Har-de-har. See ya in an hour, you cheeky wee bitch.' He strode off, his loping stride eating up the ground despite the suggestion of a limp which became more pronounced in the colder weather.

Meredith watched him go before doubling back the way they had come, past the bookmakers and out onto Castle Street again. She kept her head down and hood up, her raven locks bundled up in a loose ponytail. She was as nondescript and anonymous as the growing army of other young homeless who marred the modern, metrosexual image that the new Belfast was pitching at the wider world.

She cut down another side street where a pedestrian precinct opened out into a spacious square. Mulberry Square. It had become her Jerusalem, her Mecca in recent weeks, and she knew exactly where she was going. She crossed the square as a Guinness lorry pulled up to the right outside O'Reilly's Bar, preparing to stock the public house for the thirsty hordes who would soon be flooding the square.

Meredith didn't realise she was holding her breath until she crossed the square and entered a dog-legged alley leading back onto Royal Avenue. The walls of the alley were bedecked with vibrant hanging baskets suspended from mounted brackets at regular intervals. Between them, the walls themselves were a riot of colour, courtesy of council-approved graffiti artists, allowed to display their artistic talents as part of a massive regeneration scheme for this once run-down and most disreputable part of town. Meredith often stopped to admire the artwork, marvelling at the explosions of colour and creativity from an art form which was once regarded as an eyesore but was now seen as chic and desirable.

Not today, though. Her destination was just around the dogleg, or at least she hoped it was, hence the bated breath. Meredith rounded the corner and exhaled in relief for there it was, or rather, there *she* was.

Emily…

The graffiti was exquisite in its detail and perfectly captured the young woman, less than a year ago, had settled into a hot bath and calmly made deep incisions in both wrists with a set of scissors. Red rivulets of regret darkening the water she lay in, until her pupils were as dull and still as the murky depths she had chosen as her final resting place.

Her best friend. Her only friend.

The artist had captured Emily in profile, her delicate yet strong jaw jutting defiantly beneath cheekbones that even the finest plastic surgeon could not have replicated. Her skin was porcelain pale, thin lips hinting at a smirk which was never far from the features of the girl who had been her closest confidante. The angle of the portrait meant that only one of her brown eyes was displayed, but it glinted with a wit and intelligence suggesting the artist knew their subject intimately. A mane of spectacular, platinum-blonde hair framed these features and flowed behind her as if the sitting had taken place in a wind tunnel. A slim, elegant neck atop a bare shoulder completed the work which adorned the far wall of the alley where Meredith now stood transfixed.

She could have stared at the portrait all day, despite having visited the alley countless times to gaze upon it since it first appeared, not two months ago. It was unerringly accurate, as if a Polaroid photo had been taken of Emily and transposed onto the wall. Its origins were a puzzle and despite having made enquiries with countless graffiti artists who plied their art in the city centre, she was no closer to identifying the person who so effortlessly captured the essence of Emily. The tag line beneath provided no clues either and, if anything, its lazy, loping script deepened the mystery.

For it was her own initials.

'EO'H'. Emily O'Hara. The first time she saw it, Meredith thought the mural was some sick, intricate prank to further fuel the suspicion and paranoia that was often her most trusted companion on the streets. Was she being watched? Mocked? Had she not escaped the shadows of Ashgrove, the school where she and Emily had first met and were bullied mercilessly until that fateful Autumn evening? So, she thought at first. Until the second visit to the alley, and the one after that, and then the one after that. Messages had begun to appear beneath the tag line, in the same distinctive script. She initially thought it was the Buckfast, that her sanity was finally subsiding and crumbling like a child's sandcastle in the face of an incoming tide. Until she had dragged a grumbling Danny to the alley to confirm that the writing was there and not simply all in her head.

Three visits. Three messages. Different each time but when read in conjunction, they painted a picture more telling than even the dazzling artwork that initially lured her to this site.

Read More.

Urban Murmurs.

My Dearest.

My Dearest? Meredith had gasped. Emily was old-fashioned beyond belief. She was not one for texting and other forms of instant messaging. Instead she preferred the written word and corresponded with pen pals from all corners of the globe who she had diligently maintained contact with since a young girl. 'There's nothing more thrilling than receiving a letter from the other side of the world,' she had grandly informed Meredith, waxing lyrical about the personal connection that could never be duplicated by online communications.

She had even started writing to Meredith, despite them living less than a mile apart and seeing each other every day. Long, rambling diatribes about everything and nothing. Meredith called her a silly cow and never replied, but secretly she cherished each letter, devouring its contents. When Emily had died, Meredith had cried herself to sleep most nights, poring over the bundle of letters, which were the first items she hurriedly stuffed into her bag the night she decided to leave home.

She now bitterly regretted not replying. Could it have made a difference? She didn't know the answer to that but beat herself up about it for months after Emily's passing; until the day the messages started to magically appear on the wall of the alley. The dead girl, the girl who she had grieved the loss of for so long, was reaching out to her.

Emily wanted Meredith to write her a letter.

So that's exactly what she did.

42

CHAPTER 14

MILKY COFFEE, TWO SUGARS

10:34 a.m.

'Sorry, Brian. What time do those invoices have to be on the system by? It's just I'm doing the morning post, and there might be a few late ones I need to wing your way.'

'Noon,' Jenkins replied absent-mindedly, not looking away from the computer screen; his face a mask of concentration.

'Thanks, mate,' replied Kirkwood as he breezed past. Beneath the casual exterior he was fighting a losing battle to maintain composure. The anxiety within him was slowly unfurling like a comatose cobra stirring from a mammoth meal-induced slumber. Since retiring to his desk, he had been eyeing Jenkins constantly, waiting until the little creep was at his most distracted before making a move.

He carefully jotted down on a pad the exact wording of their exchange, while still fresh in his memory. Next to that he noted the time, just as he had done following their initial conversation when he first arrived in the office. It was crucial he recorded Jenkin's response each time he asked the question because otherwise he would hear Skelly's poisonous voice in his ears, making suggestions which jumbled his recollection of events and filled his head with doubts. His nemesis delighted in sabotaging routines and muddying the already unclear waters at every opportunity.

'Are you sure you've asked four times? Wasn't it three? Are you 100 per cent certain?'

'Did he say noon? Or was it eleven? You can't remember, can you?'

'If you can't be certain then the routine won't feel right. And if it doesn't feel right then that's when bad stuff starts to happen.'

'We wouldn't want that now, would we? Not after the last time. Terrible business that was. All those little children.'

'Tell you what? Best start again just to be on the safe side. But hurry, hurry. The clock is ticking.'

Kirkwood had been there countless times before and bore the mental scars to prove it. There was no worse feeling than having to start a routine from scratch when you thought you were on the verge of completing it. That was why he now resorted to taking notes as he went along. At least then he possessed concrete evidence should Skelly start his mind games.

Two down. Three to go.

Attempt number three was launched at 10:45 a.m. Ever the creature of habit, that was when Jenkins always rose from his labours and made his way to the vending machine in the first-floor canteen for a mid-morning snack. This routine was set in stone and neither wild horses nor a direct nuclear strike on Belfast would deter Jenkins from it. Milky coffee with two sugars, and a Mars Bar. Brian Jenkins' sour personality was only matched by his sweet tooth. Kirkwood eased alongside him as he waited in the queue behind other staff.

'Thanks for this morning, Brian.'

'What?' Jenkins turned irritably to discover Kirkwood grinning inanely at him.

'For letting me know about the invoices. Big Boss Atkins from the third floor phoned down wanting to know when they would be ready, and I picked up the call. I would have looked a proper idiot if I hadn't known.'

'I'm surprised Mr Atkins would want to know that. It's hardly a Human Resources matter.'

'Well you know what HR are like. Always sticking their noses in everybody else's business. Anyway, I put him right. Eleven o'clock, Mr Atkins. Eleven o'clock.'

Jenkins' face dropped like he had been kicked in the groin. 'Eleven? But it's noon. It's always noon. How am I meant to have them done by eleven?' He looked around the canteen like a frightened rabbit half expecting heavily armed shock troops from HR to crash through the windows at any second, having abseiled down from the third floor.

'Oh, right, I could have sworn you said eleven.' Kirkwood inched ever closer, patiently reeling in his catch now he had secured a nibble. Softly, softly, catchy monkey.

'No, you idiot. Noon. Twelve o'clock. I've told you this already today. Twice!'

Kirkwood smiled. 'That's right. Twice. I should have written it down really.' The irony of his words was not lost upon him.

'Look, don't worry. I'll phone him back and set the record straight. Just you relax. Here, let me buy your coffee. My way of saying sorry. Two sugars, isn't it?'

Jenkins' face brightened, for he was as tight fisted as he was a jobsworth. 'Well yes then,' he sniffed imperiously before quickly adding, 'I normally have a Mars Bar as well with it.'

'Not a problem,' replied Kirkwood cheerily. He began to slot coins into the vending machine as they reached the front of the queue. 'Money is no object for a fellow comrade from Business Support Two! Now, one last time, just so I'm 110 per cent certain before I ring him back. What time do the invoices have to be in by?'

Jenkins sighed as Kirkwood handed him the coffee and chocolate bar. But he answered. And that was all that mattered.

Strike three.

CHAPTER 15

MY DEAREST EMILY

18 June 2012

My Dearest Emily,

The day after the third message appeared, I worked it out. I knew what to do. I had to steal a notepad and some pens from Eason's on Royal Avenue but don't judge me. A girl's gotta do what a girl's gotta do and, anyway, you put me up to this in the first place. So here I am, sitting on Great Victoria Street, watching the world go by and wondering what to write. You were always the expert at this pen pal malarkey. I guess I should start from the beginning, or rather, the end as far as you are concerned. Bring you up to date on my wonderful life. It really is a magical tale of unicorns and pixie dust so pin your ears back and, for the first time in your afterlife, listen.

I remember the first time we met. I was sitting in the chaos that was Miss Gladstone's form class when you glided into the room. You were the new girl, but you entered as if you owned the place. You shimmered with confidence and glowed with self-belief. Everybody stopped what they were doing to stare. You just stared back before bursting out laughing and slinging your bag onto the desk next to mine. You sat down, eyed me up, and then grandly announced for all to hear, 'I'm Emily O'Hara and I'm your new best friend.' And that was that. We became inseparable. Little did I know it was the beginning of the end for in just over a year you would be gone, and I would be here. Living from one day to the next, scrounging together the money to buy my next drink.

Ashgrove College for Girls, established 1876. A magnificent red brick,

Victorian building, resplendent with exquisite, sprawling grounds which swept down to the shores of Belfast Lough overlooking the city itself. The elite of the elite were sent there, the higher echelons of Northern Irish society. Or the scum of the earth dripping with new money — dependent on your views of public-school education in the twenty-first century. The Board of Governors weren't that bothered when it came down to it. Beneath the sophisticated veneer and exquisite breeding, was a money-grabbing ethos that beggared belief. Scandal after scandal was covered up, from coke-snorting parties to unwanted teenage pregnancies. Anyone could be bought, and the Ashgrove hierarchy were infinitely resourceful when it came to keeping the excesses of their little darlings off the front pages of the Sunday tabloids.

We would come to hate that school but vowed to survive it together. And I thought we had. You wreaked havoc in those first giddy weeks, like a pebble thrown into a still, alpine lake. You were your own self-generated storm, the queen of all you surveyed. Your very presence in a room created shockwaves that sparked and crackled like home-made popcorn on the hob. You demanded the attention of everyone who entered your sphere of influence, you divided opinion, and were the talk of the place.

Yes, you were a queen but one without a throne for they hated you. Hated the fact you were prettier than them, smarter than them, always one step ahead. They chased you like a child chases a kite on a breezy afternoon. A pointless, futile pursuit, as you always evaded their jealous grasp. Or so I thought. You were like a sun to me and I basked in the warmth of your life-affirming glow. Yet you still chose, yes, chose — I cannot get away from that; to leave me in the manner you did. Without warning, without any form of explanation. No note, nothing. Until now.

I'll just spit it out, shall I? No point beating about the bush. That was never our style. We shared everything, right? There were no secrets. You killed yourself. Committed suicide. Took your own life. Whatever you choose to call it. You left me, deserted me, betrayed me when I needed you most.

You broke me, Emily.

Without you I became a lifeless lump, a dead planet spinning through the void not knowing or caring where the journey took me. There was to be no pot of gold at the end of this rainbow, only the ravages of the abyss. And as I write this I am teetering on the brink once more. I fear it, part of me craves it, yet I will not seek its cold embrace for I must exist. I must keep going. For you, you selfish bitch. When I sat beside your beautiful corpse in the funeral home, I thought it was over, for the both of us. Yet you wouldn't even allow me to quietly slip away onto the streets and wallow at the bottom of a bottle. You came back; you always had to be the centre of attention, didn't you?

Even in death.

Sasha Blackstock and her B14 coven made it their mission to torment you. Jealousy is an insatiable mistress, and it roamed the corridors of Ashgrove with a ravenous hunger which could not be sated. Their cruelty was only matched by your refusal to succumb to their belittling taunts and childish insults. They christened you the White Witch, so envious were they of your hair which cascaded halfway down your back like a silver waterfall. Sasha maintained it was out of a bottle, but it was as natural as daylight itself. I would spend hours brushing it out as you recounted that day's hostilities. You seemed immune to their barbs. You always had a comeback, a pithy retort; always had the last word at their juvenile attempts to bring you down to their own pathetic level. I didn't know their endless probing would eventually breach your defences, allowing them to pour through and overwhelm you.

Behind those proud eyes you were cracking day by day, just like me. It's just that you hid it so much better. I thought I knew you, that I could read you like nobody else, but what a deluded fool I was. I knew nothing — less than nothing, for I could have helped you. I should have sensed the distress flares you sent shooting up into the starless sky. I wore my heart on my sleeve whereas you concealed yours within layer upon layer of serene smiles. 'Man-up, Meredith,' you would lecture me. 'Those bitches are vampires. They want our blood. They get a whiff of your fear and it will be a feeding frenzy. Don't give them the satisfaction. Not an inch, you hear me. Not. An. Inch.'

But it was you who was silently yielding the inches to them. Slipping and sliding ever nearer the brink. Fighting a lonely, desperate battle which you concealed from me like you concealed your butchered heart. Cut to shreds and left to bleed out on a slab. Just like you were butchered on that mortuary slab and then laid out for all to see in a wooden box. You were the most stunning of creatures, snuffed out in her prime. They got to you and I don't know how, and I don't know when, but they did. I should have saved you like you saved me, but I did nothing; too absorbed was I with all my own petty problems. Spots and boys and all the usual teenage crap.

The police investigation found nothing, shock horror, as the Ashgrove illuminati closed ranks to protect their little darlings. Sasha and her mean girl wannabes trooped past your coffin, bawling their eyes out. It was a performance of some note, I was tempted to rise from my seat and applaud them out of the graveyard, such was their poise and panache. Butter wouldn't melt in their mouths, but the rancid taste their vacuous hypocrisy left in mine will haunt me to my own grave. No amount of wine or vodka will ever cleanse my palate of that. They disgust me, but not as much as I disgust myself. The mirror never lies, and I saw myself for the hideous coward I was when I glimpsed my haggard features reflected in the polished stained glass as we filed from the church to say our last goodbyes.

I could not look at them that day, just as I cannot look at myself today. I dream of you every night, the same dream that sucks me from my sleep screaming and shattered. You are wearing the dress they buried you in, the baby blue one that your mother adored but you changed out of, the second she turned her back. Standing on the edge of the grave, arms outstretched. I reach for you, but you silently fall, smiling all the while. Falling through time into the abyss from where there is no return. You saved me from myself, but I couldn't save you from the flames. You welcomed their caress, surrendered to the blissful silence.

Oh, I need you so much, Emily. And I am so, so sorry. I miss us. Every hour is a day and every day a year. The pain is incessant, it roars through my marrow like nothing I have experienced before. There is no respite and no relief. I couldn't be there anymore, powerless against their whispered exchanges and sly looks. If I had stayed, I know I would have taken the same option as you.

So, I ran away, I escaped. Escaped from the school, my parents, those bitches; a life that suffocated you and was doing the same to me. I ran to these streets in order to survive. And if I'm honest — to escape from you as well. To flee from the memories that were just too brutal to bear. I wanted to feel nothing. I wanted to be nothing. And it was working so well. Until you came back and started talking to me again.

I'll finish for now, 'post' this letter and see what happens. I've done what you asked of me, so I guess the ball is in your court now. Until next time, if there is a next time.

Meredith x.

CHAPTER 16

BUCKIE FOR BREAKFAST

11:12 a.m.

Meredith stopped writing and raised a hand to shield her eyes from the early morning haze that was aggravating the nagging headache which had been creeping across her forehead since her return from the alley. Across the square, Danny was deep in conversation with two other men. She recognised one of them as Colly, an equally gaunt, angular figure who had already discarded his shirt despite the early hour. It promised to be another hot day in Belfast as the 'heatwave' weather forecasters were gushing over showed no signs of abating. By heatwave, they meant the temperature had a chance of making double figures, and driving sleet was unlikely. The locals were making the most of the milder conditions and Belfast's pasty-skinned, 'tops off' brigade would be out in force again. Some people knew no shame when it came to gratuitous shows of flesh.

She didn't recognise the other male, but he looked vaguely familiar. Either way, he cut a shifty figure perched on a battered wooden skateboard. Pedestrians crossing the square eyed-up the three men warily and gave them a wide berth. A plastic looking woman in a tight-fitting blouse and skirt clutched her bag tightly to her hip and hurried past, never taking her heavily made-up eyes off Danny. He stared back aggressively until she was beyond him and then, after checking over both shoulders to ensure the coast was clear, slipped something into the hand of Skateboard Guy who paused and considered the offering before reciprocating the gesture.

Then followed the obligatory finger-clicking and fist-pumping before the three of them made off in different directions across the square — the seediest of starbursts. Meredith knew a drug deal when she saw one. Danny swaggered nonchalantly back to where she was huddled on a bench, all baggy clothing and deathly-pale skin. Despite the rising heat, she was freezing cold or 'foundered' in Belfast speak; always feeling this way before the first proper drink of the day. Her central heating system consisted of copious amounts of alcohol and had for some time. She reached into the Adidas bag between her feet and produced one of the Buckfast bottles they had purchased from Dirty Dominic. It was time to make significant inroads into the tonic wine and experience the familiar, warming glow as it seeped through her body.

She unscrewed the cap and took a mouthful of the dark liquid, closing her eyes and concentrating hard on swallowing and keeping it down. The first drink of the day was always the hardest but so worthwhile. She paused and fought the gag reflex as the liquid settled on her empty stomach and considered whether or not to remain there. One…two…three. Nothing. Meredith opened her eyes and gave a tired smile as Danny crash-landed on the bench beside her. Subtlety was not part of his admittedly limited repertoire of social skills.

'Right. That's me sorted wee girl. Sure you don't want a happy pill to kickstart another day in paradise?'

'Nah I'm fine. I'll just stick to my Buckie.' She raised the bottle to him and scanned the square nervously. The last thing they needed was an eagle-eyed cop swooping down and confiscating their carry out. Notices were dotted all around the square warning that alcohol consumption in public was prohibited. Not that anyone paid the slightest bit of attention. On long, hot days like they were having of late, it sometimes seemed as if the whole of Belfast was drunk. She wondered who was running the country at times. Maybe that explained why it was in such a mess. Oh, if Mummy and Dad could see her now, they would be *so* proud.

'Please yourself,' shrugged Danny, indifferent to her decision. 'All the more for little old me.' He produced a clear, plastic bag from a pocket of his tracksuit bottoms. It contained about a dozen tiny, white pills. Removing one, he placed it on his outstretched tongue before tipping his head back and swallowing. He gleefully turned to her and opened his mouth wide to reveal the pill was no more.

'Ahhh, just what the doctor ordered.' Danny smacked his lips and indicated for her to pass the bottle, which she reluctantly did. Taking a healthy slug of wine, he cackled, revealing a mouthful of neglected, tobacco-stained teeth. 'You don't know what you're missing out on.'

'You'll be missing what's left of your front teeth if you don't cough up what you owe the McManus Brothers. Slipping them the odd tenner now and again isn't going to keep them sweet at the rate you neck those pills. How much do you owe them now? Hundreds?'

'Oh, keep your knickers on,' Danny's voice dripped with sarcasm. 'They're hardly going to do that to one of their best customers. Talk about cutting your nose off to spite your face. I'm good with them. They know they'll get their money.'

'Your nose will be the least of your worries unless you sort it out and quick, that's all I'm saying.' He sulkily handed her back the bottle and she took a sharp nip of it before pulling a face as she realised it was already half empty, and it wasn't even ten in the morning. Binge drinking wasn't big, and it wasn't clever but, at present, it was the only coping mechanism to ensure she scrambled from one day to the next.

The rest of the morning became a toxic blur. Danny convinced her that mixing Buckfast and Smirnoff was a good idea — not that she needed much persuading. Voices and faces merged into a muddled morass and at one point she recalled dancing in the middle of the square, spinning faster and faster with arms outstretched as she flung her head back, basking in the glow of drunken oblivion. She shrieked with laughter until losing her footing and landing with a jarring thud on the concrete. The laughter ebbed away after that to be replaced with soft sobs.

By early afternoon the Buckfast and vodka had taken their toll and she found herself slumped in a shadowy corner of the square, eyes heavy with intoxicated exhaustion. She dozed fitfully, jerking awake on one occasion to spew the watery contents of her stomach into an adjacent flower bed. Shivers raked her body from head to toe as she lay motionless on one side, a globule of saliva connecting her bottom lip to the pavement. She hadn't the energy to lift her head, let alone move away. Just a girl and her vomit.

She watched as feet crossed her worm's eye view of the square, headed in either direction. A pair of expensive, polished shoes stopped, and she heard the jangle of coins landing on the ground beside her prostate form. 'I wasn't even begging,' she roared, summoning the energy from somewhere to prop herself onto an elbow and hurl the coins in the general direction of the mystery benefactor. 'I don't want your bloody money. You can shove it where the sun don't shine.' The dozen or so drinkers sitting in the beer garden outside O'Reilly's halted their conversations to look over at her, their expressions a mixture of pity and embarrassment.

She didn't care. Forcing herself to sit upright, she pulled her knees up and buried her face into them. The tears came streaking her grimy cheeks and dripping onto the concrete between her legs. 'I just want my Emily,' she whimpered inconsolably.

She sat that way for some time before slowly keeling over and falling into a deep, dreamless sleep. A blessed relief from the terrors haunting her nights of late. The men chasing her, never stopping, always hunting her and Emily down.

She somehow evaded them but Emily, she would always stumble and fall before they descended upon her like a pack of starving wolves, ripping her to pieces with their bare hands, cracking her ribcage and gorging on the still-beating heart, their hands drenched in ruby red blood. Meredith could only look on helplessly, screaming at them to stop but powerless to return to where the body of her lifeless friend lay, bloodied and broken.

She could never recall them in any detail when she jolted awake, drenched in a clammy, vinegary sweat — except for one man. The ruddy jowls and ridiculous mutton-chop sideburns; dark, deranged eyes gloating at her as he licked his lips and howled in delight at her horrified expression. His face was a mask of malice, coated in the glossy entrails of her beloved best friend. She would take that face to her grave. It was never far from her thoughts, assailing them at every opportunity. There was no therapy to make him go away. Just the numbing bliss of the wine and the letters she wrote during the brief periods of lucidity between waking up and that first drink of the day.

Letters to Emily. Describing him, detailing the horrors of the night. Hoping that her friend would offer some sort of a clue as to who this nightmarish man was, a sign from beyond that would allow a sliver of light to pierce the darkness. She had even sketched him this morning as she sat on Great Victoria Street, scraping together the coins to buy the poison which now coursed through her veins, evolving into the next crippling hangover. When she woke up, she would pocket the coins the shiny-shoed Samaritan had chucked her way. Dignity and pride would be set aside because only the next bottle mattered.

Across the square, a tall, thin man in an immaculate pinstriped suit smirked at the drunk girl slumped in the corner, before continuing on his way. He had urgent business to attend to elsewhere in the city. He looked down and frowned at a speck of dust on his exquisite Prada loafers. His reflection frowned back up at him, such was the sheen from the highly polished Saffiano leather. The man bent down to flick away the blemish before setting off briskly towards his next appointment. *This planet is vile,* he thought to himself, but work was work. And you didn't want to get on the wrong side of the Colonel.

CHAPTER 17

MR BRADLEY'S TOY SHOP

Omagh

March 1995

Kirkwood Scott was eight years old the first time he set eyes on the man who was to destroy his life.

Every month, without fail, John Scott took his only son to Bradley's Toy Shop, the only one of its kind in town. It was the highlight of the young boy's month. Katie wasted her pocket money on stupid girly magazines and eyeshadow. She was thirteen and their mother allowed her to experiment with make-up even though Kirkwood thought it made her look like a clown. He was much more disciplined with his finances and saved his precious pennies for the excursion to Bradley's. It was always a magical event and he rarely slept much the night before; such was the excitement. Kirkwood carefully set his money out the night before and woe betide Katie or anyone else who ventured near it without his express permission.

He was always first up the following morning, barely able to contain growing impatience as his father dithered over egg and toast before finally dressing and scooping the car keys up into his huge hands. 'Come on then General Kirkwood,' he would proclaim with a mischievous smirk. 'Let's get down to the recruiting station and sign up some fresh cannon fodder.' It was one of their many in jokes.

On entering the shop, Kirkwood always made a beeline past the shiny bicycles and doll's houses, to a glass cabinet at the back that contained his own personal holy grail; the finest collection of toy soldiers this side of Belfast. The metallic figures stood no more than six centimetres tall, unless they were on horseback, and each one was exquisitely hand-painted, down to heroic facial expressions and immaculate uniforms. They told stories of conflicts long gone by; from grizzled, camouflaged World War II commandos to flamboyant Crimean cavalry officers; from sturdy Cromwellian pikemen to Civil War infantrymen. Spanning centuries of warfare and bursting with tales of forgotten heroics and gallantry, the cabinet and its contents mesmerised the young Kirkwood. Inside the glass cabinet lay countless adventures of derring-do. Kirkwood was mesmerised by it all. Every single month.

The most difficult part was deciding which figures would be accompanying him home. Kirkwood wanted them all, but his budget dictated he was restricted to two purchases per visit. This led to much procrastination on his part, weighing up the priorities of his burgeoning bedroom army, against the constraints of his limited finances. No doubt Napoleon had similar difficult decisions to make in his day, but for an eight-year-old boy this was serious stuff. In the end it took a fair bit of persuasion and cajoling from his father to drag a decision out of him.

Then followed the most solemn of ceremonies, as ancient Mr Bradley produced a gargantuan set of keys, fumbling and fussing for what seemed an eternity before selecting the one which opened the cabinet. Kirkwood stood slightly behind, licking his lips in anticipation as he willed the elderly shopkeeper to hurry up as there were battles to be fought, and wars to be won. Mr Bradley dithered over opening the cabinet almost as much as Kirkwood deliberated over what to buy.

The Saturday Kirkwood first saw the Colonel was the exception. The minute he set eyes on him astride the huge black charger, his mind was made up. Call Mr Bradley what you will, but he was a wily businessman and made sure that the store was regularly restocked with all the 'must-have' goods that featured on the birthday and Christmas lists of his young customers. Every month, there would be new figures in place to tempt and entice the coins from Kirkwood's pocket into the till. Not that it took a lot of tempting, as every month there was only one place the money was going, and that was straight into the Bradley coffers. The old man took great pride in ensuring that no two months were the same when young Master Scott came to gaze upon his wares.

'Yes, I thought he would catch your eye,' smiled the shopkeeper when Kirkwood pointed towards the mounted figure on the middle shelf of the display cabinet. 'He only arrived yesterday. Nineteenth-century British cavalry officer. Not sure of the regiment, but this fellow would have fought at Waterloo with Wellington against the French. Isn't he magnificent?'

Kirkwood could only nod in stunned silence as Mr Bradley carefully removed the figure from the cabinet before placing it in a brown paper bag and handing it over with a flourish. The remainder of the shopping excursion was a blur. He hurriedly selected a second figure, a stoic Confederate infantryman, then endured his father exchanging pleasantries with Mr Bradley for what seemed like forever, before they finally headed home. The car had barely come to a halt in the driveway before Kirkwood crashed through the back door and into the kitchen past his startled mother. He hurtled up the stairs, two at a time, towards the sanctuary of his bedroom, with his newly acquired treasures.

'You're welcome,' his father shouted sarcastically after him, causing Kirkwood to halt in his tracks and skulk sheepishly back to where his parents and Katie awaited him at the foot of the stairs. His older sister leaned forward conspiratorially, never one to miss an opportunity when it came to scoring brownie points over her sibling; especially as she was usually the one on the receiving end of a telling-off.

'Sorry,' mumbled Kirkwood, both eyes firmly rooted on his father's shoes, avoiding eye contact. 'I am grateful. I really am. I just got excited. This is the best soldier I've ever owned, and I just wanted to…'

'Try and show a little more gratitude, Kirkwood,' his mother sighed, the exasperation evident in her tone. 'Your father gets up every morning and works all the hours God sends, so that you and your sister don't go without. You would do well to remember that and say thank you now and again.'

'I always say thank you,' bleated Katie, determined to raise her own profile at the expense of her beleaguered younger brother. 'Every time I…'

'That's enough, Katie,' said her mother, shooting her a look that sent the teenager scampering back to the pages of her pop magazine.

'I'm sorry, Dad,' whispered Kirkwood again, this time summoning up the resolve to lift his head and meet the gaze of his father. Beneath the stern exterior he thought he caught the semblance of a smile crossing his father's features. John Scott never could remain annoyed with the kids for long, unlike his wife who was capable of scolding for Ireland. It just wasn't in his nature. But both father and son knew they were playing to a captive audience as the former was frequently chastised by his wife for being too soft on the kids. 'Why do I always have to play the bad cop?' she remonstrated on more than one occasion. 'You're too easy-going, John. At the end of the day you're their father — not their best friend. It's not good for them in the long run.'

'It's okay, son,' his father offered as an opening gambit, before a raised eyebrow from his wife prompted him to continue. 'But your mother's right. We brought you up to have good manners and it costs nothing to say please and thank you. Now go on up to your room and stay there until you're called down for your dinner.'

'Yes, Dad. Sorry, Dad.' Kirkwood turned on his heels and took off up the stairs again before his mother or Katie could object to the leniency of the punishment. He closed the bedroom door behind him and sank to his knees on the carpet to inspect his latest acquisitions. A cursory glance at the Confederate infantryman satisfied him that he was a sturdy and reliable foot soldier who would adapt well to the demands that awaited him as part of this exclusive private army.

The fort, which had become the centre of the young Kirkwood's world, was a modest affair that arrived the previous December, courtesy of Father Christmas. A vicious rumour had swept the school playground that autumn, suggesting the big man in the red suit was nothing more than an imaginary figure concocted by adults, who all along were responsible for leaving presents under the tree on Christmas morning.

Kirkwood erred on the side of caution and played along with his own parents, fearing that to unmask their duplicity this close to the big day would be an own-goal of epic proportions. Lo and behold, come Christmas Day he received the fort he had asked for in his Santa letter, along with a selection of 7th Cavalry troopers.

The fort was a basic but sturdy construction. Four plastic sides created a square-shaped structure when slotted together via four attachable corner sections, complete with covered watchtowers. Swinging, detachable wooden gates and interior clip-on ramparts completed the stockade, which the manufacturers confidently claimed on the packaging was, 'robust enough to withstand the most ferocious Indian assault, while replicating the realistic timber log effect of a nineteenth-century American frontier fort.' Father Christmas or no Father Christmas, Kirkwood was delighted with his new command centre and spent the next ten months painstakingly assembling his forces in defensive positions within and around it. Pride of place went to the collection of metallic figures from Bradley's, now totalling an impressive twenty, which he placed inside the fort itself, as was becoming of their elite status.

Kirkwood placed the Confederate infantryman, from that day onwards known as Private O'Hara, just inside the front gates. With raised rifle, aggressive stance and steely gaze, he was perfectly suited to perform this key security detail, while at the same time supervising the less-trustworthy grey, plastic German paratroopers, who manned the ramparts on either side. Which left the Waterloo veteran. Kirkwood carefully lifted the mounted figure from the paper bag and held it delicately between right thumb and middle finger, so he could properly inspect his new leader; having already made that important strategic decision on the journey home. To be a leader you must look like a leader, he had read somewhere once, and boy, did this old fellow look like a leader.

The man sat resplendently astride the fearsome black stallion, which stood frozen on its hind legs; its front hooves lashing out at any unfortunate soul who strayed too close. The stallion's flowing mane, flared nostrils and crazed, pitch-black eyes completed the image of a ferocious beast that only a true hero could control.

The Colonel — for he looked like a Colonel and that was good enough for Kirkwood, sat steady as a rock, legs hugged tightly to the flanks of his equine companion. Knee-high black boots polished within an inch of their lives, and tight cream breeches, contrasted vividly with a scarlet tunic adorned with rows of elaborate gold buttons. These were complimented by matching epaulettes, which would have put an American footballer's shoulder pads to shame.

Topping off the uniform was a foot-high black Busby secured by a glistening silver chinstrap. In the heat of battle, the last thing you wanted to do was lose your hat — never mind your head. A flamboyant red feather sat jauntily atop the Busby like a multicoloured chocolate flake poking out the top of an ice cream cone. It was the cherry on top, and no ordinary soldier could carry off such a swaggering look. Only a man of the highest honour, integrity and social standing. Only a man like the Colonel.

The Colonel could always be found on the front line leading by example, with not a second thought for his own well-being. Charging headlong into French infantry squares, he wreaked instant havoc; slashing and stabbing with a gleaming sabre, which delivered death to all who dared challenge him. He butchered his foes with a calm and clinical brutality, which was underpinned by years of meticulous training and practice. This man had no call for muskets or pistols as only cowards resorted to such long-range devices in warfare. No, he wanted to look into the eyes of the enemy as he skewered, maimed and butchered. He needed to feel his blade sliding between ribs like the proverbial knife through hot butter; to sense its cruel point piercing vital organs like a pin bursting a water-filled balloon, spilling their entrails onto his uniform. He was merciless and majestic, an angel of death who careered about the battlefield like a spinning top.

Beneath the brim of the Busby were a set of intense, penetrating eyes that seemed to change colour depending on what angle you viewed them from; one minute as black as the deepest, darkest mine shaft, the next a delicate chocolate brown that would charm the birds from the trees. The crowning glory was a full, handlebar moustache, which started on his upper lip and swept to either side across ruddy cheeks, before sweeping along a chiselled jawbone to connect with equally resplendent mutton-chop sideburns. Kirkwood could only guess at the colour of his hair beneath the Busby, but the moustache and sideburns were an angry grey, reminiscent of a thundercloud about to empty its contents onto the unsuspecting earth.

Kirkwood gingerly placed the figure inside the fort and leaned back to admire it, amid his company of warriors. Finally, the men had the commanding officer they had been waiting for, a man who they would follow to hell and back. A man who would stand by them to the bitter end, who would die for them and with them.

'I shall call you Skelly,' murmured Kirkwood. 'Colonel Augustus Skelly.' He sat back on his haunches and blew out both cheeks in surprise. He had no idea where such a grand name originated from, it just popped into his head. But it was perfect. Absolutely perfect.

Colonel Augustus Skelly. The Company finally had their Commander in Chief.

And so, it began. The not so beautiful journey that would take Kirkwood Scott to the brink of madness.

CHAPTER 18

CARNAGE IN CUBICLE ONE

11:38 a.m.

Kirkwood lay curled in a tight ball of terror on the floor of the toilet cubicle. The stark fluorescent tube lighting above offered little comfort. Drawing both knees into his chest, he frantically sought foetal comfort within the cramped confines. The cubicle, however, reminded him more of a tomb than a womb; one reeking of cheap disinfectant bleach as opposed to decaying flesh, but a tomb, nonetheless.

He was thankful for the cold ceramic tiles against his burning cheek. His teeth involuntarily ground together as another barrage of unwanted thoughts launched a frontal assault on his teetering defences. He had retreated to the men's toilets at the far end of Business Support Two after a disastrous exchange with Jenkins while attempting to eke out the fourth answer for Routine 17. The little rodent, obviously under pressure himself, erupted at Kirkwood's continued amnesia as to when the invoices were to be processed. It rapidly deteriorated into a shouting match necessitating Laura, Kirkwood's line manager, to intervene, after Jenkins threatened to hurl a loaded stapler in his direction.

'TWELVE! TWELVE! HOW MANY TIMES DO YOU HAVE TO BE TOLD?' he had screamed, as a flustered Kirkwood retreated to his desk to jot down the fourth response but simultaneously entered full-blown panic mode as to how on earth he was going to elicit a fifth from the now enraged Smeagol. Which explained his current plight — horizontal on the cubicle floor and desperately racking his brains in order to conjure up a scenario whereby he could obtain the precious final answer without ending up in the hospital courtesy of a deranged Jenkins.

The door squeaked open and Kirkwood realised he had company. Just visible through the small gap between the floor and the bottom of the cubicle door he watched as a pair of battered trainers entered his line of sight. They supported two ankles resplendent in Rudolph the Reindeer Christmas novelty socks. The only saving grace was the battery within their lining had died, sparing Kirkwood a tinny chorus of 'Grandma got run over by a reindeer' every time their owner clicked his heels together. Kirkwood shook his head in disgust. Never mind they would have been an abomination on Christmas Day itself, it wasn't even September yet.

'Oh, for the love of God, Mulligan,' Kirkwood thought, as his oblivious colleague began to noisily relieve himself at the urinal no more than six feet from where Kirkwood lay. After what seemed an eternity Mulligan mercifully zipped up and the sound of a running tap allowed Kirkwood to alter his body position in order to ease an aching hip. He had little time for Mulligan due to his shameless farting, appalling work ethic and ability to pin the blame on other colleagues any time he messed up and required a fall guy. The Teflon Don they called him. Nothing ever stuck.

The sound of the rarely oiled door opening for a second time brought Kirkwood to his senses again. It was obviously rush hour after the earlier coffee break and full bladders were in urgent need of emptying. Kirkwood, shirt now clinging to his clammy back, began to doubt he was ever going to escape the toilet block, let alone have an opportunity to torment Jenkins again. He swallowed hard; his throat bone dry as he envisaged the consequences of a failed routine on today of all days.

'Well, well, well. Look who we have here. If it isn't Smeagol Jenkins.' Kirkwood froze as Mulligan's mocking voice indicated the identity of the new addition to their ranks.

'My name is Brian if you must know, Mulligan. Now, would you mind stepping out of my way please. I've had enough nonsense this morning without you starting.'

'Cut the attitude, you little runt. I've been meaning to have a quiet word with you.' Mulligan's voice took on a more menacing tone. Davy Mulligan was a moronic bully boy, but an eighteen stone, six-foot-three moronic bully boy. Not the sort of guy you wanted to get on the wrong side of, especially in a one to one setting.

'I hear you've been bad mouthing me to the bosses. Whining behind my back about paperwork being misfiled. You keep that up and you're going to end up eating your dinner through a straw.'

'Now look, there's no need for this. I was merely doing my job. Would you mind not…Please…Oof!' The sound of air being released from a helium balloon suggested Mulligan had resorted to less subtle tactics in his efforts to convince Jenkins that discussing such matters with management was an unwise move. Through the gap he watched Jenkins drop to his knees.

'Consider that a polite warning,' snarled Mulligan. 'If I hear of you going behind my back again, there's plenty more where that came from.' His feet passed the stricken form of Jenkins as he went to make his way out of the toilets.

'Screw you,' winced Jenkins, obviously in considerable pain. Kirkwood could scarcely believe what he was hearing. Didn't Jenkins know when to walk away? Or in this case, crawl away.

'What did you say?' There was now genuine anger in Mulligan's voice. This was not going to end well. Before he realised what his body doing, Kirkwood leapt to his feet, unlocked the cubicle door and threw it open to discover Jenkins in a heap on the floor and Mulligan towering over him, about to unload a size twelve boot into the stricken geek's ribcage.

'Wise up, Mulligan, that's enough. You're going to get yourself sacked.' Mulligan froze and let his boot fall to the ground, astounded that his conversation with Jenkins had been overheard. Jenkins looked up at Kirkwood, his dazed expression a mixture of relief and pain.

'Keep out of this, Scott. It's got nothing to do with you.' Mulligan gestured with his head towards the door, strongly advising that Kirkwood use it and forget about what was transpiring in front of him.

'I'm afraid it does now.' Kirkwood hoped his face displayed no clue that his stomach was currently performing cartwheels. If he became involved in a brawl with the man mountain Mulligan, there was going to be only one winner. 'You're already on a final written warning. Management get to hear of this and it's the end of the road for you here. Don't try me. I'll sing like a canary if it means seeing the back of you.'

Mulligan hesitated, not used to people standing up to him. And much as he would have loved to split open Scott's lip, there was a two-year-old daughter at home and another one on the way. He was a self-styled hard man but didn't relish the prospect of explaining to his frightening fiancée that their single income family was now a digit less.

'Consider this your lucky day, Jenkins,' he scowled, before turning, shooting Kirkwood a final withering look and leaving the block. Kirkwood was convinced he could hear knuckles scraping along the floor as the missing link lumbered back down the corridor towards Business Support Two.

'Here, let me help you.' Kirkwood reached down towards Jenkins who, after careful consideration, accepted the offer and allowed his former enemy to haul him to his feet.

'Thanks,' Jenkins spluttered, removing his glasses and inspecting them for damage. He squinted towards Kirkwood. 'You didn't have to do that. It's not as if we are exactly bosom buddies. Ten minutes ago, I was ready to strangle you.'

'Yeah, well, I wasn't going to stand idly by and let King Kong do that to anybody.' Kirkwood sidestepped the minor detail that he had been lying in a heap, as opposed to standing at the time, but the sentiment was there

'All the same, you didn't have to.' Jenkins extended a hand to Kirkwood. 'Thank you, Scott. I endured years of that at school. I thought maybe working here I could leave it behind, but apparently not.'

Kirkwood looked at the outstretched hand as if it were on fire before recovering his composure and reciprocating the gesture. 'You're welcome...Brian. My school years weren't exactly a barrel of laughs either. He won't bother you again, not if he wants to hang onto his crummy job.'

It was Jenkins' turn now to look embarrassed. He shuffled nervously before speaking again. 'I better get back to these invoices. I still have a good half dozen to get through.' He pointed at the door as if Kirkwood needed an explanation as to how he was going to return to the office.

'Of course. And I'm sorry about all the questions. I...er...didn't sleep very well last night and my head's like a sieve.'

'No problem.' Jenkins placed his hand on the handle and partially opened the door.

'Oh, and one last thing...'

'Yes?' Jenkins turned hesitantly.

'What time do those invoices have to be processed by?' There was a pause between them which lasted less than a heartbeat but felt like an eternity to Kirkwood, before ever so gradually Brian Jenkins allowed his normally dour expression to relax into a broad grin.

'Twelve o'clock, you loser. Twelve o'clock.' He closed the door behind him, leaving Kirkwood alone in the toilet block. Five questions. Five answers.

It was 11:45 am and Routine 17 was complete.

Thankfully nobody was walking past the toilet block, or they would have thought Kirkwood Scott had taken leave of his senses, such were the whoops of delight reverberating from within.

CHAPTER 19

KINGS FOR A DAY

11:54 a.m.

Kirkwood looked up from the memo he was pretending to read and checked the clock for the fourth time since returning from the toilets.

All around, his co-workers tapped inanely at keyboards, killing time and stifling yawns. The Friday lunchtime he had been counting down to for the last fortnight crept ever closer. It was pay day and as Gerry gleefully reminded him, this meant they were kings for a day. Kirkwood considered this a little disingenuous given his reprobate friend treated every day as if it was the end of the month. Gerry's funds were seemingly bottomless, thanks to a long-lost aunt who popped her clogs several years ago, leaving him a small fortune. This ensured there was always enough in his bank account for a pint or seven.

Kirkwood wished he possessed the same monetary freedom, although his liver begged to differ. His humble salary was nothing to write home about, even if he could afford a stamp to post the relevant letter. This month had been particularly tough, and ends ceased to meet several days ago. Katie's birthday had necessitated purchasing and mailing a present to Auckland, striking a death knell for his beleaguered finances.

He knew there were cheaper ways of sending gifts to selfish siblings who chose to up sticks to the other side of the world and live their perfect life, with their perfect family; now bolstered by his mother-come-globetrotting babysitter. Katie was married to the permanently smug Duncan, who possessed veneers which would put Red Rum to shame. Not forgetting their catalogue-model kids;

the demonic Shania and baby Darryl who Kirkwood had yet to meet.

11:55…

Five more minutes and he could go. Once the big hand struck twelve, he would be out of the door and en route to his favourite watering hole. He looked up as a fellow minion deposited a bundle of documents in his already overflowing tray.

'Thank you so much, do call again,' he hollered sarcastically after his uncaring co-worker as they trudged to their next unsuspecting victim.

'Don't worry,' laughed Laura from the desk opposite him. 'They can wait until Monday.' She nodded at the wall clock, leaning over conspiratorially. 'Besides, I wouldn't want to rain on your pay day parade,' she whispered.

'Thanks boss lady,' replied Kirkwood, mock saluting her and earning a smile for his efforts. 'Will you be joining us later this fine summer afternoon for a beverage or two?' He liked Laura. As supervisors went, she was firm but fair, and had on more than one occasion turned a blind eye when he phoned in feigning illness, knowing very well he was still in bed with a massive hangover.

He would receive a rollicking the next time she saw him, but the real reason for his absence never reached the ears of senior management. She also owned that rarest of qualities among Optima personnel — a sense of humour, which was regularly revealed when no one else was looking.

'Much as I would love to waste my weekend listening to your drunken ramblings, Mr Scott,' she replied, reverting her attention to the computer screen, 'I have this annoying thing called a *life* to attend to. Which involves rising at the crack of dawn on a Saturday morning to ferry my flock to and from ballet lessons and rugby practice. The most rock and roll activity I will be indulging in will involve a night in front of the telly with my husband, a bottle of Pinot Grigio and the biggest tub of Ben & Jerry's that money can buy.'

'You sad, sad woman,' Kirkwood snorted in mock derision. 'You know you won't have a better offer all weekend.' Beneath the theatrical disdain, however, he envied Laura's settled lifestyle. She knew what she wanted and what made her happy. He admired and respected that. There was a serenity about her that he thirsted for, himself. While he would never openly admit as much, it was all he secretly craved; a drama free, normal existence. Given the choice, he would have plumped for his ex, Natasha, on the sofa with an industrial vat of ice cream as opposed to an evening in a grotty pub with his equally grotty friends.

Natasha Agnew burst that bubble with a casual cruelty which left him speechless. When ending their relationship at the start of the summer, her words lodged in his heart like serrated shards of glass. His life had been on hold ever since, parked up in a lay-by gathering dust with only 'The 49' for company.

Which was just what Skelly wanted; his undivided attention. Nirvana Girl and her eerie sketch popped into his head again. Surely it was a trick of the light, she couldn't have been drawing Skelly, could she? Absolutely nobody knew about Skelly and how much Kirkwood had allowed his mental health to deteriorate.

'Yo, Captain Kirk,' Gerry strolled into Business Support Two, theatrically jabbing at his wristwatch. 'We're wasting valuable drinking time here.'

Kirkwood looked from his partner in crime to the clock on the wall. 'Time to hit the road,' he crowed, gathering his teetering in tray and shoving it into a drawer. He quickly saved the data on his computer screen and switched the hard drive off, before grabbing his jacket from the back of the chair.

'Laters Laura. Enjoy your hellish suburban weekend.'

Laura, immersed in a spreadsheet on her screen, waved absent-mindedly towards them. 'Laters losers. Enjoy your hangovers.' And with that they were off, half walking, half jogging out of the office and down the stairs leading to the main reception area. Grumpy Gary the security man, who appeared to have the troubles of the entire city resting on his bowed shoulders, forlornly watched them stride past. He reluctantly pushed the button beneath his desk which allowed them to exit through the glass entrance doors and out into the Belfast sunshine.

'Where to, mon ami?' Gerry fumbled with his brick of a mobile phone as he struggled to decipher an unread message. 'The big man wants to know where the festivities are commencing from?' The 'big man' was Grogan, the third member of their merry band and former colleague, who escaped Optima earlier in the year as part of, as he called it, a big money transfer to a nearby bank. They were not quite sure what the new position entailed, but it was a much sought-after permanent position. Meanwhile Kirkwood and Gerry limped from one temporary contract to the next, trying not to think too much that their services could be dispensed with at the drop of a hat.

'Tell him we will kick off in The Montreal. And not to be late,' replied Kirkwood, checking his own, much sleeker model in the vain hope Natasha might have replied to his text from the night before. No such luck. His heart deflated a fraction more as he returned the phone to his jacket pocket. That first pint couldn't come quick enough. With every passing day he realised that the 'Ice Bitch from Hell' persona she had adopted since their split was in fact her real personality; the sweet, caring girl he dated for the best part of a year had been a façade all along. How could you spend so much time with someone yet known so little about them? He silently chastised himself for allowing her into his thoughts. Nobody could ruin today. Not Natasha, not Skelly, not anyone. He didn't care if the North Koreans invaded Belfast this afternoon. He was getting royally drunk.

The two of them quickstepped across at the traffic lights and up High Street. Gangs of twenty something office workers roamed everywhere, causing Kirkwood to wonder how Belfast commerce functioned given the entire workforce appeared to have fled their workplaces for the purpose of drinking themselves into a stupor. Cutting a right onto a more scarcely populated pedestrian precinct, they arrived at their destination.

'The Montreal' was one of the few remaining bars in the city centre not converted into a metrosexual, anonymous, soulless posing palace. It was Belfast's version of the French Foreign Legion. Men went there to forget. And without sounding sexist, it was predominantly men. Even the women looked like men. The only thing you were likely to pull there was a shoulder muscle if you got on the wrong side of Mark the Bouncer and had to be 'encouraged' to leave the premises.

'Two flagons of your finest ale please, Francis,' beamed Gerry, sliding onto one of the half dozen shaky, wooden stools at the bar. Kirkwood sat alongside him, his boots adjusting to the sticky floor underfoot. The two of them had been frequenting the bar for the better part of two years but were yet to see a cleaner. Gerry claimed it added to the ambience and character of the establishment. Kirkwood just thought it was a dirty hole, but they served cheap beer and showed the horse racing, so he could turn a blind eye.

'Right you are lads,' grunted Francie the Barman. In those two years, they had never deduced his surname ('Francie's all you need to know lads') or viewed him from the waist down. He never moved from behind the bar, leaving the more mundane tasks of the trade such as clearing tables, to his common-law wife, known to all as Mrs Francie. Kirkwood once dared suggest his name was Francis Francie, only to be threatened with expulsion for extracting the urine once too often. He occasionally pondered if Francie was really an android who, unbeknown to all, operated on metal runners behind the bar which ferried him from one end to the other.

Francie began to pour two pints of Carlsberg as the rarely motionless Gerry leapt to his feet again. 'Just off to empty the old bladder,' he proclaimed for all to hear, and headed down the bar towards the only functioning toilet in the building. Francie was an advocate of unisex toilets, but only because he used the rarely-frequented ladies to store his bicycle and Mrs Francie's tartan shopping trolley. Kirkwood, loyal as he was to the Francie drinking empire, often nipped across the street to the much plusher, and more hygienic, Black's Tavern, to use their facilities.

He looked around the bar. The sun filtered through the stain-glassed front window, transforming into multicoloured shafts of light which would have been beautiful had they not further accentuated the swirling dust cloud engulfing the bar and its clientele. Old Mac sat on a stool at the far end of the bar supping a pint of Guinness he reportedly purchased in the late seventies. Kirkwood had never known him to put a hand in his pocket to buy a drink for anyone, himself included — instead relying on gullible tourists to keep him topped up on the black stuff.

Given the average age of The Montreal's clientele was well over sixty, the fact everyone referred to him as Old Mac said something of his venerable years. Kirkwood estimated he must be at least eighty, but it was hard to tell given he rarely moved or gave any indication of a functioning brain bar the occasional grunt or phlegm-filled hack into a once white handkerchief.

The other resident in situ was Dessy, whose life revolved around running between The Montreal and the adjacent bookmakers to bet on anything with four legs that cast a shadow. He was slightly more of a conversationalist than Old Mac, his sparkling repertoire extending to a series of stock phrases rolled out whenever one of his equine or canine interests failed to bring home the bacon.

'Thon donkey needs shaaaaaat!' Translation: That horse performed poorly in the 3:30 at Haydock Park and should be humanely destroyed.

'I could have ridden a better finish, the useless halliooooonnnnn!' Translation: I was bitterly disappointed with the performance of the jockey in the 2:45 at Newmarket.

And so on. Kirkwood smiled wryly to himself. Who needed fast cars and faster women when you had the dubious delights of The Montreal to look forward to every pay day? Living the dream, he was most certainly not. Francie placed a pint in front of him and he lifted it to his lips in anticipation. His first pint in the best part of two weeks. The first of many, if he had anything to do with it.

'Come to Dad.'

CHAPTER 20

BANTER

12:23 p.m.

Kirkwood didn't like the taste of alcohol but what he did like was the unmistakable effect it had on him. The first pint was always a battle and he sipped it slowly, his taste buds struggling to reacquaint themselves with the bland, insipid tang of Francie's undoubtedly watered-down lager. Gerry had already ordered a further round of drinks and was attacking his second pint with a gusto worthy of his proud declaration that every day was a drinking day. He hadn't suffered a hangover in six years because he was never sober long enough for one to catch up with him. While only thirty-two years old, he could pass for a man in his late forties and Kirkwood reckoned his liver was already old enough to have its own free bus pass.

'See if that waste of space doesn't show up soon, I'm out of here,' growled Gerry, inspecting his watch, while simultaneously draining the final third of his pint in a single gulp. He was referring to Grogan who operated on a different time/space continuum from the rest of humanity. He was always at least forty-five minutes behind where he was meant to be, which irked Gerry to no end. Hopeless, shambolic drunk that he was, he was a stickler for timekeeping; a quality he attributed to the endless hidings his mother administered during a chaotic youth which formed the prelude to many of his bar room anecdotes. 'She used to kick us out of our beds every Sunday and beat us up to Mass. I was more afraid of her than I was of God and the priests put together.'

They had relocated from the stools to one of a series of booths which ran along the back wall of the bar. Kirkwood noticed his phone vibrating and unlocked its screen to reveal a notification from Grogan:

'Running late. The downside of my fast-track corporate lifestyle. Ten minutes tops.'

By that he meant at least twenty.

'He's incoming,' Kirkwood advised, leaning over and showing Gerry the message. 'So, relax'. He forced another mouthful of Carlsberg down his throat, resisting the urge to retch and bring it back up again. By the third pint his taste buds would be numb, and he would be downing it as if beer was going out of fashion. That third pint seemed light years away at present, as he mulled over whether Skelly would keep to his word and refrain from gate-crashing the weekend. He stared glumly into the depths of his pint glass, conceding he was worrying about a man who did not exist.

Gerry's dulcet tones cut through his fretting. 'Would you stop daydreaming and horse that into you, Kirky boy. Your round.' Kirkwood hated drinking on his own with his thirsty friend. By three o'clock Gerry would be either under the table or dancing on his own to some imaginary jukebox, while Kirkwood and Grogan pretended he was not in their company. When socialising with Gerry you had to make the most of those first few fleeting hours of lucidity before he disappeared over the beer horizon. Any pressing matters were to be discussed at an early juncture. Despite his disdain for the human race, Gerry spoke a surprising amount of sense when sober. Including matters of the heart. Kirkwood had leaned on him heavily in recent months, dissecting in forensic detail the train wreck of his relationship with Natasha.

'That wee girl messed up your head no end. Sitting there staring off into the distance, wasting precious drinking time. You need to wake up and smell the coffee. She used you and she's moved on. You need to do the same.' He set his empty pint glass down on the table, ushering Kirkwood in the general direction of the bar.

'That's such a brain-dead saying. I don't even like coffee. The last thing I want to do is wake up and smell it.' He reluctantly stood and indicated the empty glass. 'Same again I take it?'

'That's the stupidest question I've ever been asked. Of course, it's the same again.'

'Yes, your Majesty,' muttered Kirkwood, gathering up the glass and shuffling off to where Francie was pretending to clean cutlery with a suspiciously stained cloth.

'You need to stop mooning over her and get back out there,' Gerry shouted after him, generously sharing his thoughts on Kirkwood's love life with the rest of the bar. 'Plenty more fish in the sea. And if I pulled her out of the water, I would have bashed her head off the side of the boat and thrown her straight back in. The nasty wee cow.'

'Yeah, but she was my nasty wee cow,' Kirkwood sniped over his shoulder. He caught Francie's eye who nodded and started pulling two fresh pints.

'Correction, you muppet. She's now a nasty wee cow for whatever mug is daft enough to buy her a vodka and tonic. Sure, it's plastered all over Facebook. You're not blind, are you?'

'Why, what has she put on?' Kirkwood spun around to face his friend in the booth. He immediately regretted nibbling Gerry's verbal bait, but the question was out of his mouth before he knew it. He was like a dog with a bone when it came to Natasha.

Gerry came as near as he possibly could to an apology. 'Look, I shouldn't have told you that. It's best you don't know, honest mate. She's a silly wee girl and it will all catch up with her one day. You deserve better and you are better off rid of her.'

'Suppose.' Kirkwood dejectedly began to tear up a cardboard beer mat as Francie planted their drinks under his nose.

'Having fun dismembering my property?' he glowered. Kirkwood meekly apologised and handed the grumpy barman a crumpled five-pound note. He continued to mope as he awaited the change, which he slipped into the pocket of his jeans along with the remains of the beer mat rather than incur further wrath from the ever-vigilant publican.

Natasha was his first serious girlfriend, not that he would have admitted that to anyone, including her. His teenage years were a whirlwind of social awkwardness, greasy hair and relentless bullying at the hands of his peers. He couldn't recall holding a meaningful conversation with a member of the opposite sex until he started university, and even then, they were few and far between. A few alcohol-fuelled skirmishes occurred in his first year at college, but they never extended beyond a drunken snog at the end of the night prior to being shunned the next day by his mortified victim in the lecture theatre.

Nope. Ladies' man he was most certainly not. The nearest he had sailed to love island was a two-year infatuation with Alison Gibson, Amazonian goddess and captain of the school netball team; and an eight year on/off relationship with Edrina WillowWand, a twelfth-level wizardess who he created and nurtured through various school and university *Dungeons & Dragons* societies. Until the unfortunate incident with the Fire Ogre that was.

As if on cue, Grogan strolled into the bar and sauntered over to where Kirkwood was standing. 'Another pint please, Francis,' he waved at the publican who shot him a look of utter loathing at being disturbed again and asked to do his job.

Grogan planted a hearty palm on Kirkwood's back causing him to spill the top inch of the pints he was holding. 'Well Mister Scott, what's the craic?' He suspiciously checked out the other booths as if at any moment he expected to be jumped by an angry husband or bull-necked bailiff. Tall and painfully thin, it never failed to amaze Kirkwood how such a puny example of manhood could be so attractive to the female species. Plus, he was a ginger, although he preferred to describe it as rustic auburn. Whatever his allure, Grogan's love life wouldn't have looked out of place in a South American soap opera.

'Yo, Fanta Head! Over here!' roared Gerry. The two had known each other since primary school and beneath the bravado and insults was a rock-solid friendship spanning the best part of three decades. Kirkwood first met Gerry through work who, in turn, introduced him to Grogan. His first name was Patrick but everybody, including his own parents, referred to him as Grogan. He just looked like a Grogan.

'You alright?' Kirkwood greeted him while mentally reminding himself that this was his weekend and he was meant to be having a good time, despite the best efforts of Skelly and Natasha.

'All right up one side and all left down the other,' replied Grogan, a line Kirkwood must have heard a thousand times, yet still managed to bring a wry smile to his face. He lifted the additional pint Francie had reluctantly poured and nodded towards the booth. 'Right then. Shall we join this halfwit and get proceedings underway?'

Kirkwood paid for the extra drink and they sat down opposite Gerry. The other booths were starting to fill up, a mixture of grizzled regulars and office workers drawn like bees to honey by the blackboard outside the bar offering pints for £2.50 until 5:00 p.m. He was no Lord Sugar, but Francie always knew how to undercut the opposition and cram them in on pay day.

Grogan took a sip of his pint and pulled a face. 'Ew, Francie seriously needs to get his pipes cleaned out. The beer in here gets worse every time I frequent it with my custom.' He stopped abruptly and ducked his head; aware Francie had overheard at least part of his critique and was now shooting daggers across the bar in their direction.

Gerry followed his friend's furtive look and guffawed loudly. 'You really are a master of tact and diplomacy, Grogan. I'm surprised the United Nations didn't snap up your services years ago.' He reached across the table and offered a high five to Kirkwood who reciprocated the gesture for fear of bursting his drinking partner's comedy bubble.

'Touché, Gerry. Or should I say Touchy.' Grogan glared at Gerry who responded in kind, and an uneasy standoff ensued before the two of them could maintain the pretence no longer and dissolved into fits of schoolboy giggling. They clinked their glasses together in mutual appreciation of each other's scintillating wit. Kirkwood smiled to himself. It was not all doom and gloom. The sun was shining, he was in the company of good friends and had money in his wallet. Alcohol was a temporary respite from the cavalcade of unwanted thoughts and corresponding compulsions which Skelly mercilessly dumped on his doorstep. A temporary respite, but one he fully intended on riding for all it was worth over the next few days.

'Right boys,' he yelled, raising his pint glass in the air. He was getting a taste for it at last. 'Let's get blocked.'

CHAPTER 21

GUNTHER

The tall, immaculately dressed businessman two booths along from Kirkwood and his friends took a measured sip of mineral water, before carefully setting it back on the table and studying the lunch menu. He could have passed for an accountant or banker given his expensive three-piece suit and tidy haircut. His black shoes gleamed impressively, suggesting here was a man who took pride in his appearance.

'What can I get you?' asked the waitress, holding a notepad and pencil stub in anticipation of his order.

'Steak,' replied the businessman brusquely. 'With a fresh, tossed salad.' He raised his head from the menu and met her bored expression with piercing, glacier-blue eyes. Blonde hair styled into a side-parting you could cut your finger on, betrayed his heritage, as did the faint German lilt to his otherwise perfect English.

'How would you like your steak done?' The waitress stood a little straighter now, as if the customer merited a better quality of service than she was previously willing to provide.

'Rare,' replied the man. 'And by rare, I mean bloody. Tell your chef no more than a light searing or I shall be forced to have words with him.' He handed the menu to the waitress and looked down the bar, effectively dismissing her. She hurried off towards the kitchen, a worried expression on her face.

Of course, the steak would not be to his satisfaction. Nothing in this stinking city ever was; all the Irish were interested in was drinking themselves into a stupor as quickly as they could, once they had a few pounds in their pockets.

The three reprobates he had been tasked to monitor were no exception. The occasional raised voice and burst of laughter from their booth indicated the watered-down, fizzy grog they were consuming at an extraordinary rate was already starting to take its toll. A fine frothy malt ale like the kind lovingly brewed by his fellow countrymen would be wasted on these savages. He raised his glass again and took another sip of water.

The first, and only, time he had ever been drunk was the morning of his death.

The fighting the previous evening had been a brutal, close quarters engagement through the narrow, cobbled streets of Quatre Bras. They had fallen back in the face of wave after wave of French assaults but, unlike those cowardly Belgian dogs, they did so in an orderly fashion ensuring every yard taken by the enemy was at a heavy price. Crack sharpshooters that they were, it had been like shooting fish in a barrel as the giant, heavily laden grenadiers presented easy targets. The drains ran red that evening and Gunther felled sixteen before finally running out of ammunition and being forced to reluctantly retreat from the village into the dank, dense forest at its rear.

They spent a wretched night beneath the sodden canopy, snatching whatever sleep they could. It was impossible to keep dry and a constant hunger gnawed at his stomach. He had not eaten since the previous morning and was ravenous. At dawn they ventured to the far edge of the forest and stumbled upon a deserted château, its owners already halfway to Brussels with whatever scant possessions they could hurriedly cram into their carriage.

The parlour had been empty but a roar of delight from the basement announced that several of his comrades had stumbled upon a well-stocked cellar. A search of the outbuildings also located a handful of unsuspecting laying hens. Within an hour they were feasting on roast chicken, boiled eggs and bottle after bottle of purloined wine.

He had eaten so much he thought his belly would explode, to the extent he was forced to undo the top button of his breeches as he lay on his back atop a bale of fresh hay in an abandoned barn. Napoleon and his Grande Armée were less than two hours march away, but if they were to die then it would be on a full stomach, with a song on their lips. His mother and father would receive his pension and he wouldn't have to worry about another night freezing in a boggy ditch. The dead don't get hangovers, they bellowed with false bravado as they sought to conceal trembling hands, clutching wine bottles ever tighter to their thumping chests.

'One steak and salad. Rare. Enjoy your meal sir,' simpered the waitress, setting his plate in front of the unnerving man, and backing away before he had an opportunity to examine the meat to establish whether or not it was cooked to his satisfaction. He smirked and cut into the steak, momentarily transfixed as a drizzle of blood seeped from it and pooled by a leaf of iceberg lettuce. In the blink of an eye he was back again in that damned village, slipping and sliding on the bloody cobbles as the lives of friend and foe alike, swirled indiscriminately in dark puddles at his feet. And that had only been the curtain-raiser. It was nothing compared to the horrors awaiting the men of the King's German Legion the next day when the real battle began, near an obscure Belgian town, named Waterloo.

Gunther von Steinbeck looked up from the steak, as the one known to his kind as Kirkwood Scott lurched from the booth towards the bar, an idiotic grin smeared across his features. Their eyes met and for an instant the younger man's grin wavered — confronted by the icy stare of the dead soldier. A flicker of recognition passed between them, but then the connection was gone as Kirkwood looked away, waiting for the barman to serve another customer before turning towards him.

'Same again, Francie, please. We're building up a right thirst today.'

Gunther smiled callously at the back of the young man standing in front of him.

'Enjoy it while it lasts, my friend,' he whispered. 'Enjoy it while it lasts.'

CHAPTER 22

MY DEAREST EMILY II

30 June 2018

My Dearest Emily,

So that's how it works then. Who needs the Royal Mail when we have your creepy, messed-up way of communicating? It's original if nothing else. I guess you received my first letter given your recent message, so I'll just carry on from where I left off. Hmmm…now let me see. You had just killed yourself and I was in a bit of a state. Like now, I spend a lot of my days imagining where you were after…you know…the whole scissors in the bath performance.

After the funeral I almost succumbed to it myself. I was wracked with guilt but angry as hell. With the bitches who drove you to it, with myself for not reading the signs, and at my Stepford parents for their utter lack of empathy or understanding. But most of all I was angry with you. You left high me and dry, stranded in a world I no longer recognised. Everything was off-kilter, ever so slightly askew and out of sync. It was as if I was half a pace and half a breath behind everyone else, yet no matter how hard I tried, I could never make up the lost ground.

I looked the same, but maybe a few pounds lighter. I sounded the same when I talked, which wasn't that often, but there the similarities ended. Beneath my skin and within my soul there had been a seismic shift. Clichéd as it might sound you were my anchor, my compass. Without you I was hopelessly adrift, spinning out of control, no longer knowing or particularly caring where I ended up. Nothing mattered, nothing could fill the Emily-shaped hole gouged deep within me. An ugly, festering wound which showed no signs of ever healing.

I craved nothing but release from the relentless pain which sat on my shoulder, pecking away with its bloody beak, sinking ebony talons ever deeper into me; piercing skin and scraping bone. A violent vulture invisible to all but me. It feasted on my flesh and the rest of the world looked on, oblivious to the agony, impervious to my muted despair.

After the funeral I was given a bye-ball by my parents and Ashgrove for a few weeks. They were all heart when it came to keeping up appearances. The Christmas break was coming up fast, so I was excused attending class for the rest of the term. The official reason given was 'exhaustion', but the reality was I was sinking into a deep depression. I was prodded and poked by various members of the medical profession, hired at great expense to pay discrete house visits. Blood samples were taken but the results all came back the same. Physically there was nothing wrong with me. Yes, I had lost a little weight but that was to be expected given the circumstances. The circumstances that nobody chose to discuss in my presence.

Heads were scratched, and brows were furrowed but I continued to shut down, bit by bit, like a city viewed from the skies during a power cut. I rarely left my room and meals went untouched. The thought of chewing and swallowing, those most mundane of biological mechanisms, were beyond me. Other basic tasks such as showering and dressing also began to be overlooked. Eventually Mother grasped the thistle and the elephant in the room was reluctantly confronted. I was hauled off to the psychiatrist's couch, some exclusive private practice in the east of the city.

I was a bit disappointed with it, if the truth be told. For a start, there was no couch on which to drape myself over and bemoan my poor, broken mind. Instead, I was seated on a regulation armchair in a bland office where an earnest, but stiff as starch middle-aged woman, attempted to drill down into my inner psyche with all the subtlety of a hammer to the back of the head.

Sixty minutes to unravel six weeks of unfathomable grief. I played the game, acutely aware that Dad was forking out a three-figure sum every hour for the displeasure of baring my soul to a complete stranger. As I walked out of that first awkward session, I knew I wouldn't be back. It was as pointless as it was pricey. My parents went through the roof when I informed them. The last time I saw Dad that angry was when his BMW had a key run up its side at a golf club function. He ranted and raved before going a most peculiar shade of purple. How I needed to wake up, pull myself together and get my head back in the game. The girl was dead, I was alive and that was that. I assumed by the girl he meant you, as he refused to dignify your death by acknowledging your name. I needed to move on, pass my A levels, go to university and meet a nice boy. Preferably one who played golf and worked in finance.

Mother didn't say much. She just sat there and brooded, the occasional carefully choreographed tear running down her immaculately made-up face. Her silence spoke volumes, however. I was an embarrassment and they had tried everything. There were no other offspring to focus their ambitions upon. I was an only child and often thought they merely tolerated, as opposed to loved, me.

They decided to make the best of a bad lot and treated me as an unexpected opportunity, a potential cash cow from which they could recoup some of the money they invested to clothe and feed me for the best part of two decades. Hence, the best of everything, including the privileged education at Ashgrove. It wasn't out of affection; it was a calculated business decision on their part. The only silver lining in that particular cloud was meeting you of course, my dearest, deadest friend.

He shouted, she sulked, I sat and said nothing, soaking up their disappointment. My decision was made, it had been made for weeks if I was honest. During the night when I was sure they were asleep, I hurriedly packed a bag, ransacked Dad's spirits cabinet and was on my way. To where I wasn't quite sure, I just knew I had to escape the suffocation of that five-bedroom, three-bathroom, two-dining-room prison. An upper middle class hell where we masqueraded as County Down aristocracy.

I walked to the nearest cash machine and withdrew my daily limit. Then thirty-seven minutes later as the clock in the middle of downtown Bangor struck midnight, I emptied the remainder of my savings account. I sat outside the train station until the first Belfast-bound express crawled onto the platform the following morning. I bought a single ticket with no intention of ever returning. I never did. Seven months ago and counting. An eighteen-year-old with the constitution of a thirty-year alcoholic.

Talking of which, I'll sign off now and deliver this as my hands are shaking and I need a drink. Classy, I know. And if you're having difficulty reading this then that's because it has started to rain and I'm all out of pretty parasols to protect myself from the charming Northern Irish climate. Don't flatter yourself that I'm crying over you, you selfish cow.

Meredith x

CHAPTER 23

THE BROTHERS FITZGERALD

11:47 p.m.

The plate glass window of the kebab shop exploded outwards, showering the pavement with a million shards of glistening glass. The already chaotic scene that was Bradbury Place on a Friday night went into meltdown. While some passing revellers hunched over and froze, others scurried for cover as bedlam descended on the heart of Belfast's Golden Mile. Amid the chaos, the two culprits who had propelled themselves through the window flailed about on the pavement, attempting to land punches on one another.

The immediate vicinity was heaving with hundreds of intoxicated thrill seekers drawn to the area's eclectic mix of bars, clubs and fast food outlets. Some congregated to watch the free entertainment on offer, but quickly thought better of it as the wail of an approaching siren forewarned that the show would soon be over. The protagonists continued to exchange blows, oblivious to all around them, as irate kitchen staff began to pour out of the kebab shop and threaten to involve themselves in the growing disorder.

Agitated Turkish accents mingled with locals firing expletives at all and sundry, as an armoured Land Rover careered around the corner, its blue emergency lights flashing. It squealed to a halt alongside the melee which was now spilling out onto the street itself. A growing queue of traffic began to form, and the night was alive with blaring horns. Two burly male officers jumped from the rear of the Land Rover into the clamour and attempted to separate the two pugilists who clung to each other like drowning sailors battling over the only remaining life jacket.

A younger, female officer emerged from the front of the Land Rover and joined the affray. She fumbled momentarily at her gun belt before unclipping a small, cylindrical object and pointing it at the maul of bodies on the ground.

'Police officer with CS spray! Stop fighting or I will use it.' She barely looked school-leaving age but her strong voice and steely, determined look indicated she meant business. Realising her instructions were being ignored, she discharged a jet of the solvent into the faces of the two men who immediately lost interest in each other and began to claw at their eyes, struggling to draw breath, as tears streamed down their cheeks. The male officers were also caught in the toxic cloud and turned away coughing and choking as reinforcements from a second vehicle disembarked and intervened. Order was quickly restored, and drawn batons dissuaded others on the fringes from becoming involved.

The instigators of the disorder were handcuffed and hauled to their feet before being led away, screaming of police brutality and demanding to speak to their solicitors. Both were guaranteed a free bed for the night and cooked breakfast for their endeavours, prior to an appearance before the resident magistrate the following morning. Within minutes they were whisked away, and the pavement was being swept clear of glass. Normality returned to Bradbury Place — or as normal as it would ever be on a pay day weekend.

Young men urinated openly in doorways and swaying couples, acquainted only forty-five minutes beforehand, declared their undying love between sucking the faces off each other. A heavily made-up woman in an outfit leaving little to the imagination, tottered across the street before an ankle gave way and she landed on her ample backside. Hoots of derision greeted her undignified downfall and blushes were only spared when two friends grabbed an arm each and dragged her back onto her feet. The three of them stumbled off into the night, cackling like wine-sodden witches on Halloween.

Kirkwood Scott weaved his way through the chaos, blissfully unaware of the bedlam unfolding around him. He only had eyes for the sausage supper he purchased from the nearby Golden Peacock Cantonese Takeaway, which he was shovelling into his mouth at an impressive rate of knots. His calorific intake since leaving work almost twelve hours ago had been primarily of the liquid variety. Besides, he was a man on a mission, so had little time for the dubious delights of the Golden Mile. A clear head was required as there were bigger fish to fry and time was of the essence. His clouded logic reasoned that greasy grub was the fast track remedy to ten pints of lager and several tequila shots. Somehow, he safely navigated Bradbury Place without incident and headed onto the Lisburn Road with only one destination in mind.

Less than two hundred yards away, Meredith Starc had jumped at the sound of breaking glass to her right as she slowly made her way along Botanic Avenue. Her finely honed survival instinct kicked in and she quickened her pace, keen to put as much distance between herself and whatever the hell was going on in nearby Bradbury Place. She had bypassed it and taken a more circuitous route and now inwardly commended herself for erring on the side of caution. Bradbury Place was always mad at this time and tonight seemed to be no exception.

After passing out in Mulberry Square she had dozed fitfully for several hours, dipping in and out of consciousness, before a passing pensioner roused her with a cup of sugary tea from an adjacent café. She had mumbled an embarrassed thanks to the kindly, old lady and gratefully sipped the tea, before making her excuses and heading in search of Danny. She spent an hour wandering around his usual haunts and phoning his mobile which constantly went to voicemail. Eventually she bumped into Colly, sunning himself on the grass outside City Hall with a handful of his downbeat mates. He evaded most of her questions but eventually conceded he last saw Danny earlier in the afternoon, heading to some dodgy block of flats in search of pharmaceutical supplies.

She gave up after that. Danny would turn up like a bad penny, he always did. He had more lives than the most accident-prone feline. She spent the remainder of the evening sobering up on Great Victoria Street and scrounging enough loose change to buy a large bottle of water and a sandwich, which she forced down into her protesting stomach. Eventually when the steady flow of punters eased to a trickle, she made her way out of the city centre. Like Kirkwood, she too had a very clear destination in mind, a safe place nobody knew of — not even Danny. If she had looked up as she passed the Golden Peacock, she might have recognised the young man at the counter, ordering a takeaway. Their paths crossed for the blink of an eye before separating again.

Neither was aware they were being followed and had been for some time. As their respective journeys passed the Golden Peacock, the scrawny spectres tailing them stopped and looked at each other in stunned silence; for they knew each other, indeed they were related — twins no less. The Fitzgerald Brothers, Declan and Dermot, hadn't expected to meet this evening, but here they were, face-to-face. They were virtually identical in appearance and the striking physical similarities were accentuated by matching garish tracksuits and baseball caps.

The brothers nodded at each other. They did not need to speak, given the telepathic connection between them. They passed without a word and continued to stalk their respective prey. Both were frustrated by the watching brief they had been given. They were itching to flex their muscles and prove to the Colonel they were worthy of higher-profile deployments. Each had said nothing; they knew which side their bread was buttered on, and to openly challenge his authority was a serious error. It would have effectively signed their death warrants, had they not already been dead.

So, they bit their tongues and bided their time, performing dull as ditchwater assignments around the dump known as Belfast. They were country boys and hated the urban setting but were also professionals who would follow orders to the letter; even if it went against their baser instincts. The time would come, hopefully soon, when their unique talents would be required and appreciated. And, at that time, they would emerge from the shadows and show the world what they were capable of; that's when the real fireworks would start. They would light up this damned city like it was the Fourth of July.

CHAPTER 24

THE DAY IT HAPPENED

18 May 1995

The day it happened started like any other. Days have a habit of doing that. They just start. It's getting them to stop when the wheels come off — that's the hard part. Kirkwood could recall precursor events in microscopic, fine-grain detail; images he had replayed in his mind countless times since. He had got up that morning, washed, dressed and bounced downstairs for breakfast. He was a good riser and only needed to be called once by his mother; unlike Katie who required at least three wake-up calls increasing in volume and intensity. Failing that, threats were lobbed up the stairs threatening suspension of pocket money or, horror of horrors, extra washing-up duties if she did not get down the stairs 'this very minute'.

School had been school. He scored a header at the thirty-five a side football free-for-all, which took place every lunchtime at the side of the bike sheds. It was the first headed goal he had ever scored, made all the more memorable as it earned him a visit to the nurse's office meaning he missed double Maths with Mr Matheson that afternoon. *Every cloud and all that* thought Kirkwood, as he sat outside Nurse Magee's office waiting to be called in by the formidable woman.

The header had not been a thing of beauty. No diving full length to power the ball past the helpless goalkeeper or towering majestically above helpless defenders to nod it into the bottom corner of the net. Instead, he had been loitering in the opposition penalty area attempting to avoid the surrounding chaos, when the ball whistled towards goal. A foot lashed out to hack away the danger only for the ball to ricochet off Kirkwood's forehead and into the net.

He celebrated the pinnacle of his footballing career by promptly keeling over where he lay in a stunned stupor, until someone thought better of it and decided to inform a teacher.

Nurse Magee had planted him in a chair and applied a cold, damp facecloth to his forehead before pulling his nose one way and then another, as part of her rudimentary triage assessment. He thought his face was sore before he entered her torture chamber, but it was nothing compared to the ensuing brutal inspection which, nowadays, would have resulted in immediate suspension and possible criminal proceedings being initiated against her.

After several minutes of death by healthcare, Kirkwood's assailant stood back and cheerfully announced that nothing was broken but he might be suffering a slight concussion. 'I'll call your mother,' she had announced, a thin layer of sweat having accumulated on the suggestion of a moustache, which was a constant feature on her upper lip. She was a large lady and the examination of Kirkwood appeared to have taken as much out of her as it did him. 'You need to go home and straight to bed. There's nothing long term but best you take it easy for a day or two. Get your belongings and I'll go up to the main office and phone her now.' And with that she was off, ample hips swaying beneath her navy-blue uniform which permanently threatened to be at bursting point.

Kirkwood stood at the school gates for only a few minutes when his mother pulled up in their beaten-up Ford Escort. 'Have you been fighting?' she snarled initially, annoyed that her strict housework regime had been disrupted by this unscheduled inconvenience.

'No Mum,' replied Kirkwood, hauling himself and his school bag groggily into the passenger seat beside her. 'I got hit in the face with a football…but you should have seen where the ball ended up. It…'

'Hmm,' she interrupted, not entirely convinced by the explanation. 'That nurse woman tells me nothing. I'm not even sure she is a proper nurse.' She leaned over and grabbed Kirkwood's chin with her right hand, twisting his head one way, and then the other, in the concerned, but slightly sadistic fashion all mothers are taught at Parent School. 'You do seem to have a bump coming up on your forehead,' she fussed, squinting at the offending area above his eyebrows before, without warning, jabbing a finger at it.

'Aah! Leave-off Mum,' squealed Kirkwood, squirming to avoid yet another assault by an overbearing female to whose care he was supposedly entrusted. 'I've got a percussion,' he whined, as irregular patterns of rainbow-tinted bubbles started to float across his field of vision.

His mother had smiled, ruffling his hair with her other hand. 'Sorry pet. I was just checking. Let's get you home and sorted out. No television though. And you need your hair cut. But that can wait until the weekend.'

Once home, Kirkwood had been frogmarched to his room, forced to down two spoons of a foul liquid that was supposedly 'good for him', and tucked into bed with all the finesse of a drill sergeant. 'And I mean it. No television,' his mother warned over her shoulder, as she closed his door and went back downstairs. The next sound he heard was the vacuum cleaner starting up in the living room, indicating that normal service had been resumed; the house needed to be cleaned and concussed schoolboys in need of rest would just have to accept that.

Kirkwood squinted at the digital alarm clock on his bedside table which informed him it was 2:27. Katie would be home in an hour or so and Dad around five. Dad was on pretend duties tonight so would be leaving the house again after he washed, had his dinner and changed clothes. Kirkwood wriggled free of the bedclothes his mother had encased him in and peered over the side of the bed, using one elbow to steady himself. Even though the room was in darkness he could just make out the outline of the fort and a sentry standing guard by the front gate.

Above and to either side, an array of helmets and weapons could be seen peeking above the ramparts. Inside, the rest of the men would be patiently awaiting their nightly deployments. And at their head would be The Colonel, seated upon his jet-black stallion, prepared for any eventuality. Kirkwood smiled drowsily before settling his head back on the cool, crisp pillow. Deployments on nights when Dad pretended to be a policeman were extra important. But he had time he had thought — plenty of time. Within seconds he had dozed off into a deep sleep.

The crazy dream that had followed was one he would never forget. He was inside the fort, lined up in formation with the rest of the men. He attempted to step forward, but his legs refused to budge an inch. He looked down and was astonished to discover that his feet were firmly attached to a metal base like all his other soldiers; bar the snipers who lay on their bellies, permanently peering through the sights of their rifles. He tried again to lift a leg but, despite straining and stretching, could not move a muscle from the neck downwards. With increasing awareness of his surroundings, he realised he was wearing the red tunic and white trousers of a nineteenth century British infantryman, right down to the rifle and bayonet which he held in a tight grip forever on the verge of uttering the classic, 'Who goes there?' line that sentries always came out with in the war movies.

An unfamiliar voice from behind had barked an order for the men to ready themselves for inspection. Unfamiliar, yet the second he heard it, he knew who it must belong to; the clipped, precise diction of an officer and a gentleman. The Colonel rode into sight, no metal base restricting his equine charge. The huge horse moved with a startling combination of grace, power and barely contained fury, yet responded instantly to the merest inflection of its master's voice or the slightest kick of the Colonel's heels into its muscular flanks.

The horse effortlessly brought the Colonel front and centre to face the assembled ranks. Their commander-in-chief steadied himself and scanned the attentive audience. His dark eyes twinkled, and darker moustache bristled. He was angry, very angry. Kirkwood was as powerless to utter a word as he was to move his body. He had always regarded The Colonel and himself as equals whose combined military intellect swept them to countless victories on the field of battle. But there was no questioning who was in charge now. Kirkwood felt drained of whatever affection he previously held for his comrade in arms. It was replaced by an icy fear and a certainty that this man was no ally of his; something had changed between them. The balance of power had tipped and was no longer in his favour.

The Colonel leaned forward in the saddle and rested his forearms across the back of the stallion's neck. He took one last panoramic view of the soldiers gathered before him, before fixing Kirkwood with a stare which turned the young boy's blood to ice.

'Oh, my dear boy. What have you done? What have you done?'

That was the day it happened.

CHAPTER 25

HELLO HANGOVER

Saturday, 30 August 2012
10:53 a.m.

The hangover flitted in and out of the dream, announcing its impending arrival seconds before Kirkwood's eyes opened. If first impressions counted, then this hangover certainly made an unfavourable one. He grew aware he was lying face down on a bed and breathed a sigh of relief when he confirmed that it was his own. He had slept for the best part of ten hours but felt as if he'd gone ten rounds with Conor McGregor. His body ached all over and he had no idea how he had made it home. A quick rummage through his dehydrated mush of a brain drew a resounding blank. He grimaced as he turned onto his side and peered over the edge of the bed, dreading to be reminded of the foul takeaway he undoubtedly consumed. And there it was. In its original container, no less. The mechanics of tipping it onto a plate must have been beyond his lager-drenched mind.

A single chip protruded in solitary defiance from a swamp of coagulated gravy; the only survivor from his feeding frenzy of the night before. Kirkwood stared morosely at the chip, resisting the urge to pluck it from the container and reacquaint it with its fallen comrades in his stomach. He threw back the covers and tentatively climbed out of bed, suddenly aware he was still wearing the clothes from the day before. The thought had barely registered when a rising wave of nausea gripped him. He bolted out of the bedroom and across the landing, just making the toilet bowl before the culinary delights of the Golden Peacock made an unwelcome return to the world.

'Better out than in.' Kirkwood watched as a handful of peas bobbed about in the porcelain bowl, like little green ducks on some alien lake in a galaxy not that far away.

He sighed and wiped a string of vomit-flecked saliva from his bottom lip with the little strength he had remaining. He crawled on his hands and knees back to bed and crept under the covers. Outside, it looked like the unusually good weather was set to continue. The view from his grimy bedroom window was one of blue, clear skies and the population of Belfast was awakening to the sight of an unfamiliar yellow ball in the sky. It was going to be another scorcher and for once, the normally woeful local weather forecasters had got it right. It was Saturday, the weekend was here, and it was a great time to be alive. Bar the mother of all hangovers.

He knew he urgently needed liquid of a non-alcoholic variety, but wild horses could not have coerced him downstairs to the kitchen. Not yet anyway. He needed time to allow his stomach to settle and attempt to thread together a timeline of what had happened last night.

They had stayed in The Montreal until five when Francie's cheap beer deal ended. During that time, he placed several doomed bets on the horse racing. He recalled consoling Dessie in an inebriated embrace after they watched their final mount succumb to a heartbreaking, half-length defeat in the 4:30 at Catterick.

At some point they had relocated to the slightly more salubrious surroundings of a lounge adjacent to the main bar. Gerry alternated between dozing fitfully in the corner and playing air guitar to the delight of a Japanese couple next to them, who shared half a pint of Guinness while taking several hundred photographs of him throwing his best shapes à la Angus Young. This abruptly ended when Big Mark intervened, telling Gerry to sit down and shut up or he would 'boot his hole from here to Dublin and back.' Point made, the imposing doorman returned to his watchful perch while Gerry sheepishly returned to his slumber in the corner of the booth they were occupying.

As the clock struck five, Grogan grabbed his coat and rose, simultaneously flicking a comatose Gerry on the earlobe with a beer mat. 'Come on you lush, we're moving on.'

'Whaaghh?' spluttered Gerry, grabbing at his ear as if he had been taken out by a CIA sniper.

'I've sat long enough in this dump watching your Sleeping Beauty routine. Time to move on. Come on, wake up.' He tugged Gerry's nose before heading for the door.

'C'mon, Gerry,' Kirkwood sighed, helping Gerry to his feet. 'Thanks Francie. Same time next month.' Big Mark held the door open for them. 'Right lads. Take it easy and make sure that balloon behaves himself. Not all door staff are as accommodating as yours truly.'

'Will do, Mark. Thanks mate.'

The gentle giant watched as the three of them staggered up the street. He shook his head and smiled. 'There's more brains in a rocking horse.'

They had predictably ended up at The Grid, an upmarket preening palace, where the deluded and the desperate congregated to exchange phone numbers and phonier chat-up lines. Grogan, whose gift of the gab and bare-faced nerve never failed to amaze Kirkwood, somehow managed to get Gerry into the bar, by slapping the backs of the besuited gorillas on the door and swearing on his granny's life (she had been dead for at least fifteen years last time Kirkwood checked) that he could vouch for his inebriated friend, and would ensure he was on his best behaviour.

Kirkwood recalled expressing his horror at having to pay £5.50 for a pint and swearing never to darken the establishment's doors again. The remainder of the evening was a blur. Packs of big-haired, short-skirted girls sashayed about the dance floor, attempting to keep pace with the clanging dance music blaring from the PA system. Kirkwood sat for most of the night nursing a pint until Grogan nagged him into talking to a petite blonde from East Belfast while he chatted up her friend. After twenty-five minutes of stilted small talk and monosyllabic responses from her, he had given up and, throwing caution to the wind, went on the tequila shots. His recollections of the evening became increasingly hazy after that.

He relied on a series of photographs which Grogan had forwarded to him at some point during the night to fill in the missing pieces of the jigsaw. Gerry asleep at the bar. Standard. Gerry on his knees, shirt unbuttoned to the waist and tongue protruding like Gene Simmons. Gerry asleep at the bar again. Gerry on his knees throwing up in the toilets while being photo-bombed by Grogan and the blonde girl that Kirkwood had failed to chat up earlier. Grogan on the dancefloor with his tongue down the throat of the aforementioned blonde, giving the thumbs up sign to the person taking the photograph.

Kirkwood shivered as another tsunami of nausea washed over him. Thankfully it passed without further incident. He checked his messages. Nothing from Gerry, which was no surprise given he was an utter technophobe who claimed the only two numbers on his phone belonged to Kirkwood and Grogan. Kirkwood dialled his number, but it went straight to voicemail. Either sleeping it off or lying dead in a doorway somewhere. Either way, he hadn't the energy to care.

Seven messages from Grogan.

8:37 – Where r u? Gerry's chucking up in the bogs!

8:38 – Serious m8. U gotta see this. I think he's just brought up a kidney!

8:39 – ????

9:45 – Where are ye? You should see this wee blonde I've hooked up with. Think I'm in. Yeeeoooooowwww!!!!!

9:47 – I'm sending you a pic of her. The Groganator strikes again!!!

10:46 – I'm away here. I've pulled.

01:12 – %teee3333>>(9

Kirkwood sighed. He vaguely recalled further shots of tequila. The aftertaste of lemon and salt lingered at the back of his palate, causing him to gag, but thankfully there was nothing left to bring up. He had a history of upping sticks and walking out of bars unannounced, so was not overly concerned by Grogan's texts enquiring as to his whereabouts. There was the vaguest recollection of walking through Bradbury Place. Something about broken glass and a fight. Nope, it was gone. He shook his head and instantly regretted it as the nausea subsided to be replaced by a throbbing headache; its epicentre just above his left eyebrow but proceeding to dance a painful path across his forehead.

He needed painkillers, fluids, food and then more alcohol. In that order. He lurched out of bed and painfully made his way downstairs, his leg and back muscles screeching in protest. Had he been beaten up last night? There were no bruises or anything to suggest an assault. He rummaged through his jacket which was hanging in the hall; the contents of which amounted to £14.67 in notes and loose change, a crumpled betting slip (Cross Eyed Colin – 3:30 Catterick – £5 win), his house keys and wallet (phew), and the torn-up remains of a beer mat.

He warily examined the contents of his wallet. Bank card. Check. Driving licence. Check. Not that he had a car to drive. And a partially ripped ten-pound note. He frowned, recalling he withdrew £150 from an ATM yesterday. He began to review his previous assertion that he had not been beaten up and robbed on the way home. Had he really blown over £120? He desperately attempted to calculate his outgoings from the tiny morsels of memory available to him, but try as he might, he could not account for the depleted finances. The Grid was a money-sucking pit of despair, of that much he was certain. Yes, his already unimpressive salary was looking even less impressive; a mere thirty-six hours into the new working month.

The doorbell rang. Kirkwood groaned. *What now?* he thought, opening the front door. It couldn't get any worse, surely?

It suddenly got a lot worse.

CHAPTER 26

NATASHA

For a heartbeat, Kirkwood's hopes soared when he saw Natasha standing in the doorway. This rapidly turned to dismay as he registered the blank expression on her face. It was patently clear his joy at seeing her was not reciprocated and she hadn't dropped by for a friendly chat or to beg him to take her back. His initial assessment of the situation was confirmed by her opening salvo.

'If you ever pull that stunt again, I will have your nuts in a sling,' she spat, before barging past into the hallway. Kirkwood jumped out of the way and the small of his back collided with the door handle, sending another jolt of pain through his already aching body.

'I…What…What are you on about?' he said, following her into the living room, while trying desperately to process her words.

'You know what I mean,' she screamed, turning on her heels and jabbing a finger repeatedly into his chest. 'Last. Night. My. House.' Each word was accompanied by another painful prod, causing Kirkwood to fall over the arm of a two-seater sofa and land on his backside in an undignified heap.

'Tash…Tasha…Seriously. I don't know what you…' his words petered out and he wracked what was left of his addled brain as an uneasy fear gripped him. What had happened?

'Don't you Tasha me, you pathetic excuse for a human being! You know exactly what you've done. Turning up last night plastered out of your skull. Hammering on my front door and waking up half the street with your antics. I mean…I mean…' she halted, partly to draw breath and partly to steady herself before launching into the next section of her tirade. She swept her hand through mousy shoulder-length hair which had been fashioned into a bob since he last saw her. *It didn't suit her*, he thought, with perverse satisfaction. Plus, it looked as if she had put a few pounds on.

'You said, "Ooh, Natasha, I love you. Ooh, Natasha, I can't live without you. Ooh, Natasha, I'll do anything" I have never been so embarrassed! I came that close to phoning the police, and how I'm going to look Mrs Millar in the eye next time I see her I don't know.'

The vaguest of recollections began to take shape in Kirkwood's head, peeking out from behind his headache; staggering past the top of his own street and continuing until he reached Rathfort Street, where Natasha lived. Fumbling about in the entry behind the terraced house she shared with Rowena from the university rowing club. Falling over a wheelie bin and then hiding inside it when a light came on in the back yard. Freezing like a French mannequin artist as he heard voices coming over the wall from the yard. Natasha's and another. A male voice.

He always had his suspicions. Natasha told him she needed space, wanting to focus on her studies. She had come out with every cliché in the book including that old chestnut 'It's not you, it's me.' Kirkwood was devastated and took to his bed for three days, surfacing only to butter toast he had placed in the fridge the night before. Cold comfort in cold toast.

His only forays into the outside world had been blitzkrieg raids to the shop at the top of the street to stock up on supplies of Diet Coke and untoasted toast, otherwise known as bread. His heart cracked a little bit more with every passing hour as he had cocooned himself in darkness and Kurt Cobain lyrics, turning his back on the outside world. He even turned off the notifications on his phone, but the world kept turning while Twitter and his twenty-seven followers stoically adapted to life without Kirkwood Scott.

His brain worked frenetically to piece together the developing horror show being exposed as Hurricane Natasha stood over him. 'You're a joke, Kirkwood. A total joke. I don't know what I ever saw in you. Everyone told me not to go anywhere near you. Everyone.'

By everyone, she meant her best friend and fellow she-devil, Abigail Clements. The meanest of all mean girls. The Regina George of their little universe. Make-up by Blue Circle cement. Nine stone of high-heeled hatred of which three stone was the block of ice encasing her heart. A total cow.

It was Abigail Clements who had introduced Natasha to the university badminton society. At first Natasha reluctantly tagged along, moaning to Kirkwood how difficult it was to say no to the princess of evil. But it gradually became more of a feature in her already hectic schedule, meaning he saw increasingly less of her. At the time he wasn't that bothered as it meant more drinking sessions with Gerry and Grogan, but when her absences began to include social functions and weekend training camps, he started to wonder.

This was badminton! For posh people who were too wimpy to go out into the cold and play tennis. He was sorry, he once told an irate Natasha, but he refused to take seriously a sport which included the word 'shuttlecock.' Kirkwood found this an endless source of amusement at the time but looking back, could see how it might have proven a little tiresome for her after, say, the 986th sniggering innuendo.

'I'm just glad Tim was there to see what a total moron you are.' The verbal assault continued unabated and more slivers of light began to illuminate the murky events of the night before.

Tim. Tim not very nice but incredibly dim. And by not very nice he meant utterly detestable. It was his voice that Kirkwood had heard from the back yard. Pennies began to drop out of the sky faster than the venom spewing from Natasha's mouth. Suddenly it all started to come back to him, every horrific, fine-grained detail. Stumbling from the entry onto the main street. Hammering the front door. Natasha and him screaming at each other. Her in tears. Abigail telling him to go forth and multiply or words to that effect. There had been other people in the house. Music. Some sort of party going on. Then the sound of knuckles scraping along the hall floor indicating the arrival of the missing link himself. Fifteen stone of muscle with the brain and temperament of a Tyrannosaurus Rex.

Kirkwood had been bullied mercilessly by the Tims of this world at school. He knew his type the moment Natasha introduced him on the only badminton night out he ever attended. Every school had a Tim and anyone who thought the world of jocks and cheerleaders was confined to Hollywood tween dramas obviously never graduated through the Northern Irish grammar school system. Captain of the 1st XV rugby team, his ball handling skills and ability to run through a brick wall earned him the fawning adoration of pupils and staff alike. Most of the lads wanted to hang out with him while the girls swooned in the corridors, fluttering their eyelashes and giggling inanely at his lame jokes and even lamer chat-up lines. The Tims of this world scraped just high enough marks to get by and were regularly excused from class to attend some sort of match or trial.

Yes, Kirkwood knew his type. The one and only time they had met he endured Tim's stereotypical laddish behaviour; politely declining downing his pint in one ('go on you wimp, chug, chug, chug!') and wincing whenever Tim launched into another boorish anecdote about the number of notches on his bedpost, winking all the while at Natasha who laughed a little too loudly for Kirkwood's liking.

Tim's rugby career had come to an abrupt end during his first match for

Queen's University, when an eighteen stone tight head prop landed on his left leg, popping the kneecap out of its socket and doing all sorts of nasty stuff to the surrounding ligaments and muscles. Unable to keep a good man down, however, Tim bounced, or rather hobbled, back and was now partaking in the much gentler pastime of badminton. His ability to bed women was undiminished, his new chat-up line being to ask unsuspecting prey if they wanted to see the scar on his knee, and then work north from there.

'Sod off buddy. Nobody wants you here and you're making a spectacle of yourself. Away home and sober up.'

'Well, look who it is, the great man himself,' Kirkwood had slurred. To be fair, describing him as drunk was a shocking understatement, as he was paralytic. The takeaway had done little to soak up the gallons of alcohol in his system, meaning he had very little control over his body movements or the words spewing from his mouth. He stepped back and executed a theatrical bow, correcting himself just before toppling over into a flower bed. 'To what do we owe this honour, Sir Timothy?'

Natasha had begun to sob, and Abigail slipped an arm around her shoulders, glaring all the while at an oblivious Kirkwood. Tim took a step forward, now flanked by two of his equally moronic mates. 'Look, if you don't move on you will end up head first in that wheelie bin we saw you falling over out the back. Except you'll have a broken nose for your troubles. Do you understand?'

'I understand that you are an utter waste of skin,' countered Kirkwood, swaying gently from side to side. 'But as much as I would love to continue our verbal jousting, I am not here to talk to you.' His countenance darkened as he turned his attention to Natasha. Any bravado he possessed beat a hasty retreat as he gazed upon her mascara-stained face. He hadn't planned it this way. 'Natasha, please. Give me five minutes. Just you and me alone. There's stuff I want to say. Things I need to explain.'

'No, Kirkwood. No'

'Please, Tash. Two minutes, that's all.'

'NO, NO, NO! Are you blind as well as stupid? Do I have to spell it out to you? I don't want to talk to you. I don't want to look at you. I don't want you anywhere near me. Is that clear enough for your tiny little brain to comprehend?'

'But I love you, Tash. I'm yours. Totally.' He felt sick and it wasn't the copious amounts of overpriced lager swilling about his stomach.

'Well, I don't love you.' She had delivered the killer blow, at least having the good grace to lower her voice and look away as she did. 'I'm with Tim now. He makes me happy. I never wanted to hurt you Kirkwood, but it just happened and I'm sorry. Now please just go.' She looked back at him, this time defiantly, and the truth smashed him in the face like a hammer. They were finished and no matter what he said, be it blind drunk or stone cold sober, it wasn't going to make the slightest bit of difference. This bridge was more than burnt. It had been bombed, strafed and razed to the ground. There was no bridge over these troubled waters.

Tim had placed a huge arm around Natasha, drawing her close to him. She buried her face in his chest and the tears began to flow again. Abigail sneered, Kirkwood's misery no doubt feeding whatever dark energy fed her twisted soul. The other apes began to turn their backs and lope back into the house, music continuing to pump out as other party goers danced to the beat, unaware of the drama outside.

'You heard the girl. Now clear off.' Tim smirked, the cat who had not only got the cream but the entire carton of milk.

Something had snapped inside Kirkwood. Or rather melted. Crumbled. Disintegrated. He stepped forward, swung back a foot and then leaned forward, every ounce of strength focusing on the kick which connected sickeningly with Tim's right kneecap. The big man went down like the proverbial sack of potatoes, howling like a newborn baby in an impressive falsetto that a teenage chorister would have been proud of.

He ran then, down the entry at the side of the house. Ran for his very life, his lungs bursting as the sounds of pursuing footsteps reverberated off the cobbles, a little too close for his liking. If they caught him, he was in for the kicking of all kickings. Thankfully, none of Tim's goons knew the area like Kirkwood. Two walls, several back gardens and a deserted primary school playground later, he had shaken them off and was home and hosed. The manic chase explained why he had woken up the next day feeling like a herd of elephants had stampeded over him.

The events on Rathfort Street gate-crashed his reeling senses with all the subtlety of a punch on the nose. Until Kirkwood blinked and realised that he actually had been punched on the nose; or rather something struck his face and was now nestling on his chest as he lay sprawled on the two-seater, his very ex-girlfriend towering over him. He looked down and saw a ring; the ring he bought Natasha for her twenty-fourth birthday not three months ago. She initially thought he was proposing and had looked mortified before he hurriedly explained it was nothing of the sort. She laughed then, flinging her arms around him and making a big joke of the misunderstanding, but it still stung, old romantic that he was. Looking back, he realised it began to fall apart from that moment onwards.

'You need to stay away, Kirkwood. Tim ended up in casualty last night. Luckily you kicked his good knee,' she paused for a second. 'Well it used to be his good knee. You have me to thank for the police not being the ones banging on your front door this morning. He wanted you hung, drawn and quartered.'

'Sorry.' He sat up, the ring now in the palm of his hand. 'It's just I don't know how I'll cope without you, Tash. I've tried, I really have but I'm just miserable all the time. There's just so much stuff going on in my head. Stuff I've been wanting to tell you for ages and...'

Skelly's face loomed large in Kirkwood's mind; a bushy eyebrow arched as he slowly shook his head in disapproval. *There will be hell to pay my boy. Hell to pay.*

'What?' Natasha's curt tone indicated she wanted to be anywhere other than having this conversation with him.

'Doesn't matter.' He sniffed but no tears came. He wanted to cry. He would probably feel a whole lot better if he could cry. But the tears dried up many years ago at that cold graveside. There was nothing left to say. There were no more tears to shed.

'Look, Kirk.' He hated being called Kirk but clung to the softening tone in her voice like a punch-drunk boxer on the ropes hanging on to his opponent. 'You're a good guy, you really are. You're funny and smart and well...' she considered her next words carefully, 'You have a lot of potential.' Kirkwood smiled wistfully at her tactical sidestep regarding his non-existent career prospects.

'You have a heart of gold and I know you've been through a lot what with your Dad and Katie and your Mum emigrating, but I'm not the one. I can't deal with all your issues. You need to let me go. You need to let us go. Just let me live my life. Please.'

With that she leaned over and awkwardly hugged him. Kirkwood never wanted it to end for he knew it would be their last hug. Uncertain as to what the social etiquette was in such situations, he awkwardly patted her shoulder until they simultaneously became aware that he was touching her bra strap, forcing Natasha to tactfully extricate herself from the embrace.

'I'm going to go now,' she said standing up and crossing her arms to erect a barrier between them and prevent him from throwing himself at her mercy in a final, pitiful act of desperation. 'Don't be worrying about Tim. I'll handle him. Just go and get yourself sorted. Maybe talk to someone. Like professionally or something...' She tailed off and the suggestion hung over them like a silent fart.

'Yeah maybe,' shrugged Kirkwood, staring at his bare feet and realising that he had no socks on and needed to cut decidedly cheesy toenails. *Nice touch you imbecile*, he thought glumly. Way to win the girl back. 'Can we stay friends or...'

'I don't think that's a good idea at the minute,' she replied, just a little too quickly for his liking. 'Maybe in time we'll see. But I really want things to work with Tim, and you and me continuing to talk would only complicate matters. Is that okay?' She cocked her head to one side and pulled a pained expression. She really wanted this conversation to end soon.

'It's okay, I get it.' With that, the surrender was unconditional.

'If I see you out and about, I won't pass without saying hello but other than that I think it's best if we cut off all contact.'

'Yup. No worries.' Kirkwood rose and stood with both hands in the front pockets of his dirty jeans, not sure as to what else he could do with them.

'Right then. I'd best be off. Badminton match later. Goodbye, Kirkwood.' She turned and walked out of the room, the house, and his life.

'Bye, Tash,' Kirkwood replied to nobody, as the living room was now empty. Just him and the gaping gash where his heart used to be.

Skelly leaned back in his armchair, a look of contentment on his face. 'Good lad. Stiff upper lip and all that. Bloody women. Better off without them I say.'

The phone vibrated in his back pocket. He retrieved it and read the notification on the screen. It was from Gerry. 'Just surfaced. Head's banging. Fancy a wee cure?'

'Sure,' Kirkwood typed back. His friend's timing could not have been better.

It felt like someone close to him had died.

CHAPTER 27

THE LION TAMER WHO COULDN'T

TAME LIONS

19 May 1995

Kirkwood knew something was wrong before they came for him. He lay in bed and waited, straining to gather as much information as possible from the whispered conversations and unnatural movements about the house. The alarm clock told him it was 5:30 a.m., way too early for this level of activity on a Friday morning. As the minutes dragged by, he started to piece together the dreadful picture which was forming in his mind. He buried his head in a pillow and prayed like never before that this was not happening.

He could hear his mother crying. Faint, soft sobs at first which gradually rose to an unhinged wailing that seemed to go on forever. He had never heard his mother so out of control as other hushed female voices tried to contain and control this unparalleled show of emotion. Next came Katie's voice, her usual cocky tone gone, as she assailed some unknown person with a barrage of questions. 'What's happened?' 'Where is he?' The voice of a man, who Kirkwood did not recognise, could be heard attempting to placate her. There followed a few seconds, hours, days of silence before her sickening screams shattered it. Nothing would ever be the same again.

'Nooo. Nooo! It's not true. Oh Dad. My poor wee Dad. What have those animals done to you?'

The men came and spoke to Kirkwood shortly after that. Mum's brother, Uncle Trevor, who he hadn't seen since the previous Easter when he had stood awkwardly in the living room as his wife embarrassed Katie and Kirkwood with chocolate rabbits more befitting a four-year-old. Kirkwood had hoped for a Manchester United egg and mug, but the chocolate tasted the same, so he hadn't minded too much.

Trevor looked just as uncomfortable as he had back then. He was accompanied by an older man with a bulbous, ruddy nose and receding strands of yellowing hair, slicked across his bald pate, like one of those 1970s footballers. Uncle Harold? Kirkwood was sure he had met the man before but could not quite place him. It would come to him no doubt.

He pretended to stir and rubbed his eyes, adjusting to the glare of the bedroom light which the men switched on upon entering. They shuffled at the foot of the bed, an uneasy standoff ensuing as to who would speak first. Trevor coughed and shifted from foot to foot while Uncle Big Nose looked as if he wanted to be anywhere but where he was at that very moment.

In the end Kirkwood decided to put them out of their misery. 'It's Dad, isn't it? He's dead.' He watched as Uncle Trevor visibly flinched at the mention of the last word and scratched his left elbow nervously before replying.

'Kirkwood. There are a lot of bad men out there and you know your father was doing his bit to stop them and to keep us all safe. Well, he was doing his job last night but the car he was in was…was…' he faltered, unable to bring himself to explain the mechanics of the attack. Kirkwood would later learn it was a massive culvert bomb placed under a narrow bridge on a desolate, country lane three miles outside the town. They had been following up a report of suspicious activity in the area. There was very little left of the car, his father, or the other two police officers who had been in it with him.

Kirkwood latched onto one phrase. 'Wait. What was he doing out in a car? Dad's job was to guard the dungeon at the police station, so the real policemen could go out and catch the bad men.' He paused, trying to process the information he was being fed. Had his father lied to him? All this time? Did that explain why he needed a gun in the house? Had the bad men been after him that night they called to the house?

A sudden, shooting pain pierced his forehead and he grimaced, recalling events of the previous day. Then his mother was upon him, burrowing his face into her dressing gown in a vice-like grip which did his headache no favours. He felt the tears transferring from her cheeks, coating his hair. He was vaguely aware of Katie by his side, her arm around his shoulders, something she had never done before. When he was finally able to extract himself and surface for air, Uncles Trevor and A.N. Other had beaten a hasty retreat from the room, no doubt making a beeline for the nearest cup of strong, sweet tea.

The remainder of the day was a procession of being fussed over by innumerable long-lost aunts and uncles while making polite, yet excruciating, conversation with cousins who he hadn't seen in years. Both sets of grandparents arrived; well, he said sets, but his paternal grandfather died decades before Kirkwood was born from some illness which nobody really spoke about but apparently was perfectly treatable nowadays. This left Granny Scott, who singlehandedly raised his father and five sisters in addition to a menagerie of stray cats, dogs, rabbits and several goats. His father once revealed to an astonished Kirkwood that Granny Scott tied him up outside with the goats when he was naughty, and Kirkwood was never quite sure if he was joking or not.

Granny Scott was accompanied by her right-hand woman, Aunt Ellen, and the two of them tactlessly removed several neighbours from sandwich-making duties in the kitchen, no doubt offending them in the process, before unpacking enough bread, milk and packets of digestive biscuits to feed several football teams many times over. It was as if they had been stockpiling for this eventuality and had broken into the 'unexpected death emergency supplies' cupboard the minute they heard the news. They had little time for sentiment and unnecessary displays of emotion. There were five loaves of egg and onion sandwiches to be made to feed the hungry hordes of mourners, who now swept through the house like swarms of famished locusts.

Extra chairs were produced from somewhere to facilitate the more elderly female visitors while the menfolk stood about and nodded earnestly at one another. Kirkwood was told his father was not coming home but was so good that God had taken him straight to Heaven. They would go to church in a couple of days and bury the coffin, but Kirkwood was not to get upset as Dad was not in it, but they had to keep the Reverend Duncan happy. Kirkwood wasn't an idiot though. He had watched enough war movies and read enough comic books to know what happened to someone when a bomb was put under their car. There wouldn't have been much of his father left, but at least it was quick, and he wouldn't have known much about it or suffered.

The Reverend Duncan arrived in the afternoon and after clasping many hands and eating his body weight in cherry scones, announced he wanted to lead the packed living room in prayer. Kirkwood thought it was a bit late in the day for that as the damage was already done but played along anyway, painfully aware several relatives, his mother included, would have him under close observation to ensure he had his head bowed and eyes closed in respectful deference to the good Reverend. And God of course. The fact their own heads were unbowed, and eyes were open during said surveillance operation, was irrelevant. They went to church every Sunday, so God would turn a blind eye on this occasion.

The Reverend Duncan could pray forever which was a good thing considering it was his job. Kirkwood was dragged along to the local Presbyterian church most Sundays where he stoically endured dreary hymns and even drearier sermons, while daydreaming about what Mother had planned for dinner. He was convinced his father fell asleep on more than one occasion during the service; yet when Kirkwood nudged him, he would jump with a startled snort and focus intently on the minister in his pulpit, nodding in agreement. He later told Kirkwood with a crafty wink that he had not been asleep but praying extra hard, which to the uninitiated observer, was very similar to sleeping. But best not mention that to Mother who was at home making the dinner and probably wouldn't understand.

The day of the funeral came. Kirkwood recalled it was bitterly cold and afterwards they served up more egg and onion sandwiches, but this time with butterfly buns which seemed to go down well. Kirkwood dissected his, removing and eating the wings first, before licking the cream off the top and devouring the remainder of the cake. His mother would have been horrified at such poor table manners but was too preoccupied weeping into endless cups of tea, which a cast of thousands were producing from the tiny kitchen at the back of the church hall.

Katie handled her grief by flirting outrageously with a second cousin who had come over on the boat from Stranraer along with a strong representation from the Glasgow arm of the Scott clan. Kirkwood couldn't make out a word he said but Katie hung on every sentence, all fawning smiles and exaggerated giggling at his jokes. Kirkwood told her it was against the law to fall in love with your cousin and you could get thrown into the dungeon at the police station for such a heinous offence. He only just managed to duck in time to avoid the corresponding backhander which she unloaded in his direction.

The Reverend Duncan ended the gathering by praying again — which went without saying, and then reading from the Bible. A book written by a man called Sam who seemed to be quite sad most of the time. Afterwards he spoke about how God would guide the family and friends of Mr Scott through this terrible time, just like he steered David through his own dark valleys. This confused Kirkwood given that the book was written by Sam. Who was this David character? He hadn't heard his name mentioned once. It didn't make sense, just like most of the bits of the Bible he had been exposed to. God seemed so angry most of the time, yet Jesus was always talking about loving your neighbour and everyone else for that matter. Kirkwood didn't know who Jesus lived beside when he was growing up in Nazareth, but he bet it wasn't Mrs McCreery, who once punctured a stray football he had kicked over her wall. Son of God or not, he would have had second thoughts about all this 'love thy neighbour' business if she was glaring over the fence at him every day of the week.

After the other mourners drifted away, Kirkwood accompanied Katie and his mother to the graveside one last time. The Reverend Duncan hung about the longest but finally left after Uncle Trevor handed him an envelope and they solemnly shook hands. It was probably a thank you card or a list of things that Uncle Trevor wanted him to pray about. The grave had been filled-in by the man with the little digger and was now covered with a ton of flowers, called wreaths. There were wreaths made up with real flowers and wreaths made up of pretend flowers; a bit like real policemen and pretend policeman.

Kirkwood was impressed by the number of real policemen who had turned up to pay their respects to his father who was, after all, only a pretend one. Many strode up to him after the service and spoke about how brave his father had been and how he had to keep going for his mother and sister, as he was the man of the family now. Kirkwood was a bit put out by that as he assumed this would have been Uncle Trevor's new job but nodded in agreement. They also told him what a good man his father had been, which irked him even more given the circumstances surrounding his death. Or murder as everyone insisted on calling it. He was becoming increasingly convinced his dead father was a liar, who did an awful lot more than shoo rats out of dungeons and open gates to let people in and out.

One of them asked Kirkwood if he wanted to be a policeman when he grew up, just like his father. Kirkwood had politely, but firmly reminded him, that Dad's main job had been driving a van and he only helped out at the police station. And no thank you, he didn't want to be a policeman, if it meant getting blown into a million pieces by a cowardly Frenchman who wouldn't stand and fight like a proper soldier. The policeman who asked the question had stared quizzically at Kirkwood for a few seconds, before smiling, patting him on the shoulder and heading off in the direction of the nearest sandwich tray.

An older man spoke to him at the grave when they all queued up and allowed the mourners to pass by and shake their hands. Kirkwood was told later that he was the top policeman in the country and had travelled all the way from Belfast for the funeral. In a helicopter, no less. Outside the church, Kirkwood had giggled out loud when a cameraman fell backwards over a cable attempting to film the top policeman's arrival. That earned a disapproving glare from his mother but even Uncle Red Nose stifled a snigger.

The older policeman only had one hand and where his left one was meant to be, he had a steel hook like the type they hung meat on at the butchers. At first Kirkwood thought it was a joke, maybe to make everyone laugh, given the day had been so sad. It was only when he didn't remove it as he stood at the front of the church to read from the Bible and nobody laughed, that Kirkwood realised it was real. After that he became convinced the older man was a pirate before becoming a top policeman and lost his hand in shark-infested Caribbean waters. Or possibly a lion tamer who had failed to live up to his job description by taming lions. Either way, he was determined to find out, so when the top policeman stopped to talk to him in the queue, he seized the opportunity with both hands. Which would have been a funny thing to say if it hadn't been such a solemn occasion.

'Hello. I know who you are. How did you lose your hand?'

The top policeman smiled at Kirkwood. 'I get asked that a lot by young men your age,' he replied, before adding, 'How do you think I lost it?'

'Was it a shark? Were you a pirate?' quizzed Kirkwood, scanning the man's features for tell-tale clues. Not a flicker.

'No, not a shark.'

'A lion, it was a lion. They have a zoo in Belfast so there must be lions living there. It bit your hand off when you went into the cage to feed it.'

The top policeman threw his head back and bellowed loudly, causing a few adjacent mourners to frown in his direction before realising who it was.

'No, no, no. I'm just an ordinary policeman. Those jobs are much too dangerous and exciting for the likes of me.' The laughter subsided but his elderly face was etched with a kindness and compassion Kirkwood hadn't seen much over the last few days. 'It just fell off one day when I was doing my job and I forgot to pick it up again. Silly old me.'

Kirkwood nodded sagely, not at all convinced by the explanation he had been given. 'Did you know my Dad?' There was a tailback snaking down the side of the graveyard caused by the top policeman stopping for so long, but he didn't seem concerned and nobody had the nerve to ask him to move along. Further on, Kirkwood was aware of his mother and Katie staring down towards where he was standing, wondering why the cavalcade of hugs, handshakes and empty platitudes had dried up at their end.

'No, I never met your father,' the top policeman replied. 'But I have been speaking to some of his friends today and they have been telling me what a wonderful man he was. You should be very proud of him.'

Kirkwood considered the answer before his next question. It was a standard response which he had heard many times over the last few days, but there was something in the way the old man spoke that made it sound different, like he genuinely meant it.

'Do you think my Dad has gone to Heaven?'

The top policeman leaned forward and placed his hand on Kirkwood's shoulder. 'Why, yes I do. Because that is where all good men go. And your father was a good man. Just like you will be when you grow up.'

'Do you think your hand is in Heaven?' continued Kirkwood, on a roll now.

'The one you lost?' The top policeman guffawed again before patting Kirkwood on the cheek with the tip of his hook and walking on, still chuckling to himself.

'I sincerely hope so, young man. I sincerely hope so.' With that he was gone, moving on to talk to Mother who bizarrely curtsied to him. Kirkwood vowed there and then never to wash his cheek again where the hook had brushed against it, as it was the closest he would ever come to meeting a real pirate.

Uncle Trevor drove them home and the remainder of the evening was spent tidying up the house and encouraging the remaining hangers-on and well-wishers that it was time to go as there were no sandwiches left, and the extra chairs had to go back to the church hall the following morning. Kirkwood retreated to his room at the first available opportunity. Katie was already barricaded in hers, and as Kirkwood passed the closed door, he heard her sobbing inconsolably. He hoped it was because of his father but had an uneasy feeling it was because the second cousin was on the 6:00 a.m. boat back to Scotland in the morning.

On entering his bedroom, he closed the door and flung himself face down on the bed, before turning onto his back and surveying his kingdom. Everything was as before. His Manchester United poster, one corner peeled back, having become unattached from the generous lump of Blu Tack used to secure it to the wall. They were playing on Saturday, but Kirkwood wasn't really that bothered. He had only pledged his allegiance to them to ensure a bit of banter with his father who was (*had been,* he mentally corrected himself), a massive Liverpool fan.

He turned his attention to the fort at the side of the bed. He had barely looked at it since the day it happened. Something wasn't right. He narrowed his eyes and leaned forward to inspect it in more detail. The outlying sentries were in position, snipers positioned on his bedside table with a clear line of fire over the approaches to the fort. The ramparts were fully manned by the German commandos, and their British counterparts were positioned at the rear in reserve. Inside the structure itself the remainder of the men were all gathered in formation for the Colonel who sat astride the black stallion, his back to Kirkwood, surveying the troops.

Then it struck him harder and more painfully than any football driven into the face. The sentries permanently on duty at the front gate; there weren't any. Kirkwood shook his head and tried to dispel the thought which was drifting slowly across his consciousness. He frantically threw back the covers and dropped to his knees beside the fort, scanning it and the outlying areas for any sign of them. His thoughts were gathering momentum now and a sick, cloying sensation began to take root in the pit of his stomach. This was his fault. He was to blame.

Then he saw them. Standing in the third row, front and centre. The two sentries. Eyes staring resolutely forward, and rifles pointed towards the open gate that they should have been standing guard over. Exactly where Kirkwood had stood in the dream. The evolving thought continued to take shape in his mind, still tantalisingly out of reach. He could almost touch it, taste it, see it, but he was not quite there yet. It drifted like cannon smoke across a desolate battlefield, caressing the dead and dying.

The day before his father died, he hadn't made his evening deployments. He had been groggy and dazed, just wanting to sleep. It completely slipped his mind. Then, as the thought began to settle over his mental landscape like a shroud of grey ash, the full horror of the omission began to overwhelm him and reveal the crushing truth for what it was. He had killed his father, not the French men. He neglected his duties by not placing the sentries at their accustomed post, like he was supposed to every night when his father went to the police station. And because of that, his father had not been on sentry duties at the police station the night he died. Because of that, his father was in a car that was blown sky high and to kingdom come.

It was all his fault.

Kirkwood closed his eyes and tried to drive the thought from his mind, but it was firmly embedded now, like a grappling hook in a cliff face. The trauma of the last few days washed away his strength and ability to fight back, as the grey ash continued to settle like a shroud, clouding and distorting every rational argument he could offer up against it. It was everywhere and it was everything. It was a voice, one that would control his every waking thought and action for the next seventeen years.

A very familiar voice.

'Oh, my dear boy. What have you done?'

Kirkwood began to cry then. It was the first time he had shed tears since the news of his father's death. Tears for his father, but also tears for himself.

What had he done?

CHAPTER 28

MULBERRY SQUARE

3:45 p.m.

'And then she left.'

Kirkwood set his barely touched pint of shandy down on the wooden table and leaned back. He had showered, shaved and even managed to locate a clean shirt but still felt like every organ in his body was sucked dry of moisture. It was developing into a hangover of epic proportions. His brain was on autopilot and the glare of another cloudless day in Belfast was doing nothing to allay the excesses of the night before.

'So, oh wise one. What do you make of all that?'

Seated opposite him, Gerry rubbed his stubbly chin and took a mouthful of Guinness. He looked as if he had spent the night in a skip, indeed he may well have, for Kirkwood had yet to broach the subject of how he got home. His multicoloured checked shirt had acquired a generous smear of dried-in curry sauce. At some stage he frequented a takeaway, but other than that there was a dearth of evidence as to his movements. Kirkwood concluded there was little point asking his dishevelled friend, as Gerry was probably equally clueless regarding his journey home.

'Way I see it,' Gerry replied, setting the pint down and adjusting his sunglasses for dramatic effect. 'You're screwed.'

Kirkwood sighed and took in his surroundings for some sort of sign that this wasn't rapidly turning into the worst day of his life. They were seated outside O'Reilly's, a traditional bar, which sat nestled off the main city centre for the best part of two centuries. Taking up one side of Mulberry Square, it drew a varied clientele of shrivelled regulars, young professionals and the occasional coachload of camera-toting tourists. 'Can you tell me how we get to the Giant's Causeway?' one rotund American enquired earlier when Kirkwood was at the bar getting beers. 'Yeah, it's about sixty-five miles that way,' he replied, pointing in no particular direction before conveying the beverages back outside to where Gerry impatiently awaited him.

Kirkwood had suggested they sit outside at one of the plethora of picnic tables in the square — not because they were sun worshippers, but rather the roaring peat fire (it was twenty-three degrees outside) and piped-in 'Irish fiddly-dee' music inside was doing nothing for the rhinoceros tap dancing about his cranial cavity. About a dozen of the tables were already occupied and the bar was doing a solid trade, situated as it was to capture the steady flow of human traffic passing through the square.

'You're best off leaving it mate,' Gerry sagely continued, swatting at a fly which was threatening to perform a kamikaze dive into the creamy head of his pint. 'Take it from one who knows a bit about women.'

Kirkwood's eyes widened in genuine surprise. He had never witnessed Gerry talk to a woman other than to order drinks. He had from time to time, when in the depths of drink, hinted darkly at a previous relationship which ended in tears many moons ago. Simone, he thought her name was.

'Thank you, Oprah Winfrey,' Kirkwood replied morosely, turning his attention back to the myriad of activity in the sun-soaked square around him. The tourist boom had replaced the boom of car bombs in Northern Ireland, and huge amounts of money were being pumped into the area in an effort to bring the metropolis kicking and screaming into the twenty-first century. This previously rundown part of the city had been transformed into a place where young families and loved-up couples could happily spend a summer's afternoon without fear of being bricked, bottled or blown up. Gourmet sandwich bars and quirky coffee shops now replaced military checkpoints and security barriers.

Opposite them, St Joseph's Chapel stood resplendent with its doors wide open, offering tourists audio tours of its magnificent interior. And on the way out why not stop at the gift store and purchase a replica key ring or bumper sticker? All proceeds towards the ongoing restoration work.

The chapel held mass three times a day and the faithful few were making their way through its cavernous entrance, much to the consternation of a group of Japanese tourists trying to take a group selfie outside. Kirkwood watched as an old man, laden down with what looked like his weekly shopping, limped out of the bookmakers beside O'Reilly's and slowly made his way across the square and up the steps of the chapel. From the sublime to the ridiculous he mused; or was it the other way around? He was never quite sure. He was brought up a

Presbyterian and frogmarched to Sunday School by his mother every week, but any fleeting interest he ever had in Jesus and all that jazz vaporised the morning Uncle Trevor walked into his bedroom all those years ago.

Good luck to the old sod, thought Kirkwood, as the pensioner reached the top of the steps and paused for breath, before disappearing out of sight into the cathedral's depths. *Let's hope he finds a crumb of solace in there for I never did. Or at least a bit of divine inspiration as to the winner of the next race at Lingfield Park.*

'Just telling it as it is,' Gerry sulkily replied. 'You can polish a turd as much as you want. At the end of the day it's still a turd.' He drained the dregs of his pint in a single gulp and rose to his feet. 'Right. My round. Same again? Or are you going to man up and have a proper drink this time?'

Kirkwood eyed the shandy, which was doing nothing to ease his alcohol induced sickness. 'Aye, go on then. Pint of Stella Artois. Might as well go down all guns blazing.' Natasha drank shandies. Everything today reminded him of Natasha.

'Good man,' chirped Gerry, 'Pint of McCartney it is then.' He made his way into the bar, pulling up saggy jeans with both hands to prevent a passing nun getting an eyeful of his builder's bottom. 'Good afternoon, Sister. Lovely day for it.' The nun tutted her disapproval and hurried on towards the steps of the chapel.

A hint of a smile played across Kirkwood's face and he turned his attention this time to the far corner of the square, diagonal to where he was sitting. Here the walls were adorned with council-approved graffiti from local talent depicting the area in days gone by. An opening here connected the square to nearby Royal Avenue via a cobbled, dog-legged alley. An Eastern European woman of indeterminable years stood selling copies of the *Big Issue* at its entrance. 'Beeg Eeshyou. Hello. Thank you. Pleaaase,' she repeated over and over. A gaggle of Love Island rejects tottered past him, all bottled tans and fake eyelashes. They looked as if they were cutting across the square towards The Grid. Kirkwood shuddered as images from the night before cut a swathe through the hangover haze currently clouding his memory.

Behind them, three teenagers, wearing the regulation Belfast street uniform of trainers, tracksuit bottoms and hooded tops, entered the square followed almost immediately by two uniformed police officers on mountain bikes, their white crash helmets glinting in the sun and wrap-around shades failing to disguise they were closely monitoring what the youths were up to. 'Go back to your own country and stop scrounging off us!' one of the teenagers roared at the old woman, who smiled back with her hand held out, unaware of the insult just levelled at her. One of his mates laughed aloud, 'Nice one, Micky,' he guffawed loudly, causing a few drinkers at the tables to look over in their direction.

'Whaa?' growled Micky, aware that he was attracting attention. He threw the middle finger in the direction of the tables and swaggered on across the square. Despite the baking heat, their hoods were up and tightly drawn over their heads. *Less easy to identify when shoplifting*, thought Kirkwood. 'C'mon boys. Hurry up,' Micky turned and sneered back towards where the police officers had stopped a short distance away. 'It doesn't smell so good round here.' One of them was speaking into a walkie talkie radio attached to his stab vest, while the other leaned over the handlebars of his bike, scribbling furiously into a notebook.

For not the first time since seeing her the previous morning, Kirkwood thought of Nirvana Girl. These were her people, the down and outs who prowled through the city causing trouble wherever they went. Yet, in the handful of seconds when their eyes met, he sensed she was different. It wasn't only the unnerving sketch which so resembled Skelly. She had looked lost, desperately lost. He wondered if she looked into his eyes and saw the same loss; longing to belong — to someone, something, anything.

Gerry slammed the pint of Stella down on the table in front of him. 'Get that down your neck, Kirky boy, and all your troubles will be no more,' he proclaimed, slurping enthusiastically at his Guinness as he took his seat again. 'You know this Guinness reminds me a bit of that nun I near knocked over a minute ago. Only less bitter.' He sniggered at his joke and Kirkwood forced a tepid smile in return. He looked over towards the teenagers, but they were gone, having turned right into Castle Street, the gateway to the west of the city. He wondered if they knew Nirvana Girl, and where she was now.

The bells of St Joseph's rang out, announcing the afternoon service was about to begin. Kirkwood looked towards the steps and watched as the last stragglers hurried into the building. He estimated the congregants inside were heavily outnumbered by those worshipping the great god of alcohol outside in the sun. For a crazy second, he considered joining them and offering up a desperate prayer for answers to the many unanswered questions he had. Natasha, his absent family, Skelly, and Nirvana Girl. Everywhere he turned there was nothing but confusion and despair. He raised the pint to his lips, nodded at Gerry and drank deeply. It was only a temporary solution but, at present, it was all he had.

CHAPTER 29

THREE'S A CROWD

7:10 p.m.

Saturday afternoon went downhill rapidly after that. The quality of Gerry's conversation deteriorated, the more pints he consumed until finally Kirkwood poured him into a taxi just after 5:00 p.m. Grogan made a special guest appearance after that to brag about his conquest from the night before. Her name was Penelope, she was a hairdresser from Lisburn, and he was meeting her later at a club on the fringes of the city centre called, The Basement; the name of which baffled Kirkwood as there were three levels to it. He declined Grogan's invitation to tag along, remarking that three was a crowd.

'C'mon man. It will be good for you. She's got a couple of class-looking mates. You can be Goose to my Maverick.'

'Aye and look how that ended up. Smashing his brains all over a cockpit while little bitty Tommy Cruise rides off into the sunset with Kelly McGillis. No, you tear on. I'll sit here for a bit and then head up the road.'

'And spend Saturday stuck in the house on your own? What are you, forty-eight years old?'

'I won't be on my own. Richard will be there.'

'Richard the Pilchard? The world's most boring human being. I'd rather watch paint dry. There's more atmosphere on the moon than a night in with him.'

Kirkwood nodded glumly, unable to argue the point any further. Although housemates, Richard and he had very little in common other than an unspoken agreement to interfere in each other's lives as little as possible. Thrown together at very short notice after other prospective house sharing plans fell through at the eleventh hour, they were ships that passed in the morning, noon and night. Richard didn't drink, worked in IT, and spent most of his spare time in his room gaming with other online recluses from around the globe.

'I'm grand, Grogan. The last thing I want to do is fork out fifteen pounds for the pleasure of standing in some murky club, watching you chew the neck off some wee girl.'

'Aye you're just jealous you didn't get off with her, that's all.'

Grogan always knew what buttons to push and today was no exception. Kirkwood was finally one drink ahead of his hangover and the fresh alcohol coursing through his veins had considerably improved his mood. Natasha still lurked on the fringes like an unwelcome house guest, waiting to pounce if the opportunity presented itself. The last thing he needed was Grogan bursting his beer bubble. It took all his resolve to refrain from nibbling at the verbal bait which his so-called friend was dangling in front of him. He decided he was left with little option but to fight fire with fire.

'Sebastian,' he declared loudly, knowing Grogan hated his first name being spoken in public; a loud roar of laughter erupted from the next table. 'My final answer is a negative. You are welcome to the young lady. I am officially celibate for the rest of my life.'

'Alright, alright,' snarled Grogan, shooting the table in question a dark look and hunching over his bottle of Budweiser in the hope there would be no fallout for having been named and shamed as the son of Brideshead Revisited fans. 'No need to fight dirty. It's not as if Kirkwood is the coolest name on the block.'

'Quite the contrary, Mr Grogan. It is a most honourable name. I come from a long line of Kirkwoods, going back to my great grandfather, Reginald Kirkwood who, as you know, was awarded the Military Medal for saving the life of an officer under enemy fire at Spion Kop in the year of Our Lord 1900.'

'Yeah, only for it to be unceremoniously ripped from his uniform for being caught drunk as a skunk on duty in the year of Our Lord 1901. And anyway, I don't believe that cock and bull story for a second. Your loon of a granny made it up. Along with that other crock of nonsense that you were related to an American president. What was his name? Woodstock Wilson?'

'Woodrow,' Kirkwood corrected snootily. 'And leave my grandmother out of this. She may have been a tad eccentric but none of her stories have been definitively disproven. God rest her soul.' He raised his pint glass to the sky in honour of the dearly departed matriarch.

'Indeed,' replied Grogan, pulling on his jacket and rising to his feet in a single, languid movement. 'Well, if I can't make you see sense then I will bid you adieu. Enjoy your evening of unbridled misery.' He saluted Kirkwood, turned and began to walk across the square already fiddling with his phone. Texting sweet nothings to the delectable Penelope no doubt.

Kirkwood watched him go. He looked at his watch and stared morosely at another empty pint glass, his sixth of the day. Grogan was right. The thought of an awkward evening exchanging small talk with Richard while watching rubbish television, was an unbearable prospect. It was still way too early. The day was young, and the world was his oyster. He was a not unattractive young bachelor with a wallet full of ten-pound notes and a belly full of beer. What woman could resist?

And failing that, there was always the horse racing.

CHAPTER 30

TRICKY TRICKSTER SAVES THE DAY

8:45 p.m.

A deafening wall of silence greeted Tricky Trickster, the 16-1 winner of the final race at Lingfield Park being displayed on the bank of plasma screens adorning one side of Westland's Bookmakers. Disgruntled regulars turned away in disgust and a blizzard of beaten betting slips were crumpled into balls and discarded on the shop floor. All bar one. Kirkwood clung onto his and resisted the urge to leap into the air and click both heels together like a demented leprechaun. At last, a winner.

The last race of the day was traditionally known as the 'get out' stakes and it was time for him to collect his winnings, the princely sum of eighty-five pounds, and get out pronto. He made his way to the counter, secreted the winnings into the front pocket of his jeans and exited the premises, studiously avoiding eye contact with the jealous glares of the remaining punters. They all hated a winner, except when it was themselves.

Although relieved his rapidly declining finances were refreshed, Kirkwood felt anything but victorious as he stepped back outside. The weakening sun had disappeared behind the spire of the chapel, but it was still a fine June evening by anyone's standards. Belfast folk equated it with sub-tropical conditions. Men who should have known better were flaunting their pasty white flesh for all to see, not that anyone wanted to. A number were already displaying lava-red shoulders and only the copious amounts of White Lightning cider coursing through their veins was saving them from a world of pain. Combined with hangovers that would no doubt stop a freight train in its tracks, they had little to look forward to in the morning.

Tricky Trickster's heroics only papered over the widening cracks in Kirkwood's day. He felt as if every last drop of cranial fluid was being sucked from his brain and knew it was only a matter of time before dehydration and fatigue caught up with him. The hangover chasing him all day was coming up fast in the rear-view mirror. And this time it wasn't stopping for anyone.

He resumed his morose watch outside O'Reilly's and within an hour was in the full throes of a pity party, which kicked off somewhere between pints seven and eight. Despite being surrounded by hundreds of people, he had never felt lonelier. 'Cheers.' He raised his pint to nobody in particular and took another swig of lager.

He checked his phone in the vain hope Natasha might have seen the error of her ways and messaged him to say it had all been a dreadful mistake, and could he call over so they could live happily ever after. Zero notifications. No, hang on, a text from his mother. He messaged her most evenings but had been putting off breaking the news that his love life was dead in the water. She would phone immediately and launch into a long-distance post-mortem of the relationship, grilling her son to a fine crisp in the process, with the savage aplomb of an Old Bailey barrister. He chose the cowardly option and messaged back saying they were at the cinema and would speak to her tomorrow.

'Ok,' was the monosyllabic response. This was the height of her texting skills which suited him fine.

A folk-rock band, Irish Charm, were setting up in the square, their lead guitarist mumbling 'one-two, one-two' soundchecks in a disinterested monotone, which did not bode well for the performance ahead.

Resisting the urge to scream 'THREE' at the top of his voice was only surpassed by his desire to message Natasha. She had probably blocked his number by now, but he was still sorely tempted to throw himself at her mercy in the unlikely hope she might respond. Grogan, who regarded himself as the font of all wisdom when it came to the opposite sex, earlier warned him against such a course of action when Kirkwood brought him up to speed on the Battle of Rathfort Street.

Setting the phone back down was a physical act of will which left him exhausted, as if he had rolled a tractor tyre across the square. He sat, legs apart and arms folded, wondering how this most perfect of weekends had gone so horribly awry. It started with such high hopes but now it was just him, his beer and the oldest rockers in Ireland. Kirkwood was aware his eyes were growing heavier as the guitarist struggled to unravel a Gordian knot of leads to find the one connecting his instrument to a battered amp, which looked almost as ancient as him. The chatter of the square began to grow distant and Kirkwood's head dropped, his chin coming to rest against his chest.

The weekend had finally ground to a halt for Kirkwood Scott.

CHAPTER 31

CASTLE STREET CAPERS

10:38 p.m.

'What about ye, Danny boy? Any fegs?'

'You know I don't smoke, Micky. It's a filthy habit. I'm not poisoning my body with that muck.'

Without a hint of irony, Danny O'Connor raised the bottle of Buckfast to his mouth before passing it to Meredith. She had awakened to several missed calls from Danny and agreed to meet him in the city centre mid-afternoon, where he treated her to a Big Mac meal from the McDonald's on Royal Avenue. Between mouthfuls of food, he regaled her with his exploits from the previous night. Meredith listened dutifully, nodding in all the appropriate places, but not wholly convinced by the veracity of his tale. Danny had a tenuous relationship with the truth at the best of times, and a tendency to exaggerate when it came to how many beers he consumed, pills he popped, and girls he snogged.

They then retired to Castle Street where Dominic Healy was as accommodating as ever in supplying beverages for the evening ahead. Meredith watched as Danny unrolled a sizable wad of notes when paying but knew better than to ask where he acquired the money. See no evil, hear no evil, speak no evil, was a mantra she adhered to religiously. People who asked too many questions tended to have a short shelf life on the streets. Besides, who was she to turn down his generous offer to drown her many sorrows? Part of her itched to manufacture an excuse to visit Emily at the wall, but she knew sloping off would only offend Danny, so she resisted the urge. Micky Mallon and two of his scumbag mates accosted them several hours later as they shared the remaining bottle from their carry-out in a doorway at the top end of Castle Street.

'Who's your wee friend, Danny?' smarmed Mallon, undressing Meredith as he eyed her up and down. 'Meredith, Micky. Micky, Meredith.' Danny returned to the Buckfast, utterly nonplussed by the new arrivals.

'Alright gorgeous. Haven't seen you about. Do you come here often?' Meredith rolled her eyes. As cheesy opening lines went, this one was off the scale. 'What's the matter? You too high and mighty to speak to the likes of me? Here, Danny is she your girl or is she fair game?'

'Nah. We're just mates,' replied Danny, suddenly more interested in something happening over Mallon's shoulder further down the street. He squinted, as blind as a bat but too vain to wear glasses; claiming it didn't fit with his street image.

'Go on, love. Give us your phone number and let's hook up. I've a girl myself but I won't tell her if you don't.' Mallon's pock-marked face broke into a leering grin which did little to improve his ferret-like features.

Meredith had dealt with clowns like this before. 'I know you are probably fighting the girls off, but I'd rather cut my thumb off with a rusty butter knife than go on a date with you.' She smiled sweetly and started to walk away.

Mallon's leer turned to a sneer. 'Where do you think you're going, you wee bitch? I haven't finished talking to you.' He placed a hand on Meredith's forearm causing her to stop and look down at it.

'If you don't get your filthy hands off me…'

'What? What are you going to do? Go crying home and tell your daddy?' With that, something snapped in her. She whipped around and in one fluid movement planted her right knee into Mallon's groin. He wheezed, before slumping to the ground where he began to turn an unflattering shade of grey.

'Wha…What was that for?' he moaned, desperately trying to suck in air as his two mates looked on uneasily, uncertain as to what they should do. 'I was only trying to be friendly.' Mallon let out a low, guttural groan as a single tear rolled down his cheek.

'Lay your hands on me again and I'll cut them off next time you dirty…'

'Er, Meredith,' Danny, still peering down the street, sounded worried.

'Not now Danny. I'm…'

'No, seriously Meredith. I think you should…'

His voice was anxious now, the usual arrogance replaced by genuine concern. She looked away from Mallon and followed Danny's gaze. Charging towards them were two of the largest men she had ever set eyes on. The dark expressions on their faces strongly suggested they wanted more than a friendly chat.

'It's the McManus brothers. RUN!'

Danny broke into a sprint in the opposite direction, leaving Meredith with no option but to grab her bag and dash after him. 'I told you this was going to happen,' she screamed at his back as they veered right, off Castle Street towards Mulberry Square.

Another fine mess he had gotten her into.

CHAPTER 32

MOVE

10:40 p.m.

Kirkwood awoke with a snort as Irish Charm's guitarist launched into one of the half dozen chords he knew. He looked about self-consciously, but nobody else in the beer garden appeared that interested in the young man snoring in their midst. An impromptu dance floor had been created in front of the band and he watched enviously as a young couple swayed and smooched no more than six feet away, lost in each other's eyes. It did little to improve his foul mood, which returned with a vengeance. Despite the steady flow of alcohol forced down his throat, the excesses of the weekend were relentlessly catching up on him.

Yes, the mother, father and second cousin of all hangovers was threatening to gatecrash the pay day party and drag him kicking and screaming into its pain cave. Every time he checked his watch another twenty minutes had passed and he resolved it was time to drag his sorry backside home to bed. He needed sleep and lots of it, or there was no chance he was making the office come Monday morning.

Despite that, he found himself at the bar ordering another pint. And, in for a penny, in for a pound; a shot of tequila to accompany it. He drunkenly reasoned that if he was going to suffer, then he might as well do so in style. It was stinking thinking of the highest order but all he had at that particular moment.

As he downed the tequila with a grimace, Kirkwood Scott had no idea his life was going to change forever in eight minutes, thirty-nine seconds.

38…

37…

He walked outside with his drinks and sullenly watched the shadows stretch and deepen across the square as the light dimmed and the beer garden emptied. As the elderly four-piece lurched into their final number of the evening, he and he alone was their captive audience. The last chord of the night rang out and Kirkwood bounced to his feet to afford them a rousing, if slightly unsteady, ovation.

'Er…thanks man,' rasped the gravelly-voiced vocalist into the microphone, not sure if the unexpected applause from the young man in front of him was genuine or not.

'We're shutting up for the night soon.' One of the bar staff had emerged from inside and was starting to clear the tables of empty glasses dotted around the beer garden. He nodded towards Kirkwood's pint. 'I can put that in a plastic beaker for you if you want?'

Kirkwood considered the offer before raising the remains of the pint to his lips and downing its contents in a solitary gulp. 'Thank you and farewell my good man,' he slurred, rising to his feet and taking an involuntary step to the left, before correcting his balance and leaning against one of the decorative beer barrels which had been fashioned into a table. Above him a bountiful hanging basket swayed in time with the inebriated young man beneath it. An angry bee orbited above, unimpressed he was threatening to intrude upon its floral feeding ground.

'Do you want me to phone you a taxi?' offered the barman with a resigned expression. He was well versed in dealing with drunken idiots at chucking out time.

'Nah, it's okay. I'll be fine.' Kirkwood steadied and attempted his best impersonation as a sober pillar of society, failing miserably in the process.

'Right you are,' replied the barman, shooting one last dubious look at Kirkwood before turning his back and striding back into the bar. Kirkwood listened to the retreating clink of glasses followed by the doors slamming shut. He looked at his watch. It was getting late and the street lighting was on, bathing the deserted square in a sickly glow. He calculated with some difficulty that he could make the last bus from the City Hall if rubbery legs would obey what was left of his saturated brain. If he caught it, then he would be at the top of Glasgow Street within ten minutes and in bed within fifteen. It sounded like a plan. Failing that, he would have to flag down a passing taxi. Five times the price of the bus fare but, hey ho, needs must.

He tentatively set off across the square, directing a final, cheery wave at Irish Charm as they packed away the last of their equipment. His destination lay in the far corner of the square, the dog-legged avenue which led onto Royal Avenue. From there it was little more than a stone's throw to the City Hall, which rose majestically above the central thoroughfare. Not that he had any intention of throwing any stones. He desperately craved a bed, but one in a police cell was not on the agenda.

Kirkwood pulled his phone from the front pocket of his jeans and began to ponderously tap out a text message to Gerry, his face creased in concentration. This most basic act of hand to eye coordination suddenly became a task of Herculean proportions.

Tap, tap. 'On my way home.' Tap. 'Utterly blocked.' Tap, tap. 'I hate my life.'

He paused in the middle of the square to consider the literary gem on the screen in front of his tired, bloodshot eyes. Yes, Kirkwood. In those nine little words you have most eloquently summarised your present plight. Welcome to Rock Bottom. Population — you.

'GET OUT OF THE FAACCKINN WAY!'

Kirkwood managed to half turn in the direction of the strangled yell before he was sent sprawling to the ground. He instinctively threw out both hands to break the fall, which resulted in skinned palms but spared his body from more serious damage. His phone spun across the square before coming to rest some twenty feet away, the message to Gerry unsent. He looked up in time to see a lanky youth disappearing into the alley which he had been intending to cut through.

'MOOOOVVVE!'

He had no more than lifted his head when he was propelled forward again, his exposed nose this time connecting painfully with the concrete. Dazed and utterly confused he squinted upwards to watch a second, smaller figure sprinting after the first one. He concluded the second psychopath must have hurdled his prone body and caught the back of his head with their trailing foot.

As they vanished out of sight into the alley, Kirkwood shook his head in a frantic effort to clear his jumbled mind. He would have made a hopeless witness were he ever asked to attend an identification parade and pick out the two assailants who had crossed his path; or rather trampled all over it.

'You want me to describe them officer? Well, okay then. One of them was tall. And scrawny. How tall? Hmm, well let me see now. Six foot? Six-foot-two? Do you want me to keep going? Well, he was white. And he wasn't wearing a hat. I'm 110 per cent certain about that last bit.'

A stillness interrupted his jumbled thoughts.

The other one was wearing a Nirvana hoodie. Just like the girl sitting outside the Tesco Express yesterday morning. The girl who was sketching in the notebook.

Sketching Skelly…

A supernova of clarity burst within Kirkwood and he burst to his feet and lumbered towards the alley as fast as his battered body could propel him. The phone would have to wait. The stinging sensation in his palms would have to wait. Suddenly, all that mattered was catching up with Nirvana Girl. The key to the mayhem that had raged in him for over a decade was now tantalisingly within reach.

'GET OUT OF THE WAY YOU MUPPET!'

Kirkwood squeezed his eyes shut and winced, fully expecting to be sent clattering to the ground again. He braced for impact and was faintly aware of large shapes passing either side of him, parting like the Red Sea in order to avoid an unsightly pile up. The pounding of footfalls was everywhere, as if a squad of booted rugby players were surging past in all directions. Suddenly ahead of him he could see the source of this latest auditory assault upon his senses. Two muscle-bound apes wearing painted-on bleached denim jeans and black bomber jackets pounded into the alley, the noise created by their Doctor Marten boots reverberating around the empty square.

Every ounce of his tattered logic screamed at him to make a rapid 180 degree turn and hotfoot it in the opposite direction. He had never been on the receiving end of a punch in his life and had no intention of starting now. Yet, the hoodie. The sketch. It was either the biggest coincidence in the history of coincidences, or something infinitely better than the hand he currently held. Before he knew it, he was fully upright, legs pumping and arms flailing as he chased the two apes into the alley. He did not know where this was going but had to somehow speak to the mystery artist. At last there was a splash of colour on the bland, featureless canvas of his life. A straw to clutch at, a piece of wreckage to keep him afloat, atop the churning, slate-grey ocean.

CHAPTER 33

SIX FEET OVER

From high above they gazed disinterestedly at the puerile human drama unfolding below. It was pathetic and utterly undeserving of their interest, but they had their orders and the Colonel always knew best. The Colonel could also turn them into a tiny pile of ash in the blink of an eye, which assisted in focusing one's concentration during mundane missions such as this.

It was probably inevitable that the one known to his kind as Kirkwood would cross paths with the street urchin. She was a revulsive specimen, but for some inexplicable reason had been chosen as a vessel. Which was a problem for the organisation but an even bigger one for her, given she was now firmly in their sights. For now, they had merely been allocated the responsibility of keeping tabs on the human from a respectful distance. Although such was their disdain for them and their filthy world, they would have taken considerable pleasure in snuffing the air from their flaccid bodies given half a chance.

Not yet though, not yet. The Colonel had unfathomable patience but had been in this business much longer and always played the long game, ever aware of the bigger picture. Which was why he was the boss, and rightly so. No, they knew their place. They were rank and file, humble foot soldiers who knew not to ask too many questions. They preferred it that way. Operating on the front line they relished the cut and thrust of the job, as opposed to a management position where they would rarely be knee deep in the chaos they so loved to whip up on the various planes they had been dispatched to down the years. So many years. Coming up on two hundred now.

They swooped low and fast across the square to gain a better angle now that the human scum below had traversed it. To think they had once been of this kind. It left the sourest of tastes. Picking up the four humans at various stages along the alley they watched the farce below closely. The urchin and her junkie sidekick separated as they emerged onto the main street, cutting left and right respectively as fast as their wretched little bodies could carry them. The lumbering oafs chasing behind stopped as they too emerged from the alley, tiny brains whirring in overdrive, deciding whether to split up themselves or concentrate on one of their prey.

After what seemed an eternity but was little more than a second, the oafs plumped for the latter option and headed left after the junkie. Despite his best efforts, they would catch him in precisely six minutes and thirty-six seconds, whereupon the beating of his life would be administered. Fists and boots were so passé to those who watched from above, who could end a life with the flick of a finger — but there was something to be said for the old methods. They could have intervened and spared the loathsome Danny O'Connor but had tired of him and his part in this sorry saga. A fractured skull, perforated liver and three weeks in an induced coma was little more than he deserved. Half a dozen cracked ribs would also ensure he wouldn't be out of hospital any time soon.

Which left Kirkwood and the urchin. The one known to her kind as Meredith Starc. They had been tailing her for several weeks and knew her loathsome routines like the back of their hands. She was no doubt already halfway to her vile lair thinking she could lie low, safe and undetected. She would keep. They watched as the one known as Kirkwood emerged from the alley and skidded to a halt, looking one way then the other in a futile attempt to determine where the others had gone. They were out of sight and he turned and walked back along the alley, his shoulders slumped in defeat. What a pathetic excuse for a human being. Imagine having to stand shoulder to shoulder with that in the heat of battle. He wouldn't have lasted two minutes before he too would have turned and fled just like those damned Fitzgerald Brothers.

Cowards, the lot of them. Which made it all the more outrageous that the enemy had chosen Scott as the last remaining obstacle between them adding this wretched planet to their already-impressive portfolio. Their employers were great believers in using local people for local jobs which was why the Company had been assigned this operation. He viewed it as a great honour and lectured the men long and hard before sending them on their way. After the initial novelty of returning to the old hunting ground wore off, however, they quickly tired of the charade. Just end it and be done. They should have struck while the iron was hot after the White Witch was dispensed with; yet the Colonel stalled and when they dared suggest they finish off the junkie, they were swiftly silenced by a hard, cold stare from the old soldier.

They refocused as the young man bent down in the alley and picked up an object. What was it? A book? They glided down until no more than six feet above the human's shoulder. They were unconcerned at the proximity for if Kirkwood looked up, he would see nothing but the bruised purple sky above the city skyline, dusted with a covering of stars. The young man shuddered but would never know it was because some primal part of him sensed death above.

The human was holding a notepad, opened to reveal a sketch, a drawing. Horribly amateurish but the subject was unmistakable.

The Boss.

The Colonel.

Skelly.

CHAPTER 34

LOST JOURNAL

10:52 p.m.

Meredith sprinted the length of Royal Avenue and along the side of City Hall before she risked a glance behind. The street was deserted but she erred on the side of caution, only slightly reducing her speed. She pounded right onto Chichester Street, the Adidas bag bouncing against her hip, its strap digging deep into her shoulder. Danny had screamed for them to separate as she followed him out of the alley, mere seconds ahead of the McManus Brothers.

He had veered left, leaving her with little choice but to gamble on the opposite direction. For once, the cards had fallen in her favour. The two dealers must have followed Danny given it was him they were undoubtedly after. Well, he couldn't say she didn't warn him. He was an utter waster but, since they hooked up several months ago, she had grown fond of him. Beneath the cocky swagger and foul mouth was another lost soul, just like her. She hoped he was okay but had learnt the hard way, you could only care so much for others on the streets before self-preservation kicked in.

She slowed gradually to a jog and then a walk, continually checking over her shoulder until convinced the coast was clear. It was dark now, but as she turned onto Great Victoria Street, it was buzzing with life. Situated at the base of Belfast's Golden Mile it hosted an array of bars, hotels and restaurants that on a pay day weekend did a roaring trade. She could have chanced setting up shop outside the heaving Crown Bar where smokers and vapers were immersed in clouds of smoke on the pavement outside. She knew she would make a killing as the well attired, but equally well oiled, punters took one look at the pale, little homeless girl and showered her in slurred sincerity but, more importantly, the contents of their pockets.

She needed to get out of the public eye, however, so planting her backside outside one of the busiest bars in the city, moments after evading a near-death experience was not the wisest of moves. She trotted across the street to the other side and walked briskly past the magnificent Grand Opera House. It held a special place in her heart, crammed with warm, comforting memories of the annual family pilgrimage to the Christmas pantomime, where they had roared with laughter at May McFettridge hamming it up as Widow Twankey, or the Ugly Godmother. Meredith stepped hurriedly past her not-so-distant past. Best not to focus on happier times. Focus on the real reason she left that life behind. Focus on Emily.

Emily. Meredith felt the familiar grief gnawing at her core. She slowed and regulated her breathing to keep the bile-coated panic down and not allow it to spiral upwards through her slight frame. She rounded the corner of the opera house and fell to both knees in a doorway near its deserted stage entrance. She pulled the bag off her shoulder and emptied its contents on the pavement, ferreting furiously for the one item she knew would calm her. Not the alcohol — their daily quota had been consumed hours ago; no, it was something more substantial than that.

Her journal. It wasn't there.

She rummaged through the upended contents again, muttering all the while to herself. 'Where are you? Where the hell are you?' Once, twice, three times she checked the inside of the bag in the rapidly diminishing hope the journal might be secreted in one of its lesser-used recesses. Finally, she threw it against a wall and stifled a scream, forced to accept the crushing certainty taking up residence in her beleaguered mind. It was gone. Her journal that she poured her heart into, was gone. It held everything and meant everything. Her thoughts, the monsters that haunted her dreams, the letters she was writing to her dead friend.

Emily O'Hara. What sort of a twisted sicko drew pictures of a dead teenage girl, then signed it off in her name? Meredith had witnessed a lot of weird stuff during her time on the streets, but this was taking it to a whole new level. And the messages below her name in the same, languid lettering, had Meredith doubting what few strands were left of her sanity.

Read More.

Urban Murmurs.

My Dearest.

CHAPTER 35

REGROUP

Sunday, 30 August 2012
10:52 a.m.

Kirkwood scoured the city centre until after midnight hunting for some sign of her, knowing in his heart there would be none. Still, he searched for he did not know what else to do. Even useless activities have their uses. The 'town' as locals referred to it, was alive and on the cusp of kicking off, as gangs of revellers assembled outside packed bars, indulging their vices.

He navigated his way through voluminous clouds of vaper's smoke, his nostrils assaulted on all sides by the saccharine aromas of vanilla and cinnamon. He emerged on the other side, faintly nauseous and yearning for the good old days when tobacco smoke was tobacco smoke, and that was that. At least you knew what you were getting when engulfed by it; a faint headache and a fair chance of secondary lung cancer twenty years down the road.

Black taxi cabs fizzed past him like angry beetles conveying tipsy fares to their favourite watering holes. Within a few hours it would be blood and vomit after the initial bonhomie soured and the pugilists emerged from their respective corners at chucking out time. Kirkwood sighed at how the tables had turned over the last forty-eight hours. He should have been in one of those bars talking utter nonsense to Gerry and Grogan, instead of plodding pitifully from one nightspot to the next, desperately seeking someone who probably wasn't called Susan.

There were a few rough sleepers about but not as many as Kirkwood would have expected. A light drizzle was starting to fall from nowhere and the streets were slick and unwelcoming. The homeless were all at home tonight or otherwise engaged. He made enquiries with the few who huddled in doorways and shop fronts, but was rewarded with a mixture of blank stares, shrugged shoulders or requests for money. Despite an avalanche of adrenaline having powered him through the alleyway and beyond, tiredness was beginning to take him. His brain dared to remind him that he had barely eaten over the last two days.

He eventually accepted defeat and hailed a taxi to take him home where, after a hastily constructed and even more hastily consumed cheese sandwich, he collapsed into bed, a beaten man. He would regroup in the morning and try to make sense of the spectacular car crash that was his life. His head barely grazed the pillow before he was sucked into blessed unconsciousness.

It was a dreamless sleep that seemed to last no more than a few seconds. The sound of a church bell calling its congregation to worship seeped beneath the surface of his slumber and brought him back to his unbelievable reality. Kirkwood yawned and pushed himself up onto an elbow. He squinted at the alarm clock which informed him it was almost eleven. Daylight valiantly struggled to penetrate the gloom of his tiny room. Rubbing the prickly stubble on his chin, he reluctantly replayed the memories of the previous day before bleakly concluding he was at a loss as to what to do. His emotions see-sawed from relief that he was not a delusional schizophrenic after all, to the burgeoning horror that Skelly could be real and not the product of his fractured psyche. Or was it a billion to one coincidence Nirvana Girl had been sketching him in her notepad? She had replicated Skelly's features in disturbing detail. But how?

He had to find her, of that much he was certain. For more than half his life, the malignant force of Skelly had loomed large over his every waking moment; an impenetrable, immovable force who barred his path from any meaningful kind of existence. Skelly was utterly devoid of pity or compassion. He existed for no other reason than to cause Kirkwood as much anguish as possible via his endless riddles and routines. Visits to the study were masterclasses in manipulation and masochism. Kirkwood had stood in front of him year after year. He had begged and screamed, wept and pleaded, it counted for nothing. Skelly never once displayed an ounce of mercy.

The vibration of his phone signifying an incoming message broke through his melancholy. He retrieved it from the bedside table. It was Gerry.

'Coffee? And by coffee, I mean tea. And a fry?'

Kirkwood considered his options which were somewhat limited to say the least. He had no family to speak of. Katie and his mother were on the other side of the world and if he recounted the events of the previous twenty-four hours to them, he was fairly certain they would have him in a secure, psychiatric unit before he could say 'would you mind loosening my straitjacket please?' He had numerous aunts, uncles and cousins but he kept in touch with none of them, only seeing them at the very occasional wedding or funeral.

His circle of friends was an equally exclusive group consisting of Gerry and Grogan, and when it came to the latter you were normally required to provide two weeks prior notice in writing to ensure his attendance. When it came to a crisis, he was worse than useless. No, Gerry was the best of a bad bunch primarily because he had an even lousier social life than Kirkwood. He sighed and began tapping out a response.

'Sure. Where and when?'

'Half past one. Scoffee,' was the almost instant reply. There was a brief pause before a further notification arrived. 'Ur buying.' Low as he was Kirkwood could not help but smile.

He tossed the phone to one side and threw the covers back, using every fibre of willpower he possessed to avoid looking at the dice which sat on the desk at the fringes of his peripheral vision. At least Skelly was keeping to his word regarding a weekend reprieve from the routines. Beside them sat the dog-eared journal he retrieved from the alley. Nirvana Girl's journal. He opened it then, but slammed it shut just as fast when he set eyes on the nightmarish visage staring back at him.

Other pages were crammed with neat, precise handwriting while others were missing, having been ripped from the spine. He checked the clock again; there was plenty of time before he was due to meet Gerry. He settled back on the bed and opened the journal at a page with yesterday's date on it.

Kirkwood began to read.

'My Dearest Emily…'

CHAPTER 36

SCOFFEE

1:27 p.m.

When Kirkwood arrived, it was standing room only in the popular coffee shop. Situated in the middle of the young professional stronghold of South Belfast, Scoffee attracted a steady stream of twenty somethings intent on soaking up the alcohol from the night before with strong coffee and greasy food. Kirkwood scanned the various booths on either side. Harassed baristas hurried from one table to the next, scribbling down orders before bellowing through a serving hatch into the kitchens where a cacophony of clanging suggested equally frenetic activity. He heard his name being hollered above the various conversations and looked to the farthest corner of the café, where Gerry gesticulated towards him from a corner booth he had commandeered, much to the chagrin of two legal types, who were impatiently waiting for a table.

'Ever the gentleman,' smirked Kirkwood as his friend lifted a coat, allowing him to slide into the booth opposite him. His friend looked perplexed until Kirkwood nodded in the direction of the two disgruntled power dressers who were muttering to each other while directing dark looks their way.

'Ach, they'll get over it,' shrugged Gerry, flicking them a cheery wave which did nothing to improve relations. He produced two menus with a flourish, thrusting one into Kirkwood's hands. 'Now, what are we having?' he enquired, considering his own menu for a full three seconds before tossing it aside. 'Who am I kidding? We'll have what we always have. Here love,' he bellowed at a passing member of staff who glared at him furiously before biting her lip and reluctantly returning to take the order.

'Hi, I'm Ashleigh. What can I get you today?' She spat the words at them, her forced smile doing little to conceal the contempt in which she held them and her millionaire Dad, who insisted she wasn't touching a penny of her trust fund until she proved to him that she could make her own way in the big, bad world.

'Two Occupied Six County Breakfasts please,' replied Gerry, beaming from ear to ear and utterly oblivious to the barrage of daggers being shot in his direction.

'What did you just say?' A mixture of horror and disbelief crossed her face as she internally processed whether she should be amused or offended by the comment. It looked as if the latter option was winning out, causing Kirkwood to intercede, for fear they would be thrown out of the café.

'We will have two Ulster fries and two pots of tea please,' he said, hoping this, combined with his most apologetic smile would defuse the situation. The waitress mulled over the proffered peace offering before nodding and jotting down the order on her pad. She afforded Gerry a final withering stare before stomping off towards the service hatch.

'So — what have you been up to since I last saw you? No doubt you've countless tales of soirées and cocktail parties to regale me with. I'm all ears.' Gerry sat back and gestured with both hands for his dining companion to open the conversation. Kirkwood swallowed hard. It was now or never. In fifteen minutes, he would either have an understanding ally or be eating brunch on his own.

'Okay, pin them back then. You might need a proper drink after you hear this one though. So, don't say I didn't warn you.'

CHAPTER 37

FOR ONE NIGHT ONLY

2:12 p.m.

By the time Kirkwood finished unburdening himself of the events of the weekend, Gerry's food sat barely touched and his mug of tea stone cold. Kirkwood eyed him anxiously. This was not a good sign. Gerry and uneaten food were a previously unknown combination. He normally hoovered up cooked breakfasts, especially after a heavy night.

'Well?' It was all Kirkwood could manage to prick the bubble of silence hanging over the booth. He pushed the remnants of a fried egg nervously about the plate as he awaited his fate.

After what seemed an eternity, Gerry stirred into life and puffed out his cheeks. 'Well,' he replied. 'You were right about me needing a drink. Tea doesn't really cut the mustard at a time like this.' The café had emptied considerably since Kirkwood started his tale. The little ray of sunshine known as Ashleigh was hovering nearby, offering not so subtle hints that they should vacate their seats, so she could clear up and finish her shift.

'You really want my honest opinion?' asked Gerry. Kirkwood was unnerved by the serious expression on his face. It was most unGerry-like and aged him considerably.

'Yes of course I do. If I wanted a yes-man, I would have spoken to Grogan who no doubt would be under the table now, laughing hysterically.' Kirkwood glumly considered this scenario before bracing himself for his best friend's verdict.

'Ok then.' Gerry dabbed a smudge of grease from the side of his mouth before speaking. 'You asked for it. I don't know which of you is the biggest eejit. This wee girl for writing those weird letters. Or...' He paused for effect. 'You for buying into all this mumbo jumbo and chasing her around Belfast. She's obviously barking mad and you're well...' He paused, and Kirkwood could see he was selecting his words carefully so as not to hurt his friend's feelings. It was almost touching. Almost.

'I'm not saying I don't believe you. You're my best mate and I'll always have your back. But you must admit you've been under a lot of pressure lately what with Natasha and your er...other problems.' He tailed off like an undercooked firework on a damp autumnal evening.

'It's called Obsessive Compulsive Disorder, Gerry. You can say it out loud you know. It's not as if you can catch it or anything. Repeat after me, O. C. D.'

'Alright, alright I apologise. I'm just trying to get my head around this. You have to admit it's a bit of a head melt.' He paused to gauge his friend's reaction. Kirkwood stared defiantly back, determined not to be the first of them to look away.

Gerry sighed and continued. 'I mean, who is this bird anyway?'

'She's a young woman. Not a canary,' corrected Kirkwood sternly.

'Bird, girl, woman, whatever. You don't know her from Adam. I mean Eve. So, you see her and her mate getting chased by some scumbags down the town and you take it upon yourself to play the knight in shining armour and save her from their vile clutches. Is that the gist of it? Please step right in if I'm missing something here.'

Kirkwood disconsolately took a mouthful of tea and stared past Gerry out the window as Sunday afternoon passed them by outside. A young couple, around his age, walked past, talking animatedly to one another. Planning their summer holiday perhaps? Or maybe there were even wedding bells on the horizon? A week ago, the sight of them would have reminded him of Natasha and sent an arrow of melancholy shooting into his heart. He realised now he hadn't thought of her since seeing Nirvana Girl last night. *Every cloud has a silver lining,* he morbidly mused. Once upon a time he had been dreaming of a fairy tale future with Natasha, but that was then, and this was a whole new now.

'And another thing,' Gerry was warming to the task and leaned over the table, wagging a finger at Kirkwood as he continued. 'Have you given any thought to the increasingly likely scenario that the peelers will cotton onto your vigilante hero routine and take exception to it? Taxi for Scott. And by taxi, I mean an armoured Land Rover, matching handcuffs and a night in the cells for your efforts. I thought I was meant to be the daft one, but you're making me look like Captain Sensible.' He took a mouthful of cold tea and screwed his face up. 'Remind me why we're not in the pub again?'

'Because for once in your miserable existence, I need you sober. This is serious. I need you to forget about your grossly distended liver for five minutes and provide me with some sound advice. Of which there is no prospect if you are your usual four sheets to the wind.'

He folded his arms and looked across the table, already regretting his decision to confide in his drinking partner. Or maybe Gerry had a point. Maybe they should retire to the nearest bar, drink themselves silly and pretend none of this ever happened. Ignorance was bliss, but inebriated ignorance was even blisser. Blissful. Kirkwood shook his head and focused again on Gerry who was wearing a pained expression on his face. He was either having an angina attack or about to dispense words of earth-shattering wisdom.

'The way I see it, this can only end badly for you. If you insist on pursuing this hare-brained scheme you will end up in a cell, a hospital bed or a cosy padded cell. None of which are going to help your already laughable career prospects. You've a degree qualification but it's not as if the head hunters are knocking down your front door. That's if you owned a front door of course, as opposed to a room in crumby rented accommodation,' he paused, as if testing the waters of their wavering friendship before deciding it was safe to continue.

'Look, neither us is going to win Young Business Person Of The Year…'

'Well you certainly won't.'

Gerry let the insult wash over him before composing himself and going on. 'We have the crappiest, most dead-end jobs in the world, but at least we have jobs. But if you continue gallivanting around the town chasing homeless hotties and their dodgy mates, then you can wave goodbye to said employment. A crappy job is better than no job at all. It pays the rent and buys the beer. Comprendez?'

Kirkwood sighed and looked around the café, which was now almost deserted. A pensioner stood at the counter paying his bill with an assortment of copper coins, much to the dismay of Ashleigh, who looked on the verge of a much-needed cry.

'I know. I know,' he conceded. 'But there's something to this. I know there is. I can't explain it, but it's important to me. She was drawing the man who I have nightmares about, the man I see in my head whenever I have the obsessive, intrusive thoughts. I'm not saying he's real but sometimes it feels as if…'

He sat back, frustrated at his lack of eloquence, only revealing the tip of the iceberg to Gerry. His friend knew nothing of his visits to the study or the extent of 'The 49'; nor the events which followed his father's death, other than the broadest of brush strokes. He doubted that Gerry, or anybody for that matter, would understand so he hesitated from opening-up any further and revealing the full madness.

'Important?' squawked Gerry, earning himself a further death stare from their charming hostess at the counter, as she shovelled up the last of the pensioner's pocket shrapnel and deposited it in the till. He looked around incredulously. 'Are we being recorded here? Is Jeremy Bloody Beadle going to jump out in a minute and tell me we're on Candid Camera?'

'Jeremy Beadle is dead. And it's You've Been Framed, not Candid Camera.'

'Well, whatever it is, you are well and truly extracting the urine now, Kirkwood. Call me an old fool, but would you care to explain your current thought processes on this one? You don't know this wee girl. She lives rough even though she's probably got a lovey-dovey middle-class family to go home to. I'm sure Mummy and Dad would welcome her with open arms if the spoilt wee cow would only swallow her pride for long enough. Yet she chooses, note the use of the word choose there, to sleep on the streets and hang out with the dregs of Belfast. Drug dealers, knife-wielding nut jobs. She's probably as high as a kite half the time. Yet you honestly believe she is the solution to your long-term mental health issues because of some grubby drawing. I mean, are you for real? I thought Grogan was the mug when it came to a pretty face and a sob story, but you really are challenging him for that title.'

His tone softened as he saw the damage his verbal punches were inflicting. Kirkwood looked crumpled, deflated. 'I'm not going to get down on bended knee to you here and profess my undying love, but you're my best mate and believe it or not, beneath this grumpy old drunken exterior, I care. I really do. But this is bad, bad, bad amigo. You need to take a step back and recognise that. Yes, the wee girl nearly got a kicking the other night and you wanted to help her. I get that. But it's not your problem. You're not Superman.'

He looked his dishevelled friend up and down. 'You're not even Banana Man if I'm entirely honest. Let's leave it to the fine men and women of our local constabulary. If it makes you feel any better, let's go to the peelers and report what happened. I'll give up my valuable drinking time to accompany you. Just leave out all the crazy nightmare stuff when you tell them alright?'

'I can't go the police. I'd be laughed out of the station.' Kirkwood started to rip his paper napkin into evenly matched strips. He knew in advance he would end up with seventeen of them. The mundane mechanics of the task began to calm him. This was going exactly as he predicted it would. Gerry thought he was a raving lunatic. But he was still his friend and had spared his feelings by not coming straight out and saying as much.

'YOU'RE A RAVING LUNATIC!'

Gerry jumped to his feet, snatching what was left of the napkin from

Kirkwood. 'Look at you. I'm offering to help, and you just sit there playing origami with tissues. I give up. I really do.' He started to leave but Kirkwood stood and barred his path. Screw diplomacy. He wasn't getting away with that.

'AND YOU'RE ABOUT AS MUCH USE AS A CHOCOLATE TEAPOT,' he roared. The pensioner, already in the process of leaving the café, upped his pace accordingly at the raised voices. Ashleigh looked like she was going to intervene but then thought better of it and beat a hasty retreat into the kitchen for reinforcements. Kirkwood and Gerry continued to spar, their noses almost touching.

'I came to you at least hoping you would hear me out, if not understand. I could be on the verge of something big here, I'm convinced of that, something a decade of medication and counselling have been unable to resolve; and all you seem to care about is getting to the pub before last orders. I might as well have confided in Grogan. At least he would have shown an interest in her. If only to find out how good-looking she was.

'Aha!' boomed Gerry, like a triumphant politician scoring a point during a parliamentary debate. 'Now we're finally getting to the crutch of the matter.' He took a step back to bask in the glory of his oratory supremacy.

'What are you on about?' Kirkwood screwed up his face as if his friend had just unleashed a particularly toxic fart. 'And it's *crux* of the matter not crutch, you idiot. C. R. U. X. CRUX! Seriously, I would have got more sense out of you if I'd waited until you were half cut. At least then I could have used alcohol as an excuse for this drivel you're coming out with.' He shook his head in resignation. This was pointless. He was wasting valuable time and it was bringing him no closer to finding Nirvana Girl. He should have gone with his gut instinct and kept it all to himself.

'You'll be leaving here on crutches if you keep this crap up,' muttered Gerry darkly. A paler than before Ashleigh, reappeared with a young man wearing a shirt and tie who looked even more scared than her at the sight of two grown men on the verge of coming to blows. He quickly assessed the situation before ducking back into the kitchens, followed by the exasperated waitress.

'This Oasis girl or whatever you're calling her. Is she good looking? I only ask because I know what terrible taste you have in women. I give you Exhibit A — Natasha Agnew.' He paused, ever the showman, before driving home his perceived advantage like a vampire hunter plunging a wooden stake through the heart of an undead foe. 'Now she was bad. Very bad. But to bounce from that lying, scheming little tart to some street urchin straight out of Oliver On Crack. Methinks that is a bridge too far, even for you.'

Kirkwood opened his mouth to respond but suddenly became aware that the nervous, young man had returned. Ashleigh was nowhere to be seen but he had summoned reinforcements from the rear of the premises in the form of two hefty looking kitchen staff, who looked in no mood to be front of house dealing with squabbling customers.

'One moment please,' said Kirkwood, flashing a smile at the young man, whose name badge indicated that he was the assistant manager, before reverting his attention back to Gerry. 'You couldn't be further off the mark if you tried.' He was trying to retain his composure and treat his friend's comments with the contempt they deserved but could feel the colour rising in his cheeks. Had Gerry struck closer to home than he cared to admit? Was there a grain of truth that he was stubbornly refusing to recognise? What if he was ill, really ill, and this fixation with the sketch merely a symptom of that malady? Was this incessant itch, this need to uncover the mystery behind the mystery girl, just a sad, lonely man attempting to fill an unseemly hole inside of him? A Natasha Agnew-sized hole?

He steeled his resolve and banished the doubts and fears to the back of his mind. Nirvana Girl and the sketch of Skelly were as real as the greasy sausages sitting abandoned on his plate. 'This street urchin you so charmingly refer to needs our help — my help.' He quickly withdrew the plural offer, seeing Gerry's arched eyebrow flaring at the suggestion. 'I know it makes no sense and I'm struggling to explain it to myself let alone you, Gerry. But this is something I need to do. And if that means going it alone, well then so be it. I promise if it gets any hairier, I'll go straight to the police, ok?'

'Gentlemen, I'm going to have to ask you to pay for your meals and leave. Now if you please.' The manager nodded to one of the kitchen heavies who moved menacingly from behind, revealing a set of biceps beneath his white T-shirt which Kirkwood had no desire becoming acquainted with. Gerry seemed to concur, pulling a crumpled twenty-pound note from his jeans and stuffing it into the manager's hand.

'Here, keep the change. It was stinking anyway.' He turned to face Kirkwood, intent on firing off a final salvo. 'I'm sorry, but you're on your own with this one. You know where I am if you come to your senses. Adios amigo.'

With that, he stalked out of the café, almost removing the front door from its hinges before disappearing out of sight up the street; no doubt heading to the nearest bar for a consolatory pint.

Kirkwood closed his eyes and counted to three before turning to the manager and mustering a weak smile. 'I apologise for my friend's behaviour. And mine as well. We just had a difference of opinion, that's all.' The manager nodded dubiously before returning to the till where he deposited the note. His heavies followed but not before giving Kirkwood a final look which informed him, he'd outstayed his welcome. Grabbing his jacket, he left the café and stood outside looking up at the sky, for no other reason than this was what actors did in the movies when they hit rock bottom. He closed his eyes.

'God, if you're up there, and I very much doubt you are — but if you are, I am in a right pickle at present.' He half opened his eyes and looked either way to be sure nobody was watching. 'A sign, a sign, my kingdom for a sign. I know that's a Shakespearean rip-off, but given my ongoing lack of inspiration, it's the best I can manage at the moment.' He stood stock-still waiting for he did not know what. *I must look a right plum*, he thought, and rotated his neck trying to work out a crick that had been there most of the morning and was now escalating into a dull ache. Tension. This was one of the many ways it materialised itself within him. He rotated again and was rewarded with a satisfying crack.

He groaned with relief and kept his face raised and eyes closed as a light breeze picked up and caressed his forehead. He sensed he had reached a crossroads. He could turn and go back to the drab life he knew, forget about the girl and tell Gerry he had been right all along. Perhaps a change of medication or another stab at counselling might finally allow him to banish Skelly for good, or at least loosen the grip he currently had on him. All he had to do was accept this was as good as it was going to get and come to terms with that.

But there was Nirvana Girl and what he had read in her journal earlier today. It was decision time for Kirkwood Carson Scott.

If he was ever going to amount to a hill of beans in the real world, he was going to have to confront and overcome the increasingly unreal aspects of his life which bombarded him from all sides. And no matter how bleak the horizon looked, at least there still was a horizon for him to march towards. A horizon from where the tiniest chink of light was protruding, dimly illuminating the path ahead. Skelly could be real and, although that was a terrifying revelation, it was nothing compared to the seventeen years of guilt and shame he had waded through, battling the thoughts and concealing the corresponding compulsions like a dirty rag.

He opened his eyes just as a sudden gust of wind from out of nowhere lifted a piece of paper from the pavement and hurled it against the side of his face with a resounding slap. He flinched before peeling it from his cheek and inspecting it. In his hand was a flyer, the type that were regularly handed out to promote cafés, restaurants and other businesses. He held it out and read its contents.

Teen Spirit

Nirvana Tribute Band

For One Night Only

Ulster Hall, Belfast

Limited Tickets Available on Night at Theatre Door

Kirkwood looked at the date of the gig. It was tonight. Call it a hunch. Call it divine inspiration. Call it a million to one shot in the dark. But suddenly Kirkwood knew, beyond all doubt, where he would find her.

CHAPTER 38

LET THEM COME

Kirkwood had no idea he was being watched as he walked purposefully away from Scoffee, clutching the flyer. When he was out of sight, an elderly figure emerged from beneath the shadows of a sprawling birch tree across the street. The old man chuckled at his unnecessary act of stealth for he could just as easily have made himself invisible. Old habits die hard, however, and part of him still relished the subterfuge and intrigue of the trade. He had made a career out of it many lifetimes ago when crowns and dynasties hinged upon such subtle machinations. How times had changed, he reflected, for now the stakes were infinitely higher. Whereas before it had been kingdoms and empires he gambled upon, now the future of an entire planet hung in the balance.

Had Cornelius Dobson spoken any of this aloud he would undoubtedly have been hauled off to the nearest asylum. He looked nothing like a shaper of worlds, instead he resembled a man who had come off second best in his dealings with the universe to date. He cut a sorry sight as he limped across the street to where Kirkwood had been standing. As he did so, he lifted an index finger a fraction and from nowhere a gust of wind swept down the street, lifting several sheets of paper from the ground. He opened a hand and they drifted effortlessly into his open palm, as if they were connected by unseen wires. He looked down at the flyers advertising wailing electrical instruments and out of tune squealing as actual entertainment. Dobson shook his head and marvelled that people actually paid good money to listen to such an ungodly din. The youth of today would forever baffle him.

The flyers served their purpose, though, for it was finally time for the two known to their kind as Kirkwood Scott and Meredith Starc, to meet. His attention to detail was second to none, but recent events had rocked the apple cart. The situation was coming to a head much sooner than he would have anticipated, meaning he was left with little option but to act now and act swiftly. It was a risk throwing them together in less than ideal circumstances and it went against his better instincts. They were inexperienced, soaking wet behind the ears and horribly out of their depth. But they were the sole option, the only recourse available to him. If he didn't grasp the nettle now, what little chance they had would vanish, and all would be lost. He was gambling it all on two unknown and untested quantities but could protect them no longer.

Yes, now was the time. An old foe was marshalling his forces and firing the opening shots in a battle that would rage across this plane like no battle had ever raged before. They had crossed swords many times and this was but the latest chapter in the conflict. He prided himself on always being one step ahead of the enemy but was acutely aware one slip on his part would mean ruin for billions of innocent and not so innocent souls. One mistake and fire would reign down from the skies, the like of which had never been seen before.

He was a born winner and had been for longer than he cared to remember; it was one of the healthier habits acquired during centuries of existence. This one would unquestionably go down to the wire, but a win was a win, be it by a country mile or the shortest of short heads. Let them come for he was ready, or as ready as he ever would be. The old man stretched and rubbed his eyes. He was getting too old for this line of work and was grateful there were others who would stand with him when all hell broke loose in the days ahead. His job between now and then was to prepare them as best he could for what promised to be the fight of their young lives.

CHAPTER 39

HERE WE ARE

7:59 p.m.

The queue outside the Ulster Hall snaked along one side of the building and around the corner for an impressive distance, indicating the gig was a sell-out. It contained all walks of life united by their love of a band that disintegrated before many of them were even born. Teenagers shrouded in black and glistening with piercings mingled with middle-aged metallers whose guts threatened to burst from faded tour T-shirts. Kirkwood walked the length of the queue but there was no sign of her. He swore quietly under his breath. He had been so sure, so certain he would find her here. Bodies began to shuffle forward slowly, indicating the doors of the venue were opening. He looked at his watch. The gig was due to start in an hour, maybe this had been a wild goose chase after all. Why had he been so stupid to think fourteen years of misery could be swept away by a chance encounter with a scruffy, malnourished wino on a street corner?

Suddenly, the tail of the queue inched forward to reveal her, buried inside a heavily-stained sleeping bag. Kirkwood tried not to think about where the stains originated from. A polystyrene cup in her outstretched hand was attracting the coins of a few gig goers, appalled by the sorry sight of the young woman. The majority, however, walked past nonplussed by the bundle of rags a few feet from them. The homeless did not register on their radars for to do so, only played upon guilty consciences, bursting cosy bubbles of domesticity.

She looked utterly lost, resembling a wraith more than a human being. She was paler than he remembered, if that was possible, and her pale-blue eyes stared straight ahead, devoid of any lustre. He considered turning and walking away but the reassuring touch of her journal inside his leather jacket strengthened a wavering resolve. He had read it from cover to cover before meeting Gerry at Scoffee, and although several pages were ripped out, the remaining words and sketches spoke volumes of the foul creature who stalked her dreams. She had described to a T, an imaginary man who lived in his head, a man he had never spoken of to another living being for fear they would think him stark-raving mad. He had to talk to her, discover the connection, dig for the truth even if it meant getting his hands dirty. It was a small price to pay.

Kirkwood took a step towards Nirvana Girl but was forced to involuntarily recoil, his nostrils overwhelmed by the sharp, unmistakable odour of urine emanating from the wall she was propped against. Lord, that's gross. Had she wet herself? Or had somebody in the line been caught short while waiting for the doors to open and relieved themselves against the old building? He looked in either direction, but the street was now empty. It was just him and her. Words suddenly failed Kirkwood, words he had been composing in his head since leaving the coffee shop. All that remained was a faltering, flaccid cliché of an opening line, which caused him to flinch with embarrassment the second it left his lips.

'Are you alright? Is there anything I can get you?'

Seconds ticked by. One...two...three. No response. She stared through him as if he was invisible. Kirkwood tried again, louder this time, and preceded with a theatrical cough.

'Hi, it's me. From last night. You knocked me over, you know, in the alley.'

This time his words registered, and she blinked before looking up at him, awakening from a dream and struggling to take in her surroundings. Kirkwood realised he was holding his breath and exhaled loudly, resulting in a flurry of activity from her, as if she had emerged from beneath water and was now gasping for air. He jumped back in alarm as the bottom half of the sleeping bag kicked out at him like a crazed caterpillar.

'Woah. Steady. I'm not going to hurt you. What do you take me for? Some sort of...'

'I've no money! I owe you nothing! Get away from me or I'll scream!'

Her eyes were suddenly ablaze and flitted everywhere, weighing up potential escape options. Now fully free from the confines of the sleeping bag she sat on her haunches like a feral animal deciding whether to fight or flee. Cascades of unkempt black hair flowed chaotically from beneath a hood which framed the palest of faces, a paleness which accentuated her other features. Her nostrils flared beneath a slim nose, its bridge sprinkled with a dozen or so freckles. A nose ring suggested a rebellious streak at some point in her past.

She was decked out in cheap nylon tracksuit bottoms and the same shapeless Nirvana hooded top as before. And a camouflage green parka with a huge fur-rimmed hood, giving her the look of an Arctic explorer who somehow got lost en route to the North Pole. Dirty trainers which were once white but now a grimy grey, and a pair of black, fingerless gloves completed the ensemble. It was unmistakably her. Now all he had to do was stall her long enough from bolting or getting him arrested, whichever came first. Think, Kirkwood, think.

'Calm down.' He attempted his most reasonable, soothing tone, extending his hands in what he hoped was a convincing impersonation of a law-abiding member of the community. 'I don't know what you're thinking but I am nothing to do with those two gorillas who chased you last night.' He looked over his shoulder and smiled at a passing couple who eyed him suspiciously before hurrying on past.

The girl rose cautiously, picking up the battered Adidas bag, while never taking her eyes off Kirkwood. She narrowed them, struggling to grasp an elusive memory which hovered just beyond reach. A gradual spark of recognition began to form on her features and replace the previous haunted animal expression.

'What do you want?' she asked slowly, clutching the bag tightly to her chest as if it held all her earthly possessions. Which it probably did. Bar one. She had long fingers and fingernails caked with dirt. 'I haven't done anything. Why are you following me?'

'I just wanted to make sure you were okay. After last night.' She blinked twice in quick succession and suddenly became aware of the rank aroma emanating from around her.

'That wasn't me, in case you're wondering,' she mumbled in embarrassment. 'I was sleeping earlier, and some manky stray must have cocked its leg up against me.' She took in Kirkwood's perplexed expression before hurriedly adding, 'I can tell the difference. Human, dogs, cats. It comes with experience. I even got sprayed by a fox once...' Her voice trailed off and an uneasy silence ensued, an oasis of awkwardness until a taxi pulled up alongside them, depositing more music lovers outside the venue.

'How's your friend?' enquired Kirkwood, feeling his way into the conversation, focusing every ounce of concentration on the smelly, dishevelled mess in front of him.

'Friend?' She looked at him quizzically until somewhere within, the penny dropped. 'Oh him.' She began to roll up the sleeping bag, fussing over it like a house-proud parishioner who had just received an unexpected visit from the local clergy. 'Yeah, he's been better. I wouldn't call him a friend exactly. We just hang out now and again. Look out for each other. Or at least try to...'

Her words trailed off and she peered at Kirkwood expectantly, the ball was in his court again. A cloud of anxiety was weighing down on his chest, as he desperately scrambled for the words to convey the message he'd been rehearsing since reading her journal. The more he went over it, the crazier it sounded and now, with a captive audience before him, he froze, unable to utter a sound. She watched him intently, head cocked to one side before a fit of coughing doubled her over.

Kirkwood edged ever closer and considered placing a reassuring hand on her forearm before thinking better of it. Her clothing looked as if all manner of tiny life forms lived within, and he was still far from convinced she wouldn't scream like a banshee if he so much as laid a finger on her. He had no desire to attract the attention of every police patrol within a three-mile radius at such a crucial moment in their fledgling relationship.

'Please,' he said as the coughing subsided, and she straightened to meet his eyes again. 'Can I get you a drink or something to eat? No strings attached. I'm Kirkwood.' He tentatively held out a hand, unsure as to what the accepted social norm was in such situations. He guessed there weren't any.

She stared suspiciously at his outstretched hand before a look of conviction crossed her face and the decision was made. She cupped her own grimy hand in his and weakly shook it.

'Buy me a burger and you can string me up like Pinocchio. Oh, and I'm Meredith.' She finished gathering up her meagre belongings and, for the first time, offered Kirkwood a sideways glance accompanied by a timid smile, which fanned a faint flicker of hope within him. He detected a delicate thread of trust between them and pledged to hang on to it for all he was worth. There was no other choice really.

Kirkwood chose the Burger King at the top of Royal Avenue for no other reason than it was the nearest fast food joint to the Ulster Hall and the shorter their walk, the less chance of Meredith changing her mind. He preferred Meredith to 'Nirvana Girl'. She looked like a Meredith. He attempted to engage in small talk, but she seemed more preoccupied with the prospect of a hot meal than his sparkling repartee. They sat upstairs, and he watched with a mixture of amusement and astonishment as she devoured a Double Whopper meal, except for the slice of mayo-coated tomato, which was offered to him because 'tomatoes are stinking.' Having demolished the food, she sat back and took a noisy, contented slurp through the straw of a large Coke.

'Pardon my table manners,' she apologised, suddenly aware that she was under scrutiny. 'They're not what they used to be. I don't eat at many posh restaurants these days,' she shrugged and stared pensively at the table as if concerned she had overstepped the mark.

'The other night. What was that all about? Who were those guys chasing you?' She paused before answering, as if mentally weighing up the pros and cons of whatever response she was formulating. Her mind made up, she fixed Kirkwood with a resolute stare. 'Let's just say it was a business transaction that went slightly awry.'

Kirkwood took a sip from his Diet Coke. She was a curious creature that was for sure. Beneath the grimy veneer and questionable personal hygiene there probably lurked an attractive young woman. He estimated she couldn't have been much older than eighteen? Nineteen? There was something else, though. While she spoke with an unmistakable Northern Irish accent, she was surprisingly eloquent, her language quaint even, which suggested an education other than the one she was currently acquiring on the streets.

'Drugs you mean?' Kirkwood tried not to come across as a disapproving older brother but knew he was failing miserably.

'What can I say? It's a jungle out there. But I don't touch them, okay? It was Danny, the other guy I was with.' She fixed him with another death stare before muttering something beyond his hearing and returning her attention to the Coke in front of her. An uneasy ceasefire descended, each of them reluctant to pop their head above their respective trench for fear it would be blown off by the other one.

It was Kirkwood who spoke first, weighing his words with care. 'How long have you been living rough?'

Meredith clutched at the proffered olive leaf. 'On and off, about ten months. Mostly on.' She paused but then frowned when it became apparent that Kirkwood had no intention of speaking again until more information was forthcoming. 'Jeez, you should be a peeler,' she sulked, before swiftly looking up and adding, 'You're not a peeler, are you?' She reached down and fumbled for her bag, ready to flee in an instant dependent on his answer.

'Do I look like I'm in the police, you numpty? I've heard of community policing, but I didn't know it extended to free burgers and fries.'

She relaxed slightly and released her grip on the bag. 'Sorry,' she mumbled like a chastised child before sniggering to herself. 'Numpty...' Meredith's voice trailed off and her brow furrowed, rebuking herself for the momentary loss of composure.

Softly, softly, catchy monkey. Kirkwood fought to dispel the image of Skelly from his mind's eye. He could sense him prowling at the edges, smell him, taste him; his rotten, tobacco-stained teeth; the sly, bloodshot eyes; the smell of expensive brandy and musky aftershave barely masking the sweet, rancid stench beneath. Was that what death smelled like? And, if so, was the scruffy girl before him his lifeline? An escape from the endless procession of dark, jagged thoughts which looped around his skull like a deranged motorcyclist on a wall of death. Endless, death-defying circuits until Kirkwood sank to his knees begging for it to end. To defy death no longer, but instead fall into its silent embrace. A place of quiet. A place of nothing.

'Are you alright?' Meredith interrupted his thoughts, bringing him back to the confines of the fast food restaurant.

'Er, yeah. Sorry. I was just…just…'

'Well if you're that bored, then maybe I should go.' She stood to leave, her expression betraying the hurt at his perceived indifference. Kirkwood hated when he drifted like this. Often the routines necessitated him diverting every ounce of attention to the task at hand. This often came across as arrogance when it was exactly the opposite. He zoned out because he had to. Skelly's will was all-consuming, a crazed beast that could only be satiated by unwavering obedience. The routines…always the routines.

'No, please don't. I'm interested really, and I want to help. It's complicated that's all. There's all sorts of stuff going on in my head.' He jabbed a finger towards his forehead for emphasis. 'It's hard to explain.' A stalagmite of icy panic caressed his spine. If she walked now, then it was game over. He might never find her again. But Skelly would find *him*. He always did.

She paused and fixed him a stern gaze before erupting into laughter and sitting down again. 'You're a bit mental, aren't you? I like that. You'd fit in well where I come from.' She sat back and began to absentmindedly tug her earlobe.

'And where is that exactly?' Kirkwood mouthed a silent prayer of thanks; grateful she had decided to remain.

'Well, buy me a coffee and maybe I'll tell you,' she smiled again, and for the first time in what seemed like forever, Kirkwood smiled back. A genuine smile. He reached for the comforting touch of her journal which sat nestled within the confines of his jacket. He was getting close. Very close.

CHAPTER 40

POSH GIRL

8:38 p.m.

'The worst part is the tiredness. I'm tired all the time,' Meredith shook her head sadly before continuing, a filtered coffee sitting untouched in front of her. 'Although, I'm not looking forward to the colder nights. It's not too bad at the minute but when the winter kicks in…' she paused and shrugged her shoulders, the magnitude of what lay ahead seemingly too much for her to express in any coherent format. 'I dunno,' she concluded tamely, looking upwards as if searching for something other than a white flag of surrender.

'Have you nowhere? There must be someone. A relative? A friend?' Kirkwood leaned forward, his voice little more than a whisper. He tended to do that when involved in a solemn conversation.

'Yeah, there are people. But they're not the right people. I'm better off where I am now. My parents don't want to know. There's nothing else to say.'

'It can't be that bad surely. All I am saying is don't cut off all your…'

'Ties?' she finished the sentence, catching Kirkwood off guard. 'Believe me, the *Good Ship Meredith* has well and truly sailed on her maiden and final voyage. The *Titanic* had better luck than me.'

'But surely…'

'But surely nothing. I live rough. Through choice. End of.' Her tone was sharper than she intended and the startled look on Kirkwood's face reined her in immediately.

'I'm sorry. That came out wrong. I'm a total bitch. I'm grateful, truly I am. But I'm alright seriously. Those guys chasing us. They weren't after me. Cliché of the year I know, but I was literally in the wrong place at the wrong time. Danny owes them money. He bought some pills and didn't settle the debt. That was no more than a gentle reminder. They weren't going to kill him. He's a customer and dead customers aren't exactly good for business. It was just a warning, a lesson for him and anyone else considering pulling the same stunt. He won't do it again. When he gets out of hospital that is.'

'But what if they had caught you as well? Those thugs meant business; I was there. I saw it.'

'I'm fine, honestly. That was just in the heat of the moment. I don't do that crap. I just stick to the Buckie. Well, mostly. Buckfast and chocolate. I'm a regular girly princess.' She fluttered her eyelashes theatrically before wiping a rivulet of mucus from a nostril with the sleeve of her hooded top.

Kirkwood pretended not to notice. 'You're living rough. Necking bottles of that muck at nine in the morning. And getting chased around the town by psychotic drug dealers. Is that your definition of fine? Seriously?' He took a sip of his Diet Coke. 'It's certainly not mine.'

'What's it to you anyway? You're not the first superhero to turn up offering to save me. I've had all sorts of offers. Some right dirty old buggers as well. Don't get me wrong, you seem alright. But I don't need your help. I don't need anybody's help.' She pushed away her coffee as if to emphasise this line in the sand and glared at Kirkwood, daring him to continue.

He could feel her drawbridges being raised. It was time to apply the brakes. If he pressed too hard, he would lose her altogether. If that happened it would be an uphill battle clawing her back.

'I just didn't like what I saw that's all. You looked scared. Flip, I was terrified myself. I just wanted to make sure you were alright that's all. I'm not some slimy sugar daddy if that's what you're thinking,' he looked away, hoping this new tactic would reap dividends.

'I don't get you.' Meredith folded her arms and continued to fix him with a withering stare that Kirkwood declined to meet. 'One minute you're coming across like my guardian angel, the next you're staring off into the wide blue yonder, playing the wounded little boy routine. It's feast or famine with you.'

'I'm sorry. I'm sorry.' He looked back and hid the smile of satisfaction threatening to settle on his features. He was back in the game. She was still on the hook. 'I have a lot on my mind, that's all. But I promise you shall have my full and undivided attention from this juncture onwards.'

'Juncture,' she snorted derisively. 'You talk like something out of one of those Dickens novels we studied for GCSE. All you're missing are the crazy sideburns and top hat.'

He laughed, glad the ice which had been forming over their conversation was thawing. 'You don't want to see my attempts at facial hair. I tried to grow a beard once, it was not a pretty sight.' He finally met her eyes. 'But I'm listening now. 110 per cent.'

'Pah. I hate that saying. 110 per cent. How can anyone give 110 per cent? It's mathematically impossible. It flies in the face of every known law of physics. – Stephen Hawking would be horrified if he heard such nonsense.'

Kirkwood considered her words. 'Imagine when he dies, he found out there was a heaven after all and ended up outside the Pearly Gates with Saint Peter. Now that would be an awkward conversation.' It was Meredith's turn to laugh and Kirkwood clenched his fist triumphantly beneath the table. Another score. He was slowly wearing her down.

'Dickens, Hawking. Who would have thought such a scruff bag could be so well read?' He was taking a chance with the cheeky jibe but sensed they had reached the point in the dialogue where it was all or nothing. He held his breath and studied her face to gauge how she would react.

'I'm glad to hear my grammar-school education wasn't a complete waste of money,' she shot back instantly, before realising the error. She bit her lip, hoping against hope he would not pick up on it, but it was too late. Kirkwood gleefully seized upon the unsolicited nugget of information.

'And where was that pray tell? If you don't spill the beans, then that…' he pointed at her cup, 'Is the last coffee you will get out of me. And I can 110 per cent guarantee that.' He hoped the quip would come across as quirky as opposed to condescending and toe-curlingly cringey.

'Ashgrove College. You heard of it?'

'Have I heard of it?' Kirkwood almost gagged. 'It's only the most exclusive girl's school in the country, posh girl.' He had passed it one morning and the cavalcade of Mercedes and Jaguars depositing their darling offspring at its gates highlighted the extravagant wealth which bankrolled the establishment. Ashgrove girls were the crème de la crème of Northern Irish society. Dad's little rich girls with their designer school bags and three foreign holidays a year. The school roll call was like a who's who of the country's elite, and an education there almost guaranteed a place at a top university. Ashgrove regularly topped the academic performance lists and their hockey team had been crowned All-Ireland hockey champions three of the last four years. If you wanted to get ahead you sent your daughter to Ashgrove.

'Posh girl, huh?' grunted Meredith, clearly unimpressed. 'Thank you for the wafer-thin stereotype but I'd like to think there's a little more to me than that. Believe it or not, I worked hard when I was there. Ten GCSEs with seven 'A' grades. Hated the place though. Load of stuck up bitches. Mean girls, one and all. Well, most of them were.'

She tailed off and stared forlornly into the murky depths of her coffee, suddenly looking very small beneath the baggy apparel. Small and fragile. She shrugged again. Kirkwood noticed she did that a lot. As if she was baffled as to how her current circumstances had come about. She looked beaten, broken, and all out of ideas.

'Why are you here Meredith? Tell me please. I'm not some creepy pervert. I want to help. Don't ask me why, but it's as if I need to. Please.' Kirkwood groped for the words like you would grope blindly for a towel in the shower with an eyeful of shampoo. Something, anything to keep her a little longer. In his heart though he knew it was too late. She was reaching down to retrieve her bag before the final words left his mouth.

'Look, I have to go,' she mumbled, jumping to her feet and swinging the bag over her shoulder, narrowly missing his head in the process. 'It's probably best we don't do this again.' She avoided eye contact and walked away but halted after a few steps and turned back to where he sat frozen at the table, powerless to halt her departure. 'Thank you for the coffee. And everything else. Thank you. You seem like a really nice guy. Too nice for the likes of me.'

She turned and headed towards the stairs. Before he knew it, he had blurted the words out.

'You dropped this in the alley last night.'

Meredith stopped and swivelled to face him, mouth ajar. In his hand was the journal, her most treasured possession. He lobbed it towards her, and she caught it, still gobsmacked at his revelation. Initial relief was quickly erased by his next incomprehensible statement.

'The man you drew. The man from your dreams. I know who he is. I think he's real.'

It was as if a dam burst within her, there was only so much crazy she could take, and that was the straw that broke the camel's back. He looked so sincere, so genuine, but these had to be the words of a madman. The room began to spin, and she couldn't breathe, she had to get outside.

'I have to go.'

'No, please!' he pleaded.

'Don't come after me.' She stuffed the journal into her bag and took the stairs two at the time, tears streaming down her face.

Kirkwood put his head in his hands. It was over.

CHAPTER 41

MY DEAREST ENEMY

My Dearest Emily.

Or should that be My Dearest Enemy?

Whoever, whatever you've become, what we have become. Is this what it all boils down to, is this how it must be?

The graffiti, the letters were my focus, my raison d'être. I thought it was you reaching out to me and I clutched your cold, dead hand with what little strength I had left. And you know what? For a while it worked. For a while it gave me what I needed. My days had purpose again, I had a reason to be here and not with you. Because for months after you died that was all I desired. To be with you. I had no idea what that reason was, I still don't really know, but you were there, just over the horizon. My own little yellow brick road. I allowed you to lead me. I trusted you.

That's just another silly kid's story though, isn't it? Another myth, another fabricated fairy tale, another pathetic dream I blindly chased. Desperate people do desperate things, Emily. You taught me that, if nothing else. And I was so desperate for you, for what we had. I needed it again, I needed you. My soul wailed for you, an itch I scratched until my skin bled and my fingernails cracked.

Don't let me go under, Emily. Where. The. Fuck. Are. You? I'm sorry. I know how much you despised the F-bomb. You always said we were better than that. We had thousands of words with which to express ourselves, so why settle for that one? Why choose vanilla when there are so many other delightful and enticing flavours to savour, to caress and allow to melt on our tongues?

Why are you doing this to me, Emily? It's been six days now. Six days! If this is how it's going to be then why couldn't you have stayed away and let me be? But no. Breaking my heart once wasn't enough for you, was it? You had to come back and crush me all over again. The second time is always easier isn't it? The fault lines remain, no matter how skilfully a broken object is glued back together. It can never be as strong as before. Gullies remain, fissures and fractures lying dormant. The weaknesses, though imperceptible to the human eye, are still there just waiting to be exposed once again. To crack and splinter, my very own personal San Andreas Fault. My heart exploding into a million shattered slivers for your enjoyment and entertainment.

I've been to your alley ten times today but there are no messages, nothing. Just you, gazing down imperiously with that mysterious smirk you perfected to an art form. I need to hear from you because, otherwise, our connection is gone and there is no point me carrying on with this morbid treasure hunt from beyond the grave you've concocted for us. Why should I keep existing? If you call what I'm doing at the minute, existing. For it's certainly not living. Yes, I breathe, I eat when I can be bothered, I drink myself stupid, and shuffle around this godforsaken hole of a city; yet inside I am dead to it all. This is nothing but a walking death, without even the satisfaction of an occasional serving of brains for breakfast. Not that it wouldn't be a welcome distraction from my current routine — get up, stash my gear, and scrape together a few pounds to invest in cheap drink at the first available opportunity. Then spend the rest of the day trying to avoid getting mugged/robbed/raped or freeze to death when the colder nights kick in.

I had another dream, Emily. Worse than the other ones, much worse. It's the same guy chasing us. Except now I'm standing before him, in some sort of creepy mansion. Seriously, it's like something out of a *Scooby Doo* cartoon. He's sitting there in a hideous old-fashioned armchair. Just leering at me like the dirtiest old man in the universe. Never speaks. Always the same. Staring. Smirking. Sipping his drink. Licking his lips. Beyond gross. Rotten teeth like the dripping fangs of a cobra. And those eyes. As dead as the night itself, utterly without emotion. I scream, and I try to turn and run but I can't move, it's as if I'm glued to the spot. I can't escape him, I'm drowning, choking, sinking.

It's gotten worse, though.

I lost the journal. It's a long story for another letter, suffice to say I couldn't find it anywhere. Until some guy turned up tonight. He bought me a coffee. There was something about him, the way he carried himself. It was as if he understood, I looked in his eyes and I saw such sadness. A sadness I thought we only knew. He was different from the other slime balls who try to chat me up on the street. So, I opened up and started talking about Ashgrove.

I said too much, it freaked me out a bit. Next thing he's waving the journal at me, saying he knows who the guy in the dreams is; saying he's real. I've seen and heard a lot of crazy stuff these last few months, but this took the biscuit. I panicked, I bolted. What else was I supposed to do? It was nuts. I don't know what to think anymore. No wonder I drink so much! Wasted is a preferable state of mind to sober, if this is what I'm going to have to face every day.

I'll 'post' this in the morning. Usual place. Please, please, please reply. I need you more than I've ever needed you before.

Dead or alive.

Meredith x.

CHAPTER 42

BIGGER FISH TO FRY

Monday, 1 September 2012
9:06 a.m.

Meredith flitted through the early morning haze like a ghost. She was not of this world, immersed in a veil of shame and pain which separated her from the mundanities of modern living. She donned it every morning and wore it throughout the day like a red badge of dishonour. It separated her from the living and stymied any desire she might have had to return to their dreary ways; to be with them, to trudge through the monotonous motions required of a functioning human being.

On the streets the veil was akin to a suit of armour. It was as if people could sense her desolation and afforded her the isolation and anonymity she craved. She wanted nothing of their world. She belonged with the dead, yet the letters held her back from taking that final leap into the unknown. She survived, she existed, she waited, but little else. Inside she was a corpse, walking the streets with the other lost souls, discarded like empty sweet-wrappers by an uncaring world.

She walked quickly and with purpose along Royal Avenue which was stretching its limbs and gearing up for another week. Translink buses trundled along, flashes of gaudy pink, advertising the latest movie releases. Walnut-skinned newspaper vendors pushed their creaking carts past, laden down with morning editions of the *Belfast Telegraph*. It had been a dry and relatively mild night yet her back ached and scalp itched. Sleep had largely evaded her, and she was in desperate need of a shower. Breakfast was a cheap bottle of cider stashed away in case of emergency. The revelations at Burger King met the necessary criteria required to crack it open. It tasted foul but would stave off the hunger pangs long enough for what she had to do.

Not for the first time that morning, she thought of Kirkwood. He seemed alright and no doubt meant well, but she had encountered his type many times before. Do-gooders who thought they could dip their well-intentioned toes into the murky waters where she floundered; throwing a handful of coins here and a few kind, but meaningless, words, there. A sticking plaster on the gaping, festering wound of her life. By nightfall they were gone, the money had been frittered away, and their words were nothing more than empty whispers in the darkness. They went back to their safe, comfortable lives and she huddled in a shopfront. Nothing changed that.

She had served him up with an appetiser of her past, but it was a lukewarm dish as opposed to the scalding truth, a truth that was too hot for even her to stomach at times. She was reluctant to spill her guts to a stranger, even though part of her craved human fellowship like an addict craves their next fix. Since Emily's death, she had shut down emotionally and entered a self-enforced season of solitude. She was as wary as ever, but Kirkwood or Scott or whatever his name was, appeared decent and genuine. She surprised herself by how much she had divulged but pulled back and fled in the end. The thought of companionship again, a friend, terrified her no matter how much she needed it.

And then there was the journal; the man in the armchair and Kirkwood's insane assertion that he knew who he was. Too much for her to take in, to process, to accept. Easier to deny, to reject, to run away.

Meredith jogged across the street towards Castle Court shopping centre. It had not long ago been the crown jewel of Belfast's shopping experience, but in recent years the sparkling Victoria Square complex had wrestled away that honour. Entering its cavernous expanse, Meredith instinctively lowered her head and pulled the hood of her parka snugly over her head. Now was not the time to be recognised by the eagle-eyed security staff who always took a close interest in the comings and goings of the rough sleepers who hung around the centre. It acted as a warm haven in the winter and had saved her from a soaking many times when the heavens opened and tipped their watery contents onto the city streets.

Shops on either side of the central concourse were preparing to open for business as staff ducked beneath half-opened shutters. Office workers queued for coffee or smoothies at the various vendors who opened early in order to catch their custom. Meredith avoided eye contact with them all. A few weeks ago, there had been an awkward incident when one of her father's work colleagues waved and shouted at her, unaware that his friend's daughter had fled the nest. She pretended not to recognise him but when he continued to holler across the concourse, causing much unwelcome attention, she cracked and sprinted outside where she was sick against a wall, breathless and shaking.

Thankfully there were no such scares this time and the journey through the concourse passed uneventfully. A minute later and she was out its rear doors and on Grantham Street, a ramshackle collection of rundown shopfronts containing a diverse range of businesses. You name it, you could buy it on Grantham Street — from snakes and iguanas to World War Two memorabilia; in addition to the grubbiest collection of adult book and video stores in the city. Meredith hurried down the street unfazed by her surroundings. A year ago, she might have blushed or giggled at some of the X-rated products on sale, but now she took it all in her stride. Ten months sleeping rough had toughened her beyond recognition. And besides, there were bigger fish to fry this morning.

CHAPTER 43

MEET CORNELIUS DOBSON

She suppressed a smirk as a smartly-dressed man struggled to open his sleek sports car while juggling a bundle of magazines nestled beneath his collection of chins. Meredith stole a peek at the one protruding from the top of the pile. *Teenage Asian Babes*.

'Dirty old bugger,' she muttered, loud enough for him to hear, as she breezed past. The next sight to greet her turned the smirk into a broad smile, although at first glance, one might have wondered why. The shapeless form occupying an adjacent doorway beneath a filthy collection of blankets was doing little to improve the downtrodden ambience of the area.

'Morning, Mr Dobson.' Meredith knelt beside the mass of unkempt grey curls poking out from under the blankets. The face beneath them was a kaleidoscope of leathery skin and wrinkles. She gently shook his shoulder and a pair of bright blue eyes opened; all the more startling given the ancient face they called home. The bags beneath them could have housed the kit of a touring rugby team and the accompanying odour stripped the paint off a wall at thirty paces. Recognition slowly registered on the face and Meredith's persistence was rewarded with a sleepy smile.

'Good morning, my dear. How are you this fine day?' Her old friend, Cornelius Dobson, had somehow survived another night on the streets.

Dobson could have been aged anywhere between fifty and one hundred and seven, nobody quite knew, and he provided different answers every time he was asked. He had been a standing, much-loved feature of Belfast street life for as long as anyone could remember; even the nastier types who normally would have robbed their own granny blind, left him alone. It was an unwritten rule and any violations were swiftly and brutally dealt with in-house by the street community. Dobson was both a protected species and a medical miracle, given the copious amounts of vodka he consumed. Meredith was convinced his internal organs were pickled and his bloodstream contained more alcohol than blood. No wonder he had survived numerous harsh winters on the streets of the city. The man was a walking radiator.

He seemed to exist in a permanent state of intoxication, blissfully unaware of the passing world, yet still with the nous to cling to a ten-glass bottle as if his life depended upon it. Which it probably did. Dobson and sobriety were unacquainted, having last spoken around 1987, when they decided it better that they go their separate ways. He was a crumbling cliff, a bag of skin and bones surgically attached to a bottle of whatever spirit was on special offer that morning. Beneath the mumbling incoherence and eye-watering body odour was a heart of gold, however, that Meredith had rarely encountered. Three months ago, he thrust a crumpled five-pound note into her hand and, despite her lengthy protests, insisted she take it. She suspected it was all he had.

'Take it,' he had rasped, his throat the ravaged legacy of a lifetime of cheap cigarettes and cheaper liquor. 'You need it more than me. Besides, I'm a man of few needs.' It was all he managed before a rattling cough took hold, forcing him to bury his face in a phlegm-stained handkerchief which he produced from the depths of his duffel coat. Meredith initially shuddered at the sight, but her heart melted when Dobson returned it to his pocket. There were flecks of dark, thick blood on it. He was obviously not a well man, which was all the more reason she made an effort to be pleasant whenever their paths crossed.

'I'm good, Mr Dobson. How are you keeping?' It was a rhetorical question as the old man was a mess, but she asked anyway.

'Oh, I'm tickety-boo. I have my bottle. I have my cigarettes, and all is well with the world. My knighthood is yet to arrive but it's only a matter of time, I imagine. And where are you off to this morning?'

Meredith smiled at the old man's humour. He always cheered her up no matter how bleak the circumstances. He was a true gentleman. An incredibly smelly, scruffy one, but a gentleman, nonetheless.

'I'm just calling into the bookshop. See if I can pick something up to keep me company this evening.' Dobson nodded in approval.

'Ah, how it warms my heart to see a young person delving into the world of literature. So very pleasing. In my day it was all we had. None of this Play Box or X Station nonsense.' She stifled a giggle.

'Yes, you can't beat a good paperback. Besides...' She leaned in closer and whispered in his wax-caked ear. 'The internet connection isn't up to much in my current penthouse.'

'Ha! Splendid. Well, enjoy my child, and drink deeply of the written word.' He unscrewed the cap of a vodka bottle produced from the depths of the blankets, took a generous swig and emitted a resounding belch, before picking at his left ear and inspecting what he'd excavated onto a filthy fingernail.

Meredith grinned, stood up and continued down the street, shooting a look over her shoulder to ensure she wasn't being tailed. She was eternally wary, but ever since Danny's demise, her finely-honed senses were on red alert. While she would never touch the toxic muck the McManus Brothers peddled, she was now, in their twisted minds anyway, linked to the unsettled debt. She had no intention of becoming caught in the crossfire of their dodgy dealings. Despite having lost many of her inhibitions, she was yet to resort to whatever pills Danny popped like they were going out of fashion. She didn't have much left, but she did have some self-respect, for what that was worth. Dirty hair and dirty clothes, but at least her bloodstream was clean.

Satisfied there was no unwelcome attention, she turned to an old-fashioned shop sign swaying gently in the breeze from a rusty bracket. 'Montague & Moore – Second-Hand Books – Established 1936'. She had reached her destination. Meredith checked her tracksuit bottoms to ensure the letter was still there which, of course, it was just as it had been the previous twenty-nine times she had checked since waking up. Her heartbeat increased and was now beating at a frenetic, irregular pace. She composed herself and with a concerted effort, succeeded in slowing it to a steady thump-thump-thump. The dirty glass of the bookshop's display window and flaking green paint surround, did little to encourage passing trade to venture inside. Yet Meredith needed no persuasion. For this was her everything. She took one final glance to either side and, inhaling deeply, pushed open the door and stepped into another world.

CHAPTER 44

WAKE UP, IT'S A BEAUTIFUL MORNING

Kirkwood watched from the other end of the street as she entered the rundown bookshop. This was not a part of the city he was familiar with, given its dodgy reputation, and he saw nothing so far to convince him otherwise. He was fairly confident it didn't feature in any of the open-top bus tours which criss-crossed the city, educating snap happy tourists about Belfast's colourful history.

Meredith had spent the night in a murky underpass which hosted upwards of a dozen other sad souls unable to find a bed. He followed her from Burger King as far as the steps leading down into it and, when satisfied she was bedded down, endured a miserable night at the base of the Albert Clock, Belfast's answer to Big Ben. Tradition had it that this was where ladies of the night congregated to ply their trade, so he was relieved to discover this was nothing more than an urban myth and he had the landmark to himself during the hours of darkness.

Despite dozing fitfully on and off, come daylight he never allowed his gaze to stray far from the steps leading into and out of, the underpass. The morning rush intensified and eased off before he finally sighted Meredith emerge and hurry off in the direction of Royal Avenue. He followed at a safe distance only taking his eyes off her momentarily to text Laura saying he wouldn't be in as 'something had come up.' Her prompt response was a curt, 'Okay,' followed by a message that he owed her big time.

Although he felt uneasy, he was determined to find out where Meredith was going. He barely knew her, yet here he was stalking her like one of the weirdos he studiously avoided eye contact with, as they slipped in and out of an adult bookstore he was loitering outside of as part of the surveillance operation. Not that he cared, for if it meant traipsing up and down every grimy street in the town, then so be it, he was prepared to do so. If there was even the slightest chance she held the key to unlocking the mystery of Skelly, then the odd dirty look from the odd dirty man was a small price to pay.

Before entering the bookshop, she stopped to speak to an old wino, slumped in a doorway looking the worse for wear. When satisfied she was not going to come back out of the shop, Kirkwood cautiously made his way down the street towards it. As he drew alongside the wino, he made a conscious effort to avoid looking at the old codger who would undoubtedly either hassle him for money or start to lob alcohol-fuelled expletives in his direction.

He knew the routine. Drunken dinosaurs like this were always on the make for the next bottle of whatever their poison of choice was. He'd been taken for a mug on countless occasions in the past and had neither the time nor the inclination for the same tedious routine today. They would swear they just needed a pound for a sandwich or cup of tea, yet next time you set eyes on them they would be downing drink purchased with your hard-earned cash. Yeah, well not this time mister.

'Did you ever stop to think that you might be the one with the problem, son?'

He stopped and looked around to see who was talking to him. The voice was deep, gravelly and cultured, as if it belonged to a venerable actor. He half expected to see Patrick Stewart facing him. Given recent events, nothing surprised him anymore, so Jean-Luc Picard teleporting onto Porno Street would have been no great surprise. Beam me up, Scotty Kirkwood!

There was nobody in the immediate vicinity except the paralytic pensioner to his left, huddled in the doorway. Except he didn't sound drunk, but instead completely lucid and in possession of his faculties. Kirkwood looked down to see the old wino looking up at him with an amused expression on his time-ravaged face. Even his wrinkles had wrinkles.

'Yes, I can talk,' the ancient lush continued, intelligent blue eyes sparkling beneath an imposing set of wild, bushy eyebrows. All thoughts of Meredith were temporarily shoved to the back of Kirkwood's mind as he forced himself to focus on this latest bizarre incursion into his increasingly bizarre life.

'I'm sorry, are you talking to me?' He pointed at his chest before realising how ridiculous he looked. He sounded like a poor man's Travis Bickle, and not a taxi in sight.

The old man erupted into a warm, booming laugh and Kirkwood was left standing at arm's length until Methuselah recovered sufficiently from whatever he had found so amusing, to continue.

'We both know I am. And you can cut the second rate De Niro

impersonation. We don't have time to beat about the bush. I might be a bit long in the tooth, but I know a fellow drinker when I see one. Looks like you've had a heavy few days of it.'

Kirkwood attempted to pull an affronted look but failed abjectly and could only offer a tame comeback.

'It's been quite a stressful time, that's all,' he recovered a semblance and added spikily, 'Not that it's any of your business.'

He was annoyed at how effortlessly the old man had pierced his defences, yet more annoyed he had judged and dismissed him as nothing but a down and out. A prickle of shame broke out across his cheeks and he blushed furiously. He sought to make amends the only way he knew how, by reaching into his jacket pocket for some loose change to ease a troubled conscience.

The pensioner raised his hands in protest. He was now sitting upright although Kirkwood hadn't seen him shift position in the brief seconds they had been talking. His short-term memory was shot to pieces. Was this how stress rolled out its luxurious red carpet when it took up residence in your brain? He no longer trusted anyone, least of all, himself.

'No, son, keep your money. You need it more than me. That young lady you are so clumsily pursuing has expensive tastes when it comes to tray bakes and coffee. And you are going to have to part with a few more shillings if you are ever going to get to the bottom of what she has to tell you.'

'How do you…?' Kirkwood made no attempt to conceal his astonishment this time. His gob was well and truly smacked out of the ball park.

'Never you mind how I know. Let's just say I've spent a lifetime people-watching. Occupational hazard.' He raised a bottle of tonic wine he produced on cue from inside a tatty overcoat and drank deeply, smacking chapped lips and closing his eyes, a look of utter contentment on his face. 'Ah, I might not agree with all their spiritual beliefs, but the good monks of Buckfast Abbey certainly know a thing or two about their blessed grapes.' He opened his eyes again and winked mischievously at Kirkwood.

'Now on your way before she manages to give you the slip…again.' Was the smelly tramp poking fun at him?

The old man started to chuckle again. 'Go. Go. I've seen elephants on roller skates conduct more discreet surveillance operations.' And with that, he exploded again, his hilarity rapidly degenerating into a coughing fit which doubled him over. Kirkwood stooped to assist but the old man waved him away before sucking in a lungful of much needed air to construct his parting shot.

'Hurry. She needs you. Despite her protestations to the contrary. Almost as much as you need her. And you won't have me to guide you next time she disappears.' He began hacking into a filthy handkerchief, somehow magicked out of thin air.

Kirkwood blinked in astonishment before reverting his attention back towards the bookshop. It had been the most incredible weekend of his life and Monday morning was proving to be no different.

CHAPTER 45

A LITERARY TARDIS

The second she stepped inside, Meredith immediately felt more at ease and in control of her emotions. She realised with some alarm she had been digging her fingernails into the palms of her hands, both of them balled into tight fists. She was grateful her nails were bitten to the quick for otherwise she would undoubtedly have drawn blood. The old Meredith always took great pride in her perfectly manicured nails, but Emily's departure put paid to that. Emily's departure put paid to a lot of stuff. Death brought finality in so many ways, yet in others it was a powerful catalyst for change in those it touched.

The bookshop had become a second home. *Make that only home,* she corrected herself, stopping to take in its interior which never failed to amaze her. The display window outside contained an eclectic array of tomes strategically placed to lure passing bookworms over the threshold. Once inside, it opened into a warren of bookcases and shelving, housing thousands of titles. There appeared to be no rhyme or reason to its layout as while some aisles ended abruptly, others meandered aimlessly around the store before depositing the hapless browser back at their original starting point. Most of the archaic wooden cases looked as if they were held together by the countless layers of dirt and cobwebs which adorned them. Although her nose regularly twitched, courtesy of the dusty interior, Meredith dared not sneeze for fear she be entombed in an avalanche of paperbacks.

The shop was jaw dropping in its apparent lack of organisation, yet ask its proprietor, Jimmy James, if he possessed a certain book, and he could lay hands on it within minutes. 'If we don't have it, then it hasn't been written,' was his stock catchphrase, there being more than a grain of truth to his words. He was a veritable bloodhound when it came to acquiring rare and highly sought after publications for his loyal band of patrons, despite the dubious structural soundness of the establishment.

A handful of customers were scattered amidst the aisles, browsing in the hope of discovering a hidden gem. Handwritten notices taped to lopsided bookcases guided them, proudly announcing that you were entering the 'Medieval History' or 'New Age Science' sections. You name it, Jimmy had it. From Mayan Architecture to UFO Sightings, Landscape Gardening to Pregnancy and Motherhood. Meredith had spent many hours wandering around it, grateful for its cosy warmth combined with the welcome respite, no matter how temporary, from the harsh reality awaiting her once she stepped outside again. She had visions one day of discovering a dusty skeleton in some gloomy corner where a hopelessly lost customer settled down to accept their fate, unable to find their way out of the labyrinth of random dead ends and dimly lit passages. Their flesh would be sucked from the bones by gigantic albino bookworms who hadn't glimpsed the light of day in countless aeons.

She shuddered at the thought and crammed her jack-in-the-box imagination back into the recesses of her mind. To the right sat Jimmy, perched on a high stool behind the counter, listening to an Irish language station. Meredith, assuming he was a fluent Gaelic speaker, once asked him what he was listening to. 'Haven't a clue,' he happily replied. 'But I love the way the language sounds and well…it just adds to the ambience of the place, right?' Meredith had shaken her head in disbelief but the more time she spent in Montague & Moore's, the more she agreed with him. The lilting, hypnotic tones of the broadcasters sounded as if they belonged and added depth and substance to the already charming atmosphere.

Jimmy doffed an imaginary cap at Meredith upon seeing her, his standard greeting to all. She had become a regular visitor in recent months and always made a point of making a purchase if in possession of the necessary funds. Which was most times, given books could be bought for as little as twenty pence. It also masked the real purpose for her visit and deflected any suspicion on the part of the proprietor. In any event, Jimmy was a kindly soul and often dismissively waved away her efforts to make payment. Rumour had it the shop was a mere distraction for him after he struck six-figure gold in the National Lottery a few years back, thanks to five correct numbers and the bonus ball.

She teasingly asked him about it once to be met with a cryptically raised eyebrow. 'Sure, isn't life itself a lottery young lady?' he replied. 'We both know that. When we go to sleep at night none of us know if we will wake up the next morning. I just take each day as it comes and spin the wheel to see where it takes me.' Meredith stopped asking after that. It was ironic given his profession, there was no book more closed than the private life of Jimmy James.

With every passing visit she delved deeper into this literary Tardis, exploring every nook and cranny, unearthing its treasures and unravelling its mysteries. Its topography was imprinted on her memory to the extent she was certain she could navigate it blindfolded. She inhaled deeply of the magical mustiness she cherished so much, tracing a finger along a section of uneven shelving as she wandered along an aisle into the bowels of the building. The aroma of ageing paper combined with creaking rafters, arising from some ancient slumber, gave the impression the place was alive. Meredith felt the same every time she was there. An hour at Montague & Moore not only thawed her frozen feet but also the chill that life on the streets brought to an aching heart. It made her feel a little more human, a little more alive.

She reached into her bag and removed the battered journal. Yes, she was alive; and where there was life, there was hope.

CHAPTER 46

URBAN MURMURS

She could have easily passed as a young woman killing time before her next lecture or shift at the coffee shop as she wandered aimlessly along the aisles. Except Meredith wasn't wandering — she knew exactly where she was going. Third aisle on the right, then left and left again. Her heart began to race as she passed familiar landmarks. She was close, just around the next corner. A blur of books fizzed past on either side as she neared her destination. A little oasis of normalcy in the otherwise acrid wasteland of her current existence. She rounded the final corner and there it was, her aisle. It was no different from any of the others but, for Meredith Marie Starc, it was the centre of the universe.

This was where she came to nibble on the few remaining crumbs of comfort she had left. This was where she concealed the broken remnants of her life; hidden away from the glare of a relentlessly unforgiving world which sought to snuff out what little she still held dear. She looked down at the journal in her hands and recalled the ease with which she stole it. She wasn't proud that she had resorted to such underhand tactics as she wasn't a thief by nature and it galled her; but needs must, the greater good blah, blah, blah. Her hands started to shake as she peered over a shoulder to satisfy herself that she wasn't being watched. Seeing the coast was clear she edged cautiously along the aisle flanked on either side by tottering shelves which looked as if they could come crashing down at any moment.

The silence was total, she could hear every croak and groan of the old shop. It was attuned to her grief and wailing in empathy at her loss. Like the banshee in old Irish ghost stories which her grandmother recounted to her with a glint in her eye when she was a little girl. The shop sensed death was near.

Concentrating hard, Meredith paced out eleven measured steps, stopped and spun to her left before counting six shelves up from the floor. It was a well-rehearsed routine, perfected in recent months. The sixth shelf was roughly at eye level and housed a selection of yellowing fantasy paperbacks sitting two rows deep.

The back row was always where you found the real gems, the books craftier customers hid from prying eyes, safe in the knowledge they could return at a later date to retrieve their secret treasures. It was this row which Meredith was interested in; a rabbit hole which led to a different reality; one she could not resist no matter where it led or what consequences it brought.

She thumbed the battered spines in the front row containing tales of orcs and dragons, quests and kingdoms which rose and fell with each well-thumbed page. Counting across this row from left to right she removed the eighth book before reaching through the gap. Panic momentarily gripped her as she fumbled around but could not place a hand on the prize she sought. Her heart somersaulted into her mouth which was growing drier by the second. Finally, she triumphantly hooked two fingers on what she was seeking, pulling it out into the murky light. She looked down and all the tension melted away like an early morning frost caressed by the first, tentative rays of the sun.

'You little beauty,' she whispered.

How could she have doubted it would be there? It always was. Yet the fear still consumed her every time she made her pilgrimage to the bookshop. There it sat, in the same aisle, on the same shelf, week after week. She had bought it three times, stolen it twice, concealed it in all manner of places around the shop on umpteen occasions. She binned the book, burnt the book, even hurled it into the nearby River Lagan. When she returned the next time, however, it was always back where it had been, gloating at her, goading her, daring her to try harder next time.

Urban Murmurs – The Poetry of Gearard Farrell: 1965-1972. It was a first edition, no less, which would have been impressive had it not been for the fact a second edition was never printed given the overwhelming lack of interest in the first one. Yet Emily had loved it. 'It's as if every word was either written for me or about me,' she had purred contentedly to Meredith, looking up from her copy over dorky reading glasses. Where she acquired it from was anyone's guess as it was hardly New York Times Bestseller material, and she doubted if it ever sat on Richard and Judy's bedside dressers. Meredith hadn't the foggiest who the turgid Mr Farrell was, but Emily loved him and his dreary poems.

After Emily's funeral, she liberated the book from her best friend's bedroom when nobody was looking and pored over every line in a pathetic attempt to stay connected to her. As she devoured the pages, she closed her eyes and could almost hear Emily reciting them aloud, in that slightly artsy manner she affected.

It drove Meredith nuts but how she wished Emily was here now, prancing around in her pyjamas, dodging a barrage of pillows launched in her direction. She would have given anything to hear such recitals one last time but all she was left with was this tatty, dog-eared collection of second-rate sonnets.

Meredith realised with a pang of longing she was alone in the aisle. She didn't know if it was lack of sleep or food, but she was increasingly losing herself, drifting off into lucid daydreams where it was just Emily and her, alone in a utopia of memories. She tore the page from the journal containing her latest letter and slipped it inside the book before returning it to its rightful place on the back row of the shelf. The front row was then restored to its former glory, covering her tracks. After a final inspection, she retraced her steps to the front of the shop, stopping briefly to chat with Jimmy and buy a Stephen King paperback to avoid suspicion; she was just another customer, and nobody needed to know the real purpose for her visit.

The light outside momentarily dazzled her after the shadows of the bookshop. Meredith shielded her eyes with a hand before turning left and striding off. She knew exactly where she was going and her fingers, toes and every other conceivable body part were crossed in the hope this would be the day when Emily replied.

'Don't let me down, Ems. I need you. Just you and me.'

CHAPTER 47

PAPER SIFT

Kirkwood had been there all along, spying from the adjacent aisle which ran parallel to where Meredith had stopped and started to randomly rearrange books. When she left, he silently counted to one hundred for fear she might return and catch him red-handed. He was convinced she wasn't coming back at eighty but kept going anyway just to be on the safe side. It had taken him forever to track her down and she possessed the uncanny ability to disappear into thin air at the slightest whiff of danger. He couldn't afford to lose her again; this was too important. Although not quite sure, he sensed he was getting ever closer to finding out.

Ninety-nine…one hundred. He emerged from his hiding place and stepped into the aisle, prior to locating the shelf that was of such interest to her. He had watched her moving books before removing something from her back pocket and secreting it between the pages of one of them. It was bizarre behaviour but who was he to talk? His nine to five for over a decade had been dictated by an imaginary tin soldier who lived in his head.

He began to rifle through the books on the shelf. Flicking through a few of them established they mostly contained airy-fairy poetry. Not even remotely his cup of tea but she didn't look the type either. Each to their own, he supposed. He screwed his face up at some of the flowery language on offer but persevered, thumbing painstakingly through each book. The first three or four yielded nothing, causing Kirkwood to doubt himself as to where she had been standing. Was he searching the wrong shelf? It had to be here somewhere. For he knew what it was, the journal having already betrayed her secrets to his greedy eyes.

Just as he was about to give up and move onto the shelf below, a sheet of paper fell from the book he was sifting through and fluttered to the ground.

Kirkwood bent over and picked up the piece of A4 paper which was folded in two. Three words were written on one side in green biro. The handwriting was instantly recognisable, and he held the sheet closer to his face in the poor light until it brushed his nose, to be certain of its contents. He swore quietly for not wearing the glasses prescribed to him seven years ago. Finally, the blurred squiggles became words that told him exactly where Meredith was headed.

CHAPTER 48

ADEUS MEU AMIGO

Dobson watched the one known to his kind as Kirkwood leave the bookshop and walk down the street towards him. He looked flustered but that was to be expected. The young man's life had been turned upside down and inside out over the last seventy-two hours. He, no doubt, had a million and one questions. They would have to wait, though, for now; it was enough he had the letter and knew where the girl was going. Dobson allowed himself a wry smile. It was slowly but ever so surely coming together. He was a past master at this and when it came to patience, he had bundles of the commodity. Centuries of it to be precise. Skelly had a fight on his hands, he could guarantee that much.

Kirkwood walked straight past Dobson as if he wasn't there. Invisibility was a cheap party trick, but effective, nonetheless. There was no need for him to engage with the young man for a second time as his work was done. The letter had been located and the paths of Kirkwood Scott and Meredith Starc were steadily converging. Despite the best efforts of Skelly and his infernal associates, satisfactory progress was being made. Yes, all in all, it had been a most successful morning, reflected Dobson with some pride.

'I wouldn't get too comfortable, Cornelius.'

Dobson spun with surprising dexterity for a man of his advanced years at the sound of the deep, accented voice which he recognised instantly. Before him stood a tall, bearded man, dressed all in black. He towered a good foot over Dobson, but the old man did not flinch from the imposing frame. If it came down to it, he was confident he could deal with this latest fly in the ointment.

'I thought he would have sent the German for such a delicate matter. He tends to adopt a tactful approach, as opposed to your more…forthright style.

But if he insists on using a sledgehammer to crack a nut, who am I to argue with the legendary Augustus Skelly.' He picked at a speck of fluff on his overcoat and waited to see if the barb had found its target.

'Gunther is otherwise engaged,' replied the bearded man, declining to rise to the bait. 'Indeed, we are all very preoccupied at present. The Colonel has even considered sending more of our kind. With the situation coming to a head, however, I have no doubt he has everything under control. After all, it won't be the first time he's got the upper hand over you,' he smiled cruelly, and Dobson bit his lip for his opening salvo had been returned with some interest. Unwanted memories formed, which took all his strength to dispel.

'I'm surprised you would be aware of that given you spent most of the engagement picking the pockets of dead Frenchmen. For one apparently held in such high esteem by your Colonel, you hardly covered yourself in glory, did you?'

His bearded opponent burst into laughter. 'Rather a low blow for a man of your rank and breeding?' The grin turned quickly to a snarl. 'I was there when it mattered. Or has the amount of wine you've consumed on this pathetic planet destroyed the few remaining brain cells you have left? Why you want to fraternise with these ingrates is beyond me. The thought that I used to be one of them utterly disgusts me.' To emphasis the point, he turned his head and spat on the pavement.

'Disgust perhaps, or maybe it's fear of what my young friends are capable of that upsets you so, Sergeant Rodriguez?' The bearded man tensed, his eyes narrowing to slits. Dobson knew he had finally slipped beneath his skin so continued, seeking to drive home the advantage.

'I think we can both agree our current interests rise above and beyond the national flags we once fought under. Just as we both know you cannot win. My advice to you, my friend, would be to leave well alone. This is happening whether you like it or not. Your Colonel has underestimated the powers he is dealing with here and he knows it. It's only a matter of time before the inevitable happens.' He started to limp away, but Rodriguez reached out and grabbed his forearm.

Dobson spoke quietly but firmly. 'I suggest you unhand me, *señor*, if you know what's best for you. We don't want to cause a scene in the street now do we?'

'Indeed.' The bearded man released his grip and regained some composure. He docked a mocking salute and backed away slowly from the older man. All around them people went about their business as if unaware of the tense confrontation unfolding before them. Which of course they were. This was a personal matter and not for their kind to witness.

'They are but two, old man, and don't you forget that,' Rodriguez sneered. 'I am sure our paths will cross again Cornelius, and soon. Until then, *adeus meu amigo.*' He turned and ambled nonchalantly down the street, his loping stride eating up the ground.

Dobson watched him go and let out a low whistle. So, it began. Skelly had raised the stakes and played his opening hand. The situation was developing faster than even he had anticipated which meant one thing. Skelly was worried. Worried enough to have 'boots on the ground'. A horrible American phrase but apt in these circumstances. First the German, then the Brothers, and now Rodriguez. He was rattled.

They had removed the girl Emily or, so they thought. A messy business and no mistake. But Skelly hadn't anticipated she would return to the game in such spectacular fashion. Nobody predicted it other than the architect behind it; one Cornelius Dobson, roaming vagrant and hopeless drunk. It had been a longshot and taken an enormous amount out of him, but it was working and that was all that mattered. He was grateful, for when battle joined in earnest there would be no prisoners taken, and no quarter given. It would be a fight to the end.

Dobson returned to the doorway and wrapped a blanket around his lower body. The bottle of tonic wine sat untouched beside him. Clear heads were required now. Very clear heads.

CHAPTER 49

TRUST HIM

10:12 a.m.

She was exactly where he thought she would be; in the alley, staring at the mural of the white-haired girl, Meredith's expression a mixture of longing and disappointment.

'So, this is where the magic happens?'

Kirkwood cringed the second the words left his mouth, an epic failure to engage brain before speaking. His disastrous dating history was peppered with such appalling lines but this one took the biscuit, and the cheesiest biscuit possible. It made him think of the brand his mother only bought at Christmas and other special occasions. Why only then as they weren't particularly expensive, he had no idea. Another inexplicable childhood mystery he would never get to the bottom of.

Meredith jumped at his voice and turned her attention from the wall. No more than a dozen feet of cobbled alleyway separated them, the girl in the mural staring down on them with a knowing smile. Although startled by his appearance, Kirkwood was thankful Meredith didn't scarper. Instead she stood rooted to the spot, waiting on him to expand upon his opening comment. She looked smaller than ever, beneath the cavernous expanse of her parka. Her eyes were rimmed in red, and drying streaks on both cheeks indicated the tears had flowed freely prior to his arrival. The silence stretched awkwardly between them, until she finally spoke.

'This is where the magic is *meant* to happen.'

She sighed and bit a chapped lower lip. Kirkwood noticed the dirt under her fingernails and wondered when she last showered. She didn't smell as bad as last time, but he was careful not to stand too close, for fear of causing her to bolt like a frightened doe. There was a connection, he knew that, but it was incredibly fragile, and could be irretrievably shattered by a wrong tone or turn of phrase. He had to tread carefully, one tentative step at a time, like a tightrope walker shuffling slowly along a wire, stretched taut between two high rise buildings. One tiny misjudgement and he would plummet to his death on the hard, unforgiving streets below.

'Meant to? What do you mean?'

She eyed him for several long, hard seconds before making the decision. Then, the floodgates opened. The barrier between them was breached and the truth flowed freely.

'This is where it should be! Why isn't it here?' Her voice rose towards the end of the sentence, unable to conceal the rising panic.

'Where what should be?' Kirkwood edged closer, no more than eight feet separating them. He looked over his shoulder, for at this time of the morning there should have been a steady flow of people cutting through the alley between Royal Avenue and Mulberry Square. He noticed for the first time she was shaking, plain to see despite her baggy clothing. Her face was drained of blood, yet those glacial blue eyes continued to blaze defiantly.

'The message. Emily's message. She always leaves a message on the wall.' She waved in the general direction of the wall, more in resignation than any actual hope he would understand. 'It doesn't matter,' she mumbled, staring at the cobbles. 'Nothing matters anymore. She's gone.'

'I've read it. The journal. I know. I know, it's a scummy thing to do reading a girl's journal but, I did it anyway. I know everything. Emily, the wall, the messages, the letters you leave in the bookshop.' To reinforce the words, he produced the letter from the pocket of his leather jacket and thrust it towards her. She hesitated, before taking a step forward and snatching it from his grasp.

He stole a look at the mural, aching to believe her. The artwork was exquisite, the more he looked at it, it was as if Emily would speak and share her sad secrets with them. Hers was a haunting, mesmeric beauty underpinned with an ineffable melancholy. He ached to believe the desperate young woman in front of him, because otherwise they both needed urgent psychiatric evaluation. But there were no messages from beyond the grave, nothing beneath the mural offering a grain of substance to the scribblings in her journal.

'Every time I leave a letter at Montague & Moore, I come here and there is a new message. Every single time. Except for the last week…' Her voice trailed off; her exasperation replaced by despair. 'It should be here. Why isn't it here?'

Her voice was raised now, the despair evident in every word. Kirkwood breathed deeply, aware she was teetering on the edge; the last thing he needed was a scene that would attract attention or send her bolting out of his life again. He imagined Skelly, leaning forward in his armchair, urging him to fail at this critical moment. He couldn't allow his own anxiety to distract from the frightened girl before him.

'Look I really want to believe you,' he implored, willing her defences to further lower and provide him with a way to explain. She was pretty in a washed up, grungy way but he dispelled the thought, such was his focus on not messing up this opportunity. 'But are you sure about all of this? You've been through a very traumatic experience. You're grieving for your best friend; you're living rough and God only knows what else. You're exhausted, stressed to the back teeth. The mind can play all sorts of tricks on people when they go through what you have.'

He paused, awaiting her reply and his fate. It wasn't long in coming.

'What, you think I'm making this up? You think I'm some sort of crazy bag lady who sees dead things. Well screw you!' She stormed past, making no effort to avoid crashing into his shoulder in the process. The contact caught Kirkwood unawares and off balance. He spun around and went down on one knee, wincing as a shard of pain danced across his collar bone and into his neck.

He looked up at the wall and was vaguely aware of a flurry of expletives from behind as Meredith stomped down the alley towards the dog leg leading onto Royal Avenue. He would have been offended had his attention not been drawn to what was now facing him. It wasn't there a minute ago and it couldn't be there now. But it was.

'Er…Meredith. You might want to see this.' Beneath Emily, two words had appeared, in swirling blue lettering, stark and unmistakable against the dull brick background.

TRUST HIM.

So, this was where the magic happened.

CHAPTER 50

CARROT CAKE CONFESSIONAL

10:48 a.m.

'Do you mind telling me what on earth is going on?' Kirkwood asked.

His head was bouncing, like he was on the receiving end of a twelve-pint hangover, even though he hadn't touched a drop. He eyed up the caramel steamer in front of him, before cupping both hands around it, lifting it to his lips and taking a lingering sip. He closed his eyes and savoured the sugary taste of the hot, frothy liquid before swallowing and looking expectantly across at Meredith.

'I'll tell you what I know but I'm not so sure it's of this earth.'

She looked up from her coffee and met his gaze before dissolving into a fit of giggles. 'You know, if you're going to pull the high and mighty act it would be better if you did so without the milky moustache.'

Kirkwood stared back quizzically before realisation dawned and the penny dropped. 'Oh, for goodness sake,' he spluttered, wiping his upper lip with the sleeve of his shirt. Meredith smirked and took a huge bite out of the chunk of carrot cake she had ordered with the coffee. Kirkwood guessed she was slim beneath the shapeless clothing but there was certainly nothing wrong with her appetite. The carrot cake was vanishing at a disturbing rate.

'Am I going to get any sense out of you today? I need answers. This is nuts. One minute the wall is blank and then...well then, this!' He lifted his phone from the table and swiped its screen, thrusting a photo of the words beneath the mural into Meredith's face. 'Care to explain how that could happen — bar witchcraft? You're not a witch, are you?'

Meredith adopted a deadpan expression. 'Yes, that's spot on, you numpty; I'm a witch. I'm the Queen of the Dead and you are under my spell. Now buy me another slice of cake before I unleash my demonic hordes upon you.' She followed her words with an angelic smile, hoping to dispel the growing frustration on Kirkwood's face. 'No seriously, I'm starving. Get me another bit and I'll tell you everything I know. But if you laugh, I'm walking out of here and you'll never see me again, okay?'

Kirkwood sighed and pushed back his chair. 'You're a bottomless pit,' he moaned, rising and walking over to the counter to place the order. As he waited to catch the eye of a passing barista, he monitored Meredith from the corner of his eye. She was unaware he was watching; such was her focus on devouring the remainder of the cake. She picked at the last crumbs on the plate and licked both sets of fingers clean before draining the remainder of the coffee. The girl was ravenous. Setting aside his own selfish interests, the least he could do was buy her something to eat.

'Wow. Thanks, Kirky.' Meredith's eyes lit up and she licked her lips as Kirkwood returned to the table and placed the slab of creamy goodness in front of her.

'It's Kirkwood,' he sighed, taking his seat again. 'Now talk.' His stern countenance convinced her now was not the time for further teasing.

'Okay. Okay. Make yourself comfortable, this might take a while.' Meredith took a deep breath and straightened her posture as if poised to huff and puff and blow Kirkwood's world apart.

'It all started the day Emily O'Hara walked into my form class…'

She stopped talking forty-five minutes later. Kirkwood scratched his unshaven chin and leaned back, attempting to process the barrage of information she had unloaded upon him.

'Wow.'

'Wow, indeed.' Meredith looked exhausted, having used up every last shred of strength in unburdening herself of Emily's death and subsequent reincarnation in the form of the mural. She had skimmed over many of the gory details of life on the streets. There were memories she never wanted to recount again, even to herself. Yet, the ice was broken. Tears were shed, secrets divulged, and even phone numbers exchanged. The bond had been established.

'So…' She was keen to divert the conversation onto other topics. 'The creepy old guy from my dreams. You reckon you know him?'

'Yeah,' replied Kirkwood nervously. The shoe was on the other foot now. It was his turn to talk. Part of him baulked at the thought of it, for to openly discuss Skelly was to make him irrevocably real. Yet he knew he had to, otherwise the nightmare of his life would never find the resolution he so desperately needed.

He talked and she listened. No questions, no looks of incredulity; just the occasional reassuring nod and encouraging smile. She didn't openly laugh in his face or run screaming from the café, she just listened. When he was done, she knew it all. The murder of his father, the fort, the soldiers, Skelly, and the infernal routines. Everything. Even his belief he was responsible for catastrophe and disaster around the globe, courtesy of 'The 49'.

Kirkwood sat there, not really knowing what to say or do. Like a modern-day Peter, he had stepped out of the boat and was now waiting to discover whether he would remain above the raging waters or sink to the bottom, never to surface again. He sat and awaited his fate. Meredith Starc was to be his judge, jury and executioner.

All he needed to hear were three words, three little words. The three most important words in the world to him. Not 'I love you', for that ship sailed long ago from the world of Kirkwood Scott. No, these words meant much more to him, he had been waiting to hear them all his adult life.

I believe you.

'I DON'T BELIEVE THIS!'

Meredith jumped to her feet and, grabbing her bag, beat a path towards swing doors leading into the café's kitchens. 'COME ON!' she roared, before disappearing into a cloud of steam belching forth from the kitchens, as if a slumbering dragon was stirring. Kirkwood needed no further invitation when he saw the reason for her rapid departure. Lumbering through the café entrance were the two apes who chased Meredith and Danny through the square, two nights ago.

They had been spotted.

CHAPTER 51

CHASE SCENE

12:09 p.m.

Kirkwood had never been behind the scenes at a busy city centre eatery, but this unscheduled tour afforded him little opportunity to take in the various stainless-steel contraptions spewing out noise and steam; like a twenty-first century torture chamber. Up ahead, Meredith wove a path through startled kitchen staff with the unnerving ease of someone well used to being chased through crammed urban environments. He imagined such a skill was an essential prerequisite for surviving street life.

He struggled to get his tired legs pumping but the presence of two muscle-bound apes hot on his heels acted as an incentive to hang onto Meredith's coat-tails. He chanced a glance behind and immediately wished he hadn't. The apes were gaining, and their angry faces offered little prospect of an amicable outcome were he to stop and attempt to reason with them.

Without warning, Meredith ducked right and burst through a fire exit onto a narrow alley which ran behind the premises. Kirkwood followed and almost fell, his trainers finding little purchase on the greasy, uneven surface. Ahead, Meredith pulled over a plastic wheelie bin, its contents spewing out onto the ground like rancid confetti. The already hazardous surface was now decorated with a mixture of squashed tomatoes and other equally vile produce.

Kirkwood hurdled the bin lying across his path, landing awkwardly on the other side. He felt his legs begin to give way before staggering, regaining his balance and finding forward momentum once again. Behind him, Ape One slowed markedly, before cautiously negotiating the makeshift obstacle. Ape Two was less careful and hurled his cumbersome frame over the bin with all the grace of a demented walrus. His trailing foot caught the lid and he went crashing chin-first to the ground, with a sickening crack. *He won't be getting up from that in a hurry*, thought Kirkwood, as Meredith, again with barely any notice, swung right again, into an even narrower alley.

Kirkwood sucked as much air into his lungs as he could to ward off a stitch, which was beginning to niggle against his ribcage with all the subtlety of a sharpened knitting needle. Ape One, showing little concern for his fallen colleague, continued with the dogged pursuit. He was gaining on Kirkwood as they careered into the second alley. So much for muscle men not being able to run the length of themselves — although a strong cardiovascular system was probably a desirable attribute for those who regularly chased junkies for outstanding payments. Meredith burst out of the enclosed entry into the lunchtime clamour of Royal Avenue. With blatant disregard for even the most basic tenets of the Highway Code, she pelted across the street, narrowly avoiding a bus as it thundered past. Horns blared and, all around, pedestrians turned their heads to locate the source of the disturbance.

Kirkwood's heart missed several beats as his view was temporarily obscured by the blur of the passing bus. It kickstarted into action only when the double-decker trundled by, revealing Meredith standing unscathed on the other side of the street. As the din of horns receded, she flicked him a cocky salute, before charging on, picking her way through hordes of shoppers.

He could only admire her nerve but had little time to consider much more as he followed in her wake, relieved there were no other vehicles in the vicinity. He struggled to keep tabs on Meredith but, through a gap in the crowds caught a fleeting glimpse of her diving into the Castle Court complex. Another stolen look revealed Ape One was temporarily delayed, attempting to negotiate a gaggle of giggling schoolgirls who had flounced across his path. Not wanting to draw unwanted attention to himself, he slowed down as opposed to knocking them over like teenage bowling pins.

Grateful for the brief respite, Kirkwood continued to track Meredith, who by now was halfway along the central thoroughfare and veering towards an exit that led back onto familiar turf. She was heading for Mulberry Square. The last time he was there, Danny and Meredith had bundled him over and this crazy carousel ride started. He thought he had problems then, but they were nothing compared to his current predicament. It suddenly occurred to Kirkwood he hadn't been aware of Skelly's lurking presence all day. Maybe there was an upside to risking life and limb with reckless young women he barely knew. His thought bubble shattered as Meredith hollered, 'Come on slow coach,' over her shoulder. She dashed out of the shopping centre and across a pedestrian precinct, leading onto the square.

'Are you actually enjoying this, you lunatic?' he gasped. He wasn't sure if she heard him, but if this was her idea of fun — she could keep it. He was rapidly running out of gas and ideas to shake off Ape One.

Meredith seemed to read his mind. 'Split up!' she bellowed. I'll see you back at HQ.' Before he could even begin to process what or where HQ was, she was sprinting across the square towards one of the myriads of alleyways which ran off it. Kirkwood summoned the last of his reserves and veered left into one which led back towards Royal Avenue. He felt a pang of guilt as he prayed the ape would follow Meredith. He had only been in her company after all. What interest could Shrek possibly have in him?

Unfortunately, logical thinking did not appear to be a bedfellow of his hulking hunter. As Meredith disappeared out of sight into the alley, Ape One skidded onto the square. He looked momentarily dejected that his dual quarry had become one, but any hopes of a reprieve were dashed as he sighted Kirkwood and zeroed in on him. He broke into a run, his muscular frame covering the ground between them in a surprisingly efficient manner.

Kirkwood sucked in another lungful of air as the stitch continued to dance a merry tune across his ribcage. He had little option but to reach the alley and hope Ape One would be delayed by a coachload of tourists taking in the various sights and sounds of the square. O'Reilly's was, as ever, doing a roaring trade and dozens of customers were making the most of the early afternoon sun in the beer garden. An Ed Sheeran wannabe, all ginger hair and horn-rimmed glasses, was making the most of an attentive audience, busking tunefully outside the bar. Kirkwood would have given his right arm to be seated in their midst sipping on a chilled pint. How times had changed.

He staggered into the cooler climes of the alley and was embraced by its shadows. With more than a dollop of irony, it suddenly hit him he felt more alive than he had in years, his senses razor-sharp. The mental treacle of Skelly and his ridiculous routines were further away than ever and, despite his malignant mentor still lurking at the fringes of his awareness, he didn't have the same hold over Kirkwood as before. If Meredith catapulting into his life had somehow unsettled and distracted his nemesis, it could only be a good thing.

He kicked on again, head down, lungs bursting, but Ape One continued to gain. His only chance was to make it back onto Royal Avenue and disappear into the crowds. If he didn't make it, he feared his blood would soon be decorating the alley; along with several teeth and possibly a kidney.

Kirkwood craved the sanctuary of the avenue, now less than twenty yards away. He could make out all walks of life going about their daily business, oblivious to the drama unfolding nearby. His attempts at acceleration, however, were short-lived as he tripped and went crashing to the ground. He threw out his hands to protect his more vital organs and was rewarded with the searing sensation of several layers of skin being removed from both palms. A nanosecond later, his knees connected jarringly with the hard surface, sending arrows of pain through his crumpled body.

That was nothing, though, to the pain he sensed was imminent when Ape One fell on him like a starving lion about to feast on a stricken antelope. It was over. Kirkwood curled into a ball like an unseated jockey awaiting the first of many hooves. He would have prayed but doubted even the Big Man upstairs could extricate him from this predicament. So instead he counted.

One…two…three… Nothing.

The overbearing silence was broken by a muffled, gagging sound. Kirkwood cautiously opened his eyes, not even realising he had shut them in anticipation of the first kick or punch. Still nothing but that noise. What was it? Rising painfully from the ground onto battered hands and knees, he scuttled in a semi-circle, so he was facing back up the alley towards the gagging. The sight that greeted him evaporated any aches and pains. He stared like a slack-jawed hillbilly for what couldn't be happening before his eyes, was happening before his eyes.

CHAPTER 52

RODRIGUEZ

Kirkwood watched in astonishment as a huge bearded man pinned Ape One against the alley wall like a six-stone weakling. The gagging sound was the ape's windpipe being relentlessly crushed in the vice-like grip of his assailant's hand. The ape looked over the bearded man's shoulder and attempted to communicate with Kirkwood. His eyes bulged from their sockets like ghoulish gobstoppers that kids stuffed themselves with at Halloween. Kirkwood watched as tiny blood vessels began to spread across the ape's eyeballs like the Central Line on a London Underground map. His hands grappled pathetically with the bearded man in a futile attempt to break free. Kirkwood let out an involuntary, high-pitched giggle as it dawned on him the bearded man was effortlessly holding seventeen stone of muscular ape four inches off the ground in one hand.

The giggle alerted this most unlikely of saviours to his attentive audience. The bearded man cocked his head to one side and gave the ape a long, quizzical look before releasing his grip. The ape dropped to the ground where he lay, desperately attempting to suck air into oxygen starved lungs, via a bruised oesophagus. The bearded man took a step back to admire his handiwork before delivering a kick to the ape's exposed side. Kirkwood winced, the closest to sympathy he could muster for a man who only sixty seconds before had been intent on dishing out the exact same punishment to him. With that, the bearded man suddenly lost interest, instead focusing his attention on fixing the lapels of an expensive black overcoat which he wore unbuttoned to the knees. Sensing an opportunity to flee, the ape staggered to his feet and, with a final wounded look at Kirkwood, scrambled down the alley back towards Mulberry Square.

Turning to face Kirkwood, the bearded man smiled, revealing a dazzling set of perfect, white teeth, and extended both arms towards him as if greeting a long, lost friend. Kirkwood looked over his shoulder for surely this sequence of events must have attracted the attention of others. But no, despite them being less than ten yards from Royal Avenue, the chaotic scenes in the alley had gone unnoticed.

'It's as if they can't see us,' whispered Kirkwood. He turned to face his guardian angel who ambled slowly towards him, arms still outstretched and sporting a television gameshow grin which was even more luminous when juxtaposed against his jet black, bushy beard and slicked-back, collar-length hair. Gleaming dark eyes, a squashed tomato of a nose and a raw, jagged scar traversing his left cheek rounded off a look which would have been more at home in the professional wrestling ring as opposed to a Belfast side street.

'Kirkwood, Kirkwood, Kirkwood…my dear, dear friend. It's been so long. How are you?' The bearded man spoke with a thick Mediterranean accent. An uneducated ear might have hazarded a guess at Spanish, but a skilled linguist would have identified the subtle intonations and inflections marking him as unmistakably Portuguese. To be more precise, from the rural north of that beautiful country, in a small village to the north of Braga. It was an accent uncorrupted by any modern-day slang. The man stopped and affected a mock expression of hurt when it became clear that Kirkwood didn't recognise him.

'What? I come all this way, save your life and you can't even welcome your old comrade in arms?' Kirkwood puffed out his cheeks and, now in a sitting position, struggled to formulate a response. He delved into frazzled memory banks but came up with nothing. He had only been to Spain once when he was eighteen, which involved a drunken week in Mallorca with school friends. Even then, he barely spoke to a local the entire time other than when ordering 'una cerveza por favor,' such was his cultural ignorance.

The bearded man soaked in Kirkwood's perplexed expression and threw back his head, emitting a deep roar of laughter which would ordinarily have been heard several hundred yards away. Nobody on the nearby street paid any heed to it. Nobody stopped, nobody turned, nobody looked. 'They can't see or hear us,' mouthed Kirkwood, his voice still barely audible.

'That's right,' grinned the bearded man. 'It was just the three of us, before your friend decided to depart at such short notice. No need for the local constabulary to get involved. Our little secret, right?'

He chuckled, eyes twinkling like a Father Christmas from an alternative greetings card. Biker Santa meets Tim Burton's, 'The Nightmare Before Christmas.' Kirkwood nodded slowly, his overworked brain trying to keep up with the increasingly unhinged series of events developing before him. His mobile phone beeped in the front pocket of his jeans, breaking the awkward silence. He considered checking the message but was finding it difficult to avert his gaze from the imposing figure in front of him, who he estimated was at least six-foot-five.

'Oh, no need to check that. It's just your beloved *mocinha* making sure you are safe and sound. She seems to care about you. So sweet.' He flashed the smile again and Kirkwood wondered why he felt so uneasy in the presence of a man who had just saved him. Shouldn't he be more...grateful? He dragged his eyes away from the man long enough to retrieve the phone from his pocket and scan the message.

'You okay, Kirky? I'm at HQ. Meet me there – M.'

The phone beeped again in his hand and a second message flashed across the screen, which he noticed was now cracked, no doubt as a result of his earlier tumble.

'By HQ I obviously mean the Burger King where we went last night. Soz – M.'

Kirkwood frowned as a third message arrived almost simultaneously.

'And by M I mean Meredith – M.'

'She's a live wire that one, and no mistake. I sense you have met your match there haven't you...Kirky.' He grinned again, but this time there was a suggestion of a sneer attached to it. There was something about this man, Good Samaritan or not, that Kirkwood couldn't warm to. He had an aura about him that was just not right.

'I'm sorry. But how did you know that was her? And why can't those people see us? And do we know each other? It's just I've had a very stressful few days and I can't quite...' His words tailed off into a bewildered silence.

'Here, let me give you a clue,' he offered, reverting to his jovial, best friend routine again. He took a huge step forward, causing Kirkwood to flinch before lowering himself with surprising agility for someone his size, onto one knee. With a cheery wink, he positioned his arms to imitate holding and aiming a rifle. He closed his left eye as if sighting a target while the other one stared unblinking at Kirkwood, an imaginary firearm pointed squarely at the young man's forehead.

'Any clearer now? How you say, has the penny dropped? *A centavo?*' He stuck his tongue out as if the comic interlude would alleviate the chill steadily descending Kirkwood's spine like a creeping frost.

At last the penny did drop. Along with Kirkwood's jaw. For he was no longer sitting on his backside in a Belfast alley. He was aged eight and back in his room, performing bedtime routines, positioning his private army in defensive positions around the fort. The same routine every night. The routine he forgot to carry out the night his father was murdered. His fault, all his fault. None of them ever said as much — his mum, his sister. They didn't know the truth like he did.

They didn't know the reality confronting him every night when he closed his eyes and tried to sleep; but instead found himself staring into Skelly's unflinching, unforgiving face. 'If only you performed your duties and stuck to your responsibilities, we could have saved him, dear boy. You deserted him in his hour of need. And now you must suffer the consequences. Take it on the chin like a man.'

His mistake would haunt him forever and every night from then he positioned the toy soldiers as they should have been on that fateful evening. Because if he didn't, bad things would happen again. He did it for his mother and for Katie and for everyone else he loved and cared for. The cavalry was brought in and formed up within the confines of the fort under the watchful gaze of Skelly, poised at a second's notice to gallop out the gates to confront any approaching enemy. The ramparts were manned by the infantry, all four sides, so a withering fire could be directed down upon a foe no matter what direction they approached from.

And beyond the fort he positioned his skirmishers. All specialised sharp-shooters, skilled in sniping at supply lines and advance parties, weakening and disrupting an opponent before the real battle commenced. He created names, personalities and complex backstories for each of them. They were his elite unit, the crème de la crème of the fort's company. His favourite had been a Portuguese irregular, attached to Wellington's ragtag army when they battled the mighty French in the scorching heat of the Iberian Peninsula. A man fighting to save his country from the devil that was Napoleon. A giant, bearded man who had followed the Iron Duke, 'Old Hooky' himself, all the way across Spain, up through France to a sleepy town called Waterloo.

The intricate metal figure was beautifully painted by a skilled hand with an eye for detail. Beyond the exquisitely rendered uniform, mud-splattered boots and musket; beyond the glistening full beard, flattened street brawler's nose and scarred cheek acquired at the Siege of Salamanca. No, it was the eyes that sparked the flicker of recognition deep within Kirkwood's mind — or rather, the eye. The dark, unblinking eye peering through the rifle sights at his next victim. The eye of a cold, calculating killer. The eye that was staring at him now in a backstreet alley in modern day Belfast.

'Rodriguez,' Kirkwood uttered the name through dry, cracked lips as the bearded behemoth nodded in recognition at his name, before shifting his aim slightly from Kirkwood's now clammy forehead to an unseen target behind him. That's when he pulled the make-believe trigger. And that's when reality crashed back in and the screaming started. Kirkwood spun around to see an elderly man lying on the street clutching his chest.

Startled passers-by buzzed around the felled pensioner and a woman kneeled beside him loosening his shirt buttons and testing for a pulse. A panicked voice rang out, 'Somebody phone an ambulance! I think he's having a heart attack.' Kirkwood knew this was no heart attack, no natural death. For the old man was dead, he was certain of that. Dead before he hit the pavement, for sharp shooters like Corporal Martim Rodriguez never missed.

He turned to say something, but the alley was empty. Rodriguez was gone, but for Kirkwood the nightmare was only beginning.

CHAPTER 53

BATTLE LINES

1:38 p.m.

'So, let me get this straight.' Meredith sat back in her chair and looked around to ensure they were not being overheard. They were back once more on the first floor of the fast food restaurant where they convened the previous night. Kirkwood had made his way there in a daze following the encounter with Rodriguez in the alley. Two teenage members of staff loitered at an adjacent table, more interested in chatting each other up, than doing anything remotely resembling work.

Content they were out of earshot, Meredith leaned forward and hissed sharply, 'You're telling me that when we split up you were on the verge of being beaten to a pulp by Jamie McManus when, out of the blue, you're rescued by some Good Samaritan who just happened to be in the area?'

'That's about right,' replied a deadpan Kirkwood. 'If that's what you call the knuckle scrapers chasing us.'

'Yeah, Jamie and Dean McManus. Two of the nastiest pieces of work you will ever meet. They're apparently not happy Danny is in traction so have now turned their attention towards yours truly.'

She stared at him intently, but he returned her gaze, determined not to be the one to look away first. He could barely believe what happened any more than her, and retelling the tale only made it sound all the more incredulous.

'So, this…Rodriguez,' said Meredith, continuing the cross examination, 'Proceeded to strike down an innocent member of the public with an imaginary

193

gun before disappearing in a puff of smoke?' She sighed and muttered something to herself which Kirkwood couldn't quite make out but was fairly certain contained the word 'bonkers'.

'In my defence, I never mentioned anything about a puff of smoke,' he countered with a weak, but hopefully, winning smile.

'Pardon my scepticism and I know I said I believed you earlier, but it all sounds plain crazy.'

'About as crazy as writing letters to a dead girl and her replying with creepy, cryptic messages.'

Meredith shifted uneasily in her chair. 'Point taken,' she conceded. 'But you have to admit, it comes across as pretty weird. I mean, where did this guy come from? What did he look like?'

'Fairly distinctive, you might say. Built like a brick you-know-what with a nose like a busted slipper. Big black beard and a scar on his cheek. I think it's fair to say I could pick him out again if he were to appear in an identification parade. He was…'

'Wait a minute,' Meredith halted him, her voice shriller than intended. She glanced warily towards Burger King's answer to Romeo and Juliet, but they were still whispering sweet nothings, oblivious to the heated conversation in progress, less than a dozen feet from them.

'Beard. Wonky nose. Scar on the cheek. I've seen this guy.'

'Maybe you saw him in the square? Before we split up.'

'No. One night I was sleeping up near Botanic Gardens. Well, I say sleeping. More trying to keep warm and not get robbed. Anyway, I was packing up my bag when, there he was standing on the grass about a hundred yards away. Just staring at me with this cheesy grin plastered across his face.'

'Sounds about right. Did he say anything to you?'

'Not a word. When he saw me looking over, he just shot me this cheeky salute and began to saunter away across the lawn. And here's the thing. It's at least a thirty second walk until you get to the trees on the other side. But when I looked up again from my bag, no more than five seconds I swear, he was gone. Just like that.' She clicked her fingers to emphasise the point.

'In a puff of smoke,' smirked Kirkwood, prompting Meredith to smack him on the arm with a clenched fist. 'Sod off smartarse. This is serious. As if it wasn't bad enough that I'm being chased for that dope Danny's debts, now we've got some insane Spanish man-mountain to contend with. You seriously couldn't make this up.' She slumped back into her chair, arms folded, a worried expression on her face.

'He's Portuguese. That's like calling an Irishman, English.'

'Whatever.'

'Skelly is behind this; he has to be.' Kirkwood was deadly serious now.

'The man in your head? Who suddenly pops up in my dreams? Correct that — nightmares. This is nuts. Totally nuts.'

'Yep,' Kirkwood sighed and rubbed a hand through his unkempt mop. He needed a haircut. He needed a lot of things. But most of all, he needed time. Time to think, to piece together the insane events of the last few days into some coherent, logical order. 'Why are you still even here? I must sound like a raving madman.'

The occasional doomed counselling session aside, he had never opened up like this to anyone. He had never attempted to explain Skelly and 'The 49' to anyone. How do you explain the inexplicable, find the words to describe the indescribable? If he didn't fully understand it, then how could he expect someone else to get their head around it?

Meredith leaned forward, took his hand in hers and looked him squarely in the eye. 'Like you said. I write letters to a dead girl — who has told me to trust you.'

She smiled reassuringly and the final barrier between them melted away. Wherever this runaway train was going, they were on it together.

Kirkwood knew he wasn't delusional because, if he was, it was now a shared delusion. She had seen Rodriguez as well. If he was going through the looking-glass, then he wasn't taking that step on his own. He had finally spoken the truth to another human being as opposed to a watered-down version to some medical professional paid to ask the same bland, empty questions and jot down his bland, empty replies. He finally had an ally, someone who believed him, someone whose very presence confirmed he was sane. He was as close as he'd ever be to finally escaping the monsters in his head.

Kirkwood Scott was done fighting, done running and hiding. The battle lines were drawn. It was time to fight.

CHAPTER 54

THE LEAFY SUBURBS

6:10 p.m.

They talked for hours after that, filling the gaps in their respective stories. It was an emotional and exhausting process, and Kirkwood was amazed to look at his watch to discover it was early evening by the time they finished. He marvelled at the amount of coffee and ice cream Meredith consumed, bouncing about on her seat, a restless ball of energy determined to eke every last scrap of information out of him.

'You should have been a police officer,' he half laughed, half croaked when she concluded the interrogation. 'I feel like I've gone ten rounds with Columbo. It's getting late. Can I walk you home?'

The second the words left his mouth he groaned with embarrassment. 'Oh God, Meredith, I'm really sorry, I didn't mean it like that.' He slapped his forehead with the palm of a skinned hand before wincing as the stinging pain brought back memories of the earlier encounter with Rodriguez. 'Aarrghh. Of all the stupid, insensitive statements to come out with. I'm such a prat.'

'It's okay. Seriously. Tell you what. I'll permit you the privilege of escorting me back to my sumptuous residence in the leafy suburbs.' Kirkwood stared at her blankly, causing Meredith to laugh. 'The park, you eejit. I'll show you my hidey hole. It's like Narnia but without the annoying posh kids and mythical woodland creatures.'

Kirkwood smiled, relieved she wasn't offended by his indiscretion. 'Well, thank God for that. After the day I've had, the last thing I need is a talking beaver.'

He offered to pay for them to catch a bus, but Meredith insisted on walking. 'You've wasted enough money on me these last few days and it's not as if you're Alan Sugar, no offence.' She rose, hooked her bag over a shoulder, and strode towards the exit. 'Come on Kirky, time you saw the less glamorous side of our wonderful city.'

'Besides,' she continued, 'I like to walk. I've got used to it. Can't remember the last time I was in a car or on a bus. That's the thing about living rough. It's as if you have to hand in your 'I'm a normal member of the human race' card even though I'm still me. I haven't changed.'

She set a furious pace up Royal Avenue and Kirkwood struggled to keep up. He was struck by her confidence and inner strength despite the drama currently dogging their every step. They passed the imposing City Hall and worked their way through tourists and red-coated tour guides, keen to lure passing custom onto the hop-on hop-off buses touring the rapidly expanding city.

In front of City Hall, green-haired skater boys sat slumped on benches, their arms slung casually around the shoulders of their skinny, deathly pale girlfriends. Marilyn Manson blasted from somewhere and dubious smelling cigarettes were passed around as they scowled at anyone who dared make eye contact with them. Meredith snorted in derision as she passed. 'Most of that lot will get picked up by their daddies in an hour or so and be whisked off home to wash their hands before teatime. They're about as rock 'n' roll as a wet weekend in Portrush.'

They walked out of the city centre and up towards Queen's University, where students bustled to and from its library, laden down with files and reading lists. Kirkwood knew the area well from numerous drunken nights spent in pubs and clubs nestled around the campus. Now that he was with Meredith, it was as if his homeless radar had kicked in, for they were everywhere. He blushed, ashamed he acknowledged their existence now, whereas before he lowered his head and hurried past, embarrassed and uncomfortable at the feelings of guilt aroused within.

Meredith nodded at a few as they neared the university but didn't stop to engage in conversation. As if feeling the need to explain herself, she told Kirkwood that, bar Danny and a few others, she preferred to keep a low profile and not build friendships.

'It's not as if we're one big happy family. A lot of these guys would rob you blind as soon as look at you. It's never personal, it's just people are desperate — for alcohol, for smack, for the money to get a night in a hostel instead of freezing to death in a doorway. I mean, this is Belfast not Beverly Hills. It snows in April.'

They passed the front of Queen's, which rose magnificently from its sumptuous grounds. Its dazzling architectural features contrasted sharply with the grotty Students Union across the road. Hundreds of students milled around both buildings, agonising over whether to hit the library or retire to the bar for cheap cider promotions and heated debates. Kirkwood recalled his own student days which seemed a lifetime ago. They had been good years, though; years when he was occupied and focused on his studies and social life. Skelly was an ever-present, but largely dormant force, only stirring when stress levels rose in his final year with exams approaching fast.

Meredith looked totally at home amidst the college throngs, like any other scruffy undergraduate going about her business. She barely afforded the students a second glance, rushing on towards the ornate gates of Botanic Gardens.

'Welcome to my humble abode,' she announced, passing through them and pointing towards a gaudily painted bandstand, in the centre of an immaculately kept lawn which was bordered on all sides by conifers and bushes. Scattered across the lawn was an eclectic mix of office workers, students, and young families. Several picnics were in process while, on the edge of the lawn, a gaggle of teenagers passed around a cider bottle, despite numerous signs proclaiming alcohol consumption was prohibited. All were united in their desire to make the most of a sunny day in Belfast.

Meredith planted herself on a bench, shadowed by an overhanging birch tree. She stretched theatrically, simultaneously emitting a yawn which could have raised the dead. 'What time is it Kirky Wirky?' she enquired, staring across the lawn as if she hadn't a care in the world.

'Firstly, my name is Kirkwood. Secondly, it's…' he glanced at his watch. 'Just gone twenty to eight.'

'My, how time flies when you're having fun. The park closes at sunset which I reckon will be an hour or so. See that monstrosity over there?' She pointed towards the bandstand which shone like a giant Kinder Egg as the rays of the evening sun bounced off it. 'That is my bedroom for the night. All I have to do is evade the park warden when the gates are locked. He's meant to check everyone has left before he locks up, but it's easy to hide in a place this big. Once he's gone, I can retire to my luxurious abode. Ain't life grand?'

Kirkwood stared at Meredith, blinked and studied the bandstand, before blinking again and studying the curious young woman before him. He opened his mouth to speak but could find no words.

'Oh, relax, it's perfectly safe, Dad,' sighed Meredith, rolling her eyes and aiming a kick at his shins, causing Kirkwood to jump back from where he was standing in front of her. 'There's a loose panel in its base. If you pull it back, you can crawl inside. I've been sleeping there on and off for weeks. There's no

Wi-Fi or en suite, but it's quite cosy when I get wrapped up in my sleeping bag. I'm as happy as Larry with my torch and a crappy paperback. Nobody else knows about it. I've even stored some stuff there. If nobody sees me coming or going, then I'm safe as houses. Or as safe as a creaky, smelly Victorian bandstand can be.' She shrugged and looked up, daring Kirkwood to challenge her logic.

'That's all very well but you seem to have overlooked the small matter of the psychotic drug dealers still after our blood. Plus, our Portuguese friend, Señor Rodriguez, who also appears to have an unhealthy interest in our current whereabouts. Had you forgotten about him? The living, breathing six-foot-five toy soldier turned man-mountain with the power to inflict serious damage with a click of his fingers? Until we figure out what the hell is going on, the least you can do is spend the night at my place.'

He realised his verbal blunder, as Meredith shot him a horrified look, before bursting into laughter. 'Well, I've certainly had subtler propositions but aren't you the silver-tongued charmer.' Kirkwood turned the colour of a sunburnt beetroot, before she decided to take pity on his plight and refrain from any further teasing. 'That's kind of you but this is who I am now. I've coped for ten months and I'm perfectly capable of managing another night. Besides, who's to say Beardy McBeardface isn't on our side? After all, he did save you from the mother of all beatings back in that alley.' She stretched like a satisfied feline and smiled up at Kirkwood — pleased with her summary of their current predicament.

'I might not know much but I know this. Rodriguez is one of Skelly's men, so my wellbeing is not a priority for him. These guys have haunted me for over twenty years. Call it OCD, call it PTSD, call it whatever you want, but I know what I saw in that alley. I don't know why, and I don't know how, but this guy is here and means us nothing but harm. So, stop playing the tough little street urchin. We need to stick together tonight. You can have my bed and I'll sleep on the floor,' he paused, and a shadow of a smirk crossed his features. 'I might even show you my dice collection if you play your cards right.'

Unable to keep a straight face, Meredith exploded into laughter again. The tension was released like air from a balloon and the two of them giggled until tears rolled down their cheeks. To the casual observer, they were just two young people enjoying each other's company.

Regaining some composure, Meredith swept a hand through her tatty hair. 'I know you mean well, but if this guy Rodriguez knows you that well, then he doesn't have to be Brain of Britain, or Portugal for that matter, to work out where you live. If he's the big threat you seem to think, then wouldn't you be wiser spending the night at chez Meredith? I don't snore, and I promise not to hog the duvet.'

Kirkwood stared across the lawn at the bandstand. She had a point. Maybe the only way to combat the insanity he was embroiled in, was via equally insane tactics. Three days ago, he'd been complaining about how dull his life was. He couldn't say that anymore, so why not go with the flow even if it meant sleeping under a bandstand with an extra from Oliver Twist. What could possibly go wrong?

'Alright then,' he conceded, with a sigh. Meredith stamped her feet in delight and leapt up, intent on embracing Kirkwood but he took a large step back, holding his hands out to appease her. 'Woah, hold your horses. First, I need to nip back to the house and get some of my gear. I'll be back in an hour and I'll grab some food and drinks on the way back. Deal?'

'Deal,' grinned Meredith, a look of smug satisfaction on her face. Kirkwood sighed again. It was hard to say no to her.

'Okay, I'll be as quick as I can. Wait here and don't go anywhere.'

'Yes sir, Mister Boss Man.' She performed an extravagant salute, giggling again. Kirkwood shook his head in exasperation, turned and began to walk towards the park gates. He marvelled at how Meredith could find humour in this rapidly deteriorating mess. She had lost her best friend, was estranged from her family and living a dangerous existence on the streets. On top of that, she was dodging drug dealers and figments of his imagination, come to life. The girl was either incredibly tough or incredibly deluded. Either way, he admired her resilience.

Imaginary world. He batted the words about in his head. Except it wasn't so imaginary now, was it? Following his run in with Rodriguez, what other blasts from his past were going to pop up in modern-day Belfast? Kirkwood shuddered. Rodriguez was a skirmisher, relatively small fry in the fantasy army he created in his bedroom all those years ago. What if Skelly sent others, creations who made the Portuguese giant pale in comparison? He banished the thought, realising it was pointless to speculate any further. He was desperately tired but needed to focus on the enemy he knew about, not worry about what else might be hurtling down the track towards him.

It had been the most surreal of days, but he had to accept and deal with that. Kirkwood feared for Meredith and suddenly felt a heavy responsibility towards her. She had enough on her plate without this. Was he really so selfish he was prepared to drag an already damaged young woman into even deeper waters? Did she really need this? He doubted it, but she was all he had so he saw little choice but to cling to her for all he was worth. He had doubted her fantastical story about the Emily letters and graffiti until he'd witnessed it today, with his very own eyes. It had to be more than a coincidence that their paths were now crossing. He felt a strong connection to her and was increasingly convinced Meredith was the key to answers he had been seeking for years.

Kirkwood exited the park gates and broke into a run. He had wasted enough time daydreaming. Meredith was waiting for him. Despite her protestations to the contrary, the thought of her alone beneath that bandstand did not sit well with him.

CHAPTER 55

HAVEN'T YOU FORGOTTEN

SOMETHING?

8:25 p.m.

Kirkwood half walked, half jogged the mile from the park to his house. Turning into Glasgow Street, he was relieved to see Richard's little rust bucket of a car was not parked outside. He had no time for small talk tonight and took the stairs two at a time. Entering his tiny room, he began cramming clothes and toiletries into a holdall. He added a packet of wine gums which had been sitting on his desk for a fortnight and a blanket, stashed on top of the wardrobe. Scooping up his phone, wallet, and keys, he took a final cursory look around the room, then froze.

Sitting on his bedside table were the dice. A counsellor once told him they were a physical manifestation of his disorder, that he needed to confront and overcome. Yet, try as he might, he could not throw them out. Succumbing to the gnawing, intrusive thoughts racing through his mind was easier said than done. He tried a million times to ignore them, but to no avail. Countless relaxation techniques, intensive counselling sessions, hypnosis, acupuncture — he tried them all; but always the crushing desire to roll the dice swept away his defences. He patiently sat on an NHS waiting list for nine months awaiting bespoke OCD therapy, but it was about as effective as a one-legged man in an arse kicking competition. Nothing worked and nothing would work. The dice always returned to him, just as he always returned to them. The only way to combat the terrifying anxiety and fear was to roll and be damned.

When the dice appeared, Skelly was never far away. Kirkwood let his holdall fall to the floor and stood rooted to the spot. A bitterly cold sensation began to spread from the roof of his mouth into the core of his brain before spiralling outwards, icy tendrils shooting into both eyeballs, causing his pupils to constrict until all he could see were two tiny points of light. His knees buckled, and he sank to the ground, his entire being sucked inexorably towards the dual pinpricks of white. As he drew closer to the lights they merged until he was immersed within a huge, swirling vortex of dazzling alabaster. The study beckoned.

CHAPTER 56

LAY OF THE LAND

In the seventeen years since the study became the black hub of his life, Kirkwood never discerned any difference from visit to visit. The imposing desk, the towering bookcases and heavy velvet drapes; nothing ever changed. The subdued lighting, without any apparent source, the musky aroma of the leather-bound tomes, even the arrangement of the decanter and tumblers on the table by the padded armchair, where Skelly now sat, anticipating the conversation ahead. Less than ten feet away, Kirkwood stood rooted to the spot.

Skelly eyed him from the armchair, drink cupped between liver-spotted, leathery hands, crowned with unnaturally long fingernails. He was impeccably dressed as ever; the hand-stitched, brown leather brogues, yellow woollen socks and expensive tweed suit. The socks were matched by a garish yellow waistcoat and tie flecked with red symbols. Kirkwood could never quite make out what they were, but they seemed to permanently shift and shimmer just beyond the limits of his vision. His eyesight was far from perfect, but in the study, everything seemed even more blurred and distorted. It was like a fine mist infiltrated the atmosphere, creating a milky hue which clung to his corneas, softening the horror of the surroundings.

Just as with the room, Skelly's appearance never altered either. The ruddy cheeks and flabby jowls of a once active man gone to seed after years of neglect and excess. The large, bulbous nose reddened noticeably at its tip and was traversed by dozens of broken blood vessels. Whenever he smiled, which was rarely, two rows of poorly maintained teeth were revealed, the colour of pus freshly squeezed from a ripening pimple. Slate grey, mutton chop whiskers swept down his jawline, almost converging like the clashing cliffs of Greek legend at the base of multiple chins. A chaotic mop of curly, unkempt hair sat atop bushy eyebrows which required a postcode of their own.

Skelly sighed, the sigh of a man with a packed schedule who could ill afford the time to deal with this latest distraction from his busy itinerary. 'You know this is starting to become quite tiresome young man,' he droned, raising the tumbler to his lips and taking a healthy sip from it. 'I've gone above and beyond my pay grade today to ensure your well-being, and this is the thanks I get.' When Kirkwood gave no indication he would respond, Skelly frowned, for a second looking genuinely wounded. He afforded Kirkwood the long, hard stare of a disappointed uncle before speaking again. 'Rodriguez? Saving your bacon from a sound thrashing?' he grunted before turning his attention back to his drink.

'You've never been interested in my welfare,' Kirkwood finally spoke, no longer able to bite his tongue. 'Since the night my father was murdered, you've been nothing but a thorn in my side. You've made my life a living hell, so don't come out with your concerned routine now. Rodriguez might have saved me from a kicking but I'm sure it's nothing compared to what you've got lined up for me.'

Skelly let out a disturbing guffaw, unveiling a mouthful of rancid enamel. 'Oh, how I enjoy your more theatrical outbursts. You really are quite the thespian at times. But, despite your protestations to the contrary, I can assure you that your best interests have always been at the heart of all my actions.' He raised a bristly eyebrow as if challenging his guest to argue the point. Kirkwood realised he had overstepped the mark and reined his temper back.

'I thought not.' Skelly uncrossed his ankles and sat upright in the armchair, planting both feet on the deep, plush carpet before setting his drink back down. The old goat meant business, which was never a pleasant proposition. Kirkwood braced himself for both barrels of the Skelly shotgun.

'So, I'm a thorn in your side, am I? I think we both know that's not the case. If it weren't for the timely actions of my sergeant, this meeting would more than likely be taking place in a hospital bed, as opposed to your bedroom. When I send you back there, feel free to check the news as to the current whereabouts of one Jamie McManus, the gentleman who was pursuing you and your young lady friend at the time of said intervention. Ward 4C of the Royal Victoria Hospital, in a serious, but stable, condition. Police believe he was the subject of a savage assault in the city centre earlier today and are appealing for witnesses. There won't be any of course.'

Kirkwood would have shifted his feet uncomfortably, were they not set in invisible concrete. He shivered involuntarily. With Rodriguez roaming the streets of Belfast, Meredith was now more vulnerable than ever. The only saving grace was that Skelly could not read his mind. He had come perilously close through the years, but never managed to breach his mental defences. He was desperate to somehow end the conversation and get back to Meredith and saw no option but to take the fight to his decrepit opponent.

'I don't know what you're up to this time, Augustus, but I'm getting fed up with your pathetic mind games. You don't like Meredith, do you? And you don't like me spending time with her, either. You're frightened that you'll lose control of me, that the bond between us will break whatever sick hold you've had over me.' He paused, surprised at the ferocity of his words. He had never dared speak to Skelly so bluntly before.

It was a mistake he would regret.

Skelly leaned forward and snarled, revealing teeth which seemed sharper than before, jagged rocks glistening with saliva, that shimmered and then vanished with a viperish lick of his lips. Kirkwood didn't know if his nemesis had any nerves but, if so, he had just struck one.

'Don't you threaten me, boy or I'll have you tied up in so many knots you'll never set eyes on that little tart again,' he growled, his voice a gravelly rasp. 'You have no idea what I'm capable of. I've been toying with you since the day they dumped your beloved father into that hole in the ground. The father who died because of your own incompetence and indifference.' He recognised his own momentary loss of composure and sank back into the deeper recesses of the armchair. A sickly grin crossed his face as he waited for the verbal arrow he had unleashed to find its target. Which of course, it did. Bullseye.

'Don't you dare speak about my dad like that! You're not fit to lace his boots — you evil lump of lard.'

Skelly broke into a sadistic snigger. 'That's more like it. Good lad. Give it to me with both barrels. Your old man would be proud of you. That's if he were still about to hear all this.' He let the final few words drip slyly from his mouth like a faulty tap leaking poison. Drip. Drip. Drip.

It took every ounce of fortitude Kirkwood owned not to respond this time. It was pointless to argue back. He silently cursed himself for rising to the bait his ancient adversity had so cleverly cast.

'Are we done here?' He hoped his words masked the rage consuming him. He wanted nothing more than to sink his fists over and over into Skelly's soft, repugnant face. Focus Kirkwood. Think of Meredith, not your own stupid male pride. She needs you more than you need this.

Skelly was suddenly distracted — bored even. He waved nonchalantly to where Kirkwood stood frozen to the spot. 'You may leave but know this,' he raised his glass and took another generous mouthful. It never seemed to empty. What was in it anyway? Brandy? Port? 'The game is fully afoot. Everything up until now has merely been us testing the lay of the land. You've seen nothing yet. Nothing.'

He threw the glass and its contents into the fire and a wall of flame shot out towards where Kirkwood stood helplessly. He scrunched his eyes, anticipating both searing heat and unimaginable pain but when neither came, opened them to find Skelly smirking at him from the armchair.

'Oh, and one more thing,' the old man purred, his soulless eyes suddenly sparkling with premeditated malice. 'Don't be getting any ideas about scuttling off to your little girlfriend when you get back. There's the small matter of your daily routine which you've conveniently overlooked. Your weekend pass has expired. Never let a woman get between a man and his work. Mark my words. It will be the death of you.'

'But...' protested Kirkwood, a wave of bile rising from his stomach at the thought of Meredith alone under the bandstand as the last light of the day ebbed from the park.

'But nothing,' countered Skelly sharply, lifting a finger in the air to cut off Kirkwood's remonstrations. 'Rules are rules for a reason. You will roll the dice, or you will face the consequences.' His voice dropped to a waspish whisper and his next words turned Kirkwood's blood to iced slush.

'And worry not. We will make sure your little friend is looked after.'

CHAPTER 57

ROUTINE 64

8:47 p.m.

Kirkwood had escaped relatively unscathed and knew it. Rolling a four with the four-sided die and a 16 with its twenty-sided compatriot, he breathed a sigh of relief and knuckled down to the task at hand. Routine 64 — Red Door Knocking. There were dozens more tortuous routines he could have rolled. Despite his desperation to get back to Meredith, he knew it was futile ignoring the pounding insistence. To resist would have resulted in his physical symptoms escalating rapidly to a prickly, restless sensation in his arms and legs, a clammy sweat oozing from every pore, and a tightening sensation of the chest, like a belt being tightened notch by notch. The routine always won out. Always. Even the thought of Meredith being alone and vulnerable could not outweigh it.

Taking the stairs from his room three at a time, he hurtled down the hallway, out the front door and onto the street. He activated his stopwatch and walked briskly towards the bottom of the street, trying to look as inconspicuous as possible. Thankfully, it was largely deserted. Darkness was descending and the street lights were on, casting their artificial light on the scattering of cars parked on either side of the terraced street. Ninety-four houses in total, twenty-six of which had red doors. Kirkwood knew this, having visited them all on many occasions before, as part of this routine.

Compared with some of the other horrors he had carted around since childhood, 64 was relatively recent.

The routine involved Kirkwood visiting any address in the street with a red front door and rapping it a predetermined number of times, depending on the house number. Number 5 required five knocks, Number 12 a dozen, and so on, up until a seemingly never-ending stop at Number 87. Each knock had to be performed with his right fist and counted aloud, but not so loud as to alert the occupants. Lose count and he had to start again. Accidentally touch a door with any other part of his body, and he had to start again. If the door was open or there were people at it, he could move on to the next address but had to revisit it once the coast was clear. The routine had to be satisfactorily carried out at each door within a challenging seventeen minutes. Failure to do so, and he had to start again — until it was done.

His record was thirteen minutes and twenty-nine seconds on an unforgettable June morning the previous year, when everything seamlessly fell into place; while his darkest was a hellish four hours the previous November, where one mishap after another resulted in him performing the routine an agonising twenty-three times until it was completed satisfactorily. It made no sense; it wasn't meant to.

Tonight required four attempts. His first run was aborted within five minutes when he was disturbed mid tap, at Number 20, by a startled pensioner, who opened her door to find Kirkwood standing there, clenched fist in mid-air. His face as red as the door itself, he mumbled an apology about being at the wrong address, before skulking out of sight, until the bemused lady got into her car, and drove away.

Because of that, it was back to the start again. Kirkwood had trudged disconsolately down the street, eyes fixed on the ground to avoid any curious looks from other residents. He stole a look at his watch. Time was marching on and it was fast approaching the time he had assured Meredith he would return. He cursed Skelly and, arriving back at Number 5, began the laborious process again.

Eventually, he completed his eighty-seventh rap at Number 87 and looked at his stopwatch, prompting a small whoop of delight — fifteen minutes and forty-seven seconds. Tapping his nose three times, he recited aloud, 'It's finished…It's finished…It's finished,' and waited. Nothing. No recall to the study. Skelly was silent, meaning the routine was completed to his perverted satisfaction. Kirkwood turned and began to run as hard as he could.

With every passing stride he drew closer to Meredith but as he did so, a gathering unease began to form within. He was late, and all he could think of was Skelly's parting shot before he dismissed Kirkwood from the study.

'And worry not. We will make sure your little friend is looked after.'

Something was wrong.

Something was very wrong.

CHAPTER 58

ABDUCTION

9:04 p.m.

Meredith weighed up the pros and cons of leaving the park to search for Kirkwood, as the time of his promised return came and went. But where to look? She knew he rented a room somewhere on the Lisburn Road but beyond that, it was the proverbial needle in the haystack. The road stretched for miles out of the city, and he wasn't answering his phone.

When he left, she had melted into the trees which bordered the lawn and waited until the last of the day's visitors left via the main gates. When she was certain the coast was clear, she moved swiftly and silently in a crouching run, back towards the bandstand that kept a solitary vigil in the centre of the lawn, a silent sentinel about to be engulfed by the encroaching gloom. Arriving at it, she scanned the surrounding area to ensure she was not being watched. There was nobody about; both the park and the night were hers. She dropped to one knee and began to root about inside her ever-present Adidas bag.

After a few seconds, her fingers closed around a slim pen torch which she flicked on, and clenched between her teeth in a single, fluid movement. She directed the thin beam of light it emitted onto one of the metal panels which formed the base of the structure. Next to be produced from the bag was a metal spoon which she used as a lever to pry the panel loose. It was a tried and tested technique that granted access to her secret den beneath the stage. Only the closest of inspections would reveal that the screws attaching the panel to the framework of the bandstand had been previously loosened. Within seconds, the end of the panel came away in her hand.

'Bingo,' she grunted in satisfaction. Setting the panel to one side, she lay on her back and started to wriggle feet-first through the gap she had created, into the black expanse beneath. Once inside, she rolled onto her stomach and, holding the torch in her left hand, dragged the Adidas bag behind her, refitting the panel in a manner which gave no clue as to her intrusion. The space she now occupied was cramped. Resting on both elbows, her head was no more than six inches from the floorboards above. Sitting was out of the question, but it provided a dry, safe place to crash for the night, despite the musty smell permeating the cavity. Even though she had explored every nook of the enclosed space, she was still to be convinced someone or something had not once crawled inside to die.

It brought back memories of a particularly cold winter when her parent's house, for she could no longer refer to it as a home, was invaded by a family of field mice who took refuge inside from the freezing conditions. Her father had set poison in every room, which she diligently inspected each day for signs of activity. One morning, the poison was gone, and she had gasped in astonishment, akin to Christmas morning when she bounded into the kitchen to see if Father Christmas had consumed his mince pie and glass of milk. A week or so later, the same gassy stench as was under the bandstand started to seep through the house, an olfactory osmosis of decay. The offending aroma had been eventually traced to the rear of the airing cupboard where her father removed the corpse of a tiny mouse from beneath a bundle of towels.

Meredith imagined lying amid a graveyard of dead vermin, before banishing the disturbing image from her mind. There was worse company than a dead mouse or two and, besides, beggars could not be choosers. The dubious fragrance of her humble abode was more than compensated for by the security the bandstand provided. It was dry, reasonably warm, with just enough space for her and a few belongings. It also acted as a storage space for the items she didn't wish to lug about the city centre during the day.

She stretched out a hand and, guided by the sliver of light, retrieved a sleeping bag, blanket, and pillow that had been squirrelled away for safe keeping. Burrowing deep within the sleeping bag, she wrapped the blanket around her body and settled back on the pillow. It was a far cry from her old bedroom, but it beat huddling in a doorway, vulnerable to the attentions of any passing deviants.

Closing both eyes, she tried to relax, but Kirkwood's face persistently projected onto her cerebral cinema screen. Where was he? Had she scared him off with the mad talk of Emily and the letters? She had to tell someone, or the secret would have split her open like a ripe nectarine. He seemed to care and, more importantly, witnessed the miracle that was Emily's wall. Besides, when it came to tales of lunacy, his tale of toy soldiers morphing into gigantic guardian angels, took some beating. They made a bizarre pairing, but she sensed he needed her as much as she needed him. Emily, Skelly, the graffiti, the bearded Portuguese brute — it was all somehow connected. They just needed time and a huge slice of luck to survive long enough to figure it out.

Yes, she needed him. Not in a boyfriend-girlfriend way, jeez, that was the last thing on her mind. But she craved a friend. Someone who believed her, who she mattered to, someone who could keep her going from hour to hour, and day to day. She wasn't sure she believed in fate, but they had been thrown together and surely there was a reason as to why. It was just a case of fitting it together. All the pieces were there, she was certain of that. But where was he?

A sudden sound from outside made her freeze. All thoughts of Kirkwood, Emily and their supporting cast scattered like a frightened flock of starlings, exploding into the night sky. She caught a breath and strained her ears to somehow gather information as to the source of the noise. It was close, she was sure of that much. Was someone outside? She had discovered the cubby hole four months ago and, to date, nobody had unearthed her sanctuary, despite there being a few close calls.

On one occasion, a group of drunken teenagers occupied the bandstand for several hours, rowdily consuming their cider and alcopops to a soundtrack of clanging techno music. Then there was the time a courting couple scaled the park gates and indulged in enthusiastic, but thankfully brief, love making, inches from where Meredith lay helplessly beneath them, horrified at his guttural grunts and her high-pitched encouragement.

She considered saying something but thought better of it, erring on the side of silent caution. Outside she could discern a faint scratching, scraping sound coming from the other side of the panel. Her shoulders relaxed slightly. Most likely a stray dog pawing at the ground, or a squirrel that had ventured out from the cover of the trees on a foraging mission. She realised she was holding her breath and exhaled as quietly as she could. A few more minutes and whatever it was would hopefully move on and leave her in peace.

Then she heard the voices. At least one, possibly two of them. She struggled to make out what was being said amidst a series of harsh and indecipherable whispered exchanges. Male, she thought. And were they arguing? One of the voices rose momentarily and she detected an accent of sorts before the other one hissed irritably, followed by silence. If Meredith possessed a pin at that moment, she would have undoubtedly heard it drop. She could feel fear rising like an icy vapour within her and squeezed both eyes shut, mouthing a silent prayer for them to go, to leave her be. If there was a God, then now was the perfect time for him to get acquainted with her needs — starting with this one, right here, right now.

The loose panel was suddenly wrenched away and the screech of protesting metal cut through the air like a wailing siren. Before Meredith could utter a sound or escape their grasp, a pair of filthy, calloused hands reached through and grabbed the bottom of her sleeping bag, pulling hard. She belatedly found her voice and unleashed a withering scream, simultaneously kicking out at her invisible assailant from within the confines of the bag.

'Let go of me! Piss off!'

Her protests were in vain for, despite wriggling furiously, her opponent proved too strong. Within seconds, she had been partially hauled from beneath the structure. She flung her arms out to either side, desperate to gain a purchase on anything within reach that would frustrate the persistent efforts to haul her into the open. Another pair of hands appeared, and sharps nails dug into her forearms, tugging and pulling. One by one, each of her fingers were prised away from the base she was desperately clinging to. With a final tug, she was wrenched free, finding herself on the lawn staring up at two of the ugliest faces she'd ever had the misfortune of setting eyes upon.

Leering down at her were a pair of gaunt faces, sporting the patchiest of wispy beards, which looked like they could be whisked off their chins by the first half decent breeze. Matching blue eyes and jutting cheekbones convinced Meredith her assailants were related, more than likely, brothers. They wore dirty, hooded tops, frayed polyester tracksuit bottoms, and cheap looking trainers that convinced her they were fellow rough sleepers, who had somehow stumbled upon her hidey hole. They must have watched her go beneath the bandstand and were now claiming it as their own. At least she hoped that was all they were after.

'Look, I've no money and my phone was stolen the other week. I've a bottle of water and half a ham sandwich in my bag. That's it,' she lied, hoping to buy some time in the rapidly evaporating hope that Kirkwood might reappear.

The two men looked at each other and exchanged slack-jawed grins which exposed mouths devoid of teeth, bar a smattering of black stumps jutting from their gums. Meredith persevered. Had they even understood what she just said?

'If you want to sleep here tonight, that's fine with me. There's plenty of room for us all in this park. Just let me get my gear and I'll be on my way...'

She was cut off mid-sentence as, without warning, one of the men spat in her face. Meredith gasped and spluttered, more out of shock than anything else. She had witnessed a lot living rough, but this was a new low by anyone's standards. It dawned then that she was in serious trouble. The time for talking was over.

She arched her back and, propelling both hips forward, planted the sole of her right boot forcefully into the groin of the gimp who had just emptied the contents of his throat into her face. Despite still being restricted within the confines of the sleeping bag, she watched as the stick man doubled over, dropping to his knees like a felled tree. There was a split second of silence as he stared at her in wide-eyed astonishment before unleashing a high-pitched squeal, reminiscent of a sow in childbirth. The second stick man was momentarily torn between restraining Meredith or attending to his stricken colleague.

It bought Meredith the precious time she needed. In the blink of an eye she slithered free of the sleeping bag and was on her feet, catching the other stick man completely off-guard. As he turned away from his accomplice, now rolling around on the grass clutching his nether regions, he was rewarded with Meredith's free boot connecting with his left shin. The crack of leather on bone reverberated around the park as he collapsed beside his stricken partner in crime. 'Jeeezus Dermot. She's broke me leg!' he wailed, in a rough Southern Irish brogue, indicating they were not locals. He clutched his shin, face contorted in agony. Neither of them was getting up in a hurry.

Meredith was off and running, sprinting across the lawn towards the main gates, her beloved bag and other belongings forgotten about. Kirkwood was nowhere to be seen and her survival instinct, now finely tuned after so long on the streets, had well and truly kicked in. She would worry about the other stuff only when satisfied the coast was clear and she was out of danger.

Her freedom was short-lived. The next she knew she was lying winded on the lawn as if mown down by a truck. She gasped for a breath, but none was forthcoming, the wind completely knocked out of her. A sharp pain began to form at the base of her ribcage, and she moaned, her vision crashing in and out of focus. She blinked furiously to expel the blurriness and became aware of heavy downward pressure on her chest. She blinked again and as the fogginess cleared, observed a large, black boot pinning her to the ground. She followed it upwards, along the finely tailored trouser leg attached to it. Upwards again, beyond a muscular torso until she finally found herself staring into a vaguely familiar bearded face framing a set of perfect teeth which sparkled brighter than the starry sky above.

'Ah señorita, I must apologise for the behaviour of my colleagues. These Irish, they are savages. They do not know how to treat a beautiful lady.' His deep, seductive voice caressed each word as it left his mouth, and Meredith felt powerless to think of anything beyond the melodic, dulcet tones.

'What…What do you want?' was all she could manage, struggling to inhale the air her lungs so desperately craved.

Rodriguez's features softened in what appeared genuine sympathy at the plight of the young woman beneath him. 'Shushhh señorita,' he implored. 'You have had the most stressful of days. There will be plenty of time for questions later. For now, you must rest.' He waggled the fingers of his right hand and, before she could protest, Meredith felt her vision receding again. This time there was to be no return, as unconsciousness claimed her.

CHAPTER 59

PARK LIFE

9:18 p.m.

Kirkwood cut a sorry figure by the time he reached the park gates, the excesses of the last few days well and truly having caught up with him. He was panting like a dehydrated pug with the pained expression to match, having shifted his lardy frame down the Lisburn Road and along Eglantine Avenue in record time. He narrowly avoided a couple of head-on collisions, earning unrepeatable expletives for his troubles but hurtled on, shedding them like water off a duck's back. All he could think of was Meredith alone in the park and how he'd failed to keep his promise to her. Thanks to Skelly and his stranglehold, he might just have blown his one chance at freedom and answers to a lifetime of questions.

Skidding to a halt in front of the gates he bent over, resting his hands on aching thighs, trying to regain a breath. Now he had reached his destination it suddenly dawned he was only halfway to reaching the bandstand. He still had to figure out how to haul his sorry backside over the gates and into the grounds. He looked up, to be greeted by a solid padlock and chains securing the twelve-foot high gates, topped with lethal-looking spikes. A professional pole-vaulter would have struggled to negotiate them, so there was little hope of a slightly pudgy, lover of all things sedentary, doing so. He looked to either side of the gates to be greeted by equally high-spiked fencing. This was hopeless. It was going to take a circus cannon or the loan of a giraffe to get him in there tonight. He put his head in his heads. What was he going to do? Why, why, why had he left her in the first place?

His miserable vigil was interrupted by a voice from the shadows on the other

215

side of the gates. 'That was quite an effort, young man. Care for a cigarette? I find them very invigorating after any form of physical exertion.'

A figure stepped out from beneath the foliage to face Kirkwood. A tall, painfully thin man immaculately attired in a black three-piece suit with a subtle chalk-grey pinstripe running through it. A fetching black trilby and navy-blue tie in a perfect Windsor knot, completed the look. Walking through the grounds of the university earlier that day, the man could have passed for an eccentric mature student or visiting professor. Little did they know the polite gentleman who smiled and doffed his hat at them would have been 216 years old — were he still interested in keeping track of birthdays.

'Well that makes sense.'

Kirkwood straightened and looked through the bars of the gates, where the tall man stood like an imprisoned Hannibal Lecter on the other side. 'I might have guessed that where Rodriguez was, you wouldn't be far away. You two were always a team. Hello Gunther.'

'Good evening, Herr Scott,' Gunther replied in a clipped, measured German accent. He pursed his bloodless lips, considering how to frame his next words before continuing. 'As you are no doubt aware, the Colonel is not overly pleased with your relationship with the young Fraülein.' He lifted a hand to his mouth and took a leisurely drag from the unfiltered cigarette. He sucked hard, pallid cheeks collapsing further into a cadaverous skull. Instantaneously, a plume of smoke was unleashed squarely into Kirkwood's face. Gunther smiled without humour as the younger man spluttered from the effects of the nicotine-tinged cloud.

'So, he has asked us to intervene on his behalf. I know this is an unusual step on our part but, given recent developments, you have left Colonel Skelly with little other option. I can assure you we always act with your best interests at heart. That might not seem so at present, but we hope in the years to come you will look back on this unpleasant period of your life and reach the same conclusion.' He stopped, allowing Kirkwood to ask the only question bursting inside his chest, screaming for release.

'Where is she? What have you done with her?!'

Gunther smirked. 'The young Fraülein is safe and unharmed, you have my word on that. As to where she is, well that is a slightly more complicated question to answer. Let's just say she is no longer in this horrid city.' He wrinkled his nose in displeasure before continuing. 'I do not know how you can exist here. The food is revolting and as for the coffee…' he paused for dramatic effect, 'The muck they served us in the ranks was preferable to that. Did you know we bombed Belfast in 1941? It's a pity our boys in the Luftwaffe never came back to finish the job properly.'

Kirkwood shook his head in exasperation. 'She's just a friend. How the hell does Skelly have a problem with that? Why has he sent Rodriguez and you here? I suppose next thing he will be sending the rest of the...' He halted as a flicker of a smile crossed Gunther's face. 'What, there are more of you here? In the city?' He spun wildly, not knowing what other abominations from his childhood days were going to suddenly reappear.

'Yes. Unfortunately for you, the Colonel felt it necessary to devote considerable resources to this matter and has therefore deployed accordingly. I am hopeful, however, it will only be a temporary visit and we can then return to our normal duties.' He paused and took another long drag on his cigarette before adding ominously, 'That depends entirely upon you though.'

'What do you mean?'

'We have a proposition and would ask only that you consider it. End this silly dalliance and go back to your normal life, with your drinking friends, and your safe job. The girl is no good for you. She keeps bad company as you discovered to your peril earlier today. Thankfully Rodriguez was at hand to dissuade that thug from removing your head from your shoulders. Those silly letters, the drawings on the wall, they are not your concern and will only bring you harm. Let us deal with them. We have unique talents and are more than capable of resolving the matter to the satisfaction of all concerned. We will return the girl to her family unscathed once we have convinced her that the dead should be left well alone. Disturbing them only ever results in unpleasantness, I tend to find.' He removed a fleck of dust from the lapel of his suit jacket before flicking it to the ground.

'You're lying. Skelly hasn't a considerate bone in his oily body. He's only interested in himself and what he can get out of a situation. I don't know what's going on here, but I know Skelly doesn't like it and that's all the incentive I need to continue. No deal Fritz.'

Gunther's upper lip curled into the tiniest of snarls at the rebuke before he regained his composure and replaced it with a benevolent smile. 'Very well. I shall notify the Colonel of your decision. But may I just add that...' He flinched, as a bright light from somewhere behind Kirkwood swamped the shadows, exposing his anaemic features. Kirkwood spun to see the silhouette of a figure holding a torch.

'What are you two doing here?' a voice barked out. 'The park is closed to the public. How the hell did you get in?'

Gunther squinted into the light and raised a hand to shield his eyes. 'I strongly suggest that you switch off your torch, turn around and forget this little gathering ever took place.' The deadpan delivery did little to mask the chilling malice in his voice. 'Now, repeat what I've just said to make sure we are all very clear on this matter.'

To Kirkwood's astonishment the man began to speak, a robotic quality to his voice.

'I'm going to switch off my torch, turn around and forget this little gathering ever took place.' He stood, still as a statue, as if awaiting further instructions.

Gunther smiled again, one that could have curdled milk. 'Good man. A wise choice. On your way now.' He made a shooing gesture with both hands and, without another word, the security guard turned obediently and walked away, back towards the university complex. Kirkwood stared in astonishment at the German who now sported a slightly bored expression. 'As I was saying, before we were so rudely interrupted. This is only going to end one way. We will win and you will lose. Never say you weren't warned.' With that, he stepped back into the shadows, leaving Kirkwood alone with only his thoughts to accompany him. So many thoughts.

CHAPTER 60

ABYSS

Meredith gradually became aware of being, but little else. She was engulfed in a black blanket which offered no clue as to her whereabouts. Utter disorientation. She initially thought she was blindfolded, but after blinking and straining her eyes repeatedly, realised they were wide open, bulging from their sockets — yet nothing. The panic began to unravel within her.

I'm blind, she thought. *I can't see a frigging thing.*

She began to twist and squirm, fingers frantically searching for any form of purchase. She craved a solid surface more than she ever desired anything in her entire life. Her senses were starved and urgently required sustenance as fear threatened to overwhelm her. Even the feel of a hard, cold floor would have been a comfort. Yet there was nothing. No floor, no walls, nothing.

Was she suspended? She arched her back and contorted her body first this way and then the other to gauge if there were any wires or harnesses holding her aloft. There was nothing. Just her and her thoughts, suspended in whatever void she was currently inhabiting. Was she dead? She struggled to bring her rampaging breath under control and focus on where she had been prior to this. Her heartbeat provided the pounding backbeat as memories hovered tantalisingly out of reach like a desert mirage; fuzzy and unattainable.

Bandstand. The word gate-crashed her consciousness like a startled pony, and she clung to its mane with what little mental strength she retained. The bandstand. She had been under the bandstand waiting for Kirkwood. Yet he hadn't turned up, instead those two morons had. She had escaped from them and then…and then…think Meredith, think! She wrestled with the elusive, fragmented thoughts as they slipped through her fingers like water from a tap.

Then it came to her.

The bearded man. The final frame slid into place. He was real. She'd harboured hopes Kirkwood was mistaken, that the giant from the alley might be an ally. She never doubted a word of his story, but elements of it sounded…well…a tad exaggerated. Meredith put it down to his heightened adrenalin levels at the time. But now she knew what Rodriguez was capable of and realised he was no friend of theirs.

The bubble of panic, floating inside her mind, burst into a million shards, penetrating every cell of her body.

'HELLLLP!!!' She screamed until she thought her lungs would haemorrhage and her mouth fill with thick, dark globules of blood. Choking on it. She screamed the word over and over until she could scream it no more. And then she screamed again anyway, variations of a theme until her throat was stripped raw and her lungs were a vacuum; a guttural, piercing shriek that eventually dissolved into pitiful sobbing when finally spent.

She knew instinctively there would be no response to her cries but, even then, the deafening silence overwhelmed her with despair. She wasn't even rewarded with an echo which at least would have provided some boundaries, parameters to this desolate expanse. She needed to know there was something tangible beyond, to which she could pin her hopes; hopes which were currently being crushed on all sides by an impenetrable gloom.

Any further movement was pointless. When she kicked out her legs it was as if she was wading through thigh-high water. They were sluggish, there being no surface beneath them from which she could gain traction and gather momentum. And even if there had been, where would she run? There were no landmarks, no points of reference as to what direction she should take to escape this nightmarish void.

She felt the panic surging again, unravelling oily tentacles from its lair in the pit of her stomach. She resisted the temptation to scream again, to succumb to the unshackled beast within and allow it to surge upwards, spiralling and spinning like a ceremonial water fountain, bursting into life.

Get a grip, you stupid cow, she seethed, struggling to apply rational thinking to this most irrational of situations; to locate a strand of logic and pull herself along it towards the truth, no matter how devastating that might be. The most likely explanation was usually the most straightforward one. She read that somewhere once. What was it called? Occam's razor, that was it. So, concentrate girl, suck it up and figure this out.

If she had been asked a year ago, was there an afterlife, she would have rolled her eyes and promptly changed the subject. She didn't have a view, one way or the other, and was too busy surviving the very real day-to-day hell at Ashgrove to worry about little red men with pitchforks, sixty or seventy years down the road.

Even when she started writing the letters to Emily, she didn't seriously believe her friend was out there somewhere floating on a cloud while plucking on a harp. That was just plain daft. No, the letters were more her sad little way of keeping alive the spluttering flame of Emily's memory before it was extinguished for good. The first piece of graffiti threw the largest of spanners into that cognitive cog. When she overcame the initial fear that she was losing her mind, she was left with the once unpalatable possibility that there was something beyond this life. Although what it was, she did not know.

She sensed she was about to find out.

CHAPTER 61

JIMMY JAMES

Tuesday, 2 September 2012
10:11 a.m.

Jimmy James was many things, but a creature of habit he was not. When it came to opening and closing times at Montague & Moore, it largely depended upon his frame of mind and other competing priorities on any given day. That Tuesday was no different, as he rolled up the shutters mid-morning to be greeted by the sight of a young man pacing impatiently up and down outside. Jimmy vaguely recognised him as having been in the shop yesterday, or was it the day before? Either way, it was a rarity for customers to be queuing outside, waiting for him to open. Second-hand books were hardly a priority on anyone's shopping list, but the young man looked as if he was about to burst into tears of gratitude at the sight of him.

'Good morning. You're keen. Cramming for exams, are we? Never worry. I'm sure I have just what you're looking for. Just give me a minute to get set up.'

'Thanks,' replied Kirkwood awkwardly. 'A friend recommended you to me. She…I mean they, said you would have what I was after.'

'Oh, *did* they now?' Jimmy accentuated the second word, chuckling at the awkwardness of the young man. 'Well come on in. You have the place to yourself. Let me know if you need any help. I'll just get sorted and then you can…'

He didn't have time to finish the sentence as the young man hared down an aisle and disappeared out of sight. Jimmy smiled and busied himself behind the counter, counting out that day's float into the till. A most peculiar young man, but a customer was a customer all the same.

Kirkwood barely noticed the stark, fluorescent lighting flickering into life above him as he turned a corner, banging off a shelf and sending a handful of books clattering to the floor. He hurried on, focused on nothing but the aisle where Meredith had deposited her letter to Emily the previous day. Reaching it, he began to toss paperbacks aside, not caring where they landed. He was only interested in one. There it was, staring him in the eye, daring him to place all his cracked eggs in this one crazy basket of hope.

Urban Murmurs, I love you.

He removed the book from where it sat and kissed the cover before opening it. For an instant he panicked. Was there a section of the book where Meredith secreted the letters? A page or poem holding a sentimental value for Emily or her? He considered his options briefly; painfully aware he was attempting to second-guess a dead girl and her borderline alcoholic friend who he barely knew. It was an impossible task. Sighing, he steeled his flagging resolve and rifled through the book until reaching the page he had decided upon.

Skelly would have appreciated the irony of the choice. Kirkwood paid scant regard to its contents. Wishy-washy, bleeding heart poetry was most definitely not his cup of tea. Depressed teenage girls were welcome to it. All he was interested in was finding out where Meredith was and bringing this whole insane escapade to a speedy conclusion. Part of him mourned the mundanity of the life he was leaving behind; the drinking sessions with Gerry and Grogan. It already seemed so long ago, even though it was less than a week since the three of them gathered at The Montreal, setting the world to rights.

This new life refused to go away, nagging at him incessantly like a neglected tooth flaring into lurid life, causing him to scuttle off to the dentist's chair, tail well and truly tucked between his legs. He had stumbled along for years now, barely getting by, existing rather than living. He coped with, as opposed to controlled, the voices and routines that shackled and stymied his every move. Skelly reigned supreme, a malignant benefactor who claimed he was keeping Kirkwood from the brink, when really, he was staked to the ground, slowly wasting away; his very essence seeping between the cracks of an arid existence.

Pulling the crumpled piece of paper from his jeans, Kirkwood smoothed it out and laid it flat on page sixty-four before closing the covers and carefully returning the book to the shelf. He then spent a frantic few minutes retrieving books from the floor and hurriedly covering his tracks. Finally, satisfied that all was in order he retraced his steps to the front of the shop where the owner was still behind the counter, fussing over the till.

If Meredith could write letters to the dead, then so could he.

'Did you find what you were looking for, son?' Jimmy noticed the young man was returning empty-handed.

Kirkwood suddenly realised he hadn't picked up a book to cover the real reason for his visit to the store. Idiot! He racked his brain for a response to the innocuous question.

'Er...no...I couldn't find it. My friend must have been mistaken. It's okay, I'll get it somewhere, thanks anyway.'

'Well, maybe if you tell me the name of it, I could order it in for you. I get new stock twice a week.'

'No, it's alright, honestly. But thanks again.'

Kirkwood forced himself to make eye contact with the man to convey his appreciation at the offer, even though all we wanted was to get out of the shop and back to the alley where the graffiti had appeared before his disbelieving eyes, as Emily had looked down serenely at the unfolding chaos.

'Okay. Well drop in any time. You know where we are.' The young man muttered a farewell and was gone. *Kids*, Jimmy thought to himself. He would never figure them out. In a world of his own, that one.

Outside, Kirkwood walked purposefully, a mixture of hope and belief fuelling his steps. Yes, he did live in a world of his own. A world that he was finally starting to understand.

CHAPTER 62

REVELATION

10:24 a.m.

Kirkwood reached the alley off Mulberry Square in record time to find Emily, as ever, gazing down on all who passed; but no message, no response to the hurriedly scribbled note he left at the bookshop. He circled the square several times but always returned to the same, disappointing scene. He had loosened and retied his laces, pretended to be in deep conversation on his phone, and even feigned interest in an antique lamp post until a passing stray almost christened his jeans when it cocked a leg there to relieve itself; anything to justify his presence in the alley and lessen any suspicion from passers-by. The last thing he needed right now was a roving police patrol taking an interest in his increasingly bizarre behaviour. He could barely explain his actions to himself let alone under caution at the local station.

He had almost given up hope when, on his sixth loop of the square, he noticed the finest outline appearing on the wall beneath Emily. So fine, he initially thought it was his imagination willing into existence words that were simply not there. He decided to make one last loop of the square to be certain, heart thumping against his chest and his stomach performing backward flips. His arms and legs wobbled like jelly. This had to work.

'Please let this be real. Please let this be real,' he pleaded, negotiating the final corner and turning back into the alley. It was thankfully deserted on this occasion. Raising his eyes from the pavement, he fully expected the outline to have vanished along with any fragile hopes he still retained.

This time there was no doubting it. As clear as could be, she was there on the wall, dark eyes surveying his approach. He marvelled at the paleness of her skin, so opaque it looked as if her flawless cheekbones could burst through at any time. Her platinum-coloured hair fanned out in all directions like a blazing halo. It was as if the artist, if this indeed had been painted by human hands, insisted she pose in a wind tunnel.

An elegant nose swept downwards to slightly flared nostrils, hinting at a rebellious nature which its creator was determined to capture. The same applied to her mouth. Thin lips framed a knowing smile but refused to reveal any more. A slightly prominent chin rounded off the image of a young woman challenging the viewer to dispute her outlook on the world. Her bare neck and shoulders merged with the words which Kirkwood now focused his attention on. He imagined the bold, sweeping script being painstakingly penned by a robed monk cocooned in an ancient monastery, perched atop a mountain.

'Rockwood. Find me, and you will find her. For we are one and they are many. Hurry. They are coming.'

As soon as the final words registered with him, they began to fade. Kirkwood fumbled for his phone to capture the message, but only succeeded in allowing it to slip through his fingers, hitting the ground with a worrying crack. By the time he bent down to retrieve it and looked up again, the message was gone. He started to furiously punch the words into his phone and then googled 'Emily O'Hara. Death. Rockwood'. Of the 1567 resulting hits, he only had to read the first to determine where he was heading next.

'28 September 2011. The funeral of teenager Emily O'Hara (18) will take place today at Fulton Memorial Presbyterian Church in Bangor, followed by a private burial service at Rockwood Cemetery. Emily was found dead at her home address in the early hours of...'

Kirkwood tucked the phone into his jacket pocket. He didn't need to read on as he was already calculating the best way to get to the cemetery, on the outskirts of the city. It was at times like this he wished he had invested in a second-hand car instead of donating his monthly wages to the publicans and bookmakers of Belfast. Hindsight was a wonderful thing though, and what he was facing now was far from wonderful. Emily's message merely confirmed what he already knew. Skelly and his ghouls. They were coming.

CHAPTER 63

REHANNA

Eventually, despite her best efforts not to, the tears came. Meredith cursed aloud as she prided herself on never succumbing to such displays of weakness. She had cried rivers following Emily's death, but they were shed in private. To the watching world there wasn't a flicker of emotion, even at the pantomime of a funeral. 'Resting Bitch Face,' Emily had called it, when the Ashgrove coven were at their most brutally vindictive. 'Don't give those witches an inch, Meredith. Never.'

But that was then, and this was now. A now of nothingness. No Emily, no Kirkwood, no clue as to her whereabouts. So, she cried. A low sobbing at first, evolving into a guttural roar of rage that went unheard and unheeded. When there was no more, her ribs ached, and throat throbbed. Cheeks stained with salty tears; tracks of misery which marked them as indelibly as the current predicament scarred her heart. She was broken, bereft. Out of ideas and devoid of hope.

'Help me, Emily. Please,' she whimpered into the abyss.

The words were barely audible even given the stifling silence all around. How long had she been here? Hours? Days? Weeks? Initially she thought her eyes would adjust to the lack of light, allowing her to deduce some understanding of the surroundings. Fat chance. The darkness remained absolute, firmly beyond her perception no matter how hard she willed some form — even the faintest of outlines, to emerge from the blackness. She grew exhausted, raking over every conceivable scenario until morbidly concluding she was either blind, or dead. Possibly both.

Following Emily's suicide, she also craved death, so she could be with her best friend. That desire gradually waned in the months that crawled by, to be replaced by a need for nothing but the comforting warmth of a wine bottle, as the sobering truth Emily was never returning settled on her like a blanket of bitter, acrid ash. The letters changed all that, opening a channel of communication she clung to desperately. She believed; believed that somehow Emily was looking over her, protecting her and guiding her slowly, hand over fist, back towards a life worth living. Ghost? Angel? Figment of her battered imagination? It mattered not to Meredith.

All she knew was it was enough.

An almost imperceptible breath of air brushed against her left cheek, causing Meredith to jump and then freeze, too frightened to exhale in case she gave away her whereabouts to an unseen predator. She sensed the temperature around her rising and a warm glow began to creep through her, a sensation she surrendered to, gladly. Muscles relaxed as if she was soaking in a hot bath, laced with revitalising minerals and oils.

'Who's there?' From somewhere deep within, she mustered the courage to speak the words. The only reply was the faint breeze again, softly caressing her furrowed forehead like the softest of downy feathers. She instinctively sensed whoever, whatever this was, presented no danger to her. It was a comforting sensation, although she refused to relax completely for fear she was being lulled into a false sense of security by some unseen enemy.

The fragrance that next assaulted her nostrils almost knocked her off her feet, had she been on her feet, as opposed to floating in nothingness. It was instantly recognisable as Rehanna. Subtle, refreshing, vibrant. It had been Emily's favourite fragrance and she wore it religiously, never without a bottle of it in her bag and forever drowning herself in it. It was her trademark, unmistakably Emily O'Hara. Meredith's heart started to stampede afresh as she struggled to maintain what little composure she had left.

'Emily?' The tears were flowing again, no matter how hard she tried to contain them. It was all too much. Her resolve began to crumble, frayed emotions within a strand of snapping. She feared if the floodgates opened, she would never be able to close them again, and every remaining aspect of her would be washed from the face of the earth. A flood to end all floods. A blessed submersion of all the pain and grief which had eroded any resolve and left her high and dry, frozen and floundering.

The fragrance weakened slightly as if its wearer had withdrawn slightly to consider a response to her question. Then words began to form in her mind, foreign words that were not of her. Nobody had spoken, the silence was as total as before; yet someone or something was placing words and phrases in her mind that flared and fizzed like Halloween sparklers.

'Meredith. Stay calm. Please try. We are coming. Patience. Strength. We are one. There is a great evil afoot, but we can overcome. Soon. I promise. Soon.'

Afoot. It was such an Emily word. Flowery, slightly pretentious. It had to be her.

'Emily. Where are you? Where am I? I'm so scared.' She could feel the panic rising again, despite her best efforts to hold it together.

'Help is coming. But they are also near. I must go for they will destroy me. Patience. Be calm. Soon.'

Meredith's brain was a malfunctioning radio antenna, struggling to pick up a signal from a distant land. Her mind overflowed with static and interference, yet occasionally cleared enough to allow the transmission to be heard. It was enough. The breeze, the perfume, the jumbled message. Scant crumbs of comfort but she was starving and gratefully gobbled them down.

The breeze and the fragrance vanished, and she was alone again. Or was she? At the very edges of her being, she became aware of something watching. Something huge and unbearably intense. It was far, far away and only toying with her, like a rhinoceros vaguely aware of an oxpecker perched on its back, pecking at its hide.

She remained perfectly still; certain she had never encountered anything so terrifying in all her life. If it were to turn and look directly at her she would go quite mad, her sanity incinerated to a crisp like a handful of leaves thrown on top of an autumn bonfire.

She waited. That was all she *could* do.

CHAPTER 64

WET RAIN

12:19 p.m.

Harry Potter never had these problems.

Kirkwood stepped off the bus after a ponderous, stop-start journey to the outskirts of the city, where the sprawling cemetery sat nestled in rolling countryside. It was beginning to rain, a nagging, persistent drizzle which fell steadily from a monochrome grey canopy; it showed no sign of abating any time soon. When it rained in Northern Ireland it rained, and then some. Kirkwood wondered, if Darwin was so clever, then why didn't the residents of Belfast have webbed feet? His mother eloquently referred to it as a 'wet rain', a Northern Irish saying if ever there was one. There was a certain logic to her nonsense, however. It soaked you to the bone, chilled your very soul, left your spirit as dank and overcast as the sky from which it was falling.

He picked his way through a patchwork of puddles forming on the potholed driveway which led into the graveyard. He shuddered, zipped his leather jacket up, and pulled the collar tight around his neck to provide a modicum of protection from the dire conditions. The graveyard sloped gently downwards, row upon row of tombstones and monuments marking out generations of the city's citizenry. Kirkwood sighed. The grim weather and the grimmer landscape befitted his overall demeanour. The initial excitement at being a step nearer to rescuing Meredith had largely fizzled out during the tortuous journey.

His mood darkened further as he surveyed the hundreds of graves in front of him. How on earth was he going to find Emily's among this lot? It was taking needles in haystacks to a whole new level. Kirkwood sighed again, suddenly aware of how hopelessly out of his depth he was. He had naively hoped the graves would be arranged in some sort of logical order, but there appeared to be little rhyme or reason to the layout of the cemetery. Overgrown plots which had been neglected for decades sat alongside magnificent marble structures bedecked with fresh flowers and glowing with loving care. Paths branched off at regular intervals on either side of a central driveway which stretched into the distance as far as the eye could see.

'This place is a maze,' he muttered sourly, as the rain continued to cascade down, now accompanied by a cutting wind which whistled an eerie tune between the headstones.

He was on the verge of giving up any hope of finding Emily's grave when a miniature digger trundled up the driveway towards him on mud-caked tracks. Steering it was a broad-shouldered young man in a fluorescent council jacket, several sizes too small for him. Kirkwood raised a hand to catch the man's attention.

'Where would I find a grave that was dug last September?' he shouted as the digger drew alongside him. He was forced to repeat the question several times with accompanying hand gestures before the driver reluctantly turned off the engine.

'What's that?' He stared dully down from his seat at Kirkwood who quickly realised customer service skills were not high on this guy's training needs analysis; but then he did work in a graveyard, so it was hardly a must-have attribute. He repeated the question again and patiently waited for the man to process the request, an apparently herculean effort on his part. Finally, after what seemed forever, a glint of understanding registered on his face, and he responded in a slow, deliberate manner.

'What's the name?'

'Name?' Kirkwood repeated, confused. 'Er...my name's Kirkwood Scott. First name Kirkwood. Not the other way round.'

'No,' Digger Man replied, his face betraying no emotion. 'Name of the deceased.'

'Oh yes, of course,' a flustered Kirkwood replied. 'It's O'Hara.'

'First name?' The staccato delivery of the questions continued. The man had a strange lilt to his accent. Was he English? Australian? It was difficult to tell, given his robotic monotone.

'Emily.' Kirkwood was struggling to maintain his composure. Time was of the essence here. Every second spent teasing information out of this dullard was another second Meredith was in danger.

'Date of burial?'

Was this idiot taking the hand out of him? Kirkwood scanned the graveyard desperately, in the hope that someone with half a brain would come to his aid, but there was nobody else in sight. 'Er…September 2011, I think. I don't know the exact date.'

Digger Man looked slightly peeved at the lack of specific detail but, running his hand through a greasy, unkempt mullet, closed both eyes as if unravelling an unfeasibly complicated mathematical equation. He would have looked more at home in one of those psycho hillbilly movies where a campervan full of American teenagers get lost in the woods and are never seen again. Suddenly his eyes snapped open and he looked down at Kirkwood with an expression of mild triumph.

'Row 224. Plot 5783.' He waved a beefy hand in the general direction of the bottom left hand corner of the cemetery, before starting the digger and continuing up the driveway.

'You couldn't make this up,' groaned Kirkwood. As if in agreement, the wind picked up an extra notch, wailing like all the spirits in the graveyard were welcoming him to their final resting places.

Then he heard the first explosion.

CHAPTER 65

THE FITZGERALD BROTHERS

Kirkwood instinctively dropped to his haunches at the sound of a dull thud somewhere off to his left. The ground beneath him shook as shock waves surged through his body. After a few seconds, he chanced a peek in the direction of the explosion. About two hundred yards further down the driveway and to the left, a mushroom cloud of dense black smoke was drifting up into the sky. This was insane. The Troubles were over years ago, and he had already endured more than enough trouble for one day, thank you very much.

He tensed, awaiting the inevitable screams or wail of approaching sirens. Instead he was greeted with a delighted whooping that would have been more at home at a rodeo than in the middle of a terrorist attack. It was quickly followed by a second, less happy voice.

'For God's sake. I told you to wait until I gave the signal!'

'Did you see it though? Did you see it? Must have sent that box thirty feet in the air. Some shot boy, you can't deny that.'

'Next time, you will wait until I give the instruction as your older brother and Commanding Officer.'

'Commanding Officer, my backside. You can take that stripe and shove it where the sun don't shine. And you popped out of our Ma precisely seventy-five seconds before me, so you're neither my elder nor my better, you lying dog. Sure, everybody knows she saved the best for last.'

Kirkwood was creeping slowly towards the sound of the voices, though he couldn't quite believe his legs were propelling him in that direction. Even less believable were the voices themselves. He was transported back to his childhood, playing make believe in the sanctuary of his bedroom. Except he would never have dared use the swear words that these brothers were now liberally flinging around.

It was the twins. Brothers who, until recently, he regarded as nothing more than a distant memory from a fractured upbringing. The not so delicious irony was that now, surrounded by thousands of buried bodies, his past was being resurrected in spectacular fashion. Rodriguez. Gunther. He should have known it was only a matter of time before others returned, and now they had. The Fitzgerald Brothers, Declan and Dermot; the runts of Skelly's Company, were back. And if he was to save Meredith, it looked like he was going to have to go through them first.

CHAPTER 66

FOR THE KINGDOM

Kirkwood crawled as close to the voices as he dared. His knees and elbows were soaking wet from his amateur efforts to covertly creep between the lines of graves, towards the brothers. His commando crawl would never win any awards for speed or technical ability, but was clumsily effective. He found himself huddled behind a headstone less than twenty feet from where the Fitzgerald Brothers, unaware of his presence, continued to bicker.

'I should thrash your skinny backside for dragging the good name of our Mammy through the dirt,' snarled Dermot, the older of the two. 'If the old fella were standing here now, his belt would be tanning your hide, good and proper.'

Kirkwood glimpsed from behind the headstone. The twins were squaring up to each other on the pathway. Beyond them, about thirty feet further down the slightly sloping cemetery, the last tendrils of smoke were floating across his line of vision, presumably from where the seat of the explosion had been.

He took a moment to mentally adjust to the sight of nineteenth century infantrymen in modern day attire, just as he had struggled to adapt to Rodriguez and Gunther. At least they had displayed a semblance of style when selecting their modern-day wardrobes. The same could not be said for the Fitzgerald Brothers. They were decked out in matching garish green polyester tracksuits, gleaming white 'box fresh' designer trainers and baseball caps bearing the skull and crossbones motif of the Los Angeles Raiders American football team. It was the standard uniform of a certain type of Belfast youth; the type that stole cars and burgled little old ladies. Chunky gold chains and chunkier sovereign rings topped off an undeniably expensive, but also undeniably naff, look.

'Jesus wept,' exclaimed Kirkwood under his breath. 'It's Kevin and Perry.'

Both brothers were painfully thin and stood a good two inches over six-foot, Dermot marginally the taller of the two. If you were to compare them to a member of the animal kingdom, then weasels or ferrets immediately sprang to mind. Beady dark eyes that were a fraction too close together and wispy tufts of facial hair with a suggestion of ginger, which certainly exempted them from the category of 'eye candy'. Their crowning glory, however, if you pardoned the pun, were their teeth, or rather, lack of them. A handful of rotten stumps sat like isolated crags of rock, rising from infected gums. The pride of County Kerry, their birthplace, they were most certainly not. When the Iron Duke, Wellington, had referred to the British Army as the scum of the earth, he probably was thinking of Dermot and Declan Fitzgerald.

'Well he isn't here. And I don't see Mammy either, so I believe I can do whatever I so desire.'

Declan took a step towards his brother as if spoiling for a fist fight before thinking better of it, instead jutting his chin out defiantly before continuing.

'What's more, the Colonel gave specific instructions we were to use whatever means at our disposal to ensure the success of the operation. I am merely following orders, or would you care to challenge him on that particular point?'

Dermot bit his lip uncertainly before clearing his throat with a thunderous gulder. He turned to one side and unleashed an impressive mouthful of black, bubble-flecked phlegm, striking the base of a nearby headstone. 'Bullseye,' he declared proudly before turning to scan the cemetery, eyes little more than slits in his pockmarked face.

'Yee Ha,' hollered Declan, clearly overjoyed at the moral victory over his sibling. He began to dance an inane jig, circling Dermot like a marionette controlled by an inebriated puppeteer. Kirkwood would have sniggered at the ridiculous sight, had the situation not been so serious. He knew the brothers were as dangerous as they were mentally unhinged. In the fantasy world he constructed as a child, they had operated to deadly effect whenever deployed against enemy forces. He had no reason to doubt they were any less lethal in the flesh. If Meredith was in their hands, then he had to act, and soon.

Without warning, Declan flung out his right hand and a grave forty yards away erupted, flinging huge clods of earth and masonry high into the sky. Kirkwood ducked behind the headstone and was showered with debris. A sizable chunk of headstone embedded itself in an adjacent grave, missing him by no more than a few feet. He stared in horror at the lump of expensive black marble, the words 'Loving father of…' engraved on it in gold-embossed script.

'You bloody lunatic,' roared a clearly rattled Dermot. 'You're going to get the two of us killed before he even gets here! That's if the Colonel doesn't nail our nuts to the ground first. The boy will run a mile if he hears this commotion.'

'Stop spouting like a jabbering fool, Dermot. He's close. I can smell him. And when he arrives, I'm going to show him who's the new sheriff in town. I'm gonna blow him and his little missy sky high. Yee Ha!'

'Quit it!' Dermot hissed. 'Or so help me, you'll be the one getting blasted to kingdom come.'

There was no stopping Declan now. 'Here little missy. I know where you're at. How's about I heat up that chilly old box those nasty boys have buried you in.' He let out another insane shriek and stretched out an arm, pointing his index finger at an ornate memorial positioned towards the end of the row which housed Kirkwood's observation point. Kirkwood's mouth dropped open when he read the inscription etched upon it:

Emily Sylvia O'Hara

Born 19th August 1993

Died 15th September 2011

Dearly Beloved Daughter and Granddaughter

The Lord Is Thy Shepherd

The impressive monument towered above all the other plots in the immediate area. It reeked of money and privilege, but no amount of veneer could mask the sorrow and heartache underpinning the grandeur. Kirkwood instinctively realised Meredith was close, just like he knew if Declan was allowed to continue this destructive rampage, then it would be too late to save her. Before his brain could quite comprehend what his legs were doing, he launched from his hiding place to stand in the pathway between the younger brother and Emily's memorial.

'STOP! You want me, you've got me. Just no more. Please.'

He paused, and a heavy silence hung in the air between him and the soldier who had died over two hundred years ago at Waterloo. A dead soldier, now alive and kicking in a Kappa tracksuit, laying waste to a cemetery with the power of his mind. Kirkwood felt a bizarre out of body experience, like this was happening to someone else and he was merely a stunned onlooker.

Declan let out a low whistle, followed by a whoop of delight. 'Well look who we have here, Dermot. If it isn't Master Kirkwood, signed, sealed and delivered as requested. Now who says my tactics don't work? Me being only a dumb country boy, good for nothing but feeding the crows,' he smirked, looking beyond Kirkwood's right shoulder, towards Emily's final resting place.

Dermot, standing slightly behind Declan, now moved alongside him. He removed his baseball hat to reveal a thinning thatch of fine, sandy hair. He mopped his grimy brow with a forearm, the heat from Declan's most recent thermal assault having raised the air temperature around them.

'I'll give you this one little brother,' he reluctantly conceded, eying Kirkwood with a cunning intelligence that reeked of venomous intent. 'You were a scrawny, snotty-nosed kid last time I set eyes on you, Kirkwood Scott. All grown up now though, aren't you? Well, the time for playing games is over cos we aren't your little tin soldiers anymore,' he sneered, revealing a mouthful of rotten teeth which Kirkwood doubted had ever seen a toothbrush.

'Where is she? You better not have hurt her or I'll…I'll…' his words petered out tamely. Kirkwood hadn't a clue what to do next and for not the first time in recent days, realised how horribly inadequate he was to overcome the challenges being hurled in his direction.

'You'll do what?' taunted Declan, puffing his chest out like a prize fighter strutting around the ring. 'Pack us away in your toy chest until the next time you want to play war? Well, this is real war. Something a little toad like you would know nothing about. My brother and me though, at eighteen, when you were still hanging on your mammy's apron strings, we were fighting Bonny and his boys, toe to toe, across the continent.'

'Oh really? And there was me thinking you were two good-for-nothing conscripts who couldn't be trusted with anything beyond the most basic sentry duties. Sorry, I must have been thinking of another pair of thieving cowards who never got within two miles of the front line.' Kirkwood wasn't sure where he dragged the memory from, but suddenly the legend he created for the Fitzgerald Brothers all those years ago, came flooding back.

'You better watch that smart mouth of yours or the little lady you've swaggered down here to save will be plastered all over this graveyard. And I promise you she won't be such a pretty sight then.'

'What do you want from me?' Kirkwood decided to adopt a different approach. Winding up the Fitzgerald Brothers was probably not the wisest tactic given their volatile natures, but he was unable to resist, nibbling at the bait the moronic Declan dangled in front of him. He silently resolved to rein in his growing anger. There was too much at stake here.

'Well, that's just the beauty of our little drama,' Dermot interjected with a sickly smile. 'All you have to do is turn around, go back to your safe little life and forget the last few days ever happened. Forget about the little lady, forget about her dead as a doornail friend, and forget about acting the conquering hero. Go home, have a beer and everything will be just as it was before.' He leaned back, obviously pleased with the eloquent delivery of his proposal.

Kirkwood mulled the offer over, then threw back his head, laughing. He had no idea why he was, given the gravity of the situation, but the release of tension was palpable.

'Yeah. Go back to a life of being Skelly's pet monkey, jumping through hoops for him. Every second for the rest of my life. Grinding me into the ground, day after day after bloody day with his endless routines. No thanks, I think I'll take my chances with Meredith. I haven't worked it out yet, but your esteemed leader doesn't like the two of us together. And if Skelly doesn't like something, then I'm inclined to like it very much.'

He took a step forward towards the brothers and spoke in a low voice, slowly and carefully emphasising each word. 'Now for the last time. Where is she?'

Dermot emitted a dramatic sigh. 'I must admit. I am disappointed that an educated young man like yourself has declined this most generous offer on the table. Especially as from where I'm standing, you haven't a leg to stand on. But as you wish. Don't say I didn't warn you.'

He turned his head and nodded towards Declan who, during this latest verbal exchange, had stood rooted to the spot with a slack-jawed expression on his face. 'Light her up little brother. Light her up.'

Declan smiled. He liked to leave all the fancy pants talking to his brother. He was more a man of action. Lifting his right arm, he extended it, pointing a dirt-caked finger towards Emily's memorial.

'This one's for the Kingdom of Kerry.'

'NOOOOOO!!' shouted Kirkwood, powerless to intervene. He had no idea where Meredith was but sensed if the memorial was destroyed, then he would never see her again. He had gambled and lost.

CHAPTER 67

MAKE IT END

It could have been an hour; it could have been a year after the presence of Emily departed, when Meredith heard the explosion. It was ever so faint, yet this time she was certain her mind was not playing tricks. The sound was akin to clashing cymbals, but she was clueless which direction it came from, given her complete disorientation. She twisted one way, then the other like a blindfolded trapeze artist. Both nostrils twitched as the muscles in her throat began to constrict. What was that? Smoke? Her deprived senses latched onto it, desperate for anything other than the void.

She began to inhale and exhale deeply to ward off the rising tide of hysteria threatening to overwhelm her. Her eyes began to sting and water, but this time it was the effects of the smoke, rather than any internal waterworks. Her already raw throat began to tickle, as it permeated her lungs. What on earth was going on and what wouldn't she give for the largest glass of chilled white wine right now. She was parched and panicky, at her wit's end.

'Please make this end. Just make it end,' she whimpered, never having felt so alone in her life.

CHAPTER 68

SAMUEL

Kirkwood flinched as something — he did not know what, flashed past his right shoulder. He instinctively reached for the corresponding earlobe which flared in pain, as if the flame of a lighter had been held to it. At the same time, he watched in horror as what little hair Dermot Fitzgerald had on his head burst into flames. Kirkwood had heard of the phenomenon of spontaneous combustion but discounted it as just another urban myth. But here it was, right before his eyes in vivid technicolour. Dermot emitted a high-pitched squeal and began to pathetically flap at his head, falling to the ground where he writhed around in agony. The smell of burning flesh began to assail Kirkwood's nostrils and it took all his willpower not to retch violently.

Declan fell to his knees beside his stricken brother. Removing his tracksuit top, he attempted to smother the flames, at the same time searching the surrounding area for clues as to what had befallen Dermot. He did not have to look far. Kirkwood stared in amazement as, striding towards them, came the gravedigger he had spoken to earlier. The vacant stare was gone now, replaced by a fierce intensity in his brown eyes. Still a good thirty feet away from them, he hurled a shovel he was carrying like an Olympic javelin thrower, towards the brothers. Kirkwood ducked and felt the air around him divide as the unlikely missile hurtled towards its target.

It would have removed Declan's head from his shoulders, had he remained where he was, desperately tending to his shrieking brother. Kirkwood closed his eyes, waiting for the sickening connection followed by the sound of a lifeless body falling to the ground in front of him. He counted two seconds in his head. Nothing. Opening an eye, he looked towards where the brothers had been, no more than a few feet away from him on the path.

Dermot was lying motionless on his back, his head and upper torso a charred lump of blackened flesh and bone. The liquified remains of his eyeballs were dripping down what remained of his cheeks like two fried eggs, their yolks pierced with a fork.

Declan was nowhere to be seen, yet there was no way he could have evaded the shovel given the frightening speed it had been travelling. It was as if he vanished into thin air. Kirkwood would have considered this impossible, had he not accepted he was now living the impossible. He spun on his heels as the gravedigger bounded past, towards Emily's memorial. His long legs effortlessly covered the ground, before crouching at its base beside a bundle of rags lying amidst the floral tributes. Or at least that's what Kirkwood initially thought; as his frazzled vision cleared, he realised it was not rags, but a person. Curled in a tiny ball and caked in mud and grass, but most definitely a human being. He ran towards the memorial and his unlikely saviour. Drawing nearer he could make out muffled, choking sobs emanating from the bundle on the ground.

Crashing to his knees, he cradled Meredith's head in his hands. She looked as if she had been dragged through several fields and, gazing up at him, seemed momentarily unaware who he was. Then recognition and awareness dawned, and she mustered a weary smile.

'Fancy meeting you here,' she spluttered, spitting mouthfuls of soil from her mouth.

'Where on Earth have you been?' Kirkwood didn't know whether to laugh or cry with relief and eventually settled on a dopey grin, which gave Meredith no option but to widen her own smile.

'I'm not sure I've been anywhere on Earth but help me up, and I'll try and explain.' Taking Kirkwood's arm, she rose shakily to her feet, to be met by the stern gaze of the gravedigger who had retrieved his shovel. He towered a good foot above her. Kirkwood looked over to where the remains of Dermot should have been smouldering, but he was gone. It was as if the terrible twins had never been there.

'Who...What...?' Kirkwood struggled to formulate a coherent sentence but was unable to find the words so, instead, fell into a bewildered silence. He looked at Meredith for a lifeline but, for once, she too was incapable of speech. The recent barrage of incredible events had finally overwhelmed the two of them. They looked at the gravedigger who now stood in front of them, muscular forearms folded across a broad chest.

'We will answer all your questions in good time,' he said in a strong, clear voice, a million miles from the drooling bumpkin Kirkwood encountered at the cemetery gates. 'But for now, you must come with me. Time is not on our side and there is someone who wants to talk to you.' His stern tone left them in no doubt he meant business. He turned and began to walk back up the path towards the central driveway.

'But who are you?' Kirkwood finally found his voice again.

'My name is not important,' he replied, not allowing the question to break his stride. 'But for now, you may call me Samuel.'

Kirkwood and Meredith exchanged puzzled looks and, more supporting one another than walking independently, followed the strange man. He had saved their lives and was their best and probably only means of answering the multitude of questions forming a not so orderly queue on their lips.

They followed; exhausted, but hopeful.

CHAPTER 69

THE GATEHOUSE

1:11 p.m.

'Drink this. It's not cordon bleu, but it's hot and nourishing. Your bellies need filling for what lies ahead.'

Samuel handed them two chipped mugs into which he had ladled steaming broth from a pot, simmering on a small stove. He had led them to the gatehouse, inside the front gates of the cemetery. Kirkwood cradled the mug between his fingers and eyed its lumpy contents with suspicion. Suddenly realising he was ravenous, he allowed the hunger pangs to overcome his reticence and, shrugging at Meredith, took a tentative sip. She watched cautiously as he swallowed, before an affirmative nod convinced her it was safe to follow suit.

Whatever the concoction was, it received their seal of approval. It was warm and thick, full of chunks of meat and vegetables. The next few minutes were spent in silence, bar the occasional contented slurp. The gravedigger busied himself about the stone gatehouse; a clutter of work tools and gardening equipment. He initially waved away their questions, insisting they eat first and talk later. Amidst the chaos, there was a camp bed and gas stove, on which he had heated their broth in a dented saucepan.

Scattered clothing and toiletries suggested Samuel spent more time here than your average nine-to-five employee. Draining his mug, Kirkwood shifted awkwardly in the deckchair he was sitting on, before deciding to tackle the gigantic elephant in the room.

'Thank you. For everything. You saved our lives, but can I ask why the place isn't swarming with police right now? You could have heard those explosions a mile away. Not forgetting the small matter of the imbecile who you fried to a crisp out there. Local law enforcement tends to take a dim view of decapitating people with lightning bolts or whatever it was you had up your sleeve. Even if it was for the greater good.'

The gravedigger, who had been tidying a workbench as they ate their broth, now turned, leaned against it, and folded two impressive forearms against his barrel of a chest. He fixed them with an intense stare. 'You need not worry about the police or that imbecile, as you so charmingly described him.' All semblance of the goofiness he displayed when first meeting Kirkwood, was gone. He now spoke assuredly, and every word was carefully considered before being delivered with gravitas, despite the ridiculous brown mullet of hair which sat atop chiselled features. Kirkwood still struggled to place the accent, which seemed to shift every time Samuel spoke. English was definitely his first language, but the nationality continued to elude Kirkwood.

'Need not worry?' he replied in astonishment. 'Correct me if I'm mistaken, but I believe we managed to blow up half the city cemetery out there. I suspect the peelers might be a tad curious as to how that happened, don't you?'

The gravedigger casually cupped a hand to his ear. 'Do you hear any sirens? No, me neither.' He dropped the hand, his expression remaining as unreadable as before. 'I know this will be difficult for you to understand, but as far as the outside world is concerned, none of the events you just witnessed took place. If you were to walk outside now, the cemetery would be just as it was before. No explosions, no lightning bolts as you call them, and most definitely no decapitated bodies.'

'But…I saw it with my own eyes. You killed him right in front of me. I could smell him burning.' Kirkwood crinkled his nose in disgust at the memory of it.

'It's difficult to kill somebody who wasn't alive in the first place,' replied the gravedigger. 'Dermot Fitzgerald died at the Battle of Waterloo on 18 June 1815. As did his twin brother, Declan. Shot in the back by their commanding officer during the act of desertion. What you encountered out there were not the Fitzgerald Brothers. They may have looked like them, talked like them, even thought like them, but it was not them, let me assure you.'

'Well if it wasn't them, then who was it?' persisted Kirkwood. 'Because they sure as hell had an unhealthy interest in ending our lives.'

He nodded towards Meredith, including her in the statement, but she did not appear to be listening, instead staring into the bottom of her mug, lost in thought. It suddenly struck Kirkwood he had yet to establish how she was, or where she had been, such was his haste to quiz Samuel about his own near-death experience. He suddenly felt selfish and more than a little foolish.

As if reading his thoughts, the gravedigger leaned forward and gently placed a large, calloused hand on Meredith's knee. It broke whatever memory she was reliving, causing her to look up and smile at the man. It was a tired but grateful smile. The gravedigger smiled back, and his rugged features softened. 'You are safe here. No harm will come to you in this place.' He studied her face with sombre brown eyes to ensure she understood him. Meredith hesitated slightly but then nodded and, content she was reassured, Samuel removed his hand and turned to face Kirkwood, who was already priming the next salvo of questions.

'Who are you?' he asked. 'Who are…were…they? And why am I caught up in the middle of this unholy mess?'

Samuel chuckled as if amused by Kirkwood's choice of words.

'I'm sorry, but do you find this funny? From where I'm sitting, I see nothing remotely humorous about our current plight.' He was angry now, his cheeks flaring red.

The gravedigger held up his bucket-like hands in a placatory gesture. 'Okay. Okay. I apologise and will do my best to answer at least some of your questions. But you hit the nail on the head when you referred to what just transpired as an unholy mess.' He started to laugh again, but realising the stern expression on Kirkwood's face, thought better of it and reverted to his default hangdog expression.

'As I said, you can call me Samuel. It is not my real title, but I know that your kind place great importance on putting a name to a face.'

'Our kind?' Meredith shot him a perplexed expression. 'What do you mean, our kind?'

Samuel was silent for some time before speaking again. It was as if he was weighing up what he could and could not tell his young interrogators.

'I will do my best to make this as simple as I can. You live in the present, within the three dimensions of which you are aware. Your scientists have made some steps towards discovering there is more, much more, beyond your home world. They have discovered other planets, stars and galaxies which stretched your greatest minds to their limits. I'm afraid, however, that they have only dipped their toes in the waters of understanding, and barely scratched the surface of what there is to know.'

'For a higher, sentinel being who is trying to impart understanding…' Kirkwood raised inverted fingers as he sarcastically accentuated the last word, before continuing. 'You aren't currently doing a very good job of it. So far it's about as clear as mud.' He folded his arms and waited for the gravedigger to continue.

'Very well then. I will cut to the chase as your kind say. Time is short, and you will have to grasp what you can now; as for the rest, we will fill in the gaps as we go along. You are correct when you refer to me as a higher being. I am not what you would consider human, although once I was. Before I moved on.'

'Moved on?' gasped Meredith. 'As in died?'

'We prefer "moved on". Death is such a finite expression. But yes, "died" will suffice if it helps you understand. There are many of my kind and, when required, we visit your plane. Some of you refer to us as angels, others spirits or ghosts. We have many names, depending upon the belief systems held by your kind; none of which are totally accurate or totally inaccurate. You do your best, given your limited intellect.' He paused to gauge whether Kirkwood and Meredith were still following him.

'Highly patronising, but feel free to continue, oh mighty one,' replied Kirkwood, directing a sweeping bow towards Samuel. A well-placed elbow in the ribs from Meredith made him wince and focus on the big man standing in front of them.

'For many millennia we have been waging a war. For while you would describe my kind as good…' this time he inverted his fingers, earning a grudging smile from Kirkwood. '…There are others like us who do not have such honourable intentions. They are driven by a terrible darkness. So deep and ancient, that even I struggle to comprehend its origin and motivations.'

'Like the Devil?' suggested Meredith. 'Satan, Lucifer, Beelzebub?'

'Some of your kind refer to it by those titles. This darkness has many monikers. If you can even refer to such a force by name. All I know is that it is intent on sweeping all before it, until it desecrates the known planes and there is nothing left. Until existence ceases to be and we are all no more.'

'Planes?' asked Meredith, warming to her inquisition of the big man. 'As in parallel worlds or something? You don't mean to tell me there is more than one Kirkwood Scott out there? I've been through a lot lately, but I think that would be a bridge too far.' She sniggered as her jibe was rewarded with a dark scowl from Kirkwood.

Samuel nodded. 'Again, it is a somewhat simplistic interpretation, but essentially, yes. There are many planes and we have the ability to move between them at will.' A smirk flitted across his face and he looked at Kirkwood before continuing. 'On the bright side, no two planes are the same, so I can assure you the mould was broken when your friend was created.'

Meredith erupted with laughter and the tension in the gatehouse palpably lessened. Kirkwood tutted and, choosing to ignore the ribbing, resumed his inquisition of Samuel.

'So, you guys are flying around in the clouds, firing laser bolts or whatever it is you do in some never-ending battle of good versus evil?' He ran a hand through his mop of hair, ruffling it furiously, in a futile effort to cram this fresh torrent of information into an already overflowing brain.

Samuel nodded. 'The battle, as you call it, has been raging across many planes for many aeons. Some have been lost to the darkness, while others we barely retain a foothold on. Planes, such as the world you inhabit, have been largely untouched. Until recent generations, that is. Initially, it was just the occasional foray by the enemy, as if it was sounding out our defences. But of late, it has been a more sustained intervention. Which brings me to you two.'

Kirkwood and Meredith exchanged puzzled looks. 'What do you mean…us?' Kirkwood finally asked.

Samuel stretched and straightened out his back. He stood well over six feet tall and a muscular physique threatened to burst from beneath the confines of his work shirt. *There wasn't an ounce of fat on him*, thought Kirkwood jealously.

'I will leave that for someone else to explain.' He covered the distance from the stove to the gatehouse's only door in two giant steps and opened it, despite neither Kirkwood nor Meredith having heard a knock.

An elderly figure stood in the doorway. Instantly recognised by Meredith although the weathered face beaming at them was also vaguely familiar to Kirkwood.

'Dawson!' she exclaimed, jumping to her feet, the mug in her hand falling to the floor and splintering into several pieces.

Kirkwood suddenly realised that the scruffy, old man in the doorway was the wino he had spoken to when following Meredith to the bookshop. He sat back in his deckchair and puffed out both cheeks.

Could this day get any weirder?

CHAPTER 70

THE SCOURGE

Dobson hobbled slowly into the gatehouse allowing Meredith to reflect that this was possibly the first time she had seen the old man standing upright. Normally he was slumped in a doorway, reeking of alcohol and other odours she cared not dwell upon. He winked playfully at her, a broad smile lighting up his wrinkled features.

'Greetings, Meredith. I see that Samuel is taking good care of you. Any of that delicious broth left, my young friend?' He removed a battered trilby to reveal a mass of unkempt grey curls which cascaded over both stooped shoulders. It had been many years since Cornelius Dobson had seen the inside of a barber's shop.

'Of course.' Samuel closed the door behind Dobson, returning to the stove where he began ladling the still-bubbling broth into another mug produced from behind the remnants of a lawnmower. Dobson had already taken up residence in a tatty armchair facing Kirkwood and Meredith. He gratefully accepted the steaming mug from Samuel who stood back, waiting for the older man to speak. Kirkwood sensed that whoever or whatever they were, Dobson was the senior figure in the partnership.

They looked expectantly towards Dobson as he settled into the armchair before draining the contents of the mug in one noisy slurp. Seemingly impervious to the heat of the broth, he smacked his lips contentedly before emitting a cavernous belch which threatened to bring the walls of the gatehouse crashing down upon them.

'Excellent. Excellent. Now down to business. Where were we?' He rubbed his hands together enthusiastically and surveyed each of them in turn, his eyes twinkling like an excited puppy waiting for a ball to be thrown in its direction.

'You're in on this?' Meredith pointed at Samuel, struggling to contain her shock. 'You're one of them?'

Kirkwood took up the baton of incredulity. 'But I saw you yesterday. You were outside the bookshop when I followed Mere…' He stopped in his tracks, all too aware of his gaff. It was too late as Meredith spun around to face him.

'You followed me to the bookshop? Who the hell do you think you are? I'm not your property and I'm more than capable of fighting my own…' Her pale blue eyes flared angrily as Dobson looked on in delight, enjoying the show. Samuel remained as impassive as ever.

'Yeah, because you've been making such a good job of it.' Kirkwood took the verbal bait, hook, line, and sinker. 'If it weren't for Emily and I, you would still be wherever the Brothers Grimm had you holed up.'

'I think you'll find *he* rescued me,' Meredith pointed at Samuel who shifted uncomfortably at suddenly being the centre of attention. 'And hang on. Emily? What's this got to do with her?'

Kirkwood realised he was fighting a losing battle and gestured towards Dobson, desperate for a reprieve from the verbal onslaught.

'Oh, I can speak, now can I?' The old man smirked, before a more serious expression replaced it. 'It may be hard for you both to take in, but everything Samuel has told you so far is unfortunately true.' He paused to let the words sink in. Kirkwood wondered how Dobson knew what they had been discussing prior to his arrival but decided to let it go. Nothing surprised Kirkwood Scott anymore when it came to this bizarre new world he had stumbled upon.

Dobson handed the empty mug to Samuel before speaking again. 'Now, I could sit here talking all night and you would still only grasp a fraction of what is at stake here. I will tell you what I can but also ask that you trust me, for we will have to move soon. Word of Dermot's demise will have reached our enemies and they will be seeking swift retribution. We may have won this skirmish, but the battle is only just beginning.'

Kirkwood's ears pricked. 'Skirmishers. That's what I called them. The brothers, Rodriguez, Gunther. When they were…' He looked towards Dobson, desperate for some sort of sane explanation.

'Your toy soldiers,' the tramp sombrely finished the sentence. 'Our enemy can manifest itself in any form it wishes. It often chooses disguises that will have the greatest emotional impact upon those it targets.'

'Targets?' Meredith didn't like the direction the conversation was taking.

'I'm afraid so, young lady. They have been watching the two of you for many years.' He cleared his throat and glanced at Samuel who suddenly developed an intense interest in his work boots. 'As have we…'

'But why?' asked Meredith, failing to comprehend what she was hearing. 'Why us?'

Dobson crouched over and took her hand in his. 'My dear, I know this is difficult to understand but please bear with me. For just a few more moments.' He patted it softly before addressing them again.

'As Samuel explained before my arrival there has been a war raging for millennia across the planes between the darkness and our kind. These planes are many. I suppose the easiest way to describe them to you are as parallel worlds. Some are similar to your own, whereas others are different in every way imaginable.'

Kirkwood nodded slowly while Meredith started to nervously chew on a fingernail.

'The planes are separate yet also linked, some directly and others less so. For example, there are pathways from the plane known as Earth to sixteen others. From them, you could access hundreds of others again. And so on, until eventually you would travel to countless worlds.'

He paused to let the information sink in. 'Well, I say countless. They are a finite number. But if I tried to explain it via your rather basic mathematical models, I fear your brains would leak out of your nostrils. Einstein came the closest to getting his head around it, but he's moved on now.'

Kirkwood sniggered nervously but stopped when a stony look from Dobson indicated the old lush was not joking.

'We had been holding our own on this plane. It was something of a sleepy backwater to be honest, but for whatever reason our enemy has decided to raise the stakes as far as dear old planet Earth is concerned. The situation was bubbling under for a while but the arrival of these skirmishers as you call them indicates a new offensive is imminent.'

'More broth?' offered Samuel. The words barely left his mouth before Dobson was nodding vigorously. Kirkwood and Meredith declined the offer, somewhat more politely.

'Hungry work, this talking business,' explained the old man. 'Why you humans haven't evolved beyond verbal communication is beyond me. I find it all awfully tiresome.' He gratefully accepted the replenished mug Samuel handed him and took another large slurp before continuing.

'Which is where you two come in.'

'Us?' Kirkwood and Meredith replied simultaneously before, not for the first time, exchanging baffled looks.

'Yes, I'm afraid so. Although I like to look upon it as more a once in a lifetime opportunity that you'd be mad to miss out on.' He held out both arms expectantly, expecting a rousing response from the young man and woman sitting before him. When it was not forthcoming, he returned his hands to his lap and sighed quietly.

'Oh, alright then, maybe not. But I cannot stress how important the two of you are. Especially since your friend moved on.' He looked sadly at Meredith and paused as if in silent tribute.

'Emily? What's this got to do with her? She never hurt anyone.' Meredith fought back the urge to burst into tears. This was simply too much to take in at the one sitting.

Dobson produced a filthy handkerchief from the depths of his overcoat and offered it to her. She studied the rag with some horror before waving it away. Seeming slightly offended, the old man continued. 'Us higher beings, as you like to call us, do what we can to protect each plane. But this is a war of attrition and our enemy is incredibly strong. Every plane it occupies is drained of all life, which it then uses to fuel its own reserves. It is breeding and multiplying far quicker than we previously thought possible.'

He inspected the handkerchief as if aghast that anybody would consider it dirty, before emptying the contents of both nostrils into it with a thundering honk. Kirkwood and Meredith flinched in revulsion while even the normally implacable Samuel seemed mildly embarrassed.

'Every plane has portals which provide doorways to other planes. As I said, your planet has direct access to sixteen such…'

'Sixteen other planes. Yes, yes, we get that,' interrupted Kirkwood, his impatience growing at the meandering way Dobson was imparting such life-changing information. 'But where do Meredith, Emily and I fit into all this?'

'Planes are accessed by portals. They're a bit like supernatural doorways if that makes it any easier to understand. The portal for your beautiful world is located on the fair island of Ireland. Hence, the arrival of our skirmishing friends. But they are only the advance party. We have yet to experience a fraction of what the enemy is capable of unleashing. If it is successful, I fear for the future of your planet. Other front lines have quietened, suggesting this is its priority at present. We are currently trying to figure out the significance of Earth to it, for it does nothing without very good reason. Its cunning is only matched by a malicious intelligence.'

'Perhaps you could explain to our young friends their role in all this,' Samuel softly suggested, aware of the growing frustration in the room.

Dobson shot him an ominous look before carrying on, clearly displeased his ponderous delivery was being critiqued by a subordinate. 'That's the problem with young people today. No patience,' he tutted. He paused, as if re-boarding a train of thought, before plunging once more into the insane tale.

'As you have no doubt gathered, this war had been raging for many, many generations. Long before the two of you were born, and Samuel and myself, for that matter. Our enemy is not for ceasefires, negotiations or treaties. It does not recognise flags of truth, only total destruction and unconditional victory. Prisoners of war are an utterly foreign concept to it. We are facing an uphill battle against an unrelenting, merciless enemy. We cannot fight it alone and are thankful for any allies we can find.' He looked at them, as if inviting a response but was met with blank expressions.

Samuel sensed the confusion and stepped into the fray. 'What my colleague is trying to say is that we need your help. Without your assistance, this planet and its population have little hope of surviving what is to come.'

'Let me get this straight. You're telling us we are on the verge of Armageddon Day but rather than appeal to the United Nations, you ethereal beings are pinning your hopes on a homeless, drunk girl, and a depressed paper-pusher from Belfast? Correct me if I missed anything there?'

'Hey, less of the drunk girl!' snarled Meredith. 'I can take it or leave it. It's just I choose to take it most days given my current circumstances.'

Samuel ignored her, instead addressing Kirkwood's retort. 'This battle goes far beyond what your conventional armies can offer in resistance. If they were all that stood between us and our enemy, then your plane would be swept away in the blink of an eye.'

'Which is why we need you,' implored Dobson, seizing the initiative once more. 'There are powers at work here far beyond your comprehension. As we proceed, more will be revealed, but for now you must accept what we are saying. Every generation of your kind throws up those whose responsibility it is to protect their plane from outside influences. They often live lives oblivious to their calling and, on their own, are unremarkable. Our kind are aware of them, however, and watch over them throughout their earthly existences.'

'I've had a guardian angel looking over me all these years?' Kirkwood spoke the words a little louder than he intended to. 'Well, can I just say they haven't been doing a very good job of it so far if that's the case.'

'We have to be careful as to when and how we intervene in the lives of your kind. It cannot be too obvious so as to draw unwanted attention. We prefer to keep as low a profile as possible, hence the humble lifestyles Samuel and I presently lead on your world. Likewise, there is this bothersome concept of free will that your kind insist upon retaining. Believe it or not, my friend, but much of what befalls you is of your own making. If we intervened all the time, it could lead to all kinds of nasty repercussions further down the road.'

Samuel picked up the thread. 'Every portal on every plane has three guardians or protectors at any given time. In the case of your world, it was yourselves and the one you knew as Emily.'

'Emily!' Meredith looked aghast and on the verge of tears again, causing Kirkwood to awkwardly place a hand on her arm.

'I'm afraid so,' replied Dobson dourly. 'As individuals, there is little to distinguish you from others of your kind. On your own you are three perfectly normal young persons. However, when the three of you align together, you unlock a power which is capable of defending the portal from external attack. We call it, The Presence. Our enemy recognises this and has been desperately trying to keep the three of you from coming together in recent years.' He paused and hung his head. 'In the case of your friend Emily, I am sorry to say they were successful.'

'But I don't understand,' wailed Meredith, her faltering fortitude dissolving quicker than a spring frost caressed by the morning sun. 'Emily slit her wrists because of those bullying bitches at Ashgrove. That had nothing to do with this enemy or whatever the hell you call it.' She turned abruptly and buried her head in Kirkwood's shoulder, the tears finally flowing freely. Kirkwood patted the back of her head and whispered meaningless platitudes in a futile attempt to console her.

He only spoke over her, when the fiercest sobbing subsided, fixing Dobson with a stern stare. 'I have one word for you. One word. I just need to know if he is behind any of this...Skelly.'

For the first time since entering the gatehouse, Dobson was at a loss for words. Samuel made no effort this time to intervene and remained silent, clearly of the belief this was a thorny topic, more fitting for his senior colleague to address.

Dobson sighed before eventually speaking. It seemed even the very mention of the name weighed heavily on his spirit, as his shoulders slumped. 'Our enemy can adopt many guises, and these are carefully calculated to have the maximum emotional impact upon those it feels threatened by. For you, it is this man you know as Skelly. He is part of our enemy, just as our enemy is part of him. It is one and it is all. It has no structure, no restraints, no body; so to speak. It is everywhere and nowhere. It has no name, so we provided it with one. We call it, The Scourge. This Skelly is but a manifestation of it.'

'Could you be any vaguer?' grumbled Kirkwood, clearly unimpressed.

'I'm sorry,' said Dobson. 'But the words of your language are woefully incapable of allowing me to describe what we are currently facing.'

Kirkwood stared at his boots before lifting his head and looking Dobson in the eye. 'Rodriguez, Gunther, The Fitzgerald's? They're all part of this?'

'That is how The Scourge has chosen to present itself to you. It seizes upon an inherent weakness or character flaw within an individual and preys upon it. In your case, it was your childhood experiences and subsequent feelings of guilt and shame. The persistent, intrusive thoughts and your need to perform sets of routines to reduce the resulting anxiety and discomfort. Your doctors refer to it as Obsessive Compulsive Disorder, if I'm correct? You have been diagnosed, yes?'

Kirkwood paused, nervously scratching the bridge of his nose. Now it was Meredith's turn to squeeze his hand. 'Not formally,' he conceded. 'I've been pretty good at hiding it down the years. I'm not an idiot, though. I've googled it, read the books, I even went to a support group once, but it wasn't for me. I prefer to fight my own battles. And anyway, Skelly — my blackouts where I end up in his study, it all kind of suggested I was beyond help. Washing your hands religiously or refusing to step on cracks in the pavement, I get that. But me? That was just a whole new ball game of lunacy. I couldn't explain it to anyone, not least myself, without looking like a raving nutjob. So, I just muddled along on my own.' He shook his head sadly, before fiddling with a loose button on his shirt.

Dobson smiled sympathetically. 'I can assure you, Kirkwood, you are anything but a nutjob. Foolish yes, for not seeking professional help, but not a nutjob. Your illness is as real and as credible as the common cold or a broken bone. Millions of your kind struggle with it daily. Our enemy has seized upon it, however, as a prize fighter would seize upon a weakness in their opponent. It uses your illness as a tool, a means of incapacitating you so you no longer pose a threat. But you are not just anyone, Kirkwood Scott, and the sooner you realise that, then the better for all of us. You were chosen from long before you were formed in your mother's womb, for today.' He turned his attention to Meredith. 'As have you, Meredith Starc.'

Meredith stared blankly at the grizzled old man, desperately trying to process the avalanche of information being hurled at her. A blanket of silence fell over the four of them before Kirkwood sat bolt upright and stared at her. 'Wait a minute, your surname is Stark? As in Game of Thrones, Stark? That's my favourite show. Although I was well into the books before they started filming it here and changed all the storylines.' He sniffed contemptuously at the very thought of it.

Meredith rolled her eyes. 'That's Starc with a *c*. As in the County Down Starcs. We existed centuries before that big guy with the beard started peddling his trash and making a mockery of our fine name. And anyway, you can't talk. Your parents got your name the wrong way around when they were registering the birth.'

Kirkwood resisted the urge to scream and gritted his teeth. 'Oh, har de har har. I've never heard that one before. Excuse me, while I die laughing over here.' He dared Meredith to respond but, before she had an opportunity to do so, the ever-stoical Samuel intervened.

'We have no time for bickering. The Scourge is closing again. I've gained us some time but now you must come with us. The portal is increasingly in danger so long as The Presence is but two.'

'Two?' queried Kirkwood, not for the first time none the wiser.

'Yes,' confirmed Dobson, rising to his feet with surprising dexterity for such a venerable man. 'It's high time we made tracks. The portal awaits us.'

CHAPTER 71

COUNCIL OF WAR

Skelly sighed and looked up from his broadsheet. England had collapsed at Lords again. Decades passed, empires rose and fell but the English cricketing tail still resolutely refused to wag. 'They would have been hung, drawn and quartered in my day, every damned last one of them,' he muttered angrily to himself. 'It's a bloody disgrace.'

He breathed deeply, as this was doing nothing for his mood. Folding the newspaper precisely and setting it on his lap, he reached at the same time for the tumbler and decanter on the adjacent circular table. 'I predict I'll need a stiff drink to get me through this latest debacle,' he snarled, pouring himself a generous measure. His hospitality did not extend to a nervous Rodriguez who stood before him.

The Portuguese giant cleared his throat to speak. 'With hindsight, sir, I should have personally handled the graveyard operation. Or at the very least, sent Gunther in a supervisory capacity. However, we did not anticipate the enemy becoming aware of our intentions and dispatching one of their own to intercede on behalf of the boy.' He shifted weight uneasily to his other foot, uncertain how the wizened pensioner seated before him in the plush armchair would react to this explanation.

'Yes, hindsight is a wonderful thing,' conceded Skelly, taking a leisurely sip from his drink. He smacked his lips and Rodriguez allowed himself to relax a fraction. Maybe the Colonel was mellowing a little in his dotage. His hopes were short lived as Skelly drained the dregs of the glass, before launching it with alarming ferocity towards his subordinate. Had it not been for sharp reflexes, the missile would have connected squarely with Rodriguez's forehead, but he narrowly avoided it, jerking to one side as it whistled millimetres past his left ear.

Rodriguez tensed, waiting for the sound of smashing glass behind him, but there was nothing. The glass either vanished or continued on an unknown trajectory, of which he had no desire to know about. He remained rooted to the spot, unable to move. Things were going badly, very badly.

'You dare to come here and report to me that (*a*) you have permitted the White Witch to somehow still remain on this plane and influence events upon it, (*b*) allowed her whiny little friend to escape from the abyss, and (*c*) watched as that vile vagrant Dobson waltzed off into the sunset with them, headed for pastures new. You should consider yourself fortunate I'm not forwarding this information to our superiors because believe me, Señor Rodriguez, they do not share my conciliatory and forgiving nature.'

Skelly prided himself on remaining calm in a crisis, but this was testing his patience. If the powers that be were to get wind of the shambles in the graveyard then he would be summoned to answer some very awkward questions. Throwing tantrums, however, was not the solution. He was disappointed in himself at the glass throwing incident. He was better than that. Showing emotions to the junior ranks was a sign of weakness and unbecoming of a man of his stature. He closed his eyes for a second and composed himself before opening them and adopting a different approach.

'So, how are we going to extract ourselves from this mess, Sergeant?'

Rodriguez grimaced. This was going much worse than anticipated. He had never known the Colonel to raise his voice before, let alone attempt to assault one of his own. It was time to apply some much-needed damage limitation and extract himself from the predicament as best he could. He would have Declan Fitzgerald's head on a stick the next time their paths crossed.

'I believe the situation is still retrievable, sir. The involvement of the White Witch was unforeseen, but I believe we have her contained now. Dobson and the others have left the city known as Belfast and are headed west. While she did not fully move on following her demise, and remnants of her aura remain, there is no indication she can affect proceedings regarding The Presence. The other two are completely isolated in that respect. It cannot be fully released as long as they remain but two.'

'Isolated? Oh, I see. How very clever of you and remiss of me to not identify your masterful strategy. By allowing Meredith to be liberated and uniting her with Kirkwood and the others we have in fact seized the initiative. Everyone home for tea and crumpets by Christmas then. I can pass the message up the chain that all is in hand and proceeding as planned.' He raised a bushy eyebrow to underline the sinister sarcasm in his voice.

'I accept it is a setback sir, but plans are afoot to rectify the situation, if you would only allow me to explain.' He looked desperately at Skelly who sniffed and waved a hand. Rodriguez interpreted it as a sign to continue and plunged ahead.

'As I said, isolated. Isolated as in there are two of them as opposed to three. As you know, The Presence cannot be fully released without three vessels, and the one known as Emily is no longer on the play of field in that regard.'

Skelly's stare bored into his soul, giving the bearded giant no indication whether or not his words were having any effect. 'Yes, they are in the company of The Forsaken — but Gunther and I are confident we retain the beating of them.'

'And the Toxic Twins?' enquired Skelly, sweetly. 'What of them?' He drummed a set of long, bony fingers on the arm of the chair and crossed his feet.

'Dermot has returned to the source where his energy will be redistributed as deemed necessary by those responsible for such logistical issues. Declan has been removed from the plane and will be redeployed in a less taxing role, once the appropriate disciplinary action has been taken against him.'

He paused, as the thought of disciplinary action caused a trickle of sweat to form between his shoulder blades and trace an icy finger downwards, coming to rest in the small of his back. He almost felt sorry for the halfwit. Almost.

'Well, at least you've got that side of it sorted, I suppose,' conceded Skelly reluctantly. 'When then, do you plan to intercept? We cannot delay much longer. Those up the chain are working to a tight timetable. There is a bigger picture to consider here. But nothing can happen until that damned portal is breached. It's a logjam which needs to be cleared and if it isn't, then both of our heads are going to roll.'

'I fully appreciate that, sir,' oozed Rodriguez, sensing for the first time he might survive to fight another day after all. 'Gunther is currently tailing them, and I intend to join him as soon as I have finished briefing you. We are unaware of any other Forsaken operating on the plane and, as I said, Gunther and I are confident of nullifying the threat to the overall operation. Dobson is past his best, while Samuel is inexperienced and still learning his trade. The Presence as it stands can offer us no serious resistance. If, however...' He slyly met Skelly's expressionless eyes, '...reinforcements could be deployed, well then that would be much appreciated and further stack the odds in our favour.'

Skelly nursed the tumbler which had magically reappeared in his leathery hand and mulled the offer over. 'If I were to agree to your proposition it would in no way constitute any endorsement of your activities to date. The only reason I am protecting you is because, if I don't, my unmentionables will be on the chopping block alongside your own.'

He paused, considering his options before speaking again. 'It is blatantly clear to me that I overestimated you and placed you in a position far beyond your all too limited capabilities. For now, you may remain, but operations from this point onwards will require a much more hands-on approach on my part. The ineptitude of you and your comrades means young Kirkwood is no longer under my control. As long as he remains in the company of that itinerant girl, I cannot reach him. Thanks to you, you Iberian idiot.'

Rodriguez said nothing, nervously playing with his beard. He imagined clasping Skelly's rancid head between his two massive hands and squeezing until it spilled its contents like an overripe melon. A nice thought, but he knew that even if he could take a step towards the armchair, his internal organs would explode within a second. He had watched others lose their temper with the Colonel and meet an excruciating end. Flabby and impotent he might look, but Skelly contained a frightening power appropriate for one of his lofty position. He, therefore, chose to keep quiet and instead give the pretence of listening like an obedient lapdog. Yes sir, no sir. Three bags full sir.

Skelly reined in his burgeoning temper and nodded at Rodriguez. He had made his decision. 'Very well, you will have assistance when the time comes. One of my best men. I want to ensure there are no mistakes this time. Now get out of my sight.'

With that, Rodriguez vanished from the room, leaving Skelly alone with only his own dark machinations to keep him company. 'Bloody foreigners,' he seethed, picking up the newspaper again and returning to the demise of English cricket. 'What this requires is an injection of youth.' He smiled to himself. 'And believe me, Dobson, when this one arrives on the scene you won't know what hit you.'

CHAPTER 72

A LITTLE ROAD TRIP

Samuel led them around the side of the gatehouse where a battered Nissan Micra sat awaiting. Its red, metallic paintwork was heavily corroded, while the windscreen was caked with an army of dead flies; at least one of the tyres was perilously close to the legal limit regarding its tread.

'For all powerful, celestial beings you guys sure operate on a tight budget,' remarked Kirkwood, as Samuel opened the driver's door, pulled forward the creaking front seat, and indicated for them to get into the back. They unceremoniously squeezed in and the big man followed suit, crouched uncomfortably behind the steering wheel. Neither of them noticed Dobson getting into the car but he was already in the passenger seat; a contented smile on his face.

'Where exactly are we going?' asked Meredith, leaning forward as Samuel turned the ignition key. The engine spluttered reluctantly to life, as he engaged first gear and released the handbrake. The Micra lurched forward a few feet before stalling. Samuel repeated the process, this time with more success, and the car unenthusiastically trundled away from the gatehouse, towards the cemetery gates.

'On a little road trip,' Dobson cheerily announced, as Samuel slowly negotiated the gates and turned right onto the main road. 'Don't worry, we'll stop off at some point to refuel both body and soul. I know how much your kind rely upon your creature comforts.'

Samuel eased the Micra into fourth gear and glanced to and from the rear-view mirror as he spoke. 'You are but two. The Presence requires three. Emily is no longer fully of this plane, so we must suffice with what we have.'

An irritated Meredith piped up from the rear. 'That's my bloody best friend you're talking about, how dare you! She's irreplaceable. And she's still here. How else do you explain my letters? The graffiti?' Kirkwood nodded his assent, as they dared their travelling companions to say otherwise.

'You are quite correct of course and I apologise for my colleague's lack of tact,' replied Dobson, shooting Samuel a disapproving look. The bigger man was oblivious to it, so focused was he on the road ahead. 'The Presence is an incredibly powerful force. The three of you were born into it. It is of you and you are of it. As you matured into adulthood it naturally began to draw the three of you together. Meredith, you and Emily were the first to form bonds and, had that been allowed to develop, then your paths would no doubt have converged with Kirkwood. It should have been as inevitable as day follows night.'

'Until Skelly and his mates got involved,' growled Kirkwood.

'Skelly, The Scourge — whatever you wish to call it, regards the three of you as a threat. If there is no Presence, this portal will fall, and your plane will be breached. I only dread to think what will happen then. You are all that stands between your planet being consumed by an unfathomable evil.'

'Unfathomable evil.' Meredith had calmed down slightly after her stinging rebuke to Samuel who seemed none the worse for it. 'What is this? Night of the Living Dead?'

'In its own subtle, discreet way it has probed and tested your defences, seeking a chink in your armour that it could penetrate. It will find your Achilles heel, an inherent weakness, and then it will exploit that to maximum effect. With you, Kirkwood, it was your turbulent childhood and the mental health issues you have struggled with since then. The Scourge latched onto these and manipulated them, enveloping you in these tortuous routines. Left unattended, you may have never escaped them and been lost to us for good.'

Kirkwood nodded as Dobson's verbal brush strokes, broad at first and without form, began to colour in the details that had eluded him for so long. While his natural instinct was to shoot off questions and demand answers, he decided to keep quiet and allow Dobson to continue. They were now on the motorway, heading west out of Belfast. He sat back and managed a small sigh of relief. While undoubtedly headed towards grave danger, he sensed leaving the city and his troubles behind was a personal victory. Natasha, his crappy job, the argument with Gerry. For now, they were no longer his primary concern.

It was early evening and the sidelights of approaching vehicles headed city-bound, temporarily dazzled Kirkwood. Suddenly, a light bulb sparked behind his eyeballs, causing him to jump forward as far as the seatbelt would allow him.

'Wait. We need to go back. Right this very minute.'

Meredith turned to face him and was alarmed to see Kirkwood's face drained of colour. 'Are you okay? You look like you've seen a ghost.'

'My routine. With all the craziness I've completely forgotten about it. If I don't complete it then…'

Dobson finished the sentence, looking over his shoulder at the distracted young man in the rear of the car. 'Bad things will happen?'

'Yes…' Kirkwood stared in amazement at the kindly old man. 'But how do you know? And not just that. About my OCD. Skelly. Everything. Are you a mind reader?'

Dobson chuckled. 'Oh, now there's a superpower I wouldn't wish on anyone. Not mind reading, exactly, but as I said we have been watching and protecting you for a very long time. Let's just say I've picked up a bit of knowledge along the way.'

'So, you know all about the dice? The 49?'

'Indeed, I do. Skelly has led you on a merry dance for many a year and I have watched it with a heavy heart. I'm sorry I didn't intervene earlier, but we had to wait until the time was right. That time is now, and The Presence has been activated, Kirkwood. It flows within you and, so long as that remains, Skelly and his wicked routines cannot harm you. Why do you think they are only crossing your mind now? The Presence protects you from the obsessive urges and unwanted promptings.'

'So, you mean…I don't have to do them?'

'Not as long as The Presence remains. You are free of it all, including Skelly's evil insistence that people will die if you don't conform to his will. Stuff and nonsense, the lot of it.'

Kirkwood slumped back into the seat. Free? He struggled to take in what he was being told. It was as if all his birthdays had arrived at once. Next to him, Meredith grinned from ear to ear and gripped his arm. She opened her mouth to speak, only to be beaten to the punch by Dobson.

'The same applies to you, Meredith Starc. No more waking up, craving that first mouthful of wine. The Scourge used Emily's death and your despair to awaken this need within you. You too, are free to fight back at last. Doesn't it feel good?'

She smiled sadly in response. 'Of course, it does. But it would feel so much better if Emily was here to share it with me. She always seemed so strong. I leaned so heavily on her, yet all along she was the one who was crumbling. I never had a clue. I must be the worst friend in the world.'

She threw her hands up in disgust and stared outside at the passing countryside. It was beginning to rain again as Samuel pushed the Micra beyond sixty miles per hour. The little vehicle began to shake in protest and Meredith felt they were re-entering the Earth's orbit as opposed to passing the Lisburn turnoff on a dreary Tuesday in September.

Dobson sought to ease her guilt. 'You were not to know. Emily was strong, yet the Scourge is persuasive and seductive. It also manipulates others to do its bidding. The bullying, the taunts. Those were the work of others who acted as unwitting pawns. Believe me, those people will have to live with the consequences of their actions for the rest of their lives. Every war has collateral damage, and they are all victims. The Scourge cares not. Ultimate destruction and devastation are its only concern, its reason for being.'

'So, would she have been plagued by this Skelly character, the dead soldiers that Kirkwood sees? If she was, then I really have been living in a bubble these last few years.'

'It is whatever it wants you to see. To Kirkwood it is Skelly, an internal enemy. To Emily it was the cruel taunts she received from the outside world. Either way, it drove her to the edge and was driving Kirkwood and yourself in a similar direction. It is the voice in your head that suggested you leave home. It is the voice in your head that stops you from picking up a phone and telling your parents you want to come home. It is the voice in your head that tells you to buy a bottle of wine each morning and drink until the pain slips away, even for a few hours. It is what it needs to be, when it needs to be.'

Kirkwood looked out the window as a large blue motorway sign confirmed they were heading west. 'This is all very well and good, but where exactly are we going? I'm meant to be at work in the morning and still haven't paid last month's rent.'

Dobson snorted. 'Believe me, if we don't attend to slightly more pressing matters then you might well not have a job, a house, or indeed a city to return to in the morning. Worry not about these worldly concerns and trust me when I say we have it all in hand. We have a long journey ahead of us and I for one intend to get some shut-eye. Inhabiting such a decrepit body makes one appreciate the importance of rest and relaxation. I suggest you do the same.' He burrowed deep within the folds of his cavernous overcoat and was snoring within minutes, seemingly without a care in the world.

Meredith continued to stare glumly out at bleak grey skies as the countryside rolled past. She was subsumed within a world of her own thoughts and Kirkwood decided to leave her alone with them. They both needed time and space to reflect upon what had transpired, and what still awaited them.

CHAPTER 73

STRANGERS IN A STRANGE LAND

They drove for over an hour until the events of the graveyard faded to nothing more than a dull, unpleasant memory. Following the initial frantic question and answer session, Kirkwood and Meredith fell largely silent, preoccupied with their own thoughts and fears. In the front seat, Dobson lay slumped in a catatonic stupor with only the occasional bump in the road releasing a watery snort, confirming he was still alive. Samuel sat hunched over the steering wheel, gripping it tightly, his face an unblinking mask of concentration.

The monotonous motorway eventually became an equally monotonous dual carriageway at Dungannon. Despite Dobson's reassurances, Kirkwood expected at any second to be wrenched from the safety of the Micra to the terrors of the study; or gripped by an overwhelming desire to succumb to one of the routines that dominated his life. None of that occurred, though. He felt eerily calm; a serenity rarely experienced before. Yes, he was exhausted but even though danger was a constant companion, it was a price worth paying for this sense of release and relief.

The clicking of the Micra's indicator brought him back to the present, as Samuel pulled into a service station, announcing they needed petrol. As the Micra pulled up at the pumps, Dobson jolted into life and, when aware of his surroundings, declared brightly that he needed to empty his bladder. He shuffled towards the entrance, followed by Kirkwood and Meredith, while Samuel battled with a recalcitrant fuel nozzle. Once inside the central food hall, the smells wafting from various hot food outlets reawakened dormant taste buds. A mug of broth, no matter how delicious, could only keep the hunger pangs away for so long.

'Get whatever you want,' bellowed Dobson, as he made a beeline towards the gents. 'It's all on me.' Kirkwood eyed Samuel dubiously, who had joined them from refuelling the car. 'It's okay. We have money,' the big man assured him.

While Meredith buzzed about, stocking up on coffee and her now obligatory quota of traybakes, Kirkwood procured burgers, fries and soft drinks from a Burger King outlet at the rear of the main food mall. Samuel accompanied him and paid, looking increasingly awkward the longer they spent on the premises. He truly was a fish out of water, a stranger in a strange land. As they awaited Dobson's return, Kirkwood sought to break the stilted silence between them.

'Sooo, care to divulge where we are headed or is this some other intergalactic destination our tiny, ape-like brains would be incapable of comprehending?'

'Pluto actually, although we may have to stop off at Jupiter along the way,' deadpanned Samuel, enjoying Kirkwood's shocked expression before displaying a shy smile. 'Do not worry. We will be remaining on this plane unless the engineers at Nissan have conjured up something special under the bonnet of that rust bucket out there. Which I somehow doubt.'

Meredith joined them, juggling several paper bags and cups while making significant inroads into a sticky, marshmallow-based pastry. 'Wharrrtts happerrrningg?' she enquired through a crammed mouth.

'What on this earth is that?' asked Samuel in abject horror, aghast at her choice of snack.

She raised a finger for them to wait while taking a slug from her coffee. She grimaced, swallowed, and then addressed Samuel's query. 'That, my mysterious friend, is a rocky road. The finest traybake known to man.' She polished the rest off as if to reinforce the point.

'You'll be lucky if you see twenty at this rate,' teased Kirkwood, as Dobson approached them from the direction of the toilets, fumbling at his zip.

'Says you, Diet Coke Boy,' Meredith sniped back, sharp as a button. 'Have you seen what that stuff does to a copper coin? Now just imagine that's your stomach lining. Nasty!'

'At least I still have a stomach lining. Which I very much doubt you have, given your alcohol consumption in recent times. I'll take my chances with Diet Coke over Buckfast any day of the week.'

'You know, I haven't thought of the demon drink since I came around in that graveyard. And it's normally never far from my mind. That, and traybakes of course.' She produced another sticky treat from the bag she was carrying, with a satisfied expression. 'Guess you were right after all, Mr. Dobson.'

'You will find I usually am, my dear,' Dobson concluded, fixing himself in full view of the busy food mall, earning several disapproving looks in the process. A security guard hovered nearby but kept his distance once he saw the degenerate tramp alongside three relatively normal human beings. *If only he knew,* quipped Kirkwood silently to himself.

'As I said, you'll find such urges will not have the same hold on you so long as you stay in the company of young Mr Scott and vice versa,' he stated, nodding towards Kirkwood. 'One of the perks of The Presence. Your desire to consume that poison was the work of our enemy, but The Presence is more than a match for it.'

'Yeah, I never want to see old walrus chops again, as long as I live,' remarked Kirkwood ruefully.

Dobson chuckled. 'The Colonel and I go back a long way and, yes, he was near the back of the queue when looks were being dished out. But we must never underestimate him, for he is a ruthless and relentless foe. However, as long you remain within The Presence and by that, I mean in the physical company of each other, then he cannot reach you. Believe me when I say, you cannot succumb to his promptings if you remain with Meredith.'

'And if we don't...' Only part of Meredith wanted to hear the answer to that question.

'Well then, it's a much more level playing field,' Dobson replied. He reached into a pocket of his overcoat and produced a creaseless hundred-pound note, which he promptly handed to Samuel. Noticing the shocked expressions of Kirkwood and Meredith, he patted the pocket and winked. 'Plenty more where that came from,' he chortled. 'Settle our debts Samuel, there's a good man. That barista is beginning to think she's done a runner.'

'I only hope you washed your hands beforehand, that's all,' grimaced Meredith. 'Cleanliness is next to godliness after all.'

'Oh, that's all vastly overrated, believe me,' tutted Dobson, as Samuel loped back, having survived paying for the coffee and traybakes. 'Now come along. We have quite a distance to travel yet, before we stop for the night, and tomorrow is a big day. The biggest of your young lives so far, I would imagine.'

Resigning themselves that they were in it for the long haul, Kirkwood and Meredith clambered into the back seat of the car and were soon back on the motorway, headed west. Neither of them noticed the black BMW, parked at the rear of the forecourt. As the Micra pulled away it followed, and was soon tucked behind them on the carriageway, maintaining a respectful distance, concealed behind several other vehicles. Its occupants would have been familiar to Kirkwood, were he able to see beyond the tinted glass of the top-of-the-range vehicle, stolen in South Belfast not two hours previously.

A muscular, bearded man and his painfully gaunt but elegantly dressed companion.

CHAPTER 74

SKELLY'S SQUARE

Skelly rarely felt out of his depth; his job description was to make others feel out of *their* depth. He enjoyed watching them squirm in front of him, scrambling for answers and explanations to extricate themselves from the quagmire of half-truths and barefaced lies they invariably resorted to when failing to meet his exceptionally high standards.

The debacle at the cemetery had done little to further his own career prospects. The previously unblemished reputation of both the Company and his leadership of it had taken a hammering, and he was in no mood for a repeat performance. He prided himself on having fashioned them into a formidable force, one that his current employers sought out when the chips were down.

He yawned and cricked his neck. It had been a long and decidedly unpleasant day. He sat alone in what Kirkwood and other visitors referred to as a study. It was what he allowed them to see. It could be the Arc de Triomphe, the Taj Mahal, or a busy backstreet in Beijing at a whim, if required. He was not one for high drama, though, preferring a lower-key, subtle approach when conducting business. He enjoyed the trappings of the study as it exuded an ambience which served to intimidate already nervous guests.

The Company were not accustomed to failure which made recent events even harder to swallow. As ever, the full picture was well above his pay grade which suited him fine. He had no desire to know what senior management were conniving towards, other than he trusted it was for the greater good, or rather; greater evil. He would contribute in any way he could towards the success of the operation, more than happy to remain under the radar, a mere cog in the machine. Save the highbrow stuff for his elders and betters.

The Company were all young Kirkwood's own creation, that was the ironic beauty of it, he fashioned the rod that Skelly then used to beat him with, planting himself in the boy's subconscious and immediately getting to work driving him slowly insane; or at least have him believe he was. It was a matter of personal pride for Skelly, given he once inhabited the same world. He had successfully occupied numerous other planes, but this one meant more. He hated every last stinking soul on it for they were alive, and he was not — struck down in his prime by cowards and traitors. At the time he had swallowed the whole 'For King and Country' baloney. Words, meaningless words. They said he died a hero's death and indeed he had, but he had also witnessed the utter futility of it with his own eyes. Men dying in the Belgian mud, screaming for their mothers as their guts seeped through their fingers and their eyes glazed over. When the line had broken, an orderly retreat soon turned into a chaotic rout. All discipline evaporated, and men ran for their lives; easy pickings for roaming French lancers and eagle-eyed tirailleurs.

He had rallied what remained of the regiment around the colours and formed a square. There they waited, repelling wave after wave of French cavalry and praying for reinforcements from the rear, that never arrived. Skelly watched the Duke and his staff on the ridge surveying the battle raging below. A decision was no doubt taken at some point. Resources were limited and had to be deployed sparingly, sacrifices had to be made. They were expendable; what was one square when the entire campaign hinged on where the reserves were deployed to breach the numerous gaps in the Allied line? And where were those damned Prussians when you needed them? Blücher and his weasels were nowhere to be seen after the pasting they took at Quatre Bras the previous day. Bloody cowards, the lot of them.

So, they had fought and died. One by one his men fell at the hands of sabre, lance and musket ball. The square grew smaller and smaller. There was the big brave Portuguese sergeant who had been with him since they landed on the Peninsula nine long years ago. It had taken three French bayonets to bring him to his knees and even then, he refused to relinquish the colours until they ran him through.

And the Hanoverian skirmisher, who became detached from his own unit and fell back into their square before turning and facing the enemy again, rather than fleeing with his fellow countrymen. Joining the line in a distinctive green uniform and firing until he ran out of ammunition; even then he picked up the musket of the dead soldier next to him and battled on until a shot to the head killed him outright.

He remembered their ensign who lied about his age to sign up and leave behind a drab, impoverished existence for the excitement of life in the British Army. No more than twelve years old, but he led the column down off the ridge and into the fray, drumming a steady beat to ease the men's nerves and maintain order. They sang along until the French cannons found their range and the songs turned to screams.

Skelly found the boy, lying in the middle of the square, his left arm blown off by shrapnel. Propped up against a dead horse and as white as a wraith due to the blood loss. He continued to tap out an ever-weakening beat on the drum with his remaining arm until the light departed from his eyes and he stared at Skelly. It was as if he was asking him why. Why had it come to this? Why? And Skelly had no answers.

He, himself, was one of the last to fall. The artillery ripped the ranks apart, cannonballs bouncing through the mud and into them like murderous bowling balls, removing limbs and heads with sickening ease. One by one they fell. Two hundred and twelve men formed the square and they all died in that hellish acre. Skelly sat on his brave mount, urging the dwindling force to hold and fight. It made him a sitting duck for the tirailleurs sniping all around, but he was an officer and to dismount in the face of enemy fire would have been an unmentionable slur on his character. So, it was only a matter of time before a bullet found its mark, ripping into his shoulder and sending him spinning off his steed, who then bolted back towards the ridge.

The square disintegrated shortly after that. Any last vestige of order disappearing as the French infantry rolled over the survivors. Given the brutal nature of the fighting and heavy loss of life on both sides, they were in no mood for taking prisoners — not that Skelly would have acceded to such a fate. He would fight to the end. He took the first frog foolish enough to approach him, with a thrust through the heart, then lashed another across the thighs before driving the sabre deep into his belly. He was determined to take a few of them with him, and the sight of French blood on his blade heartened him to keep swinging and die a gentleman's death.

There were too many of them though, circling like hyenas. His shoulder was on fire and the strength slowly drained from his body. He twisted and parried but could not keep them at bay forever. A sly French bayonet in the back brought him to his knees before a French chasseur galloped past, leaning down and removing his head from his shoulders with a single, clean strike. The same French cavalryman fell from his mount seconds later, the first casualty of a British counter-attack that went down in history as Picton's Charge. An impetuous, heroic charge that held the Allied line when all seemed lost; the charge that would go down in the history books for all eternity. The charge that never would have succeeded, had Skelly's Square not held the enemy advance long enough for the reserve to be deployed to that part of the line.

The planet he left behind over two hundred years ago, appalled him now. Whereas thousands of young men perished valiantly at Waterloo, the youth of this twenty-first century were pampered and spoilt. He hated them — their computer games and ridiculous clothes. He hated their shallow lives, and those of their parents and grandparents who learnt nothing and repeated the mistakes of their forefathers over and over again. He hated it all. That hatred fuelled his rise to the head of the Company with many of the soldiers who had died at his side. Rodriguez, Gunther, even those idiotic Irishmen who he dispatched to their maker early in the battle when they bolted at the first sight of the French. They were reborn, and the world would pay a heavy price for failing to honour those who died in Skelly's Square.

They were the shock troops who would establish a bridgehead, through which a new order would be established. A deeper, darker order which existed millennia before man took his first, faltering steps on Earth. Skelly feared no man, but this arcane evil was beyond human. It terrified even him, meaning that when recruited to its ranks he swiftly deferred without question. He knew his place, he knew when to talk but, more importantly, he knew when to keep his mouth shut. He was his own man, but also knew how to follow orders to the letter; efficiently, effectively and cruelly if need be. He was a survivor and his rise within the organisation reflected that. His skills and experience had been noted and rewarded. The Company got results. Well, they had before today.

He almost pitied mankind and the monumental mess they were making of their planet. Countless wars, environmental carnage, indescribable hatred and horror. The human mind was a callous instrument which feasted upon itself and would not be content until it was gorged, and nothing was left. At least the dumb beasts had a self-awareness of their inadequacies and were making feeble efforts to evolve into something resembling a useful species. But such a painfully slow process. Several thousand years and they had only just figured out how to propel themselves onto the dead moon that orbited their world. They seemed more preoccupied with wiping one another out, rather than joining forces and dragging their sorry backsides off this excuse for a world.

Still, work was work and he kept the Kirkwood Scott project bubbling along nicely, in addition to the numerous other balls he was juggling on other planes. Someone of his ability was in much demand and one could never turn down work as one never knew where the next offer would come from. Skelly liked to keep busy. It was never wise to turn down gainful employment, and self-preservation lay at the core of everything he held dear.

It was a tricky business and timing was everything. He couldn't afford to draw attention to his machinations too early in the game. The emergence of the two witches as friends had been a temporary fly in the ointment. A concerted campaign against Emily soon put paid to that. Which left the other one, the vagrant. It had been too easy, like taking sweets from a baby as she fell to pieces, necking vile wine like it was going out of fashion. She was of little use to anyone, lying in an inebriated heap in some doorway, mourning her beloved friend.

Yes, less than a fortnight ago everything had been ticking along nicely. The Presence would remain dormant, the portal would be undefended, and the occupation would proceed unopposed.

That was before Kirkwood and the vagrant stumbled into each other. He had little doubt that the devious Dobson was behind an unlikely series of coincidences that led to Kirkwood and his little lady crossing paths. Dobson knew all too well that Skelly's influence on the two of them was weakened when they came together. Even worse — remnants of the White Witch had, for reasons unknown to him, remained behind. Somehow her physical demise was not enough to sever the bond with her miserable companion. This was exacerbated by the preposterous letter writing and wall paintings. The icing on this repugnant cake was Samuel's intervention and the utter incompetence of those idiotic brothers.

He was tempted to enter the arena himself and resolve the problem once and for all. If you wanted a job done, best be doing it yourself. But he was fully aware his employers were watching events unfold with increasing interest and decreasing patience. For some time now, he had been lauding the accomplishments of the Company and arguing he had developed a template capable of engaging in much more lucrative and ambitious future operations. The destruction of this plane should have been a mere stepping stone on the path to personal advancement within the organisation. They were his elite unit, and this should have been a walk in the park. All that had changed now.

It was a lapse of judgement on his part, allowing the Fitzgerald Brothers to handle the graveyard operation. Rodriguez was a knucklehead, but a brutally efficient one who followed orders to the letter. Gunther was a different beast altogether; cold, calculated and chillingly composed. He was definitely one for the future. This was the present, however, and he needed results soon. Very soon. It was time to unleash the big guns.

Rodriguez and Gunther would remain operational and were presently monitoring the movements of Dobson and his sorry companions. Skelly knew exactly where they were heading and why, but it was a futile and desperate journey on their part. Even aided by two of The Forsaken and the White Witch, The Presence was no match for what he was about to unleash. He would crush them, there was no doubt about that.

It was almost a shame. Almost. He had grown fond of the boy but there was no room for sentiment. Skelly sighed and looked up, lost in his thoughts. He had company.

'Ah, there you are. Thank you for popping along at such short notice. I have a little errand that requires attention and you are perfect for the job.' Skelly smiled with satisfaction. Oh, at times like this, he did love his work.

CHAPTER 75

THE DRUMMER BOY

Rodriguez stared morosely through the windscreen of the BMW as it sped along the dual carriageway. He was recounting his uncomfortable conversation with Skelly in the study.

'I had little choice but to accept, having no wish to go the way of that Fitzgerald buffoon. I doubt we will be seeing him anytime soon. I cannot eat this muck.' He screwed his face in disgust and dropped the half-eaten sandwich into the footwell of the car as they tracked the Micra, never more than three vehicles behind its quarry. 'These Irish. They exist on bland offal. Where is the texture, the taste, the passion in their food?' He picked a crumb from his lush, oiled beard, examining it for a second, before flicking it against the dashboard.

'That Mediterranean passion is going to be the ruin of you,' observed Gunther drily from the driver's seat. His eyes flicked constantly between the speedometer and the little red car ahead of them. He was ever wary of his speed as the last thing they needed was to be pulled over by the police. He would of course have been able to persuade the officers to be on their way and forget they had ever stopped the BMW, but it would have been time lost; time they could ill-afford to squander at this stage in the game.

'All very well for you. You weren't the one standing before the Colonel in that accursed study of his. Place makes my blood freeze, and that's saying something.'

'Dermot and Declan are in the past. Good riddance to them, I say. We carried them for long enough and it was only a matter of time before they messed up. I, for one, won't lose any sleep over them. They were unprofessional. Operations of this nature require cool, calm precision.'

Rodriguez turned his sizable bulk to face his companion. 'And how am I expected to remain cool and calm, knowing I'm being replaced as commander of the mission? I've put my neck on the line, I don't know how many times, for that withered, old man. Never let him down, not once.' His voice rose in tandem with a barely controlled rage.

'Just be grateful you still have a neck to put on the line,' Gunther replied, not rising to the bait. 'You made a bad call. Get over it. Skelly doesn't suffer fools gladly. So, keep your eye on the ball if you know what's good for you.' He meticulously checked his mirrors, before indicating and pulling out into the overtaking lane.

'The sooner we get off this lump of meaningless dirt, and on with some proper soldiering, the better.'

'Ah, but there's the rub.' Gunther favoured the Portuguese giant the briefest of looks before returning his pale, expressionless eyes to the road in front. 'Skelly obviously doesn't regard this plane as meaningless. Nor do his superiors given the resources they are devoting to breaching its portal. We are but cannon fodder, and ours is not to reason why. We swallow our pride, collect the new commander, follow his orders and complete the mission. Now is that clear? Any more outbursts when the new boss arrives, and we will both be for the high jump.'

'Oh, I'll get the job done alright. I should have snapped that little rat's neck back in the alley and be done with. I won't be so gracious next time our paths cross.' He cocked his right forefinger and took aim through the windscreen of the BMW, mimicking firing a shot at the tiny red speck they were tracking, further up the road.

'You can have your fun when the Colonel says so and not a second earlier.' For the first time during their exchange, Gunther sounded as if his patience was beginning to wear thin. 'Skelly obviously has a soft spot for the boy, but we are at the business end of this now. You will get your chance for revenge but act rashly or there will be no third chance…Wait.' He squinted and removed a hand from the steering wheel to screen his eyes. 'Up ahead. Are they pulling off?'

Rodriguez followed his gaze and, sure enough, the Micra was slowing down and veering off the dual carriageway onto an adjoining slip road. Gunther pressed gently on the accelerator of the more powerful BMW and it surged forward, effortlessly closing the distance between itself and the other car. He indicated and carefully eased off the carriageway. Ahead, at a roundabout, the Micra was indicating left onto a minor road.

'We must be getting near the portal,' Rodriguez flashed a smile at Gunther and began to drum enthusiastically on the dashboard. 'Dobson is deluded if he thinks they can stand in our way now. Kirkwood and his scruffy little girlfriend don't stand a chance. Without a third, we will crush them, and the White Witch will only be able to stand and watch from wherever her bony backside is rotting now. I'm looking forward to watching their hearts stop beating one by one in front of me.'

'And so am I.' A shrill voice from behind caused them both to start. Rodriguez swivelled around, while Gunther looked anxiously in the rear-view mirror, having safely negotiated the roundabout.

Seated behind them was a blonde-haired waif of a boy, no more than twelve years old. He was dressed plainly in a crisp white, short sleeved shirt and grey shorts which stopped just above the knees. Thick grey socks rolled down to the ankles and scuffed, but sturdy, black leather shoes completed the attire, giving him the air of a mischievous schoolboy playing truant. An unruly mop of hair threatened to overwhelm his field of vision, but at the last moment he blew it from his eyes before speaking again.

'But we are not going to get to the fun part in one piece unless you keep your eyes on the road. I'm here now, so you two focus on what you do best. Following orders and killing. Leave the thinking to me. The Colonel has made it abundantly clear what is expected of us from this point onwards, and no further mistakes will be tolerated.'

Rodriguez and Gunther exchanged a look before staring ahead. This mission was more serious than either of them previously thought. Otherwise why would Skelly have dispatched the angelic-looking child in the back seat — although angelic was the last word either of them would have used to describe him.

William had arrived. The Drummer Boy. And where he went, death was sure to follow.

CHAPTER 76

THE FOURTH CHILD

5:30 p.m.

Dobson initially became aware of the BMW tailing them shortly after they left the service station. Having made Samuel aware of the unwelcome company, they quietly discussed options, while in the rear seat Kirkwood and Meredith chatted, oblivious to the growing tension in the Micra. *It was best they didn't know,* thought Dobson; allow them some down time, as they had little idea of the massive responsibility resting upon their young shoulders. God only knew when they would have the opportunity to rest again.

Samuel maintained a steady speed, giving no clue to their pursuers that they knew of their existence. For a relative newcomer, he had impressed Dobson so far with his steady nerve and clear thinking. Yes, he had potential this one, mused the old man. That was if he survived the next twelve hours of course; if any of them survived. Dobson knew he was getting on in years even for one with his life span. In his prime, he was confident he could have tackled Rodriguez and Gunther on his own without too much trouble. The decades and centuries of constant warfare, however, had taken their toll, and in recent times he wanted nothing more than to retire and leave the dirty work to those of his kind with fewer miles on the clock.

Unfortunately, retirement was not an option to those in his line of work. The Scourge was a remorseless foe and his kind were fighting it on many fronts. Resources were sorely stretched, resulting in un-blooded types like Samuel being thrown into the fray. It was all hands to the pump, so any thoughts of retirement would have to be shelved for another day.

He calmly told Samuel to stick to the original plan, agreed by them prior to leaving Belfast. They were to follow the motorway and then continue onto the dual carriageway, as far as the Ardgallon turn-off. From there the village of the same name was less than an hour's drive away. Dobson cast his awareness further ahead and it rippled invisibly out towards their destination, like a fisherman casting his net from a boat. He was acutely aware of The Scourge circling the village, probing and pressing for the slightest opening. The portal was holding for now, but only just and it was a matter of when, and not if, a breach would occur. Time was not their friend. It had to be now; there was no other way.

He juggled competing thoughts and energies; all the while cognisant of the BMW tracking them. Despite the odds seemingly stacked against them, he had an ace up his sleeve nobody else knew about. Not even that vile beast, Skelly. The two had crossed swords on countless planes and, to date, he remained one step ahead of his nemesis. Until now, that was. While Dobson felt jaded in recent clashes, Skelly, by comparison, seemed to be growing in terms of cunning and power. He deployed his foot soldiers with devastating effect in their various guises, Dobson having no desire to know from where they were spawned. The loss of the Fitzgerald Brothers was an unexpected bonus, but little more than a flesh wound to Skelly. He would keep coming with everything he had. Skelly and his minions would chase them down, whatever it took.

Dobson finished issuing instructions and leaned back, feigning sleep. He resisted the urge to chuckle. Oh, if only Skelly knew. He thought he had Dobson on the ropes and, indeed, the loss of Emily was a crushing blow. Every good general had a Plan B, however, and Dobson was a very good general. He knew The Presence required three guardians in order to be released to its full extent. He had anticipated at an early stage, that one of the three might fall given the intense pressure being exerted by The Scourge. Skelly, therefore, believed he had the upper hand. If only he knew.

Dobson rolled his shoulders to ease a dull ache in his neck. He was very tired. It had taken considerable effort on his part to cloak the fourth child from The Scourge for all these years. For that very reason, he had kept her close to the portal, leading as quiet a life as possible. He had hoped it would remain that way and she might have lived a full and safe existence, unaware of her calling. All that changed when Emily fell. He wanted to manage the transfer of her powers to the fourth child as subtly as possible but, The Scourge, like a bloodhound, detected the power surge and chased hard, lashing out blindly at anyone in its path.

He sought to protect the fourth child and succeeded in deflecting much of the attack. The child had been saved and her anonymity preserved, but at a price. He had been unable to stem the flow entirely, as hastily established defences were partially breached. She survived — but only just. Dobson hung his head. He would have to live with the guilt of failing her, of failing them all. None of them were fully prepared for what they were about to face. None of them deserved what was about to be unleashed with an unrivalled ferocity, he knew that, but he had to work with what he had. They were raw, they were inexperienced, but they were three again, and, for that reason, they had a fighting chance.

He jolted forward in his seat as a searing pain erupted behind his eyes. Dobson doubled over, nursing his head in both hands, biting down hard on his bottom lip to prevent the screams. Then, as suddenly as it had hit him, the agony was gone; leaving him dazed and nauseous. Kirkwood and Meredith jumped forward and began to babble a thousand and one concerned questions, a cacophony of panicky noise that did little to ease his disorientation. Samuel looked across in alarm and began to slow down, prepared to pull over onto the hard shoulder.

'Keep going. Keep going. To the village,' hissed Dobson between clenched teeth. Samuel nodded and accelerated again. 'I'm fine, I'm fine,' he told his young companions, waving away their concerns and wiping a spot of blood from his nostril. 'Damn you, Skelly,' he cursed. 'Damn you to hell and back.'

The little Micra hurtled on past a sign informing its occupants they were seven miles from Ardgallon. Seconds later, the BMW followed suit, a deadly shadow in their wake.

CHAPTER 77

RAINBOW GIRL

She knew they were coming. Well, that wasn't strictly true. She didn't know who or when, but they were coming. She could feel it in her bones and the anticipation had been building for days. It was finally happening.

She sat in her bedroom, gazing out at the street below, over the same old familiar view. Her parent's grubby Audi, desperately in need of a power wash; her brother's death trap of a scooter propped haphazardly against the gable wall, helmet dangling from the handlebars. Beyond that, the usual sights she had taken in a million times before. Kids playing football on the grassy area between their house and the main road that ran through the village. If she leaned forward and craned her neck to the right, she could just make out the bright lights of the metropolis of Ardgallon. Population 1078.

Las Vegas, it was not. Beyond the local shop, which was the hub of village life, there was little to write home about. Not that she ever felt the urge to write to anyone about her drab life and even drabber surroundings. There was a doomed attempt to open a chip shop a year ago, but it folded tamely after the initial novelty wore off and everyone had concluded the Chinese takeaway in the next village was far superior. She had eaten from the chippy once, and once only. The battered sausages were indeed battered; battered beyond recognition. And as for the chips? Well, her morning cereal was less soggy.

The tiny church on the main, as in *only*, street, still drew its ageing congregation on a weekly basis. Her parents were not religious and never forced her or her brother to attend. If asked to categorise her beliefs, she would have said she was an anaemic agnostic. She didn't know one way or the other, and she didn't particularly care. You were dealt your cards and got on with it. There was nothing else for it. All the women, even the little girls, wore hats which, frankly, looked a bit silly. She wondered if they were all secretly bald beneath them. Perhaps they had been rebellious, and God summoned fire from the heavens to burn their hair off.

No, life for Harley Davison was as sleepy as life in a sleepy backwater in rural County Tyrone could be. She attended the local high school, where academically she was above average, without overly exerting herself. She was reasonably popular and could turn on the charm when required. Her passion was music and she was rarely without it; be that listening, singing or playing the keyboard. She was told she possessed a good ear, having taught herself how to play. She didn't bother with sheet music, preferring instead to listen and play. She could hear a piece only once and it would be permanently imprinted on her memory, to be recited at will. Which was all the weirder, as ask her what she had for dinner the night before, and she would have struggled to answer.

When people met Harley, they usually asked three questions. Firstly, why the multicoloured hair which she regularly changed on a whim, depending on her mood. It swept halfway down her back, a cascading river of colour that turned heads wherever she went, and earned her the nickname, 'Rainbow Girl'. She endured the moniker as opposed to embraced it. The way she saw it, there were worse nicknames a sixteen-year-old girl could have.

Second, was the ridiculous name her moronic parents had 'blessed' her with. Pat and Susan Davison must have been the only two human beings in the Western Hemisphere not to twig that christening their daughter Harley was a complete no-no. From an early age she had been subjected to largely good-natured ribbing about the name. Before 'Rainbow' stuck, 'Angel' had been her allotted nickname, as in 'Hell's'. It was the reason she started dyeing her hair to deflect attention from the questions she was bombarded with, whenever introduced to someone new.

'Why on earth did your mum and dad call you Harley? Didn't they think?' Her tetchy response was invariably, 'Because they're idiots. No, they didn't. And before you ask, no, they're not part of a satanic motorcycle gang.' While she may have passed for a biker chick given her technicolour locks, she doubted her father had ever sat astride a motorcycle — not with his sciatica. And as for her mother? Well, that was beyond a woman of her ample frame.

'I'm just making some tea, Harley. Do you want one?'

Speak of the devil. The dulcet tones of her mother wafted into the bedroom. Harley smiled. They drove her nuts, but her parents were the salt of the earth; the kindest, sweetest couple you could ever meet. She rebuked herself for thinking ill of them about her unfortunate first name.

'Yes, please Mum. Any chance of a choccy biscuit?' She grinned and waited for the now standard response. Her mother was nothing, if not predictable.

'Oh, alright then, just the one. And I suppose I could get away with one as well. My weigh-in isn't until Friday, and I've been good all weekend. It'll be ready in five minutes. Do you want it brought down to your room?'

'No, it's alright. I'm coming now.' Harley gripped both rims and manoeuvred back from the window, turning and propelling the wheelchair across her bedroom towards the corridor that led up to the kitchen.

That was the third question people always asked, of course.

'How did you end up in a wheelchair?'

Now *there* was a story.

CHAPTER 78

ARDGALLON

7:09 p.m.

They reached the village via a corridor of open fields where cattle grazed lazily. Kirkwood awoke with a snort, surprised he had surrendered so easily to sleep, given the relentless drama of late and the uncomfortable confines of the Micra. He looked around to confirm the entire journey wasn't a dream, to discover Meredith watching him, a playful smile dancing across her features.

'You have the most alluring snore,' she simpered, her voice dripping with sarcasm. 'What a catch you are. I'm surprised you weren't snapped up years ago. What girl could resist a lifetime listening to the sound of a jet engine roaring in their ear night after night?'

'I don't snore,' countered Kirkwood, defensively. 'I've just a bit of a head cold, that's all.' He wiped a sleeve across his mouth and was mortified to discover a thin trail of drool trickling down his chin.

'Yeah right. And I'm the Queen of flipping Sheba.'

'Your Majesty,' Kirkwood solemnly bowed across the rear seat towards her. For his troubles he was rewarded with a solid slap across the back of the head.

'Ach! What was that for, you wee cow?' He leaned back and rubbed where Meredith struck him. He was beginning to feel increasingly at ease with the scruffy street urchin and hoped the feeling was mutual. If they were going to save the universe together, it was preferable they could at least tolerate the sight of each other.

'If you two children have quite finished,' Dobson rotated stiffly from his vantage point in the front of the car to address them. 'We have reached our destination. Time to put your sensible heads on for five minutes, if you can fit the needs of the planet into your slapstick routine.'

His furrowed brow informed them this was not the time for a witty riposte. Despite looking and smelling like a hopeless hobo, there was an authority about the old man which spoke volumes as to his real identity, whatever that was. Samuel certainly treated him with deference and at a nod from Dobson, he pulled the Micra onto the side of the road by a sign that proudly proclaimed, 'Welcome to Ardgallon, County Tyrone. Please enjoy our beautiful village and drive carefully.'

Kirkwood took in his surroundings. They were half way down a hill which bottomed out onto a stretch of road, bordered on either side by a mix of stand-alone bungalows and two storey houses. Beyond them, and set back from the road on the left, was a stone church bordered by a tiny graveyard. Opposite it, a middle-aged woman was pulling down the shutters of a convenience store that appeared to be the only shop in the village. Beyond the final bungalow the road swept sharply to the left, where a humpbacked bridge could be glimpsed above the hedgerows. It narrowed markedly towards the top, meaning two vehicles travelling in opposite directions would struggle to pass without colliding. It looked like a car crash waiting to happen.

'So, this is where the ultimate battle between good and evil is to be played out,' observed Meredith, decidedly underwhelmed by the surroundings. 'It's hardly DC versus Marvel, is it?' She watched in silent disgust as a tan-coloured border terrier padded towards the Micra. It stopped, sniffed the front passenger tyre and after a moment's contemplation, cocked its hind leg to urinate against the stationary car.

'It might not look like much, but this indeed is where the destiny of your plane will be decided. And you, my young friends, will be at the centre of that battle, so listen very carefully to what I have to say.'

'Oh, here we go,' sighed Meredith, rolling her eyes. 'Let the sermon beginneth.'

'They are coming,' snapped Samuel. 'This is not the time for frivolity.' He looked in no mood for comedy routines, causing Kirkwood and Meredith to sit straighter in their seats and adopt what they hoped were serious expressions.

'As I was saying,' continued Dobson. 'The Scourge will attempt to breach the portal tomorrow morning. Skelly's minions are already gathering. I did not want to alarm you earlier, but we have been followed out of Belfast.'

'Followed? Who by?' Meredith was no longer laughing. Kirkwood looked across at her. She was scared; genuinely terrified. The cocky, streetwise facade was gone, replaced by the face of a very frightened teenage girl.

'Let me guess,' countered Kirkwood, trying to display enough pluck for the two of them. 'It wouldn't happen to be a giant Portuguese psychopath, a creepy German in a pinstripe suit, and an inbred farmer?' He attempted to give Meredith a reassuring smile, as she nervously curled a lock of jet-black hair around her fingers.

'You are correct with regards to Rodriguez and Gunther,' answered Samuel. 'But the brothers are no longer a concern for us.'

'Well that's alright then,' Kirkwood clapped both hands together, before giving Meredith a playful punch on the upper arm. 'Four against two. Wee buns as they say. We can live with those odds, right Sansa?'

Meredith pushed his hand away, unconvinced by his efforts to lift her gloomy spirits.

'Unfortunately, they are three,' Dobson sighed, suddenly looking extremely fatigued. 'Skelly has seen fit to send reinforcements. And a particularly nasty reinforcement at that. The Scourge means business. It will stop at nothing tonight to break through the portal and onto this plane.'

He stopped; suddenly aware he was doing little to allay the concerns of his young accomplices. He forced a tight smile. 'I know it is easier said than done, but please try not to worry. I still have a few tricks up my sleeve. Skelly doesn't hold all the cards, not by a long shot.'

Kirkwood felt his left hand being squeezed and looked down to see Meredith grasping it tightly. He had a sinking feeling it was going to be a long, sleepless night.

CHAPTER 79

SHE KNEW SOMETHING THEY DID NOT

Harley toyed with the plate of spaghetti Bolognaise in front of her and feigned interest as her brother, Aidan, regaled the family with his exploits on the football field earlier that afternoon. She felt he made most of it up as surely nobody could be that talented yet evade the notice of the top premiership clubs. She always threatened to go along to a match and call his bluff but was yet to make good on her threats. Part of her couldn't be bothered as she hated the chest-thumping bravado of the local school team. Yet another part wanted him to be that good. If bubbles were to be burst, then let that be much further down the road her family was travelling. There had been enough pain recently to last them a lifetime.

'Harley? Oi deaf lugs. Are you listening to a word I'm saying?'

Aidan was staring at her, a chip speared on his fork, which he pointed accusingly towards her. Her parents exchanged exasperated looks as only they could. Was that something you were taught when you had children, along with the uncanny ability to embarrass them, whatever the social setting?

'Sorry, I was miles away. How many goals is that now? Seven? Eight?' Aidan was oblivious to the dollop of sarcasm in Harley's voice, but her mother raised an eyebrow in gentle rebuke before encouraging Aidan to continue.

'Go on, son. If it doesn't involve boys with long hair and guitars, then your sister doesn't want to know.'

Harley rolled her eyes, an expression honed to perfection down the years. 'That's men with guitars, Mum. Men. Boys go to school.'

'It's just noise to me,' chipped in her father. Her parents performed as a highly skilled tag team during verbal jousting sessions around the kitchen table. 'In my day, we had melodies, harmonies. You could actually make out the words they were singing, with the emphasis on *singing* as opposed to roaring and wailing like a constipated goat. I'll never understand this grime music.'

'For the forty millionth time, Dad, it's grunge music. Grunge. And I can make out every word perfectly fine.' Her father looked at her and winked, a mischievous smile lighting up his face. She loved it when he did that, it took years off him. Neither of her parents smiled anywhere near enough, not since the night on the bridge. She stuck her tongue out, before turning to her mother who was sitting opposite, enjoying the banter.

'Can I be excused, please? I'm not that hungry tonight.'

'Are you alright, pet? You aren't coming down with something, are you?' Her mother was such a fusser. The slightest sneeze and you were dragged off to the doctors.

'More likely been sitting up in that room stuffing sweets into her gob,' sniped Aidan. He shot her a sickly smile as she pushed away from the table and headed back to her bedroom. Passing him, she slyly raised the middle finger, out of sight of her parents. Before he could squeal on her indiscretion, she was out of the kitchen and down the hallway. She closed the door behind her, drowning out his impassioned pleas that Harley be grounded for the remainder of the week.

She positioned the lightweight wheelchair parallel to her bed, applied the brakes and then flicked up an armrest, before transferring sideways onto it. She had worked hard on her upper body and core strength, courtesy of intensive physio sessions and additional hours in the leisure centre gym. Her consultant surgeon advised that the chances of ever walking again were slim but when she relentlessly pushed him on it, he could not categorically rule out the possibility. Both family and friends tempered positivity with a dash of realism, but it was the only goal she could focus on — to walk again.

'If I have to spend the rest of my life in this thing, then I might as well wheel myself down to the river and jump in.' Her parents and Aidan were shocked by such a blunt assessment of the situation but never again questioned her drive and determination to walk. While her father unfailingly drove her to and from various hospital appointments and gym sessions, her mother assisted in hours of online research on people with similar spinal injuries, who had defied the odds and regained some, if not all, of their lower limb functions.

It was painful, agonising at times; both physically and mentally. But Harley was tough and the more daunting the challenge, the more she rose to the occasion and battled through whatever obstacles were thrown in her path. 'Hurricane Harley', her father had christened her, yet another nickname she outwardly rolled her eyes at, but was secretly proud to bear. It was now ten months since the nightmarish evening when a drunk driver accelerated over the little humpback bridge with no consideration for the fifteen-year-old girl pushing her bicycle up the other side. On her way to the shop to buy sweets to accompany a Friday night *Pretty Little Liars* marathon. A perfect start to what should have been a perfect weekend, culminating in a long-awaited first date with Sean Hennessy the following evening. Only movie and a pizza, but it was the culmination of a term-long campaign on the part of several matchmaking friends to pair them together. Harley had been buzzing as she neared the crest of the bridge, only to be greeted by the glare of headlights, and squealing brakes being applied too late.

After that, there was nothing. For a very long time.

Well, that wasn't strictly true. There were multiple surgeries, months spent in hospital, and painful nights sobbing into a pillow, begging for an end to it. Even then, it was nothing compared to the mental anguish that couldn't be dispelled, no matter how many friends visited, or bunches of flowers and helium balloons arrived. Harley was gradually eclipsed by a powerful depression which uprooted all she once held dear, tossing it aside like a matchstick house in the path of a twister. Months of lonely rehabilitation at home and the farce of a trial where the smirking driver walked, yes walked, away with a suspended sentence; it had unerringly chipped away, until she was left empty, spent, and broken beyond repair.

Harley leaned back on the bed and stared at the ceiling, reflecting on the dark road she had travelled since that dreadful night. She worried incessantly about what, if any, future, she was left with. Despite the well-intentioned words about equality, she now knew people treated you differently when you were confined to a wheelchair. The patronising smiles, the awkward conversations, which once flowed so effortlessly. It accrued and hardened her heart like plaque on a neglected tooth. She was still Harley but to some people, who she once regarded as close friends, she was now defined by her disability.

Harley smiled to herself. For she knew something they did not.

The tingling…

The first time was just over six weeks ago. At first, she thought it was all in her head, so desperate was she for a sign, a signal — anything. But then the sensations and twinges became more frequent and pronounced. She never imagined pain could be so welcome, but the spasms that shot up both legs were like manna from Heaven. Which was apt, as she was certain it was from Heaven, having prayed to God for nothing else since the day of the accident.

Accident. How she hated the way others casually used the word, for there was nothing accidental about the events of that night. The eight pints of strong lager he consumed hadn't been an accident; nor the decision to get behind the wheel of his car rather than face the dreadful inconvenience of waiting ten minutes for a taxi. Harley stared long and hard at him every day of the trial and never once detected a shred of remorse. He had smiled and waved to friends in the public gallery when the judge dispassionately passed the pathetic sentence. Everyone in the courtroom glided through the motions, just another day at the office. Her barrister was more interested in rushing off to his next case rather than console them. Harley and her parents left the courthouse dazed and exhausted, unable to look at one another, let alone express their battered emotions.

It was no accident, just as her answered prayers were no accident. Prayers were answered for a reason and the growing sensation in her legs was no trick of the mind. It was real. She kept it a secret from her parents, initially fearing that to tell another human being would be tempting fate, returning Harley to a life of feeling nothing from the waist down; or from the neck up for that matter, enveloped by a sadness which threatened to overwhelm her.

The night the feeling first returned to her legs, gave her hope.

The night the ghost girl first visited her dreams, gave her a new life.

CHAPTER 80

PILLOW TALK

11:15 p.m.

'You're snoring again,' hissed Meredith through the darkness of the room. Kirkwood jolted awake, as a fist connected with his ribcage. Thankfully he was fully clothed which absorbed some, but not all, of the impact. He groaned, relinquishing any hopes of drifting back to sleep. He reluctantly rolled over to face the invisible assailant lying across from him; twin beds separated by a few feet of carpet.

'If you hit me one more time, I will not be responsible for my actions, end of the world or not.' Turning, he switched on a light, set in the wall above his head. They were in a bed and breakfast on the outskirts of Ardgallon, presided over by a nosy landlady who interrogated them upon arriving as to their reason for visiting the area. Meredith deflected the fusillade of questions with an impressive patience that Kirkwood would have struggled to match.

Dobson and Samuel had dropped them off outside, the former producing a holdall from nowhere which he handed to Kirkwood. 'That should contain everything you need for tonight. Samuel and I will provide your alarm call in the morning. Breakfast is included, and I heartily recommend Mrs Morgan's fry. A real belly-buster if I do say so myself,' he had chuckled, fondly recalling fat, brown sausages and runny egg yolks.

'Where are you guys going?' Meredith had asked, peering into the holdall which Kirkwood unzipped and was rummaging through.

'Samuel and I have some pressing business to attend to,' the old tramp had replied. 'Reconnaissance work if you like. All good generals scout out the terrain on the eve of battle. But worry not, we will see you in the morning. Try and get some sleep. You'll need it.'

Kirkwood had looked up from the holdall in astonishment. 'How did you know this is the deodorant I use? I've never…' Before he could finish, Samuel had released the Micra's handbrake and they spluttered down the road and out of sight, leaving him and Meredith to face the formidable Mrs Morgan. She informed them the 'nice, old gentleman' had paid in advance, before leading them to their room with parting instructions as to where they could find extra pillows.

Kirkwood now looked at his watch, which informed him it was **not even midnight**. He had been asleep for barely an hour and, even then, it was fitful and restless. He rubbed his eyes and scratched the stubble on his chin. He strongly doubted he would get back to sleep but resisted the urge to grab a pillow and smother Meredith with it.

She sat upright, staring straight ahead with a look he was becoming accustomed to; a look that strongly suggested pushing the subject of his interrupted slumber any further was an unwise move. He erred on the side of caution, opting for a more neutral approach.

'What do you think is going to happen tomorrow?' Kirkwood attempted to conceal the trepidation in his voice but was uncertain if he was successful.

She considered him for a second out of the corner of an eye. Deciding that further sulking was futile, she unfolded both arms and slid onto an elbow to face him. 'I haven't a flipping clue. It's not as if I have any experience in this field. A few days ago, I was happy in my misery, snug as a bug in a doorway with half a bottle of Buckfast inside me. Now I'm fighting to save the planet, aided by a smelly old tramp and the loudest snorer this side of Belfast. Oh, and Samuel of course. Who can barely drive in a straight line, let alone battle the armies of eternal darkness, or whatever it is they call themselves these days.'

'It's The Scourge,' Kirkwood reminded her. 'I know they sound like some second-rate thrash metal band, but I suppose we should start referring to them by their proper title,' he paused and was rewarded with the slightest of smiles from Meredith, encouraging him to continue. 'And Samuel is no mug. He was like a souped-up Wolverine back in that graveyard. Neither of us would be here now if it wasn't for him. I'm also certain there is a lot more to Dobson than meets the eye. Let's face it, bonkers as it sounds, we are not dealing with mere mortals here.'

Meredith nodded in agreement. 'Yeah, although I would hardly refer to Dobson as a heavenly body. He smells like he hasn't used soap and water since the late nineties.' She started to giggle and, try as he might, Kirkwood could not keep a straight face. Before long the two of them were howling with laughter, side by side in their beds. Eventually the hilarity subsided to the occasional hoot and snigger before Meredith raised a hand to her eyes. Kirkwood couldn't be sure if she was wiping away tears of laughter or sadness; but they were most definitely tears.

'You okay?' he asked tentatively.

'Yeah, I think so.' She turned onto her back and surveyed the ceiling. 'You know what, up until last week my sole focus when I woke up, was to get trashed. To ease the hangover, erase the memories. I just wanted to forget everything. I didn't want to go back, and I didn't want to move on. I just wanted to slide quietly to the bottom of a bottle and leave the rest of the world to get on with it.'

'Did you think of ending it?' Kirkwood wasn't sure the question was appropriate, but the words squirmed out of his mouth before he knew it. He looked edgily at the young woman beside him, braced for another thump. The calm response that followed, impressed, as much as, relieved him.

'Yeah, it crossed my mind, why lie about it? But in the end, I couldn't. Couldn't do that to my family, even though I don't want to be within a million miles of them at the minute. Running away is one thing. Disappearing forever is another.'

'Except she didn't disappear. Emily, that is. She's still here, or at least part of her is. Helping us.'

Meredith smirked. 'She always was a nosy cow, had to be in the middle of everything.' Her expression softened. 'But she had a good heart. She would have done anything for me. And when she died, part of me just refused to accept it. I knew she wouldn't leave me high and dry. I sensed some part of her was still here. There was a connection, a thread between us, that hadn't snapped. I guess that's why I started writing the letters. Stupid at the time, but when I stumbled across that first piece of graffiti well…it kind of proved me right.'

'Where do you think she is now? Do you think she can hear us?' Kirkwood took a nervous look around the room and cleared his throat, making Meredith laugh again.

'Yeah, you idiot. She's hiding in the wardrobe, waiting to jump out and shout "BOO" with a white sheet over her head. Wise up.'

Kirkwood feigned a hurt expression, before his face relaxed into a smile. 'Okay, perhaps I'm being a tad theatrical. But she's somewhere, looking out for us and that's reassuring. I suppose if we think about any of this for too long our brains will start to melt. Best just going with the flow and trying not to dwell on it. Saving the planet sure beats crunching numbers in a dead-end office job.'

'I'll second that. But as much as I'm loving our cosy pillow talk, I think we should try and get some sleep. It will be all go tomorrow. Night Kirky Wirky…No more snoring please.'

She turned on her side and within minutes her breathing slowed to a steady rhythm, indicating she was sound asleep.

Kirkwood lay staring into the gloom, his back aching slightly from the lumpy pillows beneath him. He knew sleep would not be calling his name any time soon. A million thoughts raced through his head, each one as bizarre and improbable as the last. But amidst the clutter, he felt a soothing calm which had eluded him for many years. The obsessive thoughts were gone. Well, gone was probably not the word, but they were a dull glow as opposed to the raging furnace that normally roared. It was just as Dobson said; when the two of them were together, their destructive urges were contained. He shuddered to think what would happen if they were separated again.

He suddenly realised he could not go back to the way life had been — shackled to a torture rack of routines at Skelly's beck and call. The fight had been sucked out of him but now there was an opportunity to strike back. He intended to grab that opportunity with everything he had.

CHAPTER 81

RESTORATION

The dreams. Vivid, powerful panoramic visitations that left her more exhausted on awakening, than when first drifting off to sleep. Every night the same reel played out across her synaptic landscape. It was always the night on the bridge but, unlike when it happened, she now knew he was coming. Standing, as if by appointment, listening for the grinding gears and tortured revving of the engine as the car sped through the countryside towards her.

She stood on the brow of the bridge, watching the sweeping headlights as they rounded the bend below and started the short, steep ascent towards her. She waited fearlessly as noise and light consumed her, waiting for the inevitable impact and searing pain before darkness descended. Staring straight ahead, as if time was slowed to an imperceptible crawl, allowing Harley to see the driver in minute detail. Everything was as it was that night, except for the driver. It was not the pathetic excuse of a man who stood smirking before her in the dock. It was someone else.

He was smiling, every night smiling with uncontained glee, mounting the brow of the bridge and bearing down upon her. A gleeful grin, two rows of sparkling teeth which dazzled as bright as the headlights that lit up her face. Above the grin, black eyes twinkled like polished ebony; twinkling with malicious intent. Framing the frightful visage was a black beard, giving the driver the appearance of a landlocked pirate. He was enjoying it. He wanted to mow her down, there was no doubt about that. This was calculated murder, not the actions of an irresponsible drunk.

There was no desire to jump to the side, to save her neck, back or legs. She was meant to be where she stood, rooted to the spot. It was destiny, and to even consider another course of action was ridiculous. An eerie calm descended, and she accepted her fate; knowing she was not alone. She neither saw nor heard anyone else but was not alone, of that she was certain. And sure enough, every night at the last possible second, just as the bearded assailant threatened to prevail, intervention occurred. She would rise into the welcoming darkness, above and beyond the light that sought to engulf her.

Suspended on invisible wires, she looked down as the car thundered past, its maniac driver deprived of the kill. She watched as its tail lights disappear out of sight; red, demonic eyes blazing, a frustrated hatred. She was alive, relief washing over her like an electric current, sparking and surging with a previously unknown intensity. Harley looked in amazement at the road ten feet below as she joyfully kicked out, mesmerised at how both her legs responded at will. It was as if she was watching someone else because she could move them, just like before the world had collapsed around her.

Harley raised her head and looked upwards to the cloudless sky, bedecked with a canopy of stars. She exhaled and watched as her breath rose like smoke from a chimney into the limitless expanse. Closing her eyes, she allowed the cold air to caress her exposed skin, as invisible hands silently lowered her to the ground; the same hands that had initially elevated her from the path of the smiling assassin.

The second her feet touched the bridge she opened her eyes and, as always, her wheelchair was sitting on the brow of the bridge. Standing behind it, hands resting lightly on its frame was a young woman, maybe two or three years older than Harley. Her willowy frame looked as if it could barely hold the silver locks which tumbled over slender shoulders and halfway down her back. She was beautiful, with skin as luminous as the moon, and dark, hypnotic eyes. Harley knew instinctively she was the one who saved her every night. The girl wore a flimsy, baby-blue chiffon dress but seemed oblivious to the cold, contrasting with Harley, whose teeth chattered as goosebumps broke out en masse across her exposed flesh.

'Who are you?' she asked the silver-haired girl. 'And who was that man?' she asked the same questions every night, a conversation which gradually unfurled its secrets a little more each time. Harley didn't know why, but sensed this was the night when the key would turn, and the truth would finally be revealed; for better or worse.

The girl smiled sadly at her, hinting at unspoken tragedies that would make Harley's own troubles pale into insignificance. 'Rather, you should ask, who are we?' she replied cryptically. 'For we are his enemy, and he means you great harm.'

'We? I don't understand. Why would that man want to harm me? I've never seen him before, just like I've never seen you. This is just some messed-up dream, that's all. You aren't even real.'

'I was real once, Harley Davison,' the girl stopped and, for a second, Harley thought she might start crying. She composed herself, however, before continuing. 'But you have been chosen to replace me and aid them when the time comes. And that time is now.'

Harley snagged onto the significance of the last word, like a dog with a bone. *Now.* For in previous dreams the girl said *soon.* She stood patiently behind the chair and waited, as if for Harley to process this new information and formulate the next question.

'But I'm nobody. Just some girl who was in the wrong place at the wrong time, without a guardian angel to pluck her to safety like you just have.' She stopped as the girl threw her head back and laughed, a sound like chimes tinkling on a balmy breeze.

'What's so funny?' Harley tried to conceal her irritation at the laughter. This dream was crazy enough without her behaving like a sulky teenager.

'Oh, I'm sorry. It's just I've been called many things before but never an angel. I wish it was all as straightforward as that,' she sighed and seemed to mull over what she could disclose next without confusing Harley further. 'Okay, let's run with that one if it helps you understand. I'm an angel, a fairy, a sprite — whatever takes your fancy.'

'There's no need to be patronising,' pouted Harley.

'I don't mean to be. Grrr.' The girl gripped the frame of Harley's wheelchair and bit her bottom lip in frustration. 'This is new to me and I'm still getting to grips with all the mystical, talking-in-riddles stuff they excel at. Just bear with me, I am trying. Please.' Harley nodded slowly. Tonight's dream was spiralling off in a startling new direction.

'Okay, sod it. I'll cut to the chase.' The girl looked up and whispered something into the darkness. *Was she some sort of trainee angel?* thought Harley. Turning up randomly in dreams to earn her wings?

'I'm not an angel. Or ever likely to become one, based on your understanding of what they are. But I am here to help you, just like that lunatic in the car was here to hurt you. Him and his kind will try again. You don't have to know the specifics, as there's no time, but you do need to know this. There are people coming to your village and they need your help. Desperately need it. We all need your help, otherwise…'

She paused at the magnitude of what she was saying, before continuing. 'These people are my friends. I can only do so much. I was meant to be with them, but I messed up and they need a replacement.' She fixed Harley with a pleading stare. 'That replacement has to be you, Harley.'

'But…' Harley struggled to sift through the flurry of questions buzzing around her head, to choose the one that would elicit any sort of meaningful response from the girl. Eventually, she surrendered to the only one that seemed to offer any hope of an explanation.

'What do you want me to do?' Her voice was barely a whisper. She was aware of the wind picking up and pushed a hand through her hair to brush it back from her face. Clearing her vision, she was shocked to see the girl standing in front of her, their noses almost touching. Harley was accustomed at having to look up to make eye contact with others. Life spent at waist level was a humbling experience. To some it was as if she was six years old, not sixteen; to others she had effectively ceased to exist. They only saw the chair, the person inhabiting it was a shell of the bright young woman they once knew, crushed on the bridge. She was no more; alive yet invisible, an afterthought left to pick up what little pieces of her life she could scrape together.

The girl cocked her head to one side, scrunching quizzical eyes, as if encountering some unknown resistance. She shook her head, bemused at her inability to do whatever it was she was trying to do. Harley had no idea how she had moved, without her knowledge, to within touching distance, but it was a dream after all.

'What do you want me to do?' Harley repeated, her eyes wide, frightened, but defiant.

'You need do nothing,' the girl replied. 'My name is Emily and all you need do is replace me. Be present. The rest will take care of itself.' She reached out her hands to Harley who noticed again how pale the girl's skin was, almost transparent in the starlight. Instinctively, without thinking, Harley grasped them and squeezed tightly. Something told her it was the right course of action; the only choice. For the first time since that dreadful night she felt certain about something.

Emily smiled. 'Good Harley. Very good. Now let's begin.'

It was the first of many nights they would spend together.

CHAPTER 82

FLAG OF TRUCE

11:58 p.m.

Samuel shivered involuntarily, sinking into his seat behind the steering wheel of the Micra. Sensations such as cold and hunger were alien to him, and he was looking forward to leaving Earth and returning to more civilised surroundings. Dobson lay sprawled in the passenger seat beside him, head tilted back and mouth ajar. Not for the first time, Samuel examined the old man's chest closely to ensure it was still rising and falling. Why his mentor chose to inhabit such a wreck of a body was beyond Samuel's understanding but, who was he to question the rationale of one who held such high rank within their kind. He, in comparison, was a relative novice and selected for this mission primarily to listen and learn from his esteemed companion. It was an honour to be selected, and he was determined to make the most of the opportunity. A little shivering and the occasional hunger pang were a small price to pay.

He sat up sharply as the headlights of an approaching vehicle blinded him with their harsh glare. He lifted an arm to shield his eyes. The Micra was parked up, off a narrow road no more than a mile outside Ardgallon. After ensuring Kirkwood and Meredith were settled for the night, Dobson had spent several minutes pacing up and down outside the bed and breakfast, muttering to himself. The face he inhabited grew redder, beads of perspiration forming between the creases of its wrinkled forehead. Samuel considered interrupting but then thought better of it. The old man gave the impression of a doddering fool but was sharp as a tack with powers that made Samuel's still-limited repertoire pale into comparison. It was best letting him be; he knew what he was doing.

Dobson had eventually stopped and, producing a filthy handkerchief, dabbed at his face, before indicating it was time to move on. When Samuel enquired as to what was happening, his mentor had simply replied that the humans were safe and that was all he needed to know. He then barked directions to the layby, and upon arrival had instructed Samuel to pull over, before lapsing into a deep slumber.

Samuel sensed he was now going to discover the reason for their journey. The approaching headlights grew larger, cutting a swathe through the night and illuminating overhanging branches on either side of the narrow road, which provided a ghoulish guard of honour for passing traffic. He squinted and was not in the slightest bit surprised to see Gunther and Rodriguez in the front seats of the BMW that had followed them from Belfast; no, it was the figure in the back who was the focus of his curiosity. Other than saying Skelly had dispatched a third member of the Company, Dobson had provided no further clue as to who that was.

Gunther's automatic window silently glided down, and Rodriguez shot a movie star grin at Samuel — dazzling, as it was dangerous. Gunther stared dispassionately ahead, soulless eyes scanning the road for signs of an ambush.

'Well, what have we here?' oozed Rodriguez, insincerely. 'The old master and his apprentice. Times must be hard, Dobson, if you are throwing one so wet behind the ears into the fray.' He stared directly at Samuel, a mocking smile plastered across his tanned features, daring him to rise to the bait.

Before Samuel had a chance to respond, Dobson spoke, 'This apprentice made short work of the Fitzgerald Brothers back at the graveyard, so you would do well to afford him the respect he deserves. He may be young, but he has the beating of you — you Portuguese dog.'

Rodriguez's smile shifted to a snarl. He went to open the passenger door, but Gunther placed a firm hand on his forearm, while shaking his head. The bearded man reluctantly sat back and silently seethed, never taking his glistening black eyes off Dobson, who was now wide awake and fully focused on the job at hand. *Never underestimate the old fox*, Samuel thought to himself. He was battling The Scourge when the rest of them were still crawling across nursery floors after their mothers. He was proud the old campaigner had selected him for the mission.

'I apologise, Herr Dobson, for my petulant partner. His pride and reputation have been somewhat dented by recent events in Belfast,' Gunther nodded at Dobson in a manner which Samuel thought almost suggested respect for the old man.

'No offence taken, Herr von Steinbeck,' replied Dobson. 'I'm too long in the tooth to be wound up by such nonsense, and anyway I came here to speak to the organ-grinder and not the monkey.' He smirked at the bearded man who glared out the windscreen of the BMW, cracking his knuckles in a disturbingly loud fashion. The noise echoed like gunfire across the surrounding fields that bordered the deserted country road.

'Certainly, Herr Dobson. It is a chilly night and we will keep you no longer than is necessary.' Samuel watched as the Hanoverian pressed a button and the rear window of the BMW lowered to reveal its third occupant. He flinched as he took in the angelic face topped with a mop of golden curls. The child in the back seat could easily have passed as a choir boy skiving off evening practice to attend their late-night rendezvous. This impression was only exacerbated when he addressed them in a high-pitched lilt.

'Hello, Cornelius. Long time, no see. I am so looking forward to this. I was worried I'd missed out, but Skelly eventually saw sense and called for my services. You and I are going to have so much fun. Aren't you excited as well?'

Dobson frowned before he spoke again. 'Skelly must be concerned if he sent you, William. Samuel, allow me to introduce you to William Fotheringham, formerly of the 64th Somerset. Until his demise, aged twelve, at Waterloo. Lied through his teeth to get signed up and paid the price. That bloodbath was no place for a child, even one as repugnant as you have become.'

'I'm pleased to meet you, Samuel. You are fortunate to have such a learned mentor. It's a shame his tutelage of you is going to be short-lived, but the Colonel insists this wretched little plane be subdued tomorrow. The powers that be are working to a tight timetable and cannot afford any further slippage.' His youthful looks failed to conceal a steely edge to the words, which caused the hairs on Samuel's neck to stand to attention.

'The bridge on the edge of the village. Tomorrow morning at first light,' Dobson was suddenly all business, speaking with a clarity and purpose usually masked behind a slurred veneer. 'I will expect a fair fight, or as fair as you scoundrels can manage. The normal rules apply. You have declared three, so I will expect no more. The Presence are only two but will defend the portal as best they can.'

'Agreed,' nodded William. 'Yes, I'm aware this particular Presence has had its wings clipped of late.' He uttered a giggle more befitting of the school ground than this serious discussion about the future of the planet. On cue, Rodriguez exploded into exaggerated laughter, and even Gunther smirked.

Samuel felt a previously unknown anger well within, as the occupants of the BMW openly mocked his mentor. He leaned forward to reply but this time it was Dobson placing the restraining hand on his muscular arm. 'Tomorrow lad,' the old man whispered. 'Save it for tomorrow.' Directing his gaze at William, he inclined his head politely towards him. 'Until tomorrow then. Drive on, Samuel.'

Samuel fumbled with the gear stick, eventually finding first gear. Releasing the handbrake, he drove off, watching with growing relief as the BMW disappeared from sight in the rear-view mirror. Beside him, Dobson sat in thoughtful silence, absentmindedly playing with a loose button on his tatty overcoat. Eventually he spoke.

'Well, my dear boy, best we try and get some shut-eye ourselves before the fun and games begin in the morning.'

'Why did they let him fight when he was but a child?' asked Samuel. 'That was considered barbaric, even when I walked this plane.'

'Regimental drummer. Told the recruiting sergeant he was fourteen and, to be honest, they didn't check passports or birth certificates in those days. A brave little beggar, I suppose, until the French took his arm off with a cannonball. Bled out within minutes, I believe. Probably a blessing. Nobody has much use for a one-armed drummer boy.'

'Have we any hope?' Samuel blurted out the words and instantly regretted them. Such negativity was not befitting for one of his kind. If he were to perish in the morning, he would do so honourably and without question or regret.

Dobson ignored the younger man's pessimism. 'Oh, there is always hope. The addition of William to their ranks is a blow, but such a move by Skelly was to be expected. We are far from a lost cause.' He chuckled enigmatically to himself before promptly dozing off to sleep again.

Samuel drove into the night, back towards the village. Dobson's vague responses were infuriating at times but tomorrow would come soon enough.

CHAPTER 83

SAY HELLO TO MY LITTLE FRIEND

The harder Kirkwood tried to sleep the more it eluded him, twisting and squirming through his fingers time after time. While he relished the blessed relief of a routine-free mind and the growing knowledge that Skelly could not touch him, other thoughts hurtled through his besieged brain at breakneck speed. Thoughts of hope? Thoughts of joy? Thoughts he had dared not contemplate for years, now racing untethered to, he didn't know where.

But now, for the first time, he was not alone. While a rational part of his mind still looked down upon the current situation like a surreal movie, a growing realisation was dawning that this fantasy was his new reality. And if Skelly was in fact real, if Emily was real, if beings existed beyond human understanding? What if, what if…

'What if your father's still out there somewhere?'

Kirkwood jumped as if shot, and before he could regain his bearings, bounced off the bed, landing in an undignified pile on the floor. 'What the!' he squealed, in a voice a good octave higher than it should have been. He scrabbled frantically back until he was seated against the wall, desperately trying to locate the alien voice that had drifted from nowhere across the room. How had they got in? He could have sworn he locked the door before getting into bed.

'Oh, relax, Kirky. Honestly, you're such a drama queen.' His head spun towards the voice, a female one; he was sure of that much, if nothing else. He zeroed in on the words, vaguely aware Meredith hadn't moved a muscle despite the pandemonium in progress.

'You're dreaming, you numbskull. She can't hear any of this. Which, I must say, is a blessing in disguise if you're thinking of impressing the girl. What she sees in you, I haven't a notion,' the voice was heavily laced with sarcasm and Kirkwood relaxed a smidgeon. Psychotic axe-wielding maniacs tended not to indulge in jovial banter prior to lopping off their victim's heads.

'Who...Where are you?' He struggled to form the words, his tongue having shrivelled and attached itself to the roof of his mouth, like a discarded helium balloon clinging to the ceiling at the end of a wedding reception.

'In the time-honoured tradition of every clichéd horror movie made, I can only be in one of two places — either under the bed, or in the wardrobe. You decide,' the voice now adopted a playful tone, further reassuring him it meant no harm. 'And as for who I am. Well, I thought even an idiot like you would have worked that out by now, Kirky.'

'For the last time, my name's not Ki...' The penny dropped with a resounding clang, and the metaphorical scales fell from his eyes, as the wardrobe doors swung open. A figure emerged, swathed in a dim light; the source of which he could not determine.

'Emily...'

'Yeah, sorry about all the melodrama but my new employers seem to insist upon it.' She was just as she looked in the graffiti, pale skin and platinum hair accentuating dark brown eyes, that contained a swirling pool of mirth and grief in equal measure. 'Although, I'm a big fan of their wardrobe department. This is a flipping Vera Wang original.' She flicked the hems of the floating chiffon dress outwards, performing a delighted twirl at the bottom of the bed. 'And these Jimmy Choo's cost an arm and a leg. I feel like I've died and gone to Heaven. Oh, hang on...' she paused and eyed Kirkwood mischievously, '...maybe I have.'

'Who's being the drama queen now?' Kirkwood pushed up against the wall and propelled himself to his feet. He looked towards Meredith and sighed. 'Why can't you be in *her* dream? She would give anything to talk to you, be with you. She adores you.'

'And I adore her.' It might have been a trick of the weak moonlight filtering across the distance between them, but he thought he saw a tear glisten on Emily's cheek. 'But it's you I must speak to now.'

'Hence, *The Lion, the Witch and the Wardrobe* routine?'

'Well, I'm aware your friend Skelly and his cronies have started referring to me as the White Witch, which is cool in a creepy kind of way, but I'm afraid that's about as far as it goes. That wardrobe is certainly no Narnia.' She screwed her nose up and gestured towards the woodworm-infested piece of furniture she had emerged from. 'It smells like something died in there. And I doubt if it was Aslan.'

'You've met Skelly? Do you lot all live in a magic castle in the sky or something?'

'I couldn't explain it to you even if I cared to. That might come in time but, for now, it's Supernatural Warfare 101 for you. At least until you get a bit more up to speed with all this.'

'So, Skelly and Rodriguez? Gunther? They're demons? Like with horns and pitchforks you mean? Sheesh.'

'Not quite, but if it helps your miniscule brain get to grips with this, and makes my job a little easier then, yes. Suffice to say, they are the bad guys. Very, very bad guys with very, very bad intentions for this little blue and green planet we call home. And for our sins, you and Sleeping Beauty over there are all that stands between us and oblivion.'

'But I don't understand. I'm just me. I'm nothing special.'

'And don't I know it, buddy. Much as I am…was…oh, whatever. Yet the powers that be, in their eternal wisdom, have decided that we three constituted what they call The Presence. The plan being, that when we hooked up, Skelly and his evil minions would be repelled back to whatever hole they crawled from,' she stopped and scratched an eyebrow self-consciously before continuing. 'It's just a pity they hadn't told me that before I…' her voice trailed off and she looked at Meredith with an anguish that made Kirkwood's heart twinge in sympathy.

A silence ensued, which he clumsily sought to breach. 'Look, you weren't to know. I can't imagine what you were going through and I'm certainly not going to judge you. I've been there myself, truly I have. And as for Meredith, she understands.'

Emily gathered herself and snapped back into gear. 'Yeah, time to ditch the pity party and get down to business. If we don't get this sorted, we will have a long time to ponder our what if's, and what not's. It's time for the good news and the bad news, Kirky Wirky.'

'My name is Kirkwood.'

'I don't care if it's Captain Kirkwood of the USS Enterprise. Just pin your ears back and listen.' Emily narrowed her eyes to ensure she had his undivided attention. 'The bad news is as follows. The Presence needs to be three-strong to have any chance of preventing a breach and yours truly is out of the equation. The good news though…'

For the first time in days, Kirkwood sensed a turning of the tide as the dead girl smiled mysteriously before continuing.

'We have a secret weapon ready to launch. And the Colonel and his merry band haven't a clue about it.'

'A secret weapon?'

'Yup. Let me tell you about my little friend, Harley…'

CHAPTER 84

BREAKFAST OF CHAMPIONS

Tuesday, 2 September 2012

5:09 a.m.

Kirkwood was roused by a gentle shaking of his shoulder. At first, he sought to resist the prompt by burrowing deeper beneath the covers, reluctant to face the troubles of the day ahead. His mind was awash with vivid thoughts of Emily and the revelation about Harley, the girl in the wheelchair. She had spoken long into the night about what lay ahead. Kirkwood was ready, or as ready as he ever would be. He opened his eyes to be greeted by the craggy features of Dobson staring down at him.

'Time to rise and shine, Kirkwood Scott. The day is young, but I am not. These old bones want this squalid affair done and dusted as soon as possible — irrespective of the outcome.' The leathery, weather-beaten face peering at him was tired but determined.

'Okay. Okay. I'm awake,' groaned Kirkwood, not even convincing himself as he reluctantly pushed up into a sitting position. He rubbed the sleep from his eyes and was aware of movement elsewhere in the room. Meredith was already up and busying herself in front of an archaic, full-length mirror in the corner of the room, dragging a hairbrush through her hopelessly tangled hair.

'I believe you had a visitor last night,' said Dobson softly, taking care his words were not heard by Meredith. 'There is a reason this information was disclosed to you and not the young lady. I ask for your silence on this matter until the appropriate moment.'

'Why?' hissed Kirkwood, now fully alert. 'Meredith is the one person who would do anything to hear from Emily.'

'Exactly,' replied Dobson. 'She is too emotionally involved. When the enemy descends upon us, I need clear heads, not teenage girls blubbering and wailing over their dead friends. She is calm, for now, but the sight of Miss O'Hara would do nothing to aid that.'

Unaware of their conversation, Meredith grimaced with every brush stroke before eventually admitting defeat and flinging the brush to the floor in disgust.

'Useless, stupid hair.'

'Or as calm as Meredith Starc will ever be,' said Kirkwood, throwing back the covers. 'Good morning, Meredith. How are you this fine September morning?'

'This will have to do,' she sourly informed her dejected reflection, before spinning around to face them. 'A girl always wants to look her best for the end of the world, but you can only work with what you've got.'

Dobson smiled fondly at her. 'You look wonderful, my dear. And I doubt very much if those we are soon to confront will notice if you are not at your stunning best.' He straightened from where he was crouching by the bed and winced in pain. 'Arthritis will be the death of me. This body is riddled with it. Anyway, I will leave you both to get organised. Samuel is waiting outside in the car. It's still dark so we have some time before our allotted appointment.' He started to walk stiffly towards the door. 'Make sure you get some breakfast before you leave. I will know otherwise. Who knows when you will get a chance to eat again?'

'If ever,' added Meredith glumly as the old man left the room, closing the door behind him.

Kirkwood hurriedly threw some water over his face in the bathroom at the end of the hall, before brushing his teeth and availing of deodorant from the holdall provided by Dobson.

He quickly donned clean underwear and a matching sweatshirt and jeans, both in his size, which had been neatly folded in the holdall. Nothing seemed to be a coincidence as far as their elderly travelling companion was concerned. Meredith was also attired in new clothes; black leggings and a red and black lumberjack shirt which complemented her ever-present red DM boots. A black beanie hat completed the ensemble, perched on resolutely unkempt hair.

Despite the early hour, once downstairs they found Mrs Morgan busy in the kitchen, appetising smells wafting into an otherwise deserted dining room. Neither of them had seen another guest since their arrival the previous evening. She fussed over them like a broody hen, directing them to a corner table, before grandly announcing that breakfast would be served shortly.

Kirkwood would have been content with a mug of tea and a slice of toast to nibble, his churning stomach beset with nerves. Their hostess was having none of that, though, and emerged from the kitchen with two heaped plates of hot food — bacon, sausages, scrambled eggs, baked beans, and mushrooms atop a base of potato bread and soda farls. His stomach performed a cartwheel as he watched Meredith's eyes light up at the mountains of food being placed in front of them.

Within ten minutes, she was studiously wiping her plate clean with a slice of potato bread. Kirkwood looked on with barely contained revulsion. He pushed the food about his plate but hardly touched it. Swallowing a final mouthful, she pointed her fork languidly at him. 'Are you going to eat that sausage because, if not, I can recommend a good home for it?'

'Sure. Knock yourself out.'

'Ta very much. You know, since I've started hanging out with you and the urge to drink disappeared, I've been permanently hungry. All I want to do is eat.' She speared the sausage with her fork and held it triumphantly aloft, before devouring it.

'Really? I can't say I've noticed,' Kirkwood wryly observed, before admitting defeat and pushing his plate away. 'You might as well finish it. I haven't the stomach.'

'Waste not, want not,' Meredith repositioned his plate on her side of the table before tucking in with relish.

'You're a machine, Starc. An utter machine.' He ducked to avoid a napkin propelled forcefully in his direction, before righting himself and winking playfully at her. She was smiling, a genuine smile, and her eyes seemed brighter and clearer. All along, this vibrant bundle of infectious energy had been lurking beneath the washed up drunk he first encountered less than a week ago. No rehabilitation centre could have achieved such results. Whatever was happening, supernatural or otherwise, it was producing remarkable results in the two of them.

'You never know where your next meal is coming from,' she continued, oblivious Kirkwood was looking at her in an awestruck manner. 'If nothing else, I've learnt that much, living on the streets. I eat as much as I can, when I can. An army marches on its stomach. Didn't some old general say that, once?'

'Napoleon, they reckon. Although it's never been definitively attributed to him. I'll ask Skelly next time I see him. They were probably big mates back in the day. Well, whoever said it, they had a point. Although I do feel like a condemned prisoner, about to be dragged off to the gallows to meet my maker.'

Meredith nodded. 'I felt like that last night, but the funny thing is I woke this morning feeling the best I have in ages, as fresh as a daisy. It was as if this incredible peace came over me last night that drew a line under the past year. It all seems like it was a lifetime ago now, totally irrelevant to what we need to do today. I only want us to look forward now.'

'Us?' Kirkwood was unable to mask the surprised reaction the word evoked in him. 'Since when did Meredith Starc, Lone Wolf Extraordinaire, become *us*?'

She smiled shyly. 'Since I've accepted that all of this is real, Kirky. Dobson, your friend Skelly, The Scourge — it's not some mass hysteria on our part; it's real. Everything we've been through up until now means nothing. This is why we are here. There can be no other explanation, can there, given what we've seen? Don't you agree?' She looked anxiously towards him and he nodded in agreement.

'Yeah, it's real alright. Whatever real is these days. I should be relieved, I guess. Relieved that I'm not mad after all, relieved that Skelly and his cronies aren't a figment of my imagination. For years I thought I was a basket case, a waste of space. Now I know I wasn't,' he took a deep breath before continuing. 'But that's nothing compared to the fear of what lies in wait. I mean, look at us. We haven't a clue what to do.'

Meredith shrugged. 'Yeah, it's scary, but maybe it's better this way. If we had the full picture, we might well be high tailing it out of here on the first stagecoach back to Belfast. Dobson believes in us and I know when the time is right, whatever we need to know will be revealed to us. We *are* something now, whereas we were nothing back there.' She flung her arm out to emphasise the point, narrowly missing Mrs Morgan who had appeared from nowhere to remove their plates. Meredith smiled apologetically before continuing.

'I can't go back to the way things were. Begging for loose change, only interested in where the next bottle was coming from. Can you? The OCD? The routines?'

There was only one answer he could give. He couldn't go back to the way things were. He would rather die.

'Well,' he said, straightening his shoulders and fixing her with a serious stare. 'I've given you my leftovers, so I might as well give you my word.' He rose and deepened his voice, mimicking a Shakespearean actor. 'Meredith Starc of the County Down, not the Winterfell Starks...' She giggled, encouraging him to continue. 'I, Kirkwood Scott, do humbly give my solemn word, that I am with you for the duration of this bonkers enterprise to save the known universe from the armies of darkness, even though neither of us have the foggiest idea what we are doing.'

He ached to tell her about Emily's nocturnal visit but both Dobson and the dead girl had sworn him to secrecy. It would have to wait. He raised a palm to

Meredith who sought to reciprocate with a resounding high five, before withdrawing it at the last second, leaving her swiping thin air.

'Kirkwood Scott. You really are a wally,' she laughed, as a stony-faced Samuel stuck his head around the dining room door to abruptly end the festivities. They both turned, the smiles frozen on their faces.

'It's time,' he said.

CHAPTER 85

THE BRIDGE

6:30 a.m.

Kirkwood tried and failed to strike up a conversation on the journey from the bed and breakfast back towards Ardgallon. Samuel was his usual picture of concentration behind the wheel of the Micra, and even Dobson seemed preoccupied with other matters. In the end, he conceded defeat and stared forlornly outside as the sun began to slowly rise and release the lush, green countryside from the clutches of the night. Meredith sat beside him, head bowed. He wasn't sure if she was sleeping, praying, or simply trying to block out what lay ahead.

They drove through the largely deserted village. A fat, grey cat idly observed them from the kerb as they passed, before returning to licking its front paws. It was ridiculously early, and most people were still in their beds. It would be at least an hour before the main street stretched its weary limbs. Kirkwood wished he was in bed as well, safe under the covers without a care in the world. Eventually he would rouse and face the day, but not yet, this was too soon. He wasn't ready for any of this.

At the bottom of the street, the road swung left to reveal the little humpbacked bridge he had glimpsed the previous evening. It sat perched over a murky river that unravelled its way lazily through the surrounding countryside. The bridge was even narrower up close and, in his mind, was a road traffic collision waiting to happen. Because of the steep approaches to it on either side, there was no way oncoming motorists could be sure what was on the other side until they neared the summit.

Samuel pulled over just before the bridge and turned off the ignition. His actions prompted Dobson to life, and he turned awkwardly in his seat to address Kirkwood and Meredith. 'When the sun rises over the crest of the bridge, it will be time. I reckon we have less than ten minutes. I've held some information back as I was concerned it would have frightened you, but now is the time to impart it.'

'You mean you were afraid we would leg it,' sniffed Meredith, indignantly.

'There was that as well,' the old man smiled sadly. 'But I see now that much thought has gone into your selection. Had Emily survived, you three would have presented our enemies with a formidable challenge. Alas, with just the two of you our chances are considerably less. Yet here we are…' his words tailed off and he exchanged an uneasy look with Samuel.

'Exactly,' interrupted Kirkwood. 'Here we are, but Emily isn't. Now stop rambling and tell us exactly what we have to do and how we are going to do it.' He looked past Dobson to the bridge, as the first rays of the morning began to peek over it, like a shy toddler from behind its mother. The time for talking would soon be over.

'Of course,' Dobson took a deep breath before continuing. 'As The Presence should be three, they can only send three to challenge us for control of the portal, which is situated on the crest of that bridge. Whoever is left standing at the end of this ordeal will control entry to and from the plane. If it is us, then all well and good. If it is them then…' his voice tailed off and he left the words unspoken, for there was no requirement to further elaborate. They all knew the consequences, should they fail.

Meredith took up the baton. 'Yes, yes, we know. A great harm will befall our land, yadda, yadda, yadda. Continue, please.'

'As I said, they will send three. Rodriguez and Gunther, who you are acquainted with, and one other,' he paused again, reluctant to continue.

'Go on, the suspense is killing me,' moaned Kirkwood. 'Which of my little toy soldiers is coming to rip my head off and…' He froze as a sharp sound split the surrounding silence and reverberated through the interior of the car. And again. And again. Like cracks of gunfire from afar.

'Is that…a drum?' Meredith looked quizzically from Dobson to Kirkwood and then back again.

'I'm afraid it is Meredith,' replied Dobson, visibly paler than a few seconds before. 'And that sound means they are coming. Kirkwood, the third member of the Company that Skelly has dispatched is…'

Kirkwood laughed, not sure if speaking his thoughts aloud would make them sound any less ludicrous. 'William. The Drummer Boy. He's sending a kid?'

'I wish it were so.' For the first time since Kirkwood met him, Dobson had an edge of trepidation in his voice. 'But this is no ordinary child. Of the three of them, William is the most fearsome entity we have encountered yet. I'm afraid Skelly has wheeled out the big guns for this one.'

*

Less than half a mile away, Harley was reversing as quietly as she could out onto the ramp which her parents had spent a small fortune constructing the previous summer. She shook her head to dispel any lingering thoughts of her mother and father that might cause her to turn back from such a hare-brained scheme. It was too late now.

She wasn't sure she believed everything Emily had told her but was certain of one thing. She had walked, she was as sure of that as of anything in her entire life. It hadn't been a dream, she had walked and experienced a rush she never thought she would feel again. If there was even an iota of a chance her injury could be healed, she was hanging onto it for all she was worth. Even if it meant returning to that hateful bridge because some ghost girl pleaded with her that her friends needed help and, for whatever reason, Harley was the only person who could provide it.

She closed the door as quietly as she could and silently spun the wheelchair round, pushing down the ramp and onto the main street. Swinging right, she began to glide through the village with strong, measured strokes. Emily told her to be there for sunrise. Harley estimated that was in less than five minutes.

She would be there. What happened after that, she had no idea. But she would be there.

CHAPTER 86

THE DUMMIES GUIDE TO SAVING THE

PLANET

6:35 a.m.

'All you must do is be present, when they come. Their only desire is to bring chaos and destruction to your plane, to occupy it and scourge it beyond recognition. Until there is nothing left of what you once knew. The portal is the only means by which they can enter. They are fanatical, and they believe this is their time. But we cannot allow them to succeed,' Dobson paused for breath; the exertion of his impassioned address having momentarily taken the wind from his sails. He faced the other three, who stood in a loose semi-circle before him at the foot of the bridge.

'So, we literally stand here idly and hope for the best? Is that what you are seriously expecting us to do?' Meredith stared at Dobson in open-mouthed incredulity, desperate for any crumb of reassurance he could throw her way.

Kirkwood shared her disbelief. 'Yeah, shouldn't I at least have a laser gun or something? No spells or potions to give us magic powers or superhuman strength? At the very least, a copy of *The Dummies Guide to Saving the Planet*?' He was increasingly running out of patience with their cryptic leader.

Dobson nodded sympathetically. 'I know this is frustrating for you and I can only apologise again if I appear evasive. But I cannot teach you what I do not fully understand myself. I am not of your kind. When the time comes you will acquire the knowledge you need from within, and from each other. Until then,

I'm afraid you will just have to trust me. Will you?' He looked at them and was no longer the amiable rascal they had grown so fond of, the mask having slipped to reveal a weak and frightened old man.

'Have faith,' said Samuel. The three of them turned as one to face the quietly spoken giant. His face was as impassive as ever, but the words resonated with sincerity. 'Without that, we are nothing. Believe. When the time comes you will be well-equipped with all you need.'

Another crack shattered the silence and Kirkwood and Meredith jumped as if a hand grenade had exploded in their midst. The drumbeats were drawing ever nearer.

'And that time is soon. Come, let us take our positions.' Dobson winced as he laboriously began to limp up the gradient. Samuel joined him, leaving Kirkwood and Meredith at the foot of the bridge.

'Well, so much for the seven Ps,' muttered Kirkwood under his breath.

'Seven Ps?' Meredith looked at him, a baffled expression on her face.

'Prior Planning and Preparation Prevents Piss-Poor Performance.'

She was forced to giggle. 'You and your numbers, OCD boy. Come on, let's go. It's only three psychotic higher life forms from a parallel universe. What could possibly go wrong?'

'The end of the world?' offered Kirkwood.

'Sure, it had to end someday. And at least we can tell our grandchildren we were there. That's if we live to tell the tale.' She began to follow Dobson and Samuel, leaving Kirkwood momentarily alone with his thoughts. He sucked glumly on his lower lip before realising he had little option but to follow suit.

'Sod it,' he grumbled.

*

Harley allowed gravity to do the majority of the donkey work, free-wheeling down the deserted main street, beneath the glow of the street lights which were now engaged in a losing battle with the fast-approaching dawn, for supremacy. Every fifty metres or so, she pushed down on the rims of the wheelchair to maintain momentum. A passing police patrol might have expressed an interest in her breakneck speed, but she was in total control, having hurtled down this street on numerous occasions. 'Thank God for all those hours in the gym,' she thought, as the bend in the road fast approached that would take her sweeping towards the old bridge. The bridge where she almost died.

A million thoughts flooded her overworked mind but at the forefront were the conversations she had shared with Emily since that first visitation in her dreams. Except they hadn't been dreams. Crazy as it sounded, this pale, ghostly girl was as real as anyone Harley had ever encountered in her sixteen years on the planet. Emily had been almost ever-present in her thoughts since then. Constantly educating and reassuring her as to the role she was being asked to perform very shortly. Patiently revealing plans that terrified her, yet at the same time offered her a hope, that until then had seemed impossibly out of reach. Yes, Emily was real and so was this.

The gradient levelled out as she approached the bend in the road that would take her towards the bridge. That most brutal of bridges. She leaned into the breeze and pushed down on the rims again, her breath forming in white wisps before her, as she manoeuvred before making the final approach towards her destiny. Towards a dazzling future or a dire end; whichever it was, she was ready. She was simultaneously dizzy with expectation, and near-frozen with fear. It was a mess, an intoxicating mess, and she had no idea what she was doing, but prayed it would be enough.

Enough to take the bend and face whatever was around it.

CHAPTER 87

IT IS OUR CALLING

Kirkwood stood facing the bridge with Meredith to his left. He sensed she was shivering but could not tell if this was caused by fear or the temperature which suddenly dropped several degrees, even though the sun was rising. Despite this, her chin jutted out defiantly. She caught him looking and their eyes met and held, before realising they were somehow holding hands. Neither of them had any recollection of initiating the contact.

Slightly ahead of them, Dobson and Samuel were in position. Dobson was standing straighter than ever before while his apprentice struck an imposing, muscular figure. Kirkwood drew comfort and realised without any great surprise that if he was going to die, then he could not have picked better company. He was proud of them, and prouder still as to how they had come to be here.

Another jarring beat of the drum brought him to his senses. Small stones and slivers of gravel started to vibrate and rattle down the tarmac from the top of the bridge towards them. No more than a handful at first, but increasing with every drumbeat until a miniature avalanche cascaded towards them, bouncing off his boots. A larger one ricocheted off the roadway and struck Kirkwood's shin but nothing could wrench his gaze from the summit of the bridge. With every passing second, the beat drew closer, a prelude to their foes appearing and descending upon them. With the future of the world resting on his shoulders, all he could do was squeeze Meredith's hand. He felt her reciprocate the gesture and a warm, soothing sensation went tingling up his arm and into his shoulder. It was not much but, for now, it was enough to stop him from turning, running and never stopping.

'Remember, Meredith, we are present. That's all we need to be.' It was as if someone else was speaking the words, but they tumbled out of his mouth and into the biting cold of the morning. Crack went the drum. So close now.

'Yeah,' she replied, struggling to suppress the rising panic in her voice. 'But there should be three of us. Until that selfish bitch bailed out. She knew this was coming. She must have.' It was the first time since Emily's death she had spoken aloud what had been festering inside her for months. The anger in her voice was unmistakable, but even that could not mask the swirling undercurrent of fear which threatened to wash her away at any moment.

'You don't know that.' Kirkwood turned to face her, still holding her hand. 'Whatever her reasons, she must have been tormented. God only knows what she was going through. We might not be three, but you and I are just going to have to do the best we can.' He nodded to where Dobson and Samuel were standing ahead of them. 'Plus, we've got Batman and Robin over there as our wing men.' Samuel gave no indication he had heard the quip, but Dobson let out a gruff guffaw and turned to address them.

'Now, did you really think I'd expose you to this without having a Plan B in my locker? Our friends on the other side of that bridge won't have it all their own way, I can assure you of that much.' He turned back to face the brow of the bridge as the loudest drumbeat yet, reverberated like an angry god. Kirkwood and Meredith hunched over, their hands covering their ears, but this offered little reprieve from the sensory assault. A wicked wind picked up and whipped angrily across their faces, buffeting their bodies and threatening to send them tumbling back down the road like pins in a bowling alley. Dark, ominous clouds began to unfold across the sky, blotting out the sun and immersing the bridge in a murky half-light.

'They come!' yelled Samuel, his voice barely audible above the growing tempest. He leaned into the wind, struggling to maintain his position. The slighter Meredith began to slide backwards, despite her best efforts to remain beside Kirkwood. He wrapped both arms around her waist, anchoring her the best he could. It was either that or watch as Meredith was lifted into the skies like a modern-day Dorothy on her way to Oz.

Kirkwood looked towards Dobson, only to realise he had stepped further forward. He was amazed the frail, old man was not halfway back to Belfast, courtesy of the unnatural storm that had whipped up out of nowhere and was now howling around them. His eyes stung, and he had to blink repeatedly to clear his vision. As it did, and the bridge slowly swam back into focus, he half expected the hefty, granite stones which formed its walls, to have taken flight, finally succumbing to the elements after centuries of unstinting resistance. Thankfully, the structure remained intact and Dobson with it.

The sun, which moments earlier, had been emerging from behind the bridge was now nowhere to be seen, masked by an impenetrable wall of darkening cloud. The one constant above the supernatural cacophony was the staccato beat of the approaching drum, its metronomic rhythm a ghostly reminder of why they were there and what was required of them. Loose strands of Meredith's long, black hair flapped across Kirkwood's face and once more he lost sight of the bridge where at any second, he expected the unholy trinity of Rodriguez, Gunther and William to appear.

What he saw instead caused his heart to soar. Dobson was striding forward towards the summit of the bridge, seemingly unaffected by the fierce gale buffeting him from every angle. Samuel attempted to follow his companion but only managed a few faltering steps before a gust sent him skidding back to his starting position. He shielded his face with an outstretched arm and attempted to recover the lost ground, but to no avail. Try as he might, he could not force his sizable frame much further beyond where Kirkwood and Meredith stood crouched together, helpless to intervene.

'What's he doing?' roared Kirkwood. 'He's going to get himself killed.'

'If that is what it takes then so be it,' replied Samuel. 'But whatever his intentions, I trust him, and so must you. He will do whatever is required to prevent The Scourge from entering this plane. And if that means dying, he will gladly do so. As will I. It is our calling.'

'You guys are nutters!' roared Meredith, so Samuel could hear her. 'How can he even stand upright in that, let alone do what he's doing?' She pointed at Dobson who had stopped a few steps from the summit as the incessant, relentless beat continued. Without warning, he stretched his arms out either side of his bulky body, as if preparing to take flight. Above the bedlam, they could just make out his raised voice, although not enough to determine what he was shouting.

Kirkwood strained his ears, desperate to make out the old man's words, but it was pointless. He could only watch, as Dobson confronted the desolate dawn, his tatty overcoat flapping out around him, so he resembled a vampire from one of those creepy black and white movies his father used to watch.

'What's he saying?' screamed Meredith. She was only inches away, yet he could barely make her out, such was the tumult around them. She clung awkwardly to Kirkwood, ragged nails digging into his clothing, yet her boots were losing traction and slipping from beneath her. Another few seconds of this and she was certain they would be swept off the bridge. Kirkwood shouted something in response, but it was no more than a muffled noise.

'WHAAAAT?'

'HE SAID...'

An ear-splitting wail cut him off, followed by silence. Utter, total silence. Everything stopped, and the skies cleared as suddenly as they had darkened, bathing them in the warmth of an unnaturally high sun for that time of the morning. It sat majestically within the most brilliant of blue skies. Kirkwood gazed upwards in open-mouthed astonishment, his already serrated senses struggling to keep pace with what was occurring around them. The drumming stopped but Dobson stood where he had before. Beyond him were three figures who stood in a line along the crest of the bridge. Two of them were instantly recognisable to Kirkwood, and the third sent an icy spasm down the length of his spine. It was a sight he would take to his grave whether that was today or decades down the road.

Facing them were a smiling Rodriguez and impassive Gunther. The two of them flanked a third, smaller person. A fresh-faced boy, no more than twelve years old, with a battered, metal drum secured to his neck by a length of twine. He looked as if butter wouldn't melt in his mouth, yet the sly sneer plastered across his otherwise cherubic face convinced Kirkwood — if he needed any convincing, that his intentions towards them were anything but benevolent.

William surveyed the scene in front of him like a youthful commander scanning a battlefield. He appeared to be weighing up several options before his gaze locked on Kirkwood. A sickly smile replaced the sneer. He had settled upon a course of action.

And with that, all hell broke loose.

As if in response to an unspoken prompt from the boy standing between them, Rodriguez and Gunther simultaneously sprang forward. Their synchronised acceleration meant they were within striking range of Dobson in the blink of an eye. There seemed no possible escape route for the old man, yet he did not seek one, instead standing his ground, as if resigned to his fate. Just as he was on the verge of falling into their clutches, Dobson casually flicked out both hands as if swatting away a couple of irksome wasps.

The effect was instantaneous and devastating. Rodriguez was lifted off the ground and hurled sideways into the wall of the bridge as if made of cotton candy. The impact of flesh and bone on granite resulted in a sickening crunch. Rodriguez tottered and waved his arms like a human windmill, before succumbing to gravity and falling backwards over the side of the bridge. There was silence before a hefty splash confirmed he had entered the waters below. Kirkwood silently prayed he would be swept away by the current, or sink to the bottom, never to resurface.

Gunther also staggered back under the impact of whatever force Dobson had unleashed. He managed to retain his balance, however, so was spared the same fate as his bearded companion. He dropped to one knee, shaking his head, attempting to gather his bearings. As he raised it again, Kirkwood watched trickles of blood emerge from the gaunt man's nostrils. Gunther removed an immaculate white handkerchief from the breast pocket of his suit. He dabbed at his nose, then inspected the now stained handkerchief, not quite believing what had occurred.

His expression was one of quiet fury as he slowly rose to his feet, returning the handkerchief to an inside pocket of his jacket. He looked at William, who merely nodded his assent, before taking a stride towards Dobson. It was the only stride he managed as, from out of nowhere, Samuel emerged at full tilt, slamming his shoulder into the slim chest of the Hanoverian. The impact lifted Gunther off both feet and onto his back, Samuel crashing on top of him. A vicious tussle ensued as the two foes grappled for whatever slight advantage they could gain. Samuel succeeded in straddling his opponent's chest, one knee on either side, pinning Gunther's arms to the ground. Sensing he was gaining the upper hand, he leaned back and raised a clenched fist, intent on slamming it into the face of his stricken opponent.

As he was on the cusp of delivering the hammer blow, Gunther somehow wriggled free and, using the outstretched palms of his hands, pushed upwards into Samuel's chest. The force used must have been incredible as Samuel was propelled backwards and several feet into the air, before gravity took over and brought him crashing heavily onto the road surface. His skull struck the tarmac with a sickening crack and he lay, eyes rolling in his head, as Gunther rose unsteadily.

'What do we do? What do we do?' pleaded Meredith. She started to run to Samuel's aid but then hesitated and looked helplessly towards Kirkwood. 'I don't know what to do!' Kirkwood could only stare back at her, the words she desperately needed to hear refusing to form on his lips. A funnel of water shot skywards, showering everyone on the bridge. It was like a sperm whale was announcing itself as it passed beneath. The jet continued to rise, thirty, forty feet into the sky. Kirkwood could just make out a dark shape rising within the funnel and was then further drenched as Rodriguez burst from the cascade, onto the bridge again. Revelling in the attention, he announced his return to the fray with a toothy, trademark grin.

Still astride the brow of the bridge, William took a step forward, having seen enough and was now ready to play his trump card. For the first time since the battle started, Dobson took a step back but then steadied himself as Rodriguez and Gunther approached from either side in a pincer movement. He looked hopelessly outnumbered and a still groggy Samuel was in no position to assist. He flung out his arms again to repeat the earlier repulsion of Skelly's henchmen, but this time William intervened in a manner that defied comprehension, leaving Kirkwood and Meredith frozen in horror.

Eyeing them with utter contempt, the boy produced a drumstick from a pocket and raised it, until it was parallel with his upper lip, no more than an inch separating them. Dobson's features creased in dismay, realising what was coming next. Dobson sought to intervene but managed only a few steps before Rodriguez and Gunther grabbed his shoulders. The old tramp struggled, but in vain. He could only stand and watch helplessly as William fixed him with a withering glare before speaking.

'And now old man, it ends.'

He brought down the drumstick like a blacksmith lowering a hammer to an anvil. It was a clinical, callous connection. The noise of wood connecting with the taut skin of the drum rang through the still air, a staccato death knell. Silence followed, and Kirkwood realised he was holding his breath, too scared to breathe for fear of what might happen. Meredith's hand was trembling in his again and, for not the first time, he felt utterly inadequate and out of his depth.

Seconds passed. Nothing. To their right, Samuel began to groan softly, coming around, but still incapacitated and of little use. Dobson began to shake, almost imperceptibly at first, but then increasing in velocity until his captors could no longer hold onto him and released their grip. The old man spun around, and the true impact of that final, horrendous beat was revealed to them.

Dobson jerked uncontrollably as blood poured from his ears, nostrils and eyes. The latter were a milky white as cataracts had formed on his pupils. He started to gag, as if choking on a piece of food, before his mouth opened and great globules of black bile began to spew forth, pebble-dashing the tarmac and splattering Kirkwood's boots.

'Oh sweet…' gasped Meredith, her hand going to her mouth.

Dobson dropped to his knees, convulsing at such a rate Kirkwood feared his body was going to start disintegrating. His face was streaked with blood and his previously yellowed teeth were black with whatever was now spewing from his mouth. Rodriguez and Gunther stepped away, both mesmerised at what was happening in front of them. From the brow of the bridge, William stepped forward until he was beside Dobson, who was on his knees, his body gripped by spasms.

'If this is the best your kind can offer, Cornelius, then I wonder whether this plane is even worth occupying. I had been looking forward to this contest, for your fame precedes you. You are, or should I say were, held in high esteem by those of my colleagues who you have crossed swords with before. When Skelly chose me to face you, I was truly honoured. But I have to say, I am somewhat disappointed. Oh well. I suppose they're right when they say never to meet your heroes in the flesh.'

Samuel had somehow got onto his hands and knees and was crawling towards where Dobson lay. Rodriguez stepped forward and unleashed a brutal drop kick, a black boot connecting squarely with the young man's jaw, sending him sprawling to the tarmac again. He would not be rising again in any hurry.

Something snapped within Kirkwood, releasing him from where he was rooted to the spot. With a roar that lay dormant within for many years, he surged forward, intent on nothing but causing as much pain as humanly possible to the drummer boy. His sole objective was wiping the smug grin from William's face, even if it cost him his life in the process.

He lowered his head and tensed, anticipating the satisfying contact his shoulder would make with the torso of the waifish boy. But when he should have been careering into William, he was instead stumbling through thin air. He crashed to the tarmac, managing to throw his hands out to lessen the impact. The boy had been there one second, within inches of his grasp, and gone the next. Literally. Kirkwood scrambled onto his backside as a high-pitched peal of mocking laughter rang out.

William was standing exactly where he had been prior to Kirkwood beginning his charge. It was as if he had vanished into thin air, only to reappear a millisecond later. His left hand now held Dobson by a tuft of the old man's curly grey hair, while in his right was the drumstick. Dobson had stopped bleeding as profusely, the black bile subsiding to a thin rivulet which ran from the corner of his mouth. He swayed gently from side to side and would have fallen face forward had William not held him upright. He seemed oblivious to what was going on.

'NOOOOO…'

Meredith sprinted towards them screaming, but Rodriguez barred the way, lifting her off the ground in a bear hug she couldn't break free from, no matter how much she twisted and kicked. The Portuguese giant cupped a huge hand over her mouth and Meredith's cries subsided to muffled whimpers. Tears rolled freely down her cheeks, wetting the hands of her assailant. Rodriguez looked over at Gunther and smirked. The German ignored his partner, such was his interest in William's next move.

'Say goodbye to your beloved leader.'

Before Kirkwood could utter a word in protest, William drove the drumstick into Dobson's right ear, penetrating it with such force that it broke in his hand, leaving the bottom half wedged deep inside the old man's brain. William released the handful of hair and Dobson swayed on his knees, before falling onto the roadway.

He was dead before he hit the ground.

CHAPTER 88

THESE BOOTS WERE MADE FOR WALKING

Dobson's momentum slammed him face-first onto the road. A high-pitched keening cut through the early morning calm. It was several seconds before it registered with Kirkwood that he was the one wailing, tears flooding down his cheeks. Skelly had triumphed again. He always did in the end.

'Game over, old man. Game over.'

William smiled and motioned for Gunther and Rodriguez to join him. Rodriguez effortlessly carried a struggling Meredith who, despite her best efforts, could not escape his vice-like clutches. Gunther grabbed Samuel by the collar and dragged him unceremoniously along the ground. The big man was still dazed and appeared unaware of his mentor's fate.

All Kirkwood could do was stare helplessly at the prone body of Dobson, lying in front of him. A line of blood was winding its way from the old man's ear over the tarmac to where it pooled against Kirkwood's boot. He stared at it in fascination. What had he been? An alien? A ghost or spirit? A real man?

A rattling noise from behind caused Kirkwood to twirl to determine its source. Hurtling around the bend that led back into the village, was a girl in a wheelchair. Her head was lowered, almost touching her knees as she powered towards them at an impressive rate of knots. She reminded him of a Paralympian speeding down the track, given the relentless way she was eating up the ground towards the bridge. As she drew closer, Kirkwood saw that her hair resembled a multicoloured bird's nest. The girl suddenly jerked her head up, locked eyes with him and shouted.

'I have no idea what I'm doing, but Emily told me to be here!'

'Emily?' Meredith stopped wriggling and hung suspended, a foot off the ground in Rodriguez's meaty arms.

'Oh, for goodness sake,' sighed William, rolling his eyes theatrically towards the heavens. 'What now?'

Gunther stepped forward. 'I will take care of her.' As ever, his voice was devoid of emotion.

'Make it quick,' spat Rodriguez from over Meredith's shoulder. 'The sooner the portal is opened, and we get the hell off this godforsaken planet, the better.'

'Agreed.' William threw the broken drumstick aside, producing another one from his pocket. He tapped the skin of the drum with it and looked skywards, a secretive smile forming on his features. 'Let the not so good times roll,' he beamed.

High above, a black speck appeared, barely visible to the naked eye. It started to descend, sparks of light erupting from the swirling mass, as if some mad scientist was conducting experiments deep within it.

Kirkwood was oblivious to it all. He bounded down the bridge towards the girl in the wheelchair. Reaching her, he held out a hand. She could not have been more than sixteen years old.

'Hold my hand. Just hold it.' Skidding to a halt beside him, she did as instructed.

'I take it you're Kirkwood. Emily said you were a bit of a bossy boots.'

Ignoring the jibe, Kirkwood turned back towards the bridge, reaching into the back pocket of his jeans with his free hand. 'Meredith!' he bellowed, an insane grin on his face. 'It's all about the numbers, right? Three. That's what Dobson said to me on the bridge.' He glanced down at the girl holding his hand and then back towards Meredith. 'We are three.'

For the first time, a flicker of uncertainty crossed William's young face. He looked over to where Rodriguez was still restraining Meredith. 'Three? That's impossible. The White Witch is dead. There cannot be three.' Gunther took a step towards him in a protective gesture as the swirling black mass continued to descend from above. Meredith stared up in awe at its progress. She could now make out distinct forms within it. What were they? Birds? Initially, she could only make out two or three, but as it neared, more and more became visible, like counting stars on a cloudless night.

There were dozens of them — no hundreds; entwined within the descending stack. Hairs began to stand up on the back of her neck. Whatever William was summoning, it could not be good. She looked towards Kirkwood and the girl in the wheelchair. Suddenly the confusion cleared, and she knew what must be done. She shot a hand out towards them before Rodriguez had a chance to intervene.

'We are three!' she screamed for all she was worth.

'Three,' the girl in the wheelchair repeated, sporting a manic grin before rising to her feet unaided. She looked as surprised as anyone, but there she stood, shoulder to shoulder with Kirkwood. He looked at her and smiled before producing a small, yellow object from his back pocket.

He was holding a die, but not just any die. It was the twenty-sided one that had been the bane of his life for so many years. Until today.

Kirkwood looked William squarely in the eye and winked. The odds had suddenly and irrevocably shifted and judging by the shocked expression on the drummer boy's face, he just realised they were no longer in his favour.

'Three,' Kirkwood jubilantly announced, before hurling the die towards the bridge as hard as he could. The unlikely projectile burst into flames the second it left his hand before separating into a myriad of smaller, yet no less deadly, fireballs. Before he had time to react, Gunther was struck in the chest by one of the orbs. He staggered back a step and looked down in disbelief as he was engulfed in flames. A split-second later, a second fireball connected with his face, which disappeared in an explosion of searing, white light. The Hanoverian unleashed a high-pitched scream and dropped to his knees, flapping pathetically at his head and body in a futile attempt to extinguish the raging furnace he had become.

Rodriguez hurled Meredith forward towards two of the deadly spheres, using her as a human shield to save his own skin. It looked certain she would be struck by the fiery balls, as she was directly in their path, but at the last instance they veered to either side, leaving her miraculously unscathed.

Rodriguez could only watch helplessly as a flaming missile smashed into his left forearm. The impact caused him to drop to one knee, meaning the other sphere flashed past, narrowly missing him.

The remainder of the fireballs converged upon William. He raised the drumstick and, in a blur of motion, used it to deflect flame after flame. By now, Gunther was flailing around on the tarmac like a hooked fish on the floor of a boat. His entire body was ablaze. Within seconds he was motionless, except for the occasional twitch of his left leg.

The descending vortex was now less than two hundred feet above them. Kirkwood stared upwards into its dark heart and saw grotesque, winged creatures, too ugly to call dragons. Their eyes roared with a hatred and longing to be unleashed into the sky. Veiny, webbed wings flapped soundlessly, holding them aloft while glistening black talons adorned avian feet. They remained within the vortex, some unseen force preventing them from breaking out and laying waste to the surrounding countryside.

'We are three.'

The words were barely audible as Kirkwood surrendered to a deep exhaustion that threatened to overwhelm him. Meredith had run to join them and, grasping his other hand, the three of them faced the bridge together. In front of them, their enemies, who seemed invincible minutes ago, were now in disarray. Although he wanted nothing more than to lie down and sleep, Kirkwood was seized by a previously unknown calmness, now that he was flanked by the other two. His mind was clearer than ever before, stripped clean of the sticky, cloying mesh of unwanted thoughts and compulsions that had reigned for most of his life. He began to speak, not knowing where the words originated from. They flowed, nonetheless, as if rehearsed a million times before.

'We are three. We are present. We are now.'

As he spoke, he realised that, unprompted by him, Meredith and the rainbow-haired girl were reciting the same phrase in concert with him. Before them, Rodriguez had extinguished the flames, which threatened to consume him. He remained on one bended knee, staring incredulously at the three young warriors in front of him. The perpetual smarmy grin was gone, now replaced by genuine fear.

William remained on the brow of the bridge. He was unharmed but no longer a threat, just a scared little boy out of options, who no longer knew what to do. Before him lay was what was left of Gunther, lifeless and smouldering. A charred reminder of the force now facing him.

Samuel rose slowly to his feet and limped off the bridge to join Kirkwood and the others. He was gingerly holding his right arm, but a look of steely determination suggested no trifling physical injury was going to deflect from what was expected of him. He passed the prone body of Dobson, barely affording it a glance; yet Kirkwood detected a hint of sorrow on the big man's face, before it was gone again. He gave Kirkwood a perfunctory nod before turning to face the remnants of the Company.

Above, the vortex continued to rage but its descent was halted. It hovered, the winged abominations closely studying unfolding events below, considering their next move. Their lidless, black eyes shone with an evil, ancient intelligence.

Samuel spoke, his voice strong and clear. 'I speak for The Presence. This portal is ours and you shall not cross it today and claim this plane. The three have prevailed, and you are hereby vanquished. Take your dead and let us take ours. It is finished.'

Rodriguez looked towards William for some crumb of reassurance, but the fair-haired boy could only stare helplessly back. With a disgusted grunt, the bearded giant cleared his throat and replied.

'We shall take our fallen as is the custom. For that we offer gratitude. Yet hear this, Samuel, for this is but the beginning. We shall return and lay to waste this pitiful world. I curse this plane and all who call it their home.'

With that, he offered his opponent a curt, formal nod which struck Kirkwood as faintly ridiculous, given the carnage he had just witnessed. He might have giggled, had the solemnity of the moment not precluded any such reaction.

Rodriguez shot a final, withering stare in William's direction before raising his face towards the vortex. A blinding flash of light burst forth from it, causing Kirkwood and the others to shield their eyes for fear of being blinded. When they looked again, the vortex was gone. The sun valiantly attempted to break through a wispy cloud cover to warm the cold earth from the night before. There was no sign of either William or Rodriguez and the remains of Gunther were also gone, as was Dobson. It was as if the battle for control of the portal never took place.

The four of them stood in a line, trying to process what had just happened. All manner of thoughts raced through the minds of Kirkwood and the two girls, suddenly thrown together in such bizarre circumstances. It was Meredith who finally broke the uneasy silence hanging over them.

'Well…this is awkward. I guess introductions are in order.' She turned to face the rainbow-haired girl who stood a head shorter than her. 'I'm Meredith Starc, with a *c*. Pleased to meet you.'

She was almost bowled over as the smaller girl smothered her in a tight hug and began to weep uncontrollably. 'And I'm Harley and I can walk. I can walk! The ghost girl was right.'

Meredith looked over her new best friend's shoulder at Kirkwood, desperate for some guidance as to what she should do or say. In the end, she simply returned the embrace and was soon sobbing herself, completely overwhelmed at the enormity of what they had been through.

Kirkwood turned to face Samuel, who stood slightly apart from them. His head was bowed, and he wept silently for the loss of Dobson. His shoulders rocked gently as he allowed the grief to surface. Kirkwood hesitated, uncertain as to what to do, before closing the gap between them and tentatively placing a hand on the big man's shoulder.

'I'm sorry for your loss.' The words were utterly inadequate yet were all he could muster. Samuel made no reply and Kirkwood was unsure he even heard him. Eventually he lifted his head and smiled sadly, cheeks glistening in the hazy sunlight.

'Thank you. He taught me all I needed to know following my transition. His loss will be greatly mourned among our kind, but he died as he lived. Putting the needs of others before his own. He was one of the great ones. If it were not for him the portal would undoubtedly have been breached and all would have been lost.'

Kirkwood nodded in agreement. 'He knew, didn't he? About Harley? That she would be here today to replace Emily. To make us three and activate The Presence.'

Samuel's smile thawed a little. 'He was a wily old fox. A master tactician. Always had a trick or two in reserve. He didn't even confide in me. I knew he was up to something but had no idea she would arrive in that…' He pointed towards where the empty wheelchair sat on the road as Meredith and Harley continued their mutual lovefest. 'That chariot of hers.'

Kirkwood chuckled before realising Samuel was deadly serious. 'That's not a chariot, it's a wheelchair. Where did they find you, the Dark Ages?'

'Thirteenth century, if you must know,' replied Samuel, sounding slightly offended. He noticed Kirkwood's shocked expression and, try as he might, could not refrain from laughing. 'I appreciate it's a lot to take in. We all need to sit down, and I will do my best to explain what lies ahead.'

'Ahead?' Kirkwood's jaw dropped an inch, but before he had an opportunity to probe Samuel further, Meredith unleashed a squeal of delight that caused the two of them to turn and face her. In the short time he had known her, Kirkwood had never seen her face so radiant. She bounced over and took his hand in hers. 'It's Emily. Harley has spoken to her. She's seen her. She's alive. Well, as alive as somebody I saw being buried last year can be.'

She was breathless with excitement and Kirkwood could only share in her joy. Harley stood behind Meredith, beaming with pride like a proud parent watching her child cycle unaccompanied for the first time without stabilisers.

'I'm sorry to dampen the celebrations, but when you say alive that's not strictly accurate,' Samuel looked awkwardly at Meredith, concerned he was raining on her parade. Her face dropped like a stone; the wide smile wiped away. He ploughed on, in an effort at damage control, choosing his next words with excruciating care.

'Let me rephrase that. What the charioteer says is strictly accurate,' he paused, as Meredith responded with a blank expression. 'I think it's best we all sit down, and I will try to explain recent developments. We have a lot of ground to cover.'

'You're telling me,' Kirkwood scratched the lobe of his ear, but the big man was already making his way to where the Micra was parked. Meredith looked at him quizzically but all he could do was shrug his shoulders and set off after their mysterious companion.

'Come on, Hayley.' Meredith gestured for the teenager to accompany her. 'We will get to the bottom of this insanity one day, no doubt.'

'It's Harley.' The smaller girl took one last, lingering look at the wheelchair that lay abandoned by the side of the road. She tested her legs by taking a disbelieving, faltering step. Gasping, she took another, more confident this time. Harley giggled nervously, causing Meredith to look over her shoulder.

'You okay?'

'Yeah. Yeah I am. Better than I've been in a very long time.'

Meredith smiled as Harley stared proudly at her legs, before stepping after her new-found friends.

'Guess these boots were made for walking after all.'

CHAPTER 89

GANDALF ON SPEED

10:45 a.m.

'Enough. Enough.'

Samuel raised his spade like hands aloft to stem the barrage of questions being fired in his direction. The four of them were squashed into a tiny booth at the rear of a grubby café, ten miles outside Ardgallon. Samuel had pulled off the road when their initial adrenaline was replaced by hunger pangs. A disinterested waitress with questionable personal hygiene scribbled down their hurried orders which were now forgotten as the conversation raged about the events of the morning.

'So, where exactly is Emily?'

As ever, Meredith was at the forefront of the interrogation, her voice rising above the background noise of the café. The handful of other customers stopped what they were doing to determine the source of the noisy distraction before returning to their meals.

'Let's just say, she is elsewhere. She is no longer of this plane,' Samuel replied in as quiet and conciliatory a tone as he could manage, desperate not to attract unwarranted attention.

'Elsewhere?' Meredith flung her hands up in frustration. 'What does that even mean? Enough of the riddles, Samuel. We all nearly died on that bridge and I, for one, want answers. Now please.'

She looked to Kirkwood and Harley who both nodded their support.

'I do not mean my words to come across as patronising, but your kind have such a simplistic grasp of what you know as death. To you, it is so black and white, whereas, in reality, there are a multitude of paths that can be taken when a person moves beyond this plane. Emily is on one of those paths.'

'So, how come I saw her?' butted in an equally frustrated Harley. 'How come she talked to me?'

'She retains an energy here. She is not yet ready to move on to where she will ultimately dwell.'

'So, she's a ghost?' Meredith was quieter now, half afraid to ask any more questions for fear as to what Samuel might reveal, yet desperate to learn everything she could about the fate of her best friend.

'If that helps you understand it better then yes, you could call her that. Dobson somehow ensured enough of her presence remained, so it could be transferred to Harley.'

He nodded towards the youngest member of their party. 'Without her, we would have been annihilated on the bridge.'

'You're all very welcome,' grinned Harley at her new friends, delighted to be the centre of attention.

Samuel smiled. 'Without three, Kirkwood could not have defeated the Company as he did and stop the portal from being breached.'

Kirkwood began to blush. 'Aw, shucks guys, it was nothing,' he replied with a sheepish grin.

'Are you kidding me?' Harley looked on the verge of self-combusting with excitement. 'That was un-flipping-believable. Where did you learn that party trick? It was like Gandalf on speed.'

Kirkwood pondered the question for several seconds before answering. 'I haven't a clue to be honest. It just kind of happened. I didn't even know the die was there. And you're one to talk, Little Miss "One Minute I Can't Walk, And The Next I Can". What was that all about?'

Harley suddenly became serious. 'I got hit by a car a year ago on that bridge. Broke my spine in four places. They said I would never walk again. That's why I believed Emily and came to the bridge today. I had nothing to lose.'

'You believed, Harley,' said Samuel, a deep kindness in his expression. 'You have a strong faith. You all do. Which is partly why you have been chosen. That faith will serve you well as you face what lies ahead.'

He turned to each of them in turn as he continued, his voice gruff but sincere. 'Meredith, your grief consumed you when Emily died. For many months the only solace you found was the bottom of a wine bottle. Yes?'

'I'm not proud of it,' mumbled Meredith, unable to make eye contact with the big man. 'When she died, everything else worth living for, went with her. I was lost. Utterly, utterly lost.' Her words tailed off and she stared into the distance.

'Yet, now you are found,' urged Samuel, causing her to finally meet his gaze. 'That's no coincidence, I can assure you. Everything happens for a reason, which includes why you no longer crave alcohol. When the three of you are physically together, The Presence is fully activated.'

'We're immune? As in from Skelly and his goons?'

'Precisely, Kirkwood.' Samuel paused as the waitress returned with a tray of drinks which she placed in front of them.

'Your food will be with you shortly.' She stifled a yawn and ambled back towards the counter.

Samuel lifted his coffee and sipped it, screwing his face in disgust before speaking again. He leaned across the table towards where Kirkwood and Harley faced him, eyes burning with intensity.

'You are the linchpin, Kirkwood. The hub of the wheel, so to speak. The Presence resides within you, but it cannot realise its full power and potential without Meredith and Harley. You are three, but it is one.'

'So, he can't do his David Blaine routine without us,' chirped Harley, elbowing Kirkwood in the ribs with a satisfied smirk.

'Exactly. The Presence will lie dormant unless the three of you are physically together. Just as The Scourge cannot prey upon you, as it did when you were alone and vulnerable, Skelly cannot torment you now with his wicked mind games.'

'It's called OCD, actually,' huffed Kirkwood.

Samuel pretended not to hear him, now turning his attention towards Harley. 'As it is with you, young one. As they are healed of their addictions and illnesses, so you are physically healed. The Presence can mend both body and mind. It knows no boundaries. The Scourge no longer has a hold on you, you are free of the constraints it sought to impose, preventing you from becoming who you were created to be.'

'So, what happened on the bridge? The drunk driver. This Scourge thingy was behind that?' Harley's normally brash tones were much more subdued.

'You were a threat. It uses others, often unconsciously, to fulfil its needs. Dobson must have masked your significance from it, yet it still sensed something was afoot, and lashed out.'

Harley stared at her milkshake, for once, silent.

Samuel sought to lift their pensive moods. 'Today was only the beginning. Even I have no idea what the three of you are capable of together.'

'We are three, but it is one,' Kirkwood recited, to no one in particular.

'So, what now?' Harley piped up, bursting the bubble of silence enveloping them. 'There's no way I'm going back to that wheelchair. I just can't.' She looked fearfully at Samuel, worried this fantastical interlude could come crashing to a halt as suddenly as it had started. Meredith reached across the table from where she sat beside Samuel and took the younger girl's hand. Kirkwood merely stared at his Diet Coke in stony-faced silence, lost in his own thoughts.

'Now?' Samuel sat up straighter knowing the significance of what he was about to impart to them next. He was like a world leader about to deliver a State of the Nation speech, or a general addressing his troops on the eve of a momentous battle. 'Now is but the beginning. This morning was nothing more than an opening salvo. Skelly will be in his den licking his wounds, but he and his kind are persistent, if nothing else. They will come again, only next time there will be more of them, and they will not be satisfied until this plane is their domain.'

'But why?' implored Meredith. 'What have we done to them to deserve this?'

'It is The Scourge. It knows nothing but destruction and seeks to annihilate all that is good within the planes. It will stop at nothing until that is achieved. It will come again and again and again. Skelly and the Company are only one weapon in its arsenal. Only The Presence stands between it and the end of your world.'

The grumpy waitress returned, balancing loaded plates with surprising dexterity, before confirming who ordered what and placing their food in front of them. Samuel produced a handful of notes from his coat pocket and pressed them into her hand. 'Thank you for your service. Please keep the change.' She counted the money — far more than the meals cost, before wandering off, too astonished to even thank Samuel for the biggest tip of her career.

Meredith launched with her usual gusto into the steak burger and fries in front of her. 'So, this gig is ours for the foreseeable future,' she munched, between mouthfuls of fast food.

'There is no other way,' conceded Samuel, deciding to finish the conversation before starting his own meal. 'If this plane is to survive in its current form, then you must all commit to your calling. There is much work ahead of us and we must start immediately. I will guide you as best I can. Are you with me?'

'You better believe it,' whooped Harley. 'This rocks!' She looked across at Meredith expectantly, who shrugged her shoulders, seemingly more interested in her burger than the future of the Earth's population.

'Suppose,' she said. 'Beats being urinated over in doorways.' Harley shrieked with excitement and spun round to face Kirkwood next to her. She was by now a coiled spring waiting to explode.

'Okay firstly, I am not going to high-five you, Harley.' He waited as she reluctantly lowered her hand before continuing. 'And secondly. I've been battling Skelly and the Company for seventeen years now, so what's another few decades between friends. I guess I'm in.'

The final words barely left his mouth before he was enveloped in a bear hug of Harley-esque proportions. 'Aaargh. Unhand me, you mad woman!' He rolled his eyes and pushed her away, struggling to keep at bay the smile that danced upon his lips.

Samuel sat back, a look of immense relief washing over him. 'Then it is settled. Thank you.' He suddenly looked exhausted, which was not lost on Kirkwood.

'Are you alright, Samuel? You lost a dear friend today and in all the fuss none of us have even bothered to ask.' Harley looked suitably chastised and even Meredith glanced up guiltily from her food. He realised his words were little solace, given the seismic events of earlier.

Samuel nodded in unspoken gratitude at the gesture. 'Dobson prepared me well for this day. We both knew it would come eventually. It goes with our vocation. We fight on the front line against a merciless and brutal enemy. Casualties are inevitable, and Dobson knew he would fall one day. The responsibility for guiding you lies with me now. And I accept it. I would happily fall to defend your plane from The Scourge, for it used to be mine as well.'

Kirkwood rolled his shoulders to ease the tension in them. This was heavy going. 'So, what now? Where do we go from here?'

'For now, we regroup. You must all set your affairs in order. Then I will teach you all I can. There are others of my kind I will also call upon to assist us. You are going to see and hear sights and sounds that will challenge your understanding of everything you ever knew up until now. From this day onwards, everything changes and more than likely, not for the better. There are hard times ahead, I will not lie to you. But they are nothing compared to what will befall us all should The Scourge prevail.'

'The end of the world?'

'Worse, Kirkwood. Much worse.' Samuel stared bleakly out the window of the café; his food still untouched. His face was grey and drawn and it looked as if the mantle of responsibility inherited from Dobson was already weighing heavily upon his broad shoulders.

'It will mean the dawning of a new age. An age of unspeakable horror where what is left of your kind will be exposed to an ancient evil, the like of which your world has never known.'

Kirkwood let out a low whistle. 'Wonderful,' he winced, his tone dripping with sarcasm. 'Well, considering how high we've set the evil bar down the centuries, that is quite the statement.' He noticed he was sweating and wiped his forehead with a sleeve. Suddenly he realised he needed air as a million conflicting thoughts and emotions assailed him simultaneously. He jumped abruptly to his feet. 'If you'll excuse me please, Samuel. I just need a moment to process all this. It's a bit of a head melt.'

'Of course,' replied the big man, sympathetically. 'Take as long as you require. I will supervise the children while you are gone.' He smiled at his own gentle humour and turned to an oblivious Meredith and Harley who were now bickering over the last sausage on Harley's plate.

Kirkwood suddenly felt very old. They were little more than kids. But he needed them more than he had ever needed anybody in his life, just like they needed him.

Just like every other living soul on the planet needed him.

CHAPTER 90

A TIME TO END ALL TIMES

Kirkwood stood outside the café and watched passing traffic hurtle along the busy main road. Life carried on as usual for the passing motorists, blissfully unaware of the ravenous force that had almost broken through into their reality and torn it asunder. Lives equally oblivious to the power within him, which they now relied upon for their next breath. The enormity of the thought caused his knees to buckle and he leaned against the side of the Micra to steady himself.

He looked to his right. A young family were disembarking from an adjacent people carrier. A girl, no more than eleven years old, was straining to break free from the grasp of a young woman, who battled to erect a child's buggy with her free hand. A slightly older man, with greying temples and a hangdog expression, was equally occupied unstrapping a baby boy from a car seat in the rear of the vehicle.

The man muttered to himself as the child squirmed, kicking out in the throes of a titanic temper-tantrum. Kirkwood winced in sympathy, the horrors of parental responsibilities suddenly dwarfing his own concerns. He became aware of the mother staring at him and quickly looked away, an embarrassed expression on his face.

They were total strangers to him, as were the occupants of the cars, vans and lorries flashing past on the road, a few feet from where he was standing. Strangers who owed him nothing, just as he owed them nothing; who wouldn't look at him twice if they passed him in the street. Ordinary, nondescript Kirkwood Scott, serial under-achiever and consummate loser.

Kirkwood Scott, who spent so much time wrapped up in his own mental health issues he'd been unable to snag any of the opportunities that life had thrown his way. Much like the traffic flashing past now. He was the perennial hitchhiker destined never to thumb a ride to his final destination.

Samuel had explained on the drive from Ardgallon that when the three of them next saw home, it would be as if they were never away. Be it days, weeks or months; it mattered not. The next time he saw Gerry, Grogan, his work colleagues or his flatmate, there would be no difficult questions to answer as to his whereabouts. This reassured Kirkwood and an already homesick Harley, but Meredith offered nothing more than a trademark shrug and snide remark that it made little difference, given her current circumstances.

Part of Kirkwood now wondered the same. If he were to vanish off the face of the Earth, who would genuinely miss him? He doubted there would be many. His social calendar was hardly overflowing for the remainder of the year. A temporary contract in a dead-end job paying buttons; dumped by the supposed girl of his dreams, and a family who communicated via the occasional three-line email or stilted telephone conversation. If it weren't for Gerry and Grogan, he doubted his phone would ever ring. After twenty-five years his impact on the planet had been negligible.

Until now.

He gathered his frazzled emotions and looked back towards the young family. The buggy was finally assembled, and the reluctant baby strapped into it, a dummy protruding from its mouth. He sucked on it greedily as the father began to awkwardly steer the contraption towards the café. A misaligned wheel was causing all sorts of problems and he swore under his breath, struggling to maintain a straight line.

The mother and young girl walked hand in hand behind, sniggering at his wobbly progress. Aware he was the subject of their mirth, the man looked back and stuck his tongue out. The young girl returned the gesture, before breaking into a mischievous cackle. Beyond them, Kirkwood watched Meredith and Harley wrestling in their booth, the two of them silently dissolving in fits of giggles behind the glass. Samuel looked on with a mixture of fondness and exasperation.

Once more, a flurry of emotions assailed Kirkwood, causing him to gasp with surprise as he realised tears were streaming down his cheeks. Turning his back to the café, huge, shuddering sobs engulfed him. Tears of regret. Regret that Dobson was no longer with them. Tears of fear. Fear that he wasn't equipped for the monumental challenge awaiting them. But also tears of joy. Joy that he had finally stumbled upon a reason to keep living. A purpose, a direction he had been searching for all his life.

Although he had only known them a few days, and in the case of Harley — a few hours, he instinctively knew Samuel and the two girls were now his new family. A family to replace the one that exploded in disarray the day his father died. A needless, sickening death like the thousands of others which stained this land they called home.

He steeled himself, acknowledging that he owed it to them all, new friends and total strangers alike. There had been enough loss and grief, but no more, not if he had anything to do with it. He took one last look at the green fields beyond the road, a lush carpet populated by dozing Friesians basking in the late morning warmth.

The sun was making itself known from behind a covering of plump, white clouds. He had looked upon such scenes many times before, but it was as if its stunning beauty was only being unveiled to him now, for the first time.

He had become unfamiliar with the familiar, switched off and disconnected from the pulsing urgency of a life desperate to be lived. Skelly had robbed him of that and so much more. Skelly. For all these years he had laboured under a suffocating blanket of guilt, convinced he was responsible for the death of his father.

Skelly had played him like a fiddle. The most callous of tunes, he realised that now. The architect of his despair was real. He realised now what he always suspected deep down — he had skirted around the unpalatable truth for the sake of his frayed sanity. He was forced to accept the monsters were real, and there were horrors skulking just beyond the paper-thin veneer of reality within which our warm, safe existences were cocooned.

He had refused to accept this and instead consigned himself to a life sentence of routine and ritual. OCD. Three small letters that became his god, an idol with an insatiable thirst for mayhem and misery. Yes, it was a recognised mental illness, but Skelly had latched upon that and used it to become a permanent feature in the world of Kirkwood Scott. A world where a dormant Presence would never see the light of day, if his foul cunning had anything to do with it.

He had been well and truly played, but now knew what needed to be done. He was no longer wandering like a lost child now, far from home. His father was dead, and he finally realised it was not his fault.

Nothing was his fault.

He turned and shivered as if some unknown entity had passed over his grave. Closing his eyes, the faintest of caresses crossed the back of his neck. Emily was reassuringly close. He had yet to tell the others about her visit on the eve of battle, although he suspected Samuel knew. Something held him back from telling Meredith, something that he could not quite put his finger on. Partly because Emily had revealed herself to both Harley and him, yet not her supposed best friend.

The reasons for that were unclear to him, as so much was unclear. Perhaps it was better the bigger picture was concealed, as he feared it would cause him to run screaming back to the prison cell of Skelly's study. That was not the only reason though. Part of him, a selfish part, wanted to keep the liaison with Emily a secret. For now, at least. He needed something for himself, to keep him from unravelling. He would tell Meredith when the time was right.

He started walking back towards the café. The young family had negotiated the entrance and now occupied the next booth along from his friends. As he approached, Meredith flicked him the bird while Harley roared with laughter. Samuel looked as if he wanted to be somewhere else and apologised to the waitress who was attempting to clear their table. It was a scene of utter pandemonium.

Kirkwood joined in the laughter and the worries threatening to consume him evaporated. These were most definitely his people, and this was their time. This was his time.

A time to end all other times.

CHAPTER 91

WHAT GOES AROUND

Skelly didn't do scared.

Displays of emotion were a sign of weakness and he hadn't climbed to his current position through being weak. Yet there it was, as clear as the bulbous, purple-tipped nose on his face, and there was nothing he could do about it.

His left hand was trembling.

He stared long and hard at it, willing it to stop. He gripped it with his other hand and squeezed hard until he was certain the shaking would subside. But the second he released his grip, it started again.

'Damn and blast it,' he seethed, through gritted teeth. 'Pull yourself together, man.'

Augustus Skelly had lived his entire life accustomed to an obstinate will, overcoming all adversity and obstacles placed in his path. This obstinate spirit had taken him halfway across Europe with the Iron Duke, all the way to that godforsaken ridge where he helplessly watched his men die one by one in the gluey mud and gagging smoke of battle.

All the way to his own death in the square. Clinging to the regimental colours, trapped and doomed. Hacking at the French dogs even as their bayonets pierced his body and their filthy hands rifled through his tunic pockets. They hadn't even allowed him an honourable death before robbing his corpse.

And all the while, Wellington and his staff had stood on the ridge and watched. Unwilling to sacrifice the reserve to save them. They watched him die and then wrote their accounts of the battle with puffed out chests and medals aplenty.

Accounts where Colonel Skelly and the 49th Somersets barely merited a mention. The heroic actions of his men forgotten amidst the greed and vanity of those who lived.

His anger fed on what was left of his soul for a long time. Until there was nothing left but bile, hatred, and an unquenchable desire to wreak revenge upon a world that had betrayed him. A world he craved to be no more.

The same obstinacy served him well on this latest career path as well. A man with his innate leadership skills and tactical acumen knew it was only a matter of time before his new employers recognised such talent. He had taken to it like a duck to water and soon shot up the ladder to his current lofty position. Lofty, but not lofty enough for someone with his vision and ambition. The Scourge was his life now; or rather afterlife.

The creation of the Company was a masterstroke. They had literally taken Skelly's arm off when he first suggested the concept. A highly disciplined and skilled unit, which under his inspired command, flourished and soon proved indispensable to the powers that be.

No job was too big or dirty for the Company. They were deployed as leadership saw fit and excelled at whatever was asked of them, earning innumerable plaudits and accolades along the way. Fuelled by an unerring ability to deliver results no matter what the challenge, such was their ruthless efficiency.

Until now. Damn Dobson to hell and back. Skelly bit his lip to retain a semblance of decorum and rein in the rage building within, like a black wave about to swamp an unsuspecting vessel. He had been working on the boy, Scott, for the best part of two decades; chipping away at self-esteem, gnawing at insecurities, and planting the seeds that would one day produce a rotten crop, ripe for plucking.

The human mind was a delightfully dark auditorium and Skelly had wreaked havoc within it, holding court and tying the poor, deluded fool into all sorts of knots. He reduced him to a stuttering shadow of what should have been expected of one groomed to house The Presence. Kirkwood Scott had been barely capable of holding down the most menial employment, let alone harness one of the most powerful forces in the cosmos, when Skelly was finished with him.

The death of the boy's father had been an unexpected bonus. Much as he would have liked to, Skelly could not claim the credit for that one. All the same, he was never one to look a gift horse in the mouth. All the great generals were seasoned opportunists, so, when fortune came knocking, he flung the door open and embraced it like a long-lost friend.

Yes, the boy had been a time-consuming, but wholly worthwhile, exercise. The Presence was virtually snuffed out before he even twigged that it existed within him.

The two girls were an entirely different kettle of fish. They had been a feisty pair, there was no doubt about that. Unpredictable and erratic at the best of times. The bond between them was incredibly strong and it took all his guile to loosen it. He had observed them from a distance, studying each in minute detail until he finally caught a glimpse of what he had been waiting for — the slightest of chinks in their armour, but enough for him to exploit until the floodgates opened and chaos surged through like an unstoppable current.

It was Emily, the White Witch, who had been the weak link in the end. He was slightly disappointed as he thought she was made of sterner stuff. If anything, he would have wagered the other wench would have been first to crack. But no matter, a win was a win. The sight of the White Witch in her grave had been a delicious moment for Skelly; the culmination of a masterful battle plan. With her out of the equation, it was simply a matter of waiting for the other dominoes to fall, one by one.

Meredith had been next; reduced to a shambolic street urchin whose sole concern was where the next bottle of grog was coming from. After that, the breaching of the portal should have been a formality, despite the loss of the Fitzgerald buffoons which, in hindsight, was a blessing in disguise. They had been a liability, but the deployment of William should have steadied the ship and sealed the deal. Alongside Gunther and Rodriguez, the three of them should have been more than a match for the ragtag ensemble Dobson had formed. Should have been.

Skelly took a long swig from his drink, before setting it down and rising awkwardly from the armchair. He had an appointment to keep and prided himself on his impeccable timekeeping. It was an appointment he would rather not be attending but he was a soldier and that meant taking the rough with the smooth. He winced as a familiar dull ache formed in his left side. Damned French lancers.

He had been outflanked by Dobson, which irked him immensely. Now he knew how Bonaparte felt, watching helplessly as the Prussian columns emerged from the woods to the west. The sole consolation was that William had at least dispensed with the meddling oaf, Dobson, and dispatched him to whatever rock he had crawled out from under.

It was cold comfort, however, compared to the hand his arch nemesis had played prior to his demise. Skelly was aware the White Witch's essence still lingered on the plane following her death, but how Dobson managed to transfer that to the one they were calling the Charioteer? Well…even Skelly was forced to grudgingly take his cap off to that one. He hadn't seen it coming in a month of Sundays — a year of Sundays for that matter. Somehow Dobson had wangled it, without Skelly's normally razor-sharp senses detecting it. Touché, Cornelius, Touché.

Skelly straightened his tie and took a final fond look around the study. It would be a while before he returned. The powers that be ran a tight ship and discipline was paramount. Mistakes and errors of judgement had to be punished and he was no more exempt than the next man. He would take it on the chin, roll with the punches and then start over again. It was personal now. Kirkwood Scott and his damned harem of harpies could enjoy the sweet taste of victory while it lasted, for it would be a fleeting taste. If they thought they had seen the last of him or the Company, then they were very much mistaken. A wise general always kept his best troops in reserve. He hadn't even scratched the surface of the resources available to him yet.

He licked his lips and stepped away from the armchair, walking slowly across the plush carpet of the luxurious lair. Ahead of him was nothing but dense, impenetrable darkness. He stood tall, shoulders back and strode towards it. A stiff upper lip was what was required here; there was nothing else for it. He had survived the horrors of the square and he would survive this as well. It was a mere blip, that was all — a temporary setback on an otherwise unblemished career path.

Skelly started screaming the instant his trailing foot left the carpeted comfort of the study and stepped into the void beyond. It would be a long time before he would stop.

ABOUT THE AUTHOR

Stephen Black is a Northern Irish author who lives in the rolling countryside outside Belfast, Northern Ireland. He is married to Fionnuala and they have three children Adam, Hannah and Rebecca, in addition to the world's least obedient border terrier, Charlie. By day he works as a mild manner civil servant, chained to an office desk. His dream has always been to write, however, so in 2017 he launched the Fractured Faith blog to showcase his writing. In what is left of his spare time he runs marathons and consumes ridiculous amounts of honeycomb ice cream. 'The Kirkwood Scott Chronicles: Skelly's Square' is his first novel.

Printed in Great Britain
by Amazon